I0676474

Silver kings & Sons of bitches

A Novel

By Michael D. McGranahan

Copyright © Michael D. McGranahan, 2014
All rights reserved

Without limiting the rights under copyright reserved above, no part of this publication may be reproduced, stored in or introduced into a retrieval system, or transmitted, in any form, or by any means (electronic, mechanical, photocopying, recording, or otherwise), without the prior written permission of the copyright owner.

This "second edition" has format changes and text corrections.

Printed by CreateSpace
ISBN: 978-0-9905980-3-9

Author's Note

This is a work of historical fiction based on actual events. The scanning, uploading, and distribution of this book via the Internet or via any other means without the permission of the publisher and/or author is illegal and punishable by law. Please purchase only authorized electronic editions, and do not participate in or encourage electronic piracy of copyrighted materials. Your support of the author's rights is appreciated.

To:

Mary, Andrew, and Hillary

Louisa

He curls his toes over the end of the pier, bends his knees, and dives in. The water parts for him with a great splash; it's so cold he can hardly breathe. He had forgotten how cold the water could be. His arms resist at first, but then rise and fall, the familiar crawling motion, his feet fluttering against the surface, a glaze of murky green. How long has it been? Many years. Decades even. Decades since she was taken from him, and yet he can still hear her voice, still see the garden...

"Oh, look at the peonies."

"Peonies?" he thought. He had hardly noticed the flowers, or even the garden for that matter. Which are the peonies, he wondered, in a bit of a panic. He said, *Goodness, yes*, or some such thing, and continued to walk beside her, this girl who had thrown his orderly life into a state of blissful turmoil. Startled from his reverie, he began to take in the garden, the explosion of spring color, the fragrance, the grandeur of it. Neat rows and hedges as far as he could see, each framing a grand floral display, like exhibits in a gallery. He had heard that gardens like this existed in the east, behind the great family homes.

"Are these the peonies?" he asked, pointing, deciding he would own up to his ignorance.

"Yes, aren't they wonderful?"

Indeed, they were. Bold, confident little bursts of spring that demanded your attention, while other blossoms, more subtle, merely blushed with quiet beauty. The wall surrounding the garden caught his eye, the gnarled, leafy vine covering it like a thick green icing, and two birds that bickered and squawked and thrashed about over some nest or twig or beetle hidden within. It was a majestic wall, enclosing the garden like a cocoon, protecting it from what lay without, lulling the dreamers inside into believing that all the world was enchanted and lovely.

He could not keep from looking over at her, Louisa Thorn, strolling along the path, gravel murmuring beneath her slippers, parasol swaying. And he sensed something, a hush, as if her own youthful bloom had cast a spell, distracting the bees and making the flowers swoon, stilling the crickets, bringing all to quiet so that her beauty could be considered and admired. This was her garden, she the princess and they her subjects. And he knew, behind him, upstairs in her window Mrs. Thorn would be watching, perhaps peeking out from behind a curtain, waiting, sighing, remembering. Mr. Thorn, whom he had spoken to earlier, as tradition demanded, would be in his study, preferring not to think of his young daughter and her eager suitor. His favorite daughter.

She seemed to appreciate his admission, and she pointed out the different flowers, the roses, their buds still tight in the early spring, the sweet peas, the lilacs, and oh, she loved the wild violets, so small and yet so brave. He listened, learned, was grateful for her knowledge, her kindness in teaching him, asked questions, what sort of tree is that?—it's such a grand tree, or what hedge is that, and so on. He spoke to her of his work in Panama, moving the stampede of gold seekers through the isthmus and on to San Francisco. And she listened in turn, looking over at him from time to time, wonder in her eyes that this young man had been to Panama, the Pacific, had seen the world, unlike she who had scarcely crossed the state of New York. Had he been to San Francisco? Why, certainly. Oh, she said, she wants to see it, the little city perched on the end of the peninsula. Well, he thought, it's not much to look at, mostly mud and fog, gamblers and street women, but he doesn't say these things, of course. He was so fortunate, she sighed. And so he told her what her heart was hoping for, that San Francisco was a paradise where the ladies wore bright dresses (mostly true, although *ladies* wasn't entirely accurate), the men were dashing (true of the best gamblers), and the bay churned with tall-masted ships and gallant sailors (mostly true, except the ships were all deserted, the sailors having rushed to the hills for their chance at some gold).

She stopped, bent down, and her hat blew off in a gust of wind.

"Look, a caterpillar."

She reached for the hat and her hair escaped, falling to her shoulders. He tried not to stare, felt a twinge in his stomach. Long, brown, shining in the sunlight, she was unaware of its allure, seemed only to care about the fat little caterpillar.

"Phillip will be most unhappy about you eating his chrysanthemum leaves," she scolded, scooping it up into her palm.

Oh, her hair...

"Phillip?" he said, concentrating on the insect.

She tucked the tresses back into place. "The gardener. Caterpillars are his sworn enemies. Don't tell him I said so, but I'm rather fond of the little creatures." She brought the insect up for a closer look.

"You don't mean to eat him, do you? If you're hungry, after all—"

She laughed. It was a joyful laugh, like a bright melody, and he was smitten. Again. He had been smitten before, the night of the ball at Charles Morgan's, when he'd first seen her and they had danced. Her card had been full, but she made a spot for him.

"How is the caterpillar to become a butterfly, I say to Phillip, if he can't eat? He has nothing against butterflies, Phillip tells me, but wishes they would metamorphose in someone else's garden."

"Well," he said, thinking, "it is very hard to contain Mother Nature."

She smiled at him, tilting her chin up slightly. "You are quite the diplomat, aren't you William Ralston?" And now he laughed.

He spied a bench nestled beneath a tree, its branches erupting in white blossoms. Would she care to sit for a minute? Yes, she thought that would be nice.

She settled onto the bench, adjusted her dress and the brim of her broad hat—it was almost a kite. He sat next to her, suddenly nervous. There was quiet. The first quiet, a deafening quiet. Blossoms filled the space above and around them in a great canopy.

"Dogwoods must be the happiest of all trees," she said. "Don't the blossoms look happy?"

He looked up at the tree, the white flowers smiling at him, bright and optimistic. "They do, now that you mention it."

"How did you come to be in Panama, William? I can't imagine it. It seems so brave, so adventuresome, to work in such a place."

He was embarrassed, had never thought much of it, but he sat up straight, suddenly feeling a touch of pride, glad to know she might admire his ambition. He and his mentor, William Garrison, had moved from the Mississippi Valley to Panama, he said, when the rush for California gold began, to try their hand at shipping. He told her more of the wild Isthmus, the hungry mosquitoes, the monkeys and snakes and alligators, and don't forget the bandits! And she gasped and giggled and was happy that he was so easy to talk to, glad that he had so many improbable, fantastic stories. That he could make her laugh.

Then, again, there was quiet.

She looked down at her hands. She smoothed the folds of her white cotton dress. He reached into his pocket before dropping onto one knee, his heart pounding. He told her she was the most beautiful creature he had ever laid eyes on and certainly he wasn't worthy of her, wasn't refined enough, hadn't enough money, she was, after all, Cornelius Vanderbilt's granddaughter...but then, before he knew which words came out and in what order, she was saying yes, yes, I will marry you, William.

The memories, still so vivid, and he glides slowly through the water, away from North Beach. Towards Alcatraz. There is a ship moored in the cove, a sternwheeler, its anchor line burly and taut, holding fast against time and current. He sees the ship with each breath, each turn of the head. There is no one on board, that he can see.

That summer he had waited on the dock in New York for the ship to come in. The big, famous ship. The *Northstar*. Vanderbilt's grand yacht. His trophy. And there it was, finally, sailing into the harbor, approaching the dock, and yes, it was grand, the *Northstar*, smokestack billowing, back from a tour of Europe, the entire family on board, including his fiancée.

Porters carried the luggage down the gangplank, stacking it on the dock. The family began to disembark. He searched for her face. They straggled out, two, three at a time, but no Louisa. Where could she be? Then he saw the Thorns, but still no Louisa. Mrs. Thorn came and greeted him. Her face was pale, anxious. Louisa, she told him, had taken ill with a fever. The father had a look of fear in his eyes.

He has made it beyond the ghostly ship, out into the restless bay. He feels the turbulence just beneath him. The currents tug at his limbs, his swimming attire heavy, sail-like, pulling him off course. Alcatraz lies ahead, and to his left the strait, the Golden Gate, as Fremont had dubbed it. Pacific fog is poking its long, gray finger into the harbor. He is numb to the cold now, stroking the water with heavy arms, kicking with reluctant feet. Waves slap at this face when he turns to breathe. It has been several years since he's swum and his body protests against the exercise, his lungs heave for air.

He had sat with her. She lay in bed, thin and pale, hair matted to her forehead. She was, he said, still the most beautiful thing he had ever seen, and she squeezed his hand. Her breathing was difficult, loud and wheezy. She would cough, a terrible cough. The physicians had tried their remedies and failed. It's in her lungs, they said, the pneumonia. The Thorns debated what to do, and he overheard their hushed conversation in the hallway. Homeopathy? No, that's hocus-pocus. How about phenology? Mesmerism? No, no, it's all nonsense, claimed the doctors, and yet they had no better ideas. Her body will have to fight it off, they said, stating the obvious as if it were a medical revelation. Or we could bleed her again, perhaps. No, shouted Mr. Thorn. You will not!

Damn that arrogant, selfish Vanderbilt, Will thought. If the bastard showed his face, he would likely kill him. A trip to Europe to parade his family and show off his wealth, the garish *Northstar*, and what had it proved? That Europeans thought rich Americans were peacocks, all flamboyant display but absurd in the final analysis.

They had talked, he and Louisa, made plans. He would take her to live in San Francisco, they would do great things there, build theaters and hotels and it would become the New York of the West. No, she said, the London of the West. Paris, even.

He swims on. He can see Alcatraz up ahead, under a veil of mist. Waves beat against its rocky limbs, all elbows and knuckles and foam. It seems distant and unattainable. The numbness is failing him; he can feel the cold now, icy and penetrating. The fog approaches.

That winter, in the garden, but now the life was gone out of it. The wall seemed more of a prison. There were no blossoms, only bare trees, the bees and caterpillars and crickets too had gone into mourning. Mrs. Thorn—Emily, she had insisted he call her Emily, came to him. She stood quietly, wrapped in a great fur coat.

"You should come in, Will. It's too cold out here."

"Yes," he said. "It doesn't look the same, does it?"

"No," she said, following his gaze. "It's in hibernation."

"It will snow tonight, I think."

"Will, Mr. Thorn and I want you to know that you are welcome to stay with us as long as you like. But we worry about you. Louisa would have wanted you to go on with your life. She would be terribly sad to think that you stopped living, that you didn't have a family, that you didn't see all your great dreams come true."

Yes, Louisa had told him that. San Francisco, he thought, she would have wanted him to go, to build, to make it the city they had imagined together. Mrs. Thorn reached out to him, touched his arm.

"This portrait was painted in Europe." She handed him a little porcelain tablet. "I thought I'd never part with it, but I want you to have it."

His eyes grew moist seeing her; even in miniature she was beautiful.

"I'll cherish it," he said. And he would, always.

The bay has turned wild and belligerent. Wind sweeps the water into angry whitecaps. He should turn back. But why, he asks. He pulls up, looks around, treads water. North Beach seems very far away. Too far. He touches his chest and feels the outline of the little porcelain tablet. I am exhausted, he whispers to her. I don't think I can go on.

Part One

(1854-64)

O Fortune, Fortune! All men call thee fickle—(Juliet) Wm. Shake-speare

Chapter 1

A clear blue-sky day framed the Pacific Coast. A good omen, he thought, from his lookout on the foredeck. Panama was many days behind and San Francisco lay ahead. He had broken free of the Isthmus, the jungles, the insects, the shipping business, and was moving to the American West, where all things were possible. Six years before, gold had been discovered and now the world would never be the same. It was thrilling to think of, and yet, there was guilt. She had wanted him to go, and so he was going. But he was uncertain, wracked with doubts. Going without her seemed a betrayal, selfish. And he would be lonely there without her. The very place would make him think of her.

"Make San Francisco into a beautiful city, William," she had said.

Could he do such a thing? Was it a girl's hopeless romance to believe such a thing possible?

He grasped the railing, searched the wild, rocky coastline for his new home, for the great Golden Gate that would lead to the storied Forty-Niner town. He could feel the weight of her miniature portrait in his breast pocket, as if he were carrying her to her final resting place.

And then he saw it, the chasm, the rift in the coastline beckoning the ship like a siren, her limbs spread before him, wild and irresistible. The ship began a slow turn. North northeast. Broad swells passed beneath and he listed, first to starboard, then to port...starboard...port, back and forth, up and down, the rhythm of the sea. The currents swirled and eddied as the ship breached the Gate, the captain shouting orders and the crew dashing here, there, tugging at halyards, securing lanyards, downhauls, hosting one sail, dropping another, and he thought for a minute that the siren had lured them to their death, into a mysterious vortex, but no, the ship sailed past the whirlpools and safely entered the golden harbor.

Up ahead the city clung to the tip of the peninsula like a patch of weeds. Ramshackle buildings, decaying wharves that jutted out into the Bay, and mud. Plenty of mud. Blight amid the splendor, blemishes on an otherwise flawless complexion. What man has defiled, he thought, he can also cleanse. Beautify. On Telegraph Hill, the semaphore announced their arrival in a colorful, wind-whipped display, as if to say, "William Ralston is here to lead us into the future, to fulfill his destiny."

He chose banking. Banking, he reasoned, would be the best way to influence affairs, to bring about the transformation he had imagined. By lending money to the right people and businesses, he could direct the path of progress, lead the city out of its gold fever, out of its filth and debauchery and into the modern era of great cities like New Orleans and New York. He had the connections: William Garrison, Ralph Fretz and other men of influence with whom he had worked in Panama, that knew him and his reputation for hard work. And Vanderbilt, of course. The Commodore wanted to own the Pacific, to have a presence in California. A bitter irony, Louisa's grandfather, hands unclean (to Will's way of thinking) now in need of his help. And to gain a foothold in San Francisco, of all things. He would use Vanderbilt, and Vanderbilt him, but there would be no allegiance, no false loyalty.

A town trying to become a city will suffer growing pains. There had been a Vigilance Committee in 1851, and now a second one, in the year 1856, each designed to rid the city of lawlessness and corruption. It seemed politically driven, this Second Vigilance Committee, East Coast Tammany Hall politics reinvented in the West, Protestants versus Catholics, raw distrust, shootings, hangings. He thought the cause a worthy one, a necessary evil, but remained in the background. The upheaval ran its course and power was transferred to the new People's Party, and with law and order established, the business class in control, he formed banking partnerships with Garrison, Fretz, and Donahoe.

There were problems even vigilantes couldn't solve. They had come for the gold, but now the fever had died out, leaving the city in financial ruins. Jobs were few, money was scarce, prostitution flourished, and so did gambling. The population, having exploded to 55,000 souls during the rush, had now ceased to grow. Why come to San Francisco? Not for the weather. Not the muddy streets. There were abandoned ships in the harbor, ghostly hulks that slowly sank into the Bay at the end of long, dilapidated wharfs, and he was afraid the city would go the same way.

Can this city be saved, he wondered. Recast in prosperity? Or were the obstacles too great? Perhaps. Perhaps they were.

The year 1858, four years after his arrival, and Will befriended Colonel John Fry, a distinguished gentleman with a young niece in his care. Her parents had died young. A generous uncle and a kindly man, the Colonel introduced him to his beautiful charge: Elizabeth Fry. Will was attracted to her, her dark hair, fair complexion, fine features, but he couldn't imagine marrying. He could not forget Louisa; he could not betray her by marrying someone else. He told her about Louisa, and tears welled up in her eyes and ran down her lovely alabaster cheeks as she listened to the terrible story. He showed her the little portrait that he kept in his breast pocket. Elizabeth pressed his hand. Oh, but she wanted to help him forget. Wouldn't Louisa want him to go on with his life, she asked. Wouldn't she want him to have a family? He knew that she would, yes, but, he thought to himself, I can't imagine it.

They did marry, that same year, but only after he confessed a love for Louisa that would never cease. His feelings were only natural, she said. She was certain that, given time, she would win him over, utterly and completely, and that he would forget this Louisa Thorn.

And then it happened, like a miracle, eleven years after Sutter's Mill, a new discovery, east of the Sierra Nevada Range and just beyond Lake Tahoe. There was gold, yes, but even more silver. Lots of silver. The discovery was dubbed the Comstock Lode after one of the founders, or at least ol' Comstock claimed to be a founder. Will felt a jolt at the news. This is what San Francisco needed, he thought, a second mad rush for gold (silver, also, would do). Like the Second Vigilance Committee: the symmetry was promising. Prophetic. This would turn his city around, put it on the path to prosperity. His mind, clear and focused, began to make plans: the mines would need financing, banking, abundant capital would be essential.

Government, however, stood in his way. Pesky laws and bureaucrats. He was frustrated with his new state: the constitution would not allow corporate banks—some overblown fear of corporate power and misdeeds. His bank was a partnership, like all California banking houses, while east coast banks were incorporating and had much greater access to capital, could lend far larger sums, and could invest overseas. He tried to convince his partners: we form a corporate bank first and change the laws second. The state would follow their lead. But they were content where he was not, they the stalwarts of traditional banking, he the voice of a modern era. Let someone else take the risk, they counseled. We can't have the authorities padlocking our doors and seizing our accounts.

Will was irritated, thinking, I'll do this with or without them.

It was on a walk one afternoon, grappling with his frustrations, that he first saw her down by the wharves. The girl. Louisa!, his eyes insisted. Or the ghost of Louisa. From that day on, he was haunted by her face. Somewhere in the city was a girl, a street girl for God's sake, who looked identical to his dead fiancée. He was certain of it. But, as time passed, he began to have doubts. Dreams, after all, can creep into one's wakeful hours with an unsettling effect. Now, weeks later, Elizabeth had gone to visit friends in Sacramento and so he went back to those disreputable neighborhoods: the French District, the Barbary Coast, places no respectable girl would dare show her face. And yet, it was in one of those districts he knew he would find her. If she really existed.

It was late and he was ready to give up when he found her. She stood on a corner, her dress all lace and satin in bright red and black. Her clothing, posture, everything about her was designed to attract men. Customers. He approached her, but succeeded only in frightening her with his story, his claims of her appearance, the coincidence, and when he showed her the miniature of Louisa, she cried out and fled. He caught her, spoke softly, reassuringly, convinced her to have dinner; they would dine in a fine restaurant. Reluctantly, she agreed. They went to her apartment so she could change, but he should have waited in the hallway. Behind a screen she disrobed; water splashed in a wash basin. He tried not to look, focusing his attention instead on her bookshelf. Why, he asked, does she have so many books? "A girl like me can't read?" she said. He was ashamed, but wondered, how does a street girl learn to read?

She came out from behind the screen, bare from the waist up. She was a wisp of a girl, but her breasts were full. He stared. Couldn't breathe. She was, he realized, offering herself to him. Would Louisa have looked like this? He was confused and wracked with guilt, terrified even. He looked away, insisted that she cover herself. She shrugged and did as he asked.

They took a hackney to Clayton's Restaurant, and dined in a private room. He asked her questions, pried into her background: Where was she from? Where had she learned to read? Where was her family? But she would reveal nothing. He had found the girl, knew she existed, but now he was even more vexed than before. Her name, at least, would she tell him her name?

"Jessalyn. Jessalyn Ohhlson. Some call me Jess."

This at least was a something. She ate with gusto, laughed, and enjoyed herself. She was happy, and so he was happy. When the meal was finished, she reached across the table and touched his hand. Her skin on his skin. "Thank you," she said, "the dinner was lovely." He felt something akin to electricity run up his arm and into his chest, a sensation unlike anything he'd ever experienced.

Then, after, as they waited on the corner for a hackney to take them home, a young Irishman, a hooligan really, ambled by, saw her, plucked a flower from his vest and handed it to her. She stopped, stared at the boy, and he at her. She took the flower from him and tucked it into her dress. Will was beside himself. How dare he? But she dismissed his outrage, told him she didn't mind the attention.

He walked her to her door and they said goodbye. They agreed it was best they not see each other again. Yes, he thought as he walked away, it's best. I mustn't see her again.

Chapter 2

Adolph Sutro locked the door to his Montgomery Street tobacco shop, muttering to himself in his native tongue, as he was wont to do when events conspired against him. Buffeted by a sandy blast from the Pacific, he flipped his collar and began a fretful march home. *Unglück*, he grumbled. He picked his way through crowded sidewalks, navigated intersections thick with horse traffic (and fresh manure) all the while his thoughts running to William Ralston, the banker all San Francisco was talking about. And why, he asked himself. Had not he, Adolph Sutro, studied the Comstock Lode, written an important, insightful—riveting— article for the Alta, exposing the secrets of the new and perplexing silver mines? And yet, it was Ralston, Ralston, Ralston. The genius financier, they were saying, knew more about the Comstock than anyone in town. *Kompletter unsinn!*

Sutro, an engineer in heart and soul, belonged at the mining camp, not in a tobacco shop. It was true, he did have a family, a wife. Children to feed and clothe. They needed him, yes, yes, but the Comstock needed him too; a break in the traffic, and he hurried across the busy intersection. Oh, events! A terrible dilemma. But no, he told himself, suddenly resolute and clear-thinking.

There came a time when a man had to be a man, a captain had to take the helm, an engineer had to build. And he hurried home now, anxious to see his wife, while in his mind the pieces of his plan fell into place, click, click, click, like the workings of a fine Bavarian clock.

"Poor Adolph," Leah was saying a few minutes later. She gave her husband a sympathetic pat on the arm as he stood glumly staring at the dinner table, hands resting on the finials of a chair. "I wish you could go to the Comstock, but it is not God's will. If he wanted you to be a gold miner, he wouldn't have given you a family to care for." Sutro's complex world became remarkably simple in the hands of his faithful Jewish wife.

"How do you know that God doesn't want me to go to the Comstock?" he asked.

Leah, about to place some utensils, stopped and looked at him.

"How do you know?" he repeated.

"I know," she said, as if citing the Talmud, "because God's plan for you is clear. I do not need to bother the Lord with this question because it is obvious. You have a successful business. Is that not true?" She didn't wait for his answer. "You have a family, is that not true?" Again, a rhetorical question only. "And," she said, her eyes fixed on his, "you have three beautiful young daughters that love you and need you."

Unrepentant, he pressed on. "God has given me an important gift. I am an engineer. I am good at solving problems." He paused. "Is that not also true?"

"You are very good at solving problems, yes," she said, becoming exasperated. "The problems of raising a family. Of running your tobacco shops. These are the problems God wishes for you to solve."

"But these are not engineering problems." An important distinction, he thought. "There are many great riddles to be solved in Virginia City. I feel I could be of greater service," he stopped, considering carefully, "to God…in Virginia City."

Leah put down the utensils she had been arranging. "So, you think God wishes for you to go to this Virginia City? And does he want us to go with you? Do you expect me to raise a family in that little town full of gunslingers and filthy miners and lascivious women? I read your article. I know what they say about Virginia City. It is not a city. It's a mining camp. They don't have enough food or water for proper meals. Even the horses cannot find anything to eat."

About to respond, he thought better of it.

"You cannot look me in the eye," she went on, "and tell me you think it is God's will that we move to Virginia City so you can be Herr Engineer and solve the problems of the Comstock. These are not your problems, Adolph. Your children, your wife—we are your, well, responsibilities."

Problems, responsibilities, words, they were of no consequence. The time had come for action. He took in a deep breath, then exhaled slowly. "Leah," he said, "I must go to Virginia City. You will remain here, in San Francisco, with the children."

She seemed not to have heard; continued placing knives and forks. And then, a tear rolled down her rosy cheek. "So, you have already decided this. We were only having a game here, this conversation." She took a napkin from the table and dabbed her eyes. "You knew all along you were planning to abandon us."

"Abandon, no," he murmured. "But yes—"

She began to cry in earnest.

"Leah, my little *kürbis*—" she did remind him of a pumpkin at times, "I am not leaving you. I am only leaving San Francisco."

"How can you do that?" she shouted. "You have tobacco stores to run."

He hesitated, then said, "I will sell the stores."

Crying became sobbing. Words he could reason with, but this! She was as inconsolable as he was determined, because he would go to the Comstock, no matter the tears or sobs or gnashing of teeth. Perhaps it was God's will, he thought, or Providence, but he would follow this path to its conclusion, no matter the cost. Implacable, he nevertheless wanted to give her some good news. She would be happy to learn that he would purchase, with a portion of the sale proceeds, two boarding houses in which she would live comfortably and operate profitably for their family.

Her weeping continued, unabated.

"Many wives run boarding houses," he hastened to explain. "This is a good business. There is a great need for rooms in the city. You can have the biggest room if you like, so you will be very comfortable."

She reacted with an incredulous shake of the head. "I have a beautiful home. You would have me leave my..." she struggled for breath, "my...home...the home I love. And our children will have to leave their...friends, their rooms, they, they—"

Her despair, it seemed, was turning to confusion.

"I am living a nightmare," she cried. "And for what? For what?"

"Well—" he began.

"The Comstock Lode," she said, bitterly. "The Comstock Lode."

Chapter 3

Elizabeth Ralston sat before her vanity, her toiletries spread out in a complex array atop the glossy white surface like so many potent elixirs. Will could see her reflection in the mirror as he smoothed the drape of his white silk shirt; his wife's excitement was palpable. Many, if not all, of San Francisco's most important citizens would soon be there, in her parlor and sitting rooms, to celebrate the new banking partnership, Donohoe, Ralston & Company.

"I'm so glad you're home, Toppie. I've been a nervous wreck. Last night I dreamed you left me to face Mrs. McAllister on my own. Again."

"I tossed and turned all night myself," Will admitted. Not, of course, on account of the grand dame of San Francisco society. He studied Lizzie's face in the mirror. She had protested when he snuck into her boudoir, but not too much. He found her toilette to be fascinating entertainment, and besides, enjoyed seeing her in various stages of undress.

"Well," she fretted, pretending not to notice his gaze, "I would never be able to show my face in public again if anything went wrong tonight."

That is, if Mrs. McAllister left the party less than utterly charmed by the hostess and effusive in her praise. Word, Elizabeth knew, would spread quickly in the morning. She picked up a bottle of perfume and sprayed first the inside of one wrist, then the other, then sprayed in the general direction of her perfectly coifed hair. Had he told the porter not to park carriages on the front lawn?

Yes, he had. Will began the struggle with his bowtie.

"And did you tell the butler to show the guests into the drawing room?"

He assured her it had been taken care of.

"We simply must have a ballroom, Toppie. I don't know how I am expected to entertain in proper fashion without a ballroom."

"It is hard to fathom."

"Hmpf!"

Will glanced at his wife, letting his eyes drift down to her graceful neck that rose above bare, white shoulders, her skin almost as pale as the lace of her petticoat. The undergarments she would not cover with her evening gown until the very last minute for fear of a tragic mishap, which, if it were to occur, would lead to a complex and painful chain of events including the selection of another dress, a different hair style, a change of shoes, a new combination of jewels, and possibly a dose of laudanum to stave off a nervous collapse.

He tugged at the ends of his tie and adjusted the bow one last time. "A ballroom would add a great deal of charm to our parties, I suppose. We will have one in our next home. I promise."

"What?" she said. "Are we moving?"

"I'm considering it. The Peninsula would be nice, don't you think?"

Elizabeth, it seemed, hadn't heard him and now rose from the chair without taking her gaze off the mirror. One last inspection and she would be ready for her corset and dress. She turned herself to the left while keeping eyes fixed straight ahead, then to the right, all in graceful movements, her heel rising with each turn like a ballerina performing a *pas de basque* executed to a perfection that came only from years of practice and tireless repetition.

Her feminine ways he found irresistible. He snuck up from behind and kissed her bare shoulder. She turned to face him, then leaned gingerly forward and allowed him a kiss on her waiting lips. "I'm very proud of you, opening this new bank with Joseph Donohoe. It will be a great success, Toppie."

"Donohoe is just a goods merchant with some money, it's Eugene Kelly that will decide our fate. He's our East Coast connection."

"Hmm," she said. "Is that so?"

Will knew she was much more concerned with her preparations than with the finer points of banking. He intended to spend a good portion of the evening trying to convince Donohoe and Kelley to form a corporate bank. He had found that men tended to be more agreeable when they were in your home, partaking of your food, and drinking your best wine. They had been steadfastly against the idea, but the issue was far from decided.

"Perhaps you'll be famous, Toppie."

"I'm not concerned with fame, Lizzie."

She looked puzzled. "If not fame, then what, dearest?"

"Ah, well, money I suppose." Money that he needed for San Francisco.

"But we've already got gobs of money. What good is more? I think some fame would be nice. Notoriety, even. Then we could go to Europe and dine with aristocrats, the President would ask your advice, and the First Lady would invite me to tea. Wouldn't that be lovely?"

"It would indeed," he said, though he didn't believe it. He wanted nothing to do with Washington, D.C., where the politics of slavery and abolition grew more vitriolic by the day. The great mountains between east and west, which had been obstacles to expansion, now provided California with a generous buffer against that bitter dispute.

In order that her final transformation might remain appropriately mysterious, he would go visit little Samuel in the nursery. The one-year-old was named after Will's late brother. He pulled on his suit coat and adjusted the collar, then reached for the door—

"Toppie," she said. Something in her tone held his attention. A man recognizes that tone, but doesn't know until bravely turning to face it, if it portends trouble or blessing. He turned. She stared up at him with big, adoring eyes. "Our family will soon be a little bigger."

"What? Are you…?"

Her face glowed with a lovely, shy smile.

"What splendid news, Lizzie."

He kissed her, and she kissed him back with a confidence that surprised him. No wonder she looked so radiant. Tonight, all the stars seemed in alignment.

"I'm glad to see you so happy," she said.

He slipped out into the hallway. Another son, he thought, full of hope and with a flush of pride; although, a daughter held certain charms, too. They had been married for two years and their family was growing, just like their city.

The nurse, who perhaps had dozed off, jumped up at the sight of the master strolling in the door.

"How is our Samuel this evening?"

"Resting quietly."

"Henrietta, you're a lucky woman, getting to spend so much time with such a handsome little boy."

"He is a handsome boy, Mr. Ralston. Looks just like you."

"Why thank you, Henrietta. May I hold him?"

She picked up the sleepy boy and handed him to his father. Will talked to his son about horses, great high-blooded horses that they would ride together someday, and they would have long talks about the West and California, and life, and perhaps women. He knew as much as any man about the latter, which meant he knew very little.

"Is my husband giving out advice again?"

Will glanced over his shoulder to see Elizabeth.

"It seems so, Misses," said Henrietta.

His wife came up from behind and peered over Will's shoulder. Little Sam opened his eyes at that moment and gave his mother a smile.

"How do I look?" Elizabeth stood before him, awaiting judgment.

"Beautiful. Ravishing, actually." Her dress, of rich maroon velvet, had a daringly low neckline trimmed with white lace and set off by a spectacular necklace of diamonds and rubies. His eyes drifted to the white skin of her throat, and then a little lower, to the swell of her breasts, which, knowing her delicate condition, were all the more alluring in some inexplicable way.

Henrietta took the baby, who received a careful kiss from his mother. Will offered Elizabeth his arm, then led her down the hall and to the top of the sweeping staircase. Her grip tightened on his elbow and he patted her hand. He looked at her and smiled.

"You'll be the belle of the ball, Mrs. Ralston. Look," he said, "the men can't take their eyes off you, and neither can their jealous wives." She squeezed his arm.

Down below, the guests stared up at them: the McAllisters and the Garrisons and the Mills, Mr. and Mrs. Alvinza Hayward, his old partner Ralph Fretz, and many others, all waiting for the host and hostess to join them. Will, with Elizabeth on his arm, descended the steps to a round of applause, the new partner of a prestigious bank and his beautiful wife, the youngest and brightest lights of San Francisco business and society.

***

Will hurried home. Elizabeth had gone into labor and given birth, earlier than expected. He found mother and child in the nursery. He leaned over and kissed his wife.

"You look beautiful, Lizzie."

"Thank you, Toppie. Say hello to your daughter." She was beaming.

He gazed at the newborn nestled beside her mother. She already had a fine crop of her mother's brown hair. It took but seconds and he was in love. He knew right away what they must name her. That, however, could wait. He took up his daughter, holding her in the crook of his arm, smelling that pure, untainted newborn fragrance, marveling at her perfect features. Yes, it was true, he was in love.

The next day, Elizabeth was taken aback at the thought of naming their daughter Louisa. There were tears, remonstrations, how could he consider such a thing? But in the end, a compromise. The little girl would be christened Edna Louisa Ralston.

In the following year, the year 1861, Abraham Lincoln was elected president, and soon after the Civil War began. The year after that, before her second birthday, little Louisa chewed on a matchstick, became ill, and died. Will, numb with grief, swam in the frigid bay until he was so cold he could no longer feel the pain.

Chapter 4

His men were spirited today, their conversation animated. Or, some would say, he was *their* man, rather than visa versa. Their leader. He liked to think so. They gathered round him, after all, when he held court on the sidewalk outside his bank. They, the representative local merchants of San Francisco, the leading businessmen of the West who joined him regularly to solve their common problems. Perhaps not solve, but examine, one might say. Complain about, might actually be more accurate. Horace (grocer), always opinionated, worried over high farm prices, while Griffith (baker), a more retiring sort, expounded on unreliable workers, and so on. These problems, as far as Will knew, were not unique to San Francisco, and thus solutions were rarely found, which did not in the least require that they go home an unhappy lot. Quite the contrary.

For most men, conversation was a chore. For Will, it was a form of recreation. Like his swimming, but warmer. And he needed recreation, needed to keep his mind occupied. He was still trying to get over the loss of little Edna Louisa a few months before.

Occasionally the ad hoc group actually proved itself worthy of the space it occupied on the sidewalk, which, it should be added, forced traffic to flow around it with a fair amount of grumbling, the ladies in particular being unhappy at having to step out into the street to get by; either that or pass through a gauntlet of males eyes that no decent lady wished to endure. Today's topic, a worthy one: the Comstock Lode. On the minds of merchants and laborers, the Comstock grew ever more exciting, with new discoveries and new mines seemingly every day. The Potosi, the Ophir, Savage, Gould & Curry. Did not San Francisco, Will argued, need a stock exchange so that shares of these mines could be traded? A lively debate ensued. Seymore (brewer), seconded the motion. A splendid idea, all agreed in the end, to enable the common man to invest in the rich bounty of Mother Nature's new, and evidently prolific, silver mines.

Adopted.

***

Beams of early morning sunlight sliced through the stark wooden frame of an unfinished building on Sansome Street, casting long shadows across the planked thoroughfare and up onto a vacant sidewalk. Stillness hung in the air, belying the chaos that would arrive later in the morning with swarms of bankers and clerks, litigants and lawyers, buyers and sellers arriving in the business district to pull the levers of commerce for yet another day. The captains of enterprise.

Finnian Gillespie was not such a captain, but more of a soldier, the lever itself rather than the one pulling it. While he waited for his fellow carpenters, he studied the skeleton-of-a-building with a measure of contempt: the rough-cut braces and rafters, the simple frame, like something a child would build. Mr.

Orson wanted his building rebuilt after the fire, quickly and cheaply. So be it.

"A splendid mornin', eh, Finn?"

Joseph McGinley, cigar between his teeth, head engulfed in smoke, as always, joined Finn in his patch of morning sun and took up the gaze at their unfinished work.

"Aye, 'tis splendid."

"What do you think? Will we finish 'ere the week is out?"

Aye, they would finish by week's end. The other carpenters straggled in, and the gab turned to who had what work to do next, and where, and what sort of wages would be paid. The superintendent rang the bell, signaling the end of the morning confabulation, and they split up into pairs. Finn and Joseph worked together, one cutting the boards, the other nailing them into place. Their labors continued until the water cart arrived for the morning break. They all contributed to the two-bit cost and then shared the dipper, which was passed around from hand to barrel to mouth.

"That was some fight last week, eh Finn?" someone said, and Finn shrugged.

The Irish crew always favored talk of their latest street fight with the hated Protestants, and Finn's exploits in this never-ending war were held in high esteem by his companions. He was famous for his fighting, loved for it by the Irish, and hated for it by the Protestants. Big and brawny, he should have been a boxer, except that he didn't particularly love the fighting, and thought of it as a tool, a tool to achieve a goal. And a tool, he knew, whether carpenter's or fighter's, was something to be given considerable respect.

Thinking to change the subject, Finn asked if they had heard about the new Comstock mines. They showed no interest, wanting instead to talk of fighting. But then, Joseph, loyal as a pup, said, Aye, he'd heard of the Comstock. Then O'Connell admitted that he'd had thoughts of going to Virginia City to make his fortune. Where else could an Irishman become rich in this damn Protestant world?

"'Tis true, O'Connell," Joseph lamented, "'tis true indeed."

And so, until the bell rang again, they bragged of the riches they intended to dig out of the ground below Virginia City, of the great houses they would build (out of brick, of course: wood was for the common man), the carriages and fine horses that would fill their stables.

As they readied to go back to work, Finn had a strange sensation, like hearing a whisper amidst the noise. He turned to look, and there, across the street, he saw her, the girl from Claytons. She stared, and he stared back. But then, when he blinked, she was gone. His thoughts seemed to go to her at odd times, and he wondered now if he had just imagined her. Her eyes, those big sad eyes, those especially he saw in his dreams, or when his mind wandered in the day.

He had looked into the eyes of many a colleen in his nineteen years. The girls were drawn to him, it seemed. They stood near and talked incessantly at the dances, brushed against him accidentally, gave him impish looks with smiling eyes. It made his friends jealous. Finn can have any slip in town, McGinley would complain, but won't take her behind the barn. 'Twas a sin not to, an offense to nature, for Mary's sake.

Finn would laugh. 'Twas true, he was old-fashioned and wouldn't take his advantage with a girl. His mother had taught him to be a gentleman and to respect the fairer sex. "Whether they be fair or no," she would say. So wise, his mother.

Joseph was giving Finn a queer look. "What is it, boyo? You look like you've seen a kelpie."

"Nae," Finn said. "'Twas nothing."

Chapter 5

Sutro stood on California Street, removed his hat, and gazed up at the two-story house. It was a respectable house, made of wood, steps leading up to a porch and wide front door, a mezuzah hanging from the doorpost. The tan-colored paint was peeling in spots, mainly up under the eaves, and a few of the picket railings on the porch were broken, but otherwise it was a fine, sturdy house.

It had been over two years since he'd left for the Comstock. He did come home from time to time, and he was always anxious to see his wife, but today he was more anxious *about* seeing her. It seemed the stubborn woman would never get over the sale of his tobacco shops and subsequent move to the Comstock. She had two houses, this one, the Sutro House, and the Government House a few blocks away. That they were boarding houses was true, but could she not take pride in being a successful proprietress? Many women envied her, of this he was certain.

"How is my little Leah?" he asked his surprised wife. He gave her a little kiss.

She looked him up and down. "I didn't know you were coming." She reached up and ran her fingers through his bushy sideburns. "You need to trim your beard."

"For you I will trim it."

She grunted. "Come into the kitchen and I'll get you something to eat."

Soon he was sitting at the little table in the corner of the kitchen eating bread with olive oil, slices of salami and cheese, and sipping a dark lager. His brain worked feverishly over the story he had rehearsed. The ore milling operation had become unprofitable—there were too many mills on the Comstock! It had been such a promising venture, what with his clever design and ingenious processing formula...

"How are my little girls?" he said, mouth full of bread.

They were well and would be happy to see him. Emma was a good student and her teacher had remarked on her excellent reading and writing abilities; she was also progressing well with her Jewish education at the synagogue. Rose was certain school would be a wonderful adventure and counted the days until she could accompany her older sister. Little Gussie, with her mop of curly black hair and never-ending questions, kept her mother busy.

"How is your work in Virginia City?" she said.

He chewed the last piece of bread slowly, thoroughly, then took a drink of beer.

"My mill has burned down."

Leah closed her eyes, as if praying. Finally, she said, "How did this happen?"

The furnace, he said, ignited a fire, and the building, made of dry wood, had been quickly consumed. One of his employees had died, he told her.

She let out a groan. "Oh dear me. The poor man." And then, "So all is lost?"

"No, there was insurance. All is not lost." He decided it best not to mention that the insurance claim was disputed.

"Then, you are coming home?" she said with hope in her voice.

He sat up straight. "No. Not yet."

"No? Why not?"

"Well, I have an idea. A great idea; an important idea. I must go back, Leah. But I will be home soon, I promise."

Tears bubbled up in her eyes. "Lord Jehovah, help me." She had a husband who did not want to be a husband, or a father to his children, a man who didn't respect the Sabbath, who would always have some great engineering project keeping him away.

"You do not want to be home with us, with your family, do you Adolph?"

His neck and cheeks grew hot. He could not answer that question honestly, for there are times when truth is a cruel thing, and he was not a cruel man. It was not in his desire to hurt her.

"I will go upstairs now," he said, "and see the girls before I go."

She stood up. "You must leave already?"

He smiled, sheepishly, thinking this might be an invitation. "I can wait until morning."

She brushed past him, tight-lipped, toward the nursery. With head downcast, he followed her.

***

To not see Jessalyn again was a promise Will couldn't keep. He had resisted for a month or so before his resolve had given out. He was drawn to her and she to him, each for different reasons. Hers he couldn't fathom, but his were clear. He could no more stop seeing Jess than he could stop sending flowers to Louisa's grave. When he was with Jess, he was with Louisa. It was absurd, he knew, but life did not often make sense.

The fog was dense. His trusted horse, Sir Walter, knew the way to the little blue house on Stockton Street. Likewise, Will's feet knew the way along the stone path that led to the basement. The lodgings he had secured for her in a more desirable neighborhood—he could hardly have continued to see her in the French District. He had intended to pay the higher rent, but she stubbornly refused to allow it.

He knocked on the door several times, but quietly, a knock for her ears only. She opened and he slipped inside. He was playing cards tonight; Wednesday night was card night. It was regrettable that he must lie to Elizabeth, but he saw no alternative. If she were to see Jess, she would understand, he told himself.

In silence they embraced. She pulled away, tightened her robe, then lit a second candle while he took off his coat. There was now a warm glow filling the little room.

He sat on the couch while she tidied up the room, putting things in drawers, straightening the linens, and he noticed books stacked on a table, beside her reading chair. That she was literate still surprised him: few parlor girls were. In the corner, the sewing machine he had purchased for her clutched a piece of white muslin that draped off the side and onto the plank floor. A wood stove hissed in the far corner. She came and sat beside him and they talked, easy talk, open and relaxed, he of horses and his work, she her books, stories she had read. That she never talked of friends made him wonder: did she have friends?

His eye kept going to the sewing machine. "Did you ever inquire with Mrs. Greely? About seamstress work?"

"No," she said, followed by a frosty silence.

Chastened, he looked about the room. The gifts he had given her adorned the furniture: white silk gloves atop her dresser, beside them the pearl necklace, each carefully laid out on an embroidered silk cloth; on the wall the sketch of Yosemite Valley. His gaze settled on the nightstand, beside her bed, cluttered with treasures: a thimble (from her mother, perhaps?); a delicate figurine; and a letter, with ornamental embossing, a U, or perhaps a V. From whom, that letter, and why it was important to her?

He apologized, finally, claiming he only thought of her happiness. This was partially true, but what he truly wanted was for her to find respectable employment. This was left unsaid, a matter of propriety between them, and yet they both understood his intentions. She would say she needed no help from him, he would claim otherwise, and so on. Their discussions were elliptical, avoiding the direct, but still they would often fall into passionate arguments, she complaining that he wanted to make decisions for her, or to control her life. She was not his wife, after all. But, before reaching the brink, before it came to an angry parting, they would fall into each other's arms, their attraction always overcoming any harsh words, and then onto the bed they would fall, and under the covers they would share an intimacy that he had never thought possible.

After, they lay drenched in perspiration. She often heard talk of him, she said. That he was very important. That he loved the city and would do anything for it.

It was true, he admitted.

"That you're important, or love the city?"

He laughed. "Can't it be both?"

She shifted and turned toward him, perched on one elbow. "Why do you fret so over San Francisco?"

"A gifted child must reach its potential."

"Yes, I suppose so," she said, nodding. "And Louisa?"

"Louisa? What of Louisa?"

"Did she love San Francisco too?"

"She never laid eyes on it."

She looked at him with those guileless green eyes. "You named your daughter after her, didn't you?"

He couldn't deny it.

"Louisa is a beautiful name," he murmured. *Was* a beautiful name.

"But now you have a second son," she said. "Your namesake. That should make you very happy."

"Yes," he said. "Very happy." Elizabeth had given birth to their third child a few months ago, a boy. William, Jr. It was thrilling to have another son, and yet, the missing daughter haunted him. And haunted Lizzie, too.

He lay on his back, eyes on the ceiling. What, he asked, would make a girl like Jess happy, if not a beautiful city?

"The usual things," she said.

"What usual things?" He thought he knew but wanted to hear her say it.

She fell silent, as if he had pried a little too deeply, asked too personal of a question.

"I don't know," she said finally, with a shrug. She rolled onto her side, back toward him, and he wondered what she was thinking. It was unfair that she always seemed to know his thoughts and dreams, but kept her own closely guarded. She was a closed door, a locked vault. He would continue to look for a respectable position for her, no matter the cost. It tore at his soul to think how she paid the rent.

He wrapped his arms around her and held her for a long while. Finally he rose, dressed, kissed her goodbye, and slipped out the door. Sir Walter took him home through the thick fog like a trusty navigator. Elizabeth, he knew, would be tossing in her bed, wondering where he was. He was getting too good at lying.

Chapter 6

A new era dawned over the Golden Gate. Will, at least, believed it to be so, and with the conviction of a revolutionist as he swept through the old-guard business district, ready, at last, to unveil his brave new invention. A clear Pacific morning ushered him to the banking house of Donahoe, Ralston & Company, where he found workmen atop tall ladders changing the sign above the door; it would soon read Bank of California. It was 1864, three years after Donahoe, Ralston & Co. had first occupied the building.

"Have that sign up by eight," he called to the workers.

"It'll be done, Mr. Ralston, sir."

He burst through the front door, vacillating between euphoria and anxiety. Standing at the entrance to the lobby, his confidence swelled. He liked what he saw: receiving tellers carrying bags of coin from the vault; paying tellers at their stations in suits and bow ties, assembling the coins into neat stacks; Chinese workers, their ponytails neatly braided, polishing the brass rails and doorknobs to a brilliant luster; clerks running this way and that. And his head teller, Ed Tibbey, a giant in the midst of it all, waving and shouting and orchestrating the chaos into a grand symphony.

Dressed in a staid but finely cut black suit, Tibbey greeted him from behind the mahogany counter. A fresh haircut suggested a morning visit to the barber.

"Mr. Tibbey, you look like a fine banker."

"Thank you. Are you nervous, sir?"

"What? Of course not," he scoffed with a devil-may-care grin.

"The governor wouldn't dare intervene, Mr. Ralston."

Tibbey and his employer conspired to a mutual boost of confidence with blustery words and square shoulders. The teller believed the governor wouldn't intervene due to unwavering faith in the bank's cashier (Will), though perhaps the cashier wasn't so sanguine as he let on. One doesn't open a corporate bank, in blatant defiance of the constitution of the State of California, and not worry over the consequences. Cashier and teller, however, were men of the West—let the guns blaze and the survivors tell their stories.

The clock struck ten. The doors opened. The public rushed in, ladies clutching their purses, men their black silk hats. San Franciscans ready to deposit their money, to put their faith in the new bank and its cashier. Others, with no money, but curious to see what a corporate bank looked like, milled about the lobby.

"Looks just like a regular bank."

"What's all the fuss?"

"Dunno."

Will smiled. What's all the fuss, indeed? Little did they know. Then, standing to one side, he noticed a man, over in the corner, pencil and pad in hand. Taking notes. He looked official. Black suit, white shirt, derby hat, monocle. Bureaucratic frown. Their eyes met. The man adjusted the brim of his derby with a firm tug downward, pushed out of his dim corner, and moved in Will's direction. The tellers saw it too, their eyes darting back and forth between their customers and the black derby as it moved across the floor, the State moving in to assert its authority, to squelch progress, to end the era of modern banking before it even began.

"Are you Mr. Ralston?"

"I am."

"The name's Baker. I'm with the Alta."

Will stared at him, his mind not comprehending the words, still thinking censure. Fines. State intervention.

"The Alta Newspaper."

"Yes, of course. Have I seen you before, Mr. Baker?"

"I'm new."

"Ah. I see."

"Are you the president of this bank, Mr. Ralston?"

"Mr. D.O. Mills is the president. I'm the cashier."

Baker scribbled notes. "So this is Mr. Mills' bank, then?"

"No, it's the stockholders' bank."

The bank was the fruit of Will's labors, but he wasn't one for attention and fancy titles. Mills, to be sure, was a well-respected banker, cut in the mold of a methodical and reserved financier. When he had accepted the figurehead position of president, Will knew he had scored a coup. A coup that would lend stability to the bank, and attract customers.

Baker, scribbling notes, looked up at Will. "Why did you want to form a corporate bank, Mr. Ralston?"

"Well, Mr. Baker," he began. A corporate bank, he explained, could raise far greater amounts of capital, and with that capital it could invest more aggressively, could transact business on a grander scale, even around the globe, and could thus raise the economic standing of the entire State of California.

"And San Francisco, Mr. Baker, will become a financial center, a cultural beacon. A world-class city. Another New York, or London. People will someday come from around the world just to lay eyes upon her."

The reporter glanced out the door to the muddy streets, the drunken revelers, the rats and rubbish and human filth, the bawdy prostitutes. He scratched something on his note pad, and then muttered, "If you say so, Mr. Ralston."

Yes, he did say so. And he thanked the reporter for coming, then went in search of his head teller.

"Are you ready for the shipment of bullion, Mr. Tibbey?"

The teller nodded with a wry smile. Their strategy was to direct Comstock mining accounts to the new bank. Tibbey grasped the importance of this crucial link between the new bank and the burgeoning mines east of Lake Tahoe, a link that ensured the rich silver deposits would come under the control of the one man who knew how best to utilize them: the cashier, and founder, of the Bank of California.

***

Finn raced from window to window, searching the stores and businesses but not seeing the straw-colored hair or her indigo-blue dress. He had ventured into Russian Hill, having heard of the fine houses and shops and wanting to see them for himself. The mysterious girl had appeared, or so he thought, and off he had gone after her, if for no better reason than to prove she really did exist.

A small bookstore caught his eye. He had a premonition. He ducked in the door, a little bell sounding his arrival in happy notes. The customers, mostly ladies, glanced at him warily, while the man behind the counter looked at him with suspicion. Finn searched the store, but saw no trace of a girl in a blue dress. He made his way through the shelves, examining the book spines and wondering what the letters meant, wishing now that he had learned to read. A lady and her vast hoop skirt halted his progress. She, seemingly occupied with her book, cast her eye in his direction. He squeezed by, offering his sincerest apologies. She smiled and curtsied.

At the back of the store, he noticed an archway leading to another collection. He ambled along, feigning nonchalance, then poked his head through the archway. Empty. He stepped all the way in and looked around. Shelves of books, but otherwise deserted. He sensed her presence nonetheless, those eyes, watching him—a mysterious creature, this one.

The bell jingled at the front door.

He shot out of the room, looked, but saw no new customers. Just the same ladies, reading and glancing. He dashed for the front door, but as he reached for the knob, the clerk hailed him.

"I believe this is for you."

Finn turned. The clerk looked at him, holding out a book.

"For me?"

"The young lady wanted you to have it."

He grasped the book ever so carefully, afraid lest he damage it, and stared, dumbfounded. It was small, about the size of his hand, the cover a royal blue with gold lettering. He inspected it from every angle, leafed through the pages, noted the flimsy paper imprinted with crisp black letters.

He looked at the clerk. "Young lady, you say? What young lady?"

"The one in the blue dress."

He thought about racing after her, but knew it was too late. And she didn't wish to be caught, 'twas clear as the doorbell's ring.

"What sort of book is it?" Finn asked.

The clerk stared at him with condescending eyes.

"I can't read," he admitted, leaning in toward the clerk, ashamed that the ladies might hear.

"It's a book of poems, by Thomas Moore," said the clerk.

"I'll thank you for that," he said, forcing himself to smile at the man, determined not to reveal his humiliation.

He pulled open the singing door and stepped back out onto the sidewalk. He saw no blue dress, no yellow hair. The book stared up at him, as perplexed as he, it seemed. Why would she want him to have such a thing? A fine little book, though, make no mistake. Making his way along the streets, his limbs were light, his thoughts soaring. She had given him a gift, thought him worthy of a treasure. In his exuberance, he took off running; the blocks passed by unheeded until he heard a shout.

"Hey! What are you running from?"

Pulling up, he looked back to see a group of pinch-faced boys wearing long baggy pants and black boots. Protestant boys. One big lad and three smaller, one of which carried a stick, another a club. Ya bog trotters. He continued on his way with a steady, deliberate gait.

"What are you doing around here?" one of them yelled.

He set the book down on the sidewalk, then faced them. "Mindin' me own business."

"That so?"

"Aye. 'Tis so."

The four boys approached, then fanned out, forming a semi-circle before him. He studied them. Their faces. Their eyes. The big one was cocky, arrogant. One punch and he'd run with his tail down. Another slapped a large club into the palm of his hand, anxious to put it to use. How would he do without that cudgel? One stood with clenched fists, his eyes burning like hot coals. That one he'd watch carefully. The fourth, at Finn's left, held his stick pointing down at the ground. His eyes were pale and he had wispy, girlish hair. His lip seemed to quiver. You. I'll start with you.

He fixed his eyes on the pretty boy. The stick in the boy's hand began to tremble. Finn stood perfectly still. Waiting. His heart beat quietly, his breath easy, unhurried.

"We're gonna teach you not to come around our neighborhood, Irish."

"'Tis a free country, I'm told."

"Yeah. And we're free to live without filthy Irish swine about."

Finn's pulse quickened. No Prod could call the Irish swine and remain standing. He leaned forward and spat. "Then I suppose I'm free to put yer head on a pike when I'm done with ya."

The big one let out a fierce yell and charged. It happened quickly. Within a minute, Finn had put three of the boys into the mud, leaving only the dark-eyed one still standing. Coal-eyes smoldering. Angry.

Coal-eyes stood straight. Finn's hair was caked with mud, blood dripped down the side of his face. His eye stung and he wiped the blood away with the back of his hand. He spat, then fixed his gaze on the enemy's dark, hate-filled eyes.

"You better get out of town, Irish. We'll get you sooner or later, if you don't."

Finn stood, motionless. Coal-eyes took a step toward him. Then another. Finn remained still. Waiting. His muscles twitched. Ready. Coal-eyes lunged, quicker than expected. Blows were traded, blood drawn, flesh bruised. The battle lasted longer than usual. A worthy opponent, this one. But the wiry Protestant came too close, and Finn unleashed a great uppercut that dropped him, finally, into the mud.

Finn bent forward, hands on knees, and drew several deep breaths. He glanced back to make sure his book was still there on the sidewalk. He took out a handkerchief and dabbed the cuts above his eye and cheek. Coal-eyes looked up at him through swollen eyelids: down, but not defeated, filled with even more hate. Finn picked up the book, and slowly headed up the street.

"Get out of San Francisco, Irish!"

If I get out of San Francisco, it won't be because of the Prods, he thought, his pace steady, his gait unhurried.

Chapter 7

Each morning at 8 o'clock, Will and his hostler, James Riker, rode their horses down from Rincon Hill into the business district. The unlikely pair drew glances, and even some stares, as they passed along Market Street. There weren't many Negros in San Francisco, and fewer still that rode alongside a prominent white man, laughing and telling stories to boot. They seemed the best of friends, if that were possible in the time of slavers, abolitionists, and civil war. This morning they exchanged tales of unfathomable riches gained at the stock exchange, all in Comstock mines. Mr. Freidrick's chambermaid, Riker told his boss, "made such a killin' that she quit her job, leaving poor Freidrick without no one to empty his chamber pot." Will threw back his head and laughed. "The man don't know what to do with hisself," Riker declared.

As they approached the intersection of Washington and Battery, Will saw Tibbey at the bank door. Something was amiss.

"Stocks are falling over at the exchange, Mr. Ralston. Crashing, would be more to the point."

Tibbey looked sick; Riker's eyes were as big cue balls.

"The Comstock?"

Tibbey nodded. "The Ophir is at $300 a share; the Gould and Curry at $900. Like dropping off a cliff."

Will couldn't move, as if suddenly paralyzed. But for the horses moving in the street, he'd have sworn time had ceased its eternal march. Fortunes, he knew, were disappearing as they spoke. On his advice, many friends and customers had invested in the silver mines and now stood to be ruined. And, the majority of the bank's capital was committed to Comstock mines and mills. A collapse would mean disaster for the nascent Bank of California, not yet a year old.

He went to the stock exchange to see for himself. Chaos had engulfed the entire block leading to the front door. He pushed past the curb-brokers and teary-eyed women in black silk dresses and furs: riches all bought with now-worthless securities.

Inside the hall, paper lay strewn about the floor like the aftermath of a war between bankers and accountants. The noise was deafening. Frantic investors rushed here and there, bumping into one another, cursing, screaming. Dignity, he thought, is but a word. Stocks were being sold in the pit, the caller shouting out shares of the North American mine.

"Hundred shares, sell 'em reg'lar at 350," a broker yelled.

Screams and curses answered the call, but no offers to buy.

"Two hundred, sell 'em cash at 325," another broker shouted.

A cry went up. "Hundred shares, buy 'em cash at 290."

"Sell 'em at 290," the answer came back.

A chill of fear swept over him: the day before, North American had been trading for over $5,000 a share. He did some quick arithmetic, calculating his losses. He glanced around the room until he recognized a face. One of his brokers, face streaked with perspiration, tried to explain what had happened.

"I've never seen anything like it, Mr. Ralston. There was talk of water flooding the mines and the ore being played out above the water line. The next thing I knew, rumors were swirling and everyone started selling. I had a dozen people thrusting their shares in my face, begging me to sell for them, but I couldn't keep up."

"Are the mines flooded?"

"That's what they say."

The water. It had been a nuisance since they first began dropping shafts into the lode, but now it had graduated from nuisance to curse. Was the ore played out? Above the water, perhaps, but what about below? How could one know?

He headed back to the bank, passed through the lobby, oblivious to everything and everyone, then made his way up the stairs to his office. He sat at his desk. There, staring serenely at him, was Louisa Thorn, angelic face shining out from her porcelain frame, now placed on his desk, where he could see it every day.

A knock and then Colonel Fry strode through his office door. At the sight of his wife's father, he tore his eyes away from the portrait. The Colonel's eyes, he noted with some guilt, lingered on Louisa's picture, darted to him, and then back to Louisa. They exchanged perfunctory greetings.

Will took up a piece of paper and tore a long, even strip. Hot, foul-smelling brine was flooding the Comstock. Where in the hell was it coming from? He pulled another strip from the edge of the paper, released it, then watched it float down to his desk. Despite constant pumping, the water was continuing to rise unabated. Unless it could be cleared, the deeper ore was inaccessible and that meant the Lode would be finished, the shallow ore being almost depleted.

He looked back again at Louisa. Her serenity calmed him. An idea came to him.

"I'll send someone to Virginia City," he exclaimed. All he had to go on was speculation and stock exchange rumors. What he needed were facts. "I'll send Tibbey."

Fry turned from the window. He thought that a fine idea, sending someone to Virginia City to investigate, but not Tibbey.

"I know a man better-suited to the job," the Colonel said. "His name is William Sharon. I have nothing against Tibbey. Tibbey is a fine man. But I came over on the Emigrant Trail with Sharon and acquired great respect for him during that trying journey. I can attest to his rugged constitution and sharp mind and, as it so happens, he is between engagements and available at this time. A fortunate circumstance, which I believe to be more than just mere coincidence."

Will was set on Tibbey. He made polite inquiries into this Mr. Sharon, but only to placate his father-in-law. Sharon had no banking or mining experience, Fry admitted, but he had been swindled with counterfeit Comstock shares and lost everything. To regain his fortune from the Comstock, Fry thought to be powerful motivation. Will, however, worried that retaliation might prove an even stronger one. Prim and proper Tibbey, Fry continued, would be ground into the dust by the ruffians in Virginia City. Sharon was tough, had led a party across the continent, and he was a gambler. A damn good gambler at that.

Will was incredulous. "A lawyer who lost a fortune in the stock exchange, who is also gambler? This man you think can help our bank?"

"Sharon's past is checkered, to be sure," conceded Fry. "But when you think of it, he has all the qualities you need: tough, experienced, knows when to take risks and when not to, and he's hungry. He's burning to get his fortune back. A man like that will work himself ten times harder than an Ed Tibbey."

Perhaps the Colonel had a point. Hiring a man like Sharon would be like buying stock in a sound company when the price was at rock-bottom.

He hesitated. So much on the line. Damn his bad luck. Louisa gazed at him from across the desk, her smile reassuring, calming. Follow your instincts, William, she seemed to say.

Fry stared at him. "I realize," he said, "that you have a special place in your heart for this Louisa Thorn, but I would fail in my duties as a father if I didn't say that you now owe your affections to Elizabeth. And besides, it just isn't good for one's constitution, Chap, to hold so steadfastly to one no longer of this world."

"Don't fret, Colonel, it's only that I find a calming effect in her serene face, a bromide I'm in need of at this time of crisis. It is it nothing more, I assure you."

"I hope so. For your sake, and Lizzie's."

He thanked him for the advice. He would meet Mr. Sharon first thing tomorrow.

Chapter 8

Once, when he was a boy in Aachen, Prussia, it had occurred to Adolph Sutro that he could do anything. Not in the
sense that he could have any career, although that would certainly
be true, but that he could build any machine or piece of equip-
ment, or solve any problem. He need only set his mind to the project. It had been a remarkable discovery, this realization, leaving
him in frank and unsentimental awe of his own person. To understand a steam engine, he simply took it apart and put it back together. Likewise the mills in his father's factory. A more efficient
system had been needed to increase factory profits: Adolph soon
had the solution. His ability to penetrate and solve problems was
limitless. These astonishing gifts he had brought to America, and
now the Comstock Lode and soon-to-be-grateful Virginia City,
which were about to discover the true extent of his talents.

His brawny mule slid more than stepped down the steep
sandy slopes below that bustling camp. A dog-eared canvas sheet
lay astride the mule's bristly mane. Though the animal was of an
even disposition, and terribly sure-footed, it now came to a stop,
refusing to sacrifice itself to his master's grand scheme on these
treacherous canyon flanks. He urged him on, but the beast re-

fused. They were at an impasse. He slid down, taking his canvas with him. He grumbled something in German, but the reluctant assistant was not one to take offense, and bent his head without comment to nibble on scrub brush, while swishing his tail at the occasional fly. Sutro spread the sheet, a map-in-progress, out on the ground, looked about, then twisted it clockwise until his incipient markings were oriented according to the prominent landmarks within his line of sight.

On that map, a big circle around the Savage Mine marked the center of the Comstock Lode. He took the stub of a pencil from behind his ear, and extended a jagged line from the Savage to his present location. How fortunate that his talents encompassed so many disciplines, his mind so flexible. Untaught in geography and yet able to gather the needed cartographical skills. He slung the map over the mule's back, grabbed the reins, and led the recalcitrant beast down the canyon, through passes and over crags, toward the high Washoe desert. Along the way he stopped at regular intervals, noting his location on the map, continuing the bootstrap survey until he reached the valley floor and could see Dayton off to his left. The Savage Mine was no longer visible, but the engineer and would-be cartographer had an uncanny ability to project its location through the mountains and miles of solid rock that stood in the way. He made some final calculations in his head, all the while tromping about in a dusty circle and checking his map one last time. Then, as if to honor earth's humble outcasts, he anointed the spot where he now stood, the final spot, the beginning as it were, with a stomp of his boot and a little pile of stubborn, uncompromising rocks.

He couldn't contain his excitement, and let out a holler. His partner snorted his approval, then contributed a heap of fresh dung to the celebration. It was such a remarkable idea, he thought, gazing at the little stony monument, he could scarcely believe no one had thought of it.

***

Sir Walter made his way towards North Beach with Will tugging at his reins. Larkin Street rolled up and down through a series of hills and swales. To his left, the terrain fell off into a sandy, wind-swept valley. The higher he climbed toward Russian Hill, the bigger the houses became. A garden here and there offered splashes of colorful flowers and the rare, lovely green tree.

They reached the top of the hill and began their decent to North Beach. Neptune's Beach House lay below. Will slid down onto the saddle horn, swaying back and forth as the haunches thrust up, then down, like pistons. Minutes later, having changed into his swim attire, he waded out into the icy water of the cove, gritted his teeth, and dove in. It was a familiar routine, but still surprised him, still stole his breath. He put his face down into the water, kicked his feet and forced his arms into the slow rotation of a swimmer's crawl. Out into the Bay he went, gliding quietly on the blue-green surface.

After a time he pulled up to tread water and take his bearings. He swiped at his stinging eyes. The tide was going out. He knew the currents would be strong, sweeping him out towards the Golden Gate lest he pay attention and adjust his course from time to time. He swam on with powerful strokes, churning through the icy water, pulling one hand beneath his chest, then the other, his feet doing their part, kicking and splashing, propelling him farther and farther from shore. His pace was easy, his motion fluid, skin numbed to the cold water, and he moved like an old sea creature, rising at regular intervals to steal a breath of air.

Pulling up again, he assessed his location. The currents were indeed dragging him toward the Golden Gate. He realigned himself with a point east of Alcatraz Island, then resumed his strokes, thinking of the precarious state of his bank, settled on a vague notion that the bay would have the answers, would lead him to a solution. The early days of the bank had been so success-ful, so full of promise; it had been almost too easy. Reciprocal agreements with other banks in the east and Europe, deposits outpacing expectations, capital flowing out for projects he consid-ered vital to San Francisco. Telegraph lines, railroads, new busi-nesses, hotels. Then, just when he thought his great plan was with-in reach, the Comstock Lode had suddenly faltered. Grown stingy, as if she wouldn't make this too easy.

He pushed through the white-capped waves. They jostled and rolled him at their leisure. He caught glimpses of the city and her quirky hills lined with avenues and dotted with little houses. San Francisco. Her beauty was there to see, though the miners and the shopkeepers and the politicians were blind to it. If they would just stop for a moment, look beyond their lives of toil. He could see it, despite the veneer of grotesque, man-made folly. This he would sweep away to reveal her true character. Her true beauty.

He had only to tame the Comstock Lode.

Chapter 9

It had been two months since Will had sent William Sharon to Virginia City, an excruciating two months of waiting and worrying. He kept operations at the bank as normal as possible, reassuring investors, maintaining a calm demeanor. Panic was a banker's worst enemy. These are but temporary problems, he told anxious customers.

Today Sharon would arrive with his promised report. Will kept himself occupied on the sidewalk outside the bank, surrounded by his ad-hoc committee of shop owners and businessmen. The state of the Union was explored, the fate of the West debated, the price of cattle argued over, the inevitability of prostitution conceded. San Franciscans delighted in the long October days and their warm Pacific breezes, and Will, lulled by the Indian summer, chatted and laughed as if he hadn't a care.

"Ol' Abe will never find a general that can defeat Lee."

"He could if he ceased to confuse war and politics."

Will rocked back and forth, listening, nodding, daydreaming. The War Between the States was endlessly examined and every man was an expert in some aspect of the war, or knew some colonel, or had a nephew who had died in one of its bloody battles.

"Wouldn't matter. The South is defending a way of life, the North is merely fighting for a cause."

"They fight, sir, to maintain the Union."

And on and on the debate raged. Californians, removed from the terrible carnage by wide plains and two mountain ranges, considered the war the way politicians might a piece of legislation. One has the luxury of rational discussion when one's sons are not being driven through by bayonets. Will, for his part, had placed his bet on Lincoln. The President had floated Greenbacks, hoping to raise desperately needed war funds, and he, Will, had purchased them with gusto, at cents on the dollar. Should Lincoln win the war, the greenbacks would rise in value and the bank would reap a windfall.

He gave in and checked his watch: soon he would have his answers. The intense, dark-eyed Sharon had made an impression. He had the focus of a gunfighter sighting down a barrel, a focus like nothing Will had ever seen, certainly beyond anything the mild and dependable Tibbey could ever muster. Instinct told him Sharon would find a solution to his troubles at the Comstock. After a lengthy debate with his board of directors, principally Darius Mills, he had convinced them to send Sharon to Virginia City to investigate and report back.

It was the appointed time; he made his way back to his office. Sharon was there, waiting for him with Colonel Fry. After polite greetings, Sharon handed him a thin folder.

"Here is my report," he said.

Will leafed through it, then looked up at the man he hoped would be his savior. Sharon's dark eyes gazed back at him, and the penetrating stare unnerved him a bit. What was behind those bead-black eyes?

"I'll read this later," he said. "Give me the highlights."

Sharon ran his thumb and forefinger along his thick moustaches. "In the past two months, I have gained what most would call an intimate understanding of the Comstock Lode, much the way a new husband might become intimate with his wife after during a honeymoon." Here the edge of his mouth turned up ever so slightly in what may have been, Will thought, a smile. "I have inspected the mines and mills and now possess a respectable knowledge of their workings. I have gained a passible understanding of the geology and engineering. I engaged in scholarly discourse with the superintendents—a more discerning fraternity of men, I might add, is not to be found on the Lode. As a result of these considerable investigations, Mr. Ralston, I am here to state with complete confidence that the best days of the Comstock Lode are before you."

"And by best days, you mean what, precisely?"

"That the greatest riches remain to be discovered. At depth."

"Excellent," he said, wondering if this was mere bravado. "What are your recommendations?"

The recommendations were shocking. Open a bank office in Virginia City and then take control of the camp, the mills, and as many mines as possible.

"You must be supremely confident that a great deal of ore remains at depth."

Sharon thought for a minute, then said, "The weakest kind of fruit drops earliest to the ground." With dark black eyes unblinking, Sharon looked at Will. "Shakespeare was a wise man, Mr. Ralston."

"What do you mean?"

"The easy fruit of the Comstock has fallen, now we must be careful lest another jump in to gain the true harvest."

Will glanced at Fry, who wore a silly grin, like the parent of a precocious child, delighted but not surprised at their remarkable progeny.

"Go on, please."

"Geologists are in accord on the nature of the mineral deposits. The Comstock they consider a true fissure vein that extends to considerable depth. I have studied the geology, to the extent possible with a limited knowledge of the sciences, and I've witnessed the ledges, below ground, with my own eyes. I'm persuaded that the geologists are accurate in their assessment of the subsurface. That is to say, below the water line, sir, an abundance of rich and profitable ore bodies remain to be discovered."

"But the water," he said, a bit exasperated. "We cannot simply wish it away."

"I cannot argue with your assessment, Mr. Ralston. And thus my final recommendation. Remove the water. How, I have yet to determine. Nevertheless, remove the water we must, for once that obstacle is eliminated, the riches of the Comstock will drop into our baskets like apples from a shook tree."

Will nodded slowly while his fingers tore at a piece of paper. Could they find a way to eliminate the water? Large sums have already been invested on the Lode, but this Sharon proposed to invest more. Much more. The bank would never recover from such a loss, if this man, this man with no banking or mining experience, had misjudged. He imagined Mills' reaction to this proposal.

But there was more at stake than just the bank. San Francisco rested in the balance. Without more bullion, without the enormous mining profits, the city would shrivel up and fade away, never to achieve the exalted status she deserved.

"Mr. Ralston—"

His eyes darted to Sharon.

"If you will engage my services to conduct an agency in Virginia City, I will devote five years henceforth to you, the bank, and the Comstock Lode. The water problem will yield its secrets to my investigations, and the lode will yield its treasures. I will satisfy the bank's obligations, gain control of the Comstock, and deliver its riches to you and the Bank of California."

The claim, as enticing as it was, seemed beyond the pale of optimism. But, there was no doubt in his mind: given the choice between a dim and dying future, and a courageous final grasp at glory, he would choose the latter. He stood, extended his hand to Sharon, and with their palms pressed together, they shook, setting into motion a bold, if not reckless, plan that would alter the course of their lives, the lives of all who knew them, and the youthful city with an insatiable hunger for silver.

***

Finn slid onto a barstool at the Auction Lunch Saloon.

"Mornin' to you, James."

"Finnian, my boy!" James Flood was stooped in the far corner picking up pieces of glass. Broken tables and chairs were strewn about, left over from the night's revelries. A bucket and mop stood at the ready.

Flood slipped behind the bar and pushed back his wavy brown hair. "What're ya doin' here on a Sunday mornin'?"
"Come to see you."

The proprietor opened a bottle of ale and set it on the bar. He explained the mess: Joseph McGinley and the boys went at it the night before and into the wee hours. O'Brien had been tending shop so it was Flood's half of the bargain to clean up in the morning.

Finn gulped down some ale, then told Flood he had been in a fight up on Russian hill a while back. Four Protestants provoked him. Well, he had just heard that one of them died. A fair-haired boy that had had no business street fighting, dammit. They're saying it was Finn's doing.

"Maybe you best be leaving town for a while," Flood said.

"That's what I've come to tell ya, McGinley and I are going to Virginia City."

"You intend to be a miner, then?"

"Nae. But I'm thinking Joseph does. I've a mind to stick with carpentry."

Flood poured two glasses of whiskey.

"May the Comstock be good to the both of you, and may the Protestants all go to the devil." The proprietor lifted the glass to his lips and, turning it in one motion, swallowed the whiskey in one swift gulp.

Finn did likewise. The smooth whiskey-burn in his chest was fine indeed.

Flood said he had a friend, John Mackay, in Virginia City. Been pestering him to invest in his mining claims. This Mackay was famous for solving terrible riddles, and so Flood thought he just might put in with him. He insisted Finn go see him when he got to camp.

"He's a fine Irishman," said Flood. "A sober one, to be sure, but fine just the same. Straight as an Englishman is crooked and wise as Solomon. Says Virginia City is a dacent enough place, with goodly people. Sure but they've some troublemakers, but so does San Francisco."

"Aye, it does." Finn pictured Coal-eyes. Every town had its Coal-eyes, he supposed.

"Shall I pour another?"

"Nae," he said, waiving him off. "I'll be on my way."

Flood corked the bottle and snatched up a piece of paper. He scratched out some correspondence, folded it, stuffed it into an envelope, and handed it to Finn.

"Give this to MacKay," he said.

Finn slid off the barstool and thanked him. He was thinking, though, that what every town didn't have was a beautiful, yellow-haired girl that gave him books. She had captured his fancy, there was no denying it, and if he thought he could catch the elusive colleen, he might just stay in San Francisco.

He put two bits on the counter and headed for the door. A man would be a fool to waste his youth chasing a fairie, he thought.

"Say hello to Mackay for me," Flood yelled after him. "And tell Joseph he better be back here with an eagle or two, or I'll come looking for him."

Chapter 10

Will awoke to the sound of Jess's voice. I have something to tell you, he heard her say.

He rubbed his eyes, and realized that he was in her bed. He rolled over to look at her. "What is it?"

These were the first words they had spoken that night. He had arrived, knocked as usual, she opened the door and he fell into her arms. Words were often unnecessary for them; touch, he found, seemed to be a language they both understood. Now, an hour later, his dreams were of the bank, the Comstock, William Sharon. How much longer could he hold out against falling share prices and rising water?

She sat up in the bed, pulling the sheet up to her chin. This, he thought, did not bode well. "I'm going to grant you your wish."

"What wish?" He had a number of them at the moment.

"Your fondest wish. I'm going to give it to you. I will take a new profession."

"Profession? What sort of profession?"

"Teaching. I am to be a schoolmistress."

For a moment, he thought she was teasing him, but the look on her face said otherwise.

"My God, you're serious."

She nodded yes, smiling in a shy but proud way he had never seen before.

"Which school? Where will you be teaching?"

She hesitated. "In Virginia City," she said quietly.

He fell back onto his pillow. No, anywhere but there, he wanted to shout. The sun-baked, wind-blown mining camp flashed in his mind. "Virginia City is no place for a lady," he exclaimed. Would she reconsider? He could make inquiries.

She lifted her gaze to his, but said nothing. Oh, those eyes. So clear in their silence, so unequivocal.

Of course, she might not be a lady in the sense of San Francisco society, but in Virginia City she would be the height of refinement. Cursed luck, he thought, overcome with self-pity. She touched his arm. A tender, apologetic touch, the one touch a man never wants from a woman. She leaned over and kissed him on the cheek.

He would not be mollified. He got up and dressed, went to the coat rack, absentmindedly took down his coat, placed one arm in, then the other, and tugged it onto his shoulders. This was his own fault, he knew. He had pushed her to find another profession, and she had, and it was good, and he was happy that she would be living a respectable life. But how could he fill the void she would leave behind? Seeing her was like seeing Louisa, in the flesh; but now he was losing her, yet again. She kept slipping away.

"You'll visit me, won't you?" she said.

He sighed. "My face is known in Virginia City."

He held her for a long moment, whispering that he was happy for her, and then pushed out into the cool night air. Sir Walter, tossing his head, was glad to see him. He stroked the horse's sleek neck before climbing into the saddle. If only people were as dependable as horses, he thought.

Beneath a bright moon he pictured Jess in Virginia City, then tried to wrest the thought from his mind. The Comstock. Stamp mills. Filthy miners. William Sharon. Sharon may well turn the bank's fortunes there, he thought, or he may drag it into bankruptcy. Odd: he was losing Jess to the Comstock, as if it were demanding a price. It would yield its treasures but first wanted payment. A sacrifice. Jess, perhaps, was to be that sacrifice. There was a bitter irony at work, as if choosing between Jess (and Louisa), and San Francisco. Either way, he lost.

***

Maps, drawings, cross-sections, and engineering tables covered the kitchen table, desk, and much of the dirt floor. Sutro's house in Dayton, in the desert below Virginia City, was an ideal headquarters, to his way of thinking, for his engineering company not yet formed but soon to be so, money being the only barrier between him and success, and that a mere nuisance, which would yield once the scientific and engineering principles assembled there before him were shared with the world. This, of course, was the long-term pecuniary goal. The short-term one was to recover the insurance proceeds from his mill, withheld due to outrageous claims that he had destroyed his own business. Meanwhile, with frugal living he should have sufficient funds, according to his arithmetic, be it from the sale of his shops or a few small investors, to live and meet expenses for several years.

He scratched at the scar that ran from ear to chin beneath his sideburn, a habitual exercise, now, many years after the knife attack in Portsmouth Square. While he took no notice of the scratching, the scar reminded him of his own remarkable ability to survive, and thrive, no matter the challenge, naysayer, or hostile enemy.

He stood back to take inventory: two geologic maps, three cross sections, two plan-maps, three engineering drawings, and countless ledgers of figures and tabulations. He was ready. To-morrow he would ride up to Virginia City to visit John Mackay, a Comstock superintendent and well-respected citizen in camp, and with his support, begin the fruitful process of raising funds for his great work, a work that would, he knew with swelling pride, change the face of the Comstock, the West and, quite possibly, the nation itself.

Chapter 11

Will slipped his hand into Elizabeth's. The drawing room was silent on this Sunday afternoon save the tick-tock of the Bavarian timepiece. That clock had its place among the other gifts received from diplomats and notables who had been their guests: a Napoleonic hat from France, an Etruscan artifact from Italy, silk flowers from the Orient. They gladly played host to the world for the chance to show off their city, and to promote its businesses. If once Elizabeth had been fearful of entertaining guests or giving a party, she was now a confident hostess and the proud wife of a prominent citizen. She, like Will, adored San Francisco, loved its wild energy, its society, all its stores and theatres that were springing up in the districts. But she needed to stay busy, and there had been no guests of late. The house was quiet and Elizabeth seemed restless. Since the death of little Louisa two years before, she had never been quite the same. Will agonized over how to raise her spirits.

He asked how she was feeling.

"I'm doing well," she said with a brave face.

"Perhaps you'd enjoy a carriage ride around South Park," he said. "We can take the phaeton."

"I think it's too cold," she said. She stared out into the garden. Then, after a moment, she said, "I've been thinking about a trip abroad. That would be wonderful, wouldn't it? I've always wanted to go to Paris. Why don't we take the boys and travel to Europe. It would be good for them. New Englanders take their children to the Continent all the time. It's quite educational, they say, and we'll be able to see Paris in the springtime." Her face became a hopeful smile.

He wanted nothing more than to dash off with her to exotic, romantic places. To make her forget. To make her happy.

"Lizzie, I would love to travel to Europe with you and the boys. But to leave now would be irresponsible. The bank's future, and our future, rests in the balance." He watched the hope drain from her face.

"Of course," she said. "I understand."

He couldn't bear to look at her. His duty to the bank and his wife tugged, mercilessly like Newton's opposing forces. To leave the bank in the midst of a crisis, a crisis that threatened its very existence, and the dreams it represented, was unthinkable.

In the afternoon he waited as Riker saddled a pair of horses. Together they rode along Market Street, up Larkin to Russian Hill, and down to Neptune's Beach House on North Beach. In his swimming attire, he waded into the icy water. Riker stood in the doorway of the wind-bitten house; there the sentry would watch and wait. As was his routine, Will preferred one jolt of pain to a prolonged agony, and so dove headfirst into the water.

He drew one arm through the water beneath him, the other he swung in an arc overhead, and he worried: dividends must be paid this week. One percent. Every month. Investors expected the dividends, and if they weren't paid on time, panic would ensue. He would pay them from his personal account, if necessary. He must buy time for Sharon. He waited for this man now, this man in whom he had placed great trust, great hope, and with little reason other than instinct.

The water was all peaks and swales and whitecaps. Progress was slow. He battled a strong tide. Fatigue gripped him: his arms became heavy. Suddenly the shore seemed a great distance. He could hear Louisa's voice in his head: *You find yourself caught in a menacing tide, my love. But salvation will come to you in unexpected ways. Stay afloat, persevere and soon the tide will turn.*

I cannot give up, he thought. You and I, we will succeed, or we will fail, but we will do it together.

Part Two

(1865-1869)

Chapter 12

Sutro kicked at the burned-out frame of his old mill the way a mule might kick at a pesky dog. Would he ever be rid of this thing? Almost two years since the mill had burned down, and yet, here he was. In the distance, the town of Dayton looked like a cluster of debris plopped onto the desert floor. Soon, he hoped, he would be in the saloon, drinking a beer to celebrate the settlement of his insurance claim. The insurance adjuster, meanwhile, poked and prodded his way through the wreckage, stopping once every so often to make a note in his little book. Sutro was vexed by his diligent quietude. He had answers at the ready, if only the confounded man would ask him.

The insurance money was critical to the great plans he had for the Comstock. They had been out there for hours with the afternoon sun beating down upon them. Waves of heat curled and wafted up from the desert floor. Faint music could be heard drifting from the saloon. He licked his lips, involuntarily.

"Mr. Sutro?"

Startled, he thought maybe he was hearing things. The desert can do that to you. "Yes?" he said.

"Is there a place to stay in Dayton?"

"There's a hotel in Dayton."

"I'll need another couple of days, then I'll have your answer."

An hour later, he was in the saloon, just as he'd hoped, except the beer didn't taste nearly as good as he thought it would. Damned insurance company.

***

Finn pressed his chapped lips together to spare them, if only for a moment, from the dry desert air. Between them, his dust-filled nostrils, and dry-as-lizard eyes, he wasn't sure which part of his body suffered most. He twisted around in his saddle to get a complete view of the Carson Valley, nestled below the Sierra Nevada Mountains. As far as the eye could discern, the eastern face of the Sierras was denuded of trees, covered with aught but stumps left by voracious loggers, like stubble on a giant, unshaved face.

He turned back to the east, missing the west already. The Emigrant Trail stretched out before him, a bleak highway with memories that would surely make the saints weep. All those brave wagons had rutted westward, while he and Joseph McGinley now pushed east—what fate did they tempt, which gods might they anger, by such heresy?

"We'll go through Dayton," he said to Joseph, "to water the mules before we start up to Virginia City."

The mules, either sensing a reprieve or an oasis, moved smartly now, even as the scorching sun baked the landscape to a crisp glaze. All other creatures with any common sense were hidden in repose, and so the mules and their riders intruded upon a silent and vast siesta. In the distance, to their right, a long, sinewy band of trees hugged the banks of the Carson River, a ribbon of green in a drab gray valley. On their left, across the valley, a small range of mountains rose up, dusty and treeless, where, Finn knew, they would find Virginia City and the Comstock.

In Dayton they sought out a watering hole and strong refreshment. In the saloon, an indignant Prussian complained to the thirsty but deaf patrons of an insurance conspiracy out to defile the West and deprive an honest man of his just solatium for grievous loss. Oh, but Bismarck himself couldn't have ejaculated a more passionate tirade, nor delivered it with a thicker accent. Unencumbered by self-doubt, this immigrant knew all things with utter certainty, including, they discovered, the shortest route to Virginia City. Thus it happened that Finn and Joseph became the captive audience of Herr Adolph Sutro, following him into Six Mile Canyon on the final leg of their journey up to Virginia City.

Sutro was a barrel-chested man with prodigious sideburns, one side of which he liked to scratch. His clothes were raw and heavy-cut, his boots black and polished beneath a layer of thick dust. Having listened to one another's voices for many days, Finn and Joseph were content to hear a different tongue, even one with harsh German cadences. And Sutro, they soon discovered, enjoyed the sound of his own voice. The story began in Aachen, Prussia; his father was killed in a carriage accident, the family woolen mill shut down; mother and children then emigrated to

America. Aachen, he told them, was famous for its baths. And the Great Charlemagne had lived there—did they know that?

Joseph had a devilish twinkle in his eye. "Charlie McCain, you say? But Charlie McCain lived in Cloonacarrow, Mr. Sutro, County of Roscommon, and he never partook of a bath unless a colleen was involved."

Charlemagne was a great king, Sutro insisted, looking sideways at Joseph. Ah, well, Joseph thought him a splendid fellow anyway, despite any taint of royal blood. Sutro brooded, trying to decide if he'd been insulted. The scenery drifted by, sparse cottonwood trees, weathered crags, animal skulls that stared blankly at them. Sutro, undaunted by Joseph, continued with his heroic tale. Eventually, an engineer emerged from the story, their guide's natural calling in the world. And as the narrative came to the present day, the climax of the story was revealed to be a great engineering work, a tunnel of sorts, to be dug right beneath the very scenery they were intent on traversing.

"A tunnel, you say?" Joseph sat straight in his saddle. "'Tis a fact, I'm an expert on tunnels, Mr. Sutro. Dug one 'neath Pa's steaming shed. In Ireland, that is, when I was a wee boy. Pa didn't care for it much, so I had to fill it back up. But it was a lovely tunnel, lovely indeed."

A generous offer followed to assist Mr. Sutro in the digging of his tunnel, he, Joseph, being experienced in such matters. Sutro testily declined the offer for assistance, explaining that his tunnel was of the magnitude of four miles, and not of the backyard variety.

"Four miles!" Joseph was aghast. "Jaysus. What would you be need'n with a hole like that?"

Sutro snorted, as if at an errant or dim-witted child. His tunnel would come up from the desert, he explained, beneath these very mountains, until reaching the Comstock Lode, where it would connect to the lower reaches of the mines, efficiently remove their ore, cleanse their foul air, and drain their endless water. And all, he remarked, with the aid of free and bountiful gravity.

Finn scratched his chin. Damned if there wasn't a logic to it.

But, a befuddled Sutro, after puzzling over Joseph's questions about the size of shovel and bucket he intended to use, the number of days he thought the excavation might take, and the like, brought the tale to conclusion over the sad incidence of an insurance dispute with the claim investigator, who had grave doubts about the fire that had burned the Sutro Mill to the ground. This sole obstacle remained in the path of Herr Engineer's great work, yet to be commenced.

"A bog trotter, that actuary," sympathized Joseph. "Leave me have a word with him, Mr. Sutro. I'll set him straight, ye can be sure of it."

Finn chuckled. Sutro vehemently maintained his innocence. He was confident this would resolve in his favor. They were coming into the lower-most boundaries of Virginia City and the base of Mt. Davidson. Their guide pointed out the various districts, arranged according to race and nationality, the rents of which rose steadily with elevation, as did the quality of the residents. Stamps mills banged and clanked out their processed ore with such a racket that communications became difficult. They commenced to make the last steep climb onto C Street at the southern end of camp.

The town's main street, C, ran along the strike of Mt. Davidson, and fell away in a modest down-slope going north. Clouds of dust billowed up like swarms of locusts with each passing stagecoach, until the coaches and freight wagons and mule trains became hopelessly entangled, bringing all progress to a halt. Every man seemed to have the most urgent business to attend, their red shirts and full beards caked in grime as they charged with great haste into assay shops or supply stores.

They rode through town and Sutro pointed out shops and businesses and the owners of each building. The wealthy mine-owners resided in fine houses up on A and B Streets; C Street was busy with commerce (mostly saloons). The miners lived below on D and E, while the public ladies, as he called them, could be found on North D, in case they were interested. The Irish lived even lower down on the mountain, in the vicinity of Washington Street.

They thanked Sutro for his guidance and hospitality. Joseph offered to buy him a whiskey and renewed his offer to assist with the great tunnel, but Sutro declined on both counts, then abruptly took his leave.

"In a hurry to start diggin' that tunnel, he is," Joseph said gravely. He grinned, said he'd meet Finn on the morrow, and headed to the nearest saloon.

Finn had in mind to investigate the Irish district. At least the Irish were higher on the mountain than the Chinese, he thought, observing the bleak neighborhood. Warp-sided wooden buildings, that no carpenter could take pride in, sprouted like weeds, with no particular order.

As the mules plodded wearily, the sound of childish voices suddenly danced into Finn's ears. Then, from around the corner, a flock of wee dotes appeared, all bursting with energy and

79

bouncing and jostling and gabbing. And behind the last child, the sonsy, flaxen-haired girl from San Francisco! She had been in Virginia City—a schoolmistress. Jaysus.

He stood watching. She stepped along behind her brood, eyeing them like a mother goose. Then, unexpectedly, she looked up. Her eyes met his. Over the heads of the students and across the dusty street, they stared at each other.

One of the little ones grabbed at her dress and squeaked something at her and she looked down, nodding, Yes, all right. She looked back at Finn, then hurried to catch up with her charges. They filed into the schoolhouse, and when the last one had gone inside and the schoolmistress had reached the door, she turned, as if unable to help herself, and glanced at him again.

And then she darted inside.

He stared at the closed door. Only a moment ago Virginia City had been a noisy, dusty camp of crude miners and parlor girls. Miraculously, it now seemed a fine place indeed. He examined the camp with new eyes. Where he had seen bearded miners, he now saw little cherub-faced scholars, wives and mothers instead of public ladies. Church spires drew his attention away from the saloon signs.

The home of the comely schoolmistress seemed a splendid little city.

Chapter 13

Will looked across his desk at Adolph Sutro, wondering: Was this big Prussian a genius or a madman? Stacks and rolls of maps and charts were spread out helter-skelter all over the desk. Will had been distracted by it all, by the enormous sideburns and guttural Germanic accent. But then something began to catch his attention: an outrageous scheme began to unfold. A tunnel beneath the Comstock.

"Four miles?" Will exclaimed, after hearing the intended length.

"Yes, four miles. My tunnel will allow the foul air to ventilate, and it will take the ore, and the water, down to the valley and the Carson River."

"The water?" Will rocked forward in his chair. "How much water?"

"All of it. As much as you like," said Sutro, throwing up his hands with a big laugh.

Will snatched up the proposal, rifled through the pages until he found a drawing. "Is this the tunnel?" he said, pointing to the hand-drawn map. He peppered Sutro with questions. How far was it from Virginia City to the river? Had anyone ever dug a tunnel that long? Did he need permission from the state? What fees would Sutro charge to use the tunnel?

And as he listened, he thought, this could be the answer to all my problems. If this can actually be done.

Then, suddenly, a twist in his gut. "How much will it cost?" he asked.

"I estimate three million dollars. But," Sutro quickly added, "I need to borrow only five hundred thousand to get started."

Will couldn't help but flinch. Where would he get five hundred thousand dollars? Sharon was lending money on the Comstock at two percent a month and was extending more credit every day. These profitable loans were the bank's priority. But if the tunnel worked, and, if he could somehow raise the money...

He reached for his letterhead, dipped his pen into the inkwell. Adolph Sutro's tunnel, he wrote, was an important work and men of means should consider investing, as the benefits would be substantial. The Bank of California supported the venture and would, in time, contribute capital.

He handed the completed letter to Sutro. He was to come back when he had a right-of-way from the newly formed State of Nevada. With letter in hand, Sutro dashed out of the office.

Remarkable, Will thought, watching him go, elbows, papers and map rolls all akimbo. His desk was now free of clutter, and again he could see Louisa. Thinking of her, he took up another piece of stationary.

My Dear Mrs. Thorn—

I apologize for my tardiness in responding to your most recent letter and I hope this finds you and Mr. Thorn, and your extended family, well and prosperous. It was, of course, the greatest of news to hear the Civil War had finally ended, but we were overcome with grief at the death of President Lincoln. We pray that Andrew Johnson is up to the task of pulling our country back together again.

Business matters continue to be difficult here, although with the war over, hopeful signs are on the horizon. I pray your family, and business interests, are showing improvement. I was delighted to hear of the birth of your latest grandchild and I'm certain that you are the happiest and most generous of grandparents. Someday soon I plan visit you and see all your bright-faced little ones before they are full grown and out in the world, making their mark.

Some happy news to report—Elizabeth gave birth to a fine baby girl last month and, in honor of your longtime friendship, though truthfully I think of you as family, we named our daughter Emelita Thorn Ralston. It is, I believe, a most lovely and fitting name and I know she will honor the beauty and elegance of her namesake, to whom I hope to one day introduce her. Both Elizabeth and baby are doing well. Emelita was just over eight pounds and already has a thick head of lovely, brown hair, reminding me, I can't help but mention, of Louisa's.

So we now have a bustling family of three fine children. Samuel and William, Jr., are doing well and growing into strong young men. Like their father, they are fond of horses.

I will sign off for now but will write again soon, and may I always remain—

Forever and Sincerely Yours,
William Ralston

He did not reveal that *Emily Thorn Ralston* had been his name of choice. Elizabeth had protested, rather vehemently, that he continued to be in love with Louisa, that he thought about her more than his own living wife, and she could not bear the humiliation of naming her daughter after Louisa's mother. As before, a compromise had been reached.

While he composed his letters, Sutro's tunnel kept slipping into his thoughts. It was a courageous and bold idea. The tunnel could revolutionize development of the Comstock and free up the deeper ore. It could very well save the Bank of California, and his plans for San Francisco.

Chapter 14

John Mackay, it was said about camp, could be found at the gymnasium on C Street in the wee hours of the morning. So Finn had gotten up early on his day off, and was now watching the boxers in their red gloves (mufflers, they called them) poke and dance around like dandies at a Saturday night social. Nary a serious punch was landed. Ridiculous, he thought.

He made quiet inquiries. "You mean Mackie?" they said, laughing. "Over there." Mackie, as his friends called him, was featherweight in size but wiry, strong, with a crop of boyish blond hair. At the side of the ring, he pulled off his mufflers and shook Finn's hand. Finn presented Flood's letter.

"Flood thinks highly of you," MacKay said after reading the letter. "Says you're a young man of rare character."

"I'd be thinking the same of him. Meaning his character, that is."

Mackay laughed: 'twas true, he and Flood weren't so young any more. They talked, exchanged stories. He looked Finn right in the eye, and he listened to him like a favorite uncle might, nodding and smiling as Finn spoke. He knew right off he would trust this Mackay.

85

"I'll leave you to your boxing, then," said Finn.

"An Irishman is the butt of jokes in San Francisco," Mackay told him as he turned to go. "But things are different in Virginia. Here an Irishman can own the city and everyone will step up and congratulate him."

Then Virginia City was a rare place indeed, said Finn.

"If it's employment you're in need of, then come to my office tomorrow morning."

"Thank you, Mr. Mackay."

"Call me Mackie. And be ready to box next time."

Later, in the falling light, Finn stood across from the little schoolhouse. Children began to file out the door, scampering in all directions like rabbits hopping from the gorse. He watched the door for five, ten, fifteen minutes, but the schoolmistress didn't appear. Perhaps there was a back way, he thought. He considered going inside. No, that would be scandalous, for her, if she were alone. He pulled his coat closed against the winds coming down from the mountain. He kicked rocks down the street and waited.

Then the door swung open, and out she stepped. She looked up and saw him. He headed across the street toward her. She turned away and fumbled with a key, trying to put it into the lock. When she turned back, he was standing in front of her.

"My name is Finnian. Finnian Gillespie. 'Twas you I saw in San Francisco."

"Yes, it was."

"I looked for you," he said, scarcely believing she was right in front of him. "You're as slippery as a leprechaun."

She blushed. "You gave me a flower once."

"'Tis true, I did."

He was staring. She looked away, went back to work with her key.

"May I know your name?"

"Jessalyn," she said, turning back around. "Jessalyn Ohhlson." She paused, looking at the key. "You may call me Jessie, if you like."

"Jessie is a grand name." He reached out and wrapped his fingers around her tiny hand.

"Pleased to know you, then."

She looked at her hand in his. "I have assignments to complete," she said, pulling away.

"Might I call on you, then?"

"Thank you, but it would be better if you didn't."

She turned to go. Quickly, he said, "But I hoped you would read the poetry of Thomas Moore to me."

She stopped. "You don't know how to read?"

He shook his head.

"How do you know it's the poetry of Thomas Moore?"

"That scarecrow-of-a-man at the bookstore told me."

She smiled. "He was a scarecrow, wasn't he?" She looked at him, and he waited. "All right, we'll read together, but on condition that I also give you lessons."

If it meant spending more time with her, he would accept any condition.

"I will first have to make arrangements with my landlady, Mrs. Frieda," she said.

He watched her go, wisps of yellow hair escaping beneath her bonnet. Wasn't it grand that he had never learned to read?

***

87

The Ormsby County administration building sat on Carson Street between Musser and King in downtown Carson City, and served as the temporary offices of the Nevada State Legislature. President Lincoln, needing votes for the election, had just admitted the Nevada territory into the Union.

Sutro made his way to the second floor office of Mr. Nelson Winton of the Union Party, representing Storey County. Sutro was buoyant, having finally received the disputed insurance proceeds, and now being free to travel, if need be, and to pursue reluctant investors wherever they may be hiding. Mr. Winton and the other lawmakers were working feverishly on the Statutes of Nevada, the laws necessary to function in a manner befitting a State of the Union. For Sutro, this included an efficiently-managed Comstock Lode, which inevitably led to a need for his tunnel. But the engineer thought he noticed a little grimace on the lawmaker's round face as he stepped into his office.

Winton knew without asking what he had come to discuss, and watched with tightly pressed lips while rolls and maps and papers were deposited onto his desk. On a map, Sutro pointed out the Comstock and the long, straight line representing his tunnel, the proposed right-of-way, and, of course, the town at the bottom, near the river. Winton was not aware of plans for a town. The tunnel workers, Sutro patiently explained, and eventually the miners themselves, must have a place to live. What would the place be called? Winton thought to ask.

"Why, the Town of Sutro, of course." What else could it be called? Sadly, Virginia City would become a ghost town, he pointed out, but such was the way of life and commerce.

Shaking his head, the legislator took a close look at the map.

"You know, Mr. Sutro, some people around here think you're a madman. I'm not saying I agree with them, you understand, but digging a tunnel from the desert to Virginia City does sound mighty farfetched."

People, Sutro reminded him, thought Columbus was crazy. The world is flat, they said.

The subject of cost was raised.

"Three millions dollars?" Winton smacked his fist down onto the desk. And where the devil was he going to get three million dollars?

He reached into the satchel and pulled out Ralston's letter. The Senator read, looked up at him, then read some more. "All this says is that Ralston likes the idea and may lend you some of the money. It does not guarantee a loan."

"He will lend me the money. He needs my tunnel. It will drain his mines of the water so he can explore deeper. He will lend the money, you will see. Besides, this does not affect the right-of-way, and I am not asking Nevada for money. And if I can build the tunnel," he continued before the lawmaker could find other objections, "it will be good for Nevada because the Comstock ledge will produce more silver and there will not be so much waste. And there will be many jobs for your citizens."

Winton rubbed his eyes. Fatigue seemed to have gotten the better of him.

"Mr. Sutro, I will include your project in the Nevada Act, granting you a right-of-way for a period of five years."

Sutro protested that five years was insufficient, and commenced to recite figures and times and rates of drilling and other various and sundry facts.

A few minutes later he left the Senator's office, pleased to have secured an eight year agreement, plenty of time, if his calculations were correct, to build his tunnel.

Chapter 15

Finn held tightly to the cable of the hoisting cage. The four men who shared the platform with him were at ease, like old mariners on the deck of a ship, while Finn could barely get a breath, his chest as tight as his grip. Suddenly, the cage fell into the black chasm of the mineshaft like a stone into an abyss. He had been wary of this moment, his first descent into the mines, and his fear had not been without cause. The platform shook and vibrated as it dropped. Station lights whooshed past every few seconds, the temperature rising as they went. Finn noticed an odd weightless feeling, as if he were floating, and then a little nausea in his stomach. The air grew hotter and fouler until he wondered how a man could work in such an oven.

They landed with a knee-buckling jolt at the six hundred foot station. A loud, mechanical churning noise came up from beneath the cage, down in the shaft. Sharon's water pumps, one of the men said. Finn let loose his aching grip. A water barrel, awash in light, sat in the midst of the cave-like room, a crowd of miners gathered round it. Joseph McGinley was among them and the talk was salty, washed down with draughts of icy cold water. Ian spent all his pay on D Street (Gallagher would too but the girls wouldn't have him), Sweeny was surprised to learn there were girls on D Street; Ian's mama was a Tommyknocker; better a Tommyknocker than a Cousin-jack, and so on.

The foreman, Eliot Horner, handed Finn a tallow candle. Finn would follow the miners, where he'd find timbering that needed repair. To the miners, Horner explained the general plan to be implemented. "This week, boys, you'll be marking a new drift. You'll head westward, down this crosscut. When the cross-cut hits the lode, you'll open up a north-south drift, or gallery, to work the ore, what ore you find. Assays will be taken at five-foot intervals. Eventually you'll run east-west drifts from the gallery until certain the lode is contained. We'll need winzes to the upper gallery and adits for ventilation..."

Horner continued in this manner for several minutes. Finn's head was dinnlin' with all the easts and wests, drifts and winzes. He resolved at that moment to never get lost in a mine, as he would never find his way out of such an incomprehensible lab-yrinth. Joseph's crew headed for the hoist cage. Finn and the oth-ers lit their candles and followed Horner into the crosscut, bend-ing at the waist to keep from hitting the low ceiling. Lights and a powerful stench foretold a gallery up ahead, one growing bright-er, the other more nauseating. No privies in the mines, one of the men remarked for the newcomer.

"What's a Tommyknocker?" Finn asked Gallagher, in front of him.

"They're ghosts," came the answer. "Ghosts that likes mines, guess you could say."

"They ain't ghosts," someone yelled back. "They're elves."

"The fuck they are," shouted Gallagher. "What does a Cousin-jack know about Tommyknockers?"

"We brought the devils from Cornwall," yelled the Cousin-jack. "We should know what the fuck they are."

"All right, boys," said Horner.

They reached an old, foul-smelling gallery, with the headwall in front and dark voids to either side. The ceiling and walls were buttressed with wide timbers, oriented up and down, and side-to-side, these forming a regular, square scaffolding, or lattice frame: the handiwork of a lumbermen.

Something moved near the headwall. Finn peered through the timber, a shadow perhaps, he thought, but no, it was there but not there, a ghostly lacuna. A Tommyknocker? A light flickered.

"Mornin' to ya, Mr. Sharon," Horner said.

William Sharon, with deliberation, turned his attention from the wall. He had a great bulge of tobacco in his cheek. "Mr. Horner," he nodded, leaning over to spit tobacco juice.

"Have you found anything?" Horner asked.

"Nope."

"I heard there were some streaks over in the Kentuck. Probably just bastard quartz, least-wise that'd be my thinking."

"Is that so?" Sharon said. His face was blank, expressionless.

"Yep," said Horner, "I think it's played out here. We got to get rid of the water, so we can go deeper."

Sharon looked back up the crosscut, toward the pump noise, as if to say he was working on it.

"Don't want to keep you men from your work," he said. He leaned and dribbled more tobacco juice, then headed into the crosscut.

As Sharon disappeared into the dark void, Sweeny said, "And a good day to you too, sir."

Raucous laughter broke out.

"The devil go with him," said Ian, to a murmur of approval.

Chapter 16

A fierce wind blew sheets of powdery snow down from Mt. Davidson, buffeting the stagecoach, which creaked and shivered as Will stepped out and onto a dark and frozen C Street. Behind him the lights from the International Hotel cast an inviting glow. The stalwart driver took his bags down and a quavering bellman took them inside. Will was generous with his tips.

Entering his usual room on the fifth floor, he found a note under the door. From Sharon: "Please meet me at the bank office upon your arrival." He groaned. Perhaps the manager should come see *him*? Sighing, he retraced his steps through the gilded hotel lobby and out into the freezing wind. Sharon had recently sent a request for fifty thousand dollars and Mills had objected. The president, and largest shareholder, wanted a more traditional approach to banking. They should extract themselves from the Comstock quagmire, he was insisting. For nearly two years, he said, almost since the day the bank had opened, the Comstock anchor had been keeping dragging them down.

With his coat pulled tight and his head down, Will tromped through the snow down C Street, able to see by the saloon lights that dissected the darkness. He reached Taylor a few minutes later. In a howling wind, a key rattled in the lock and Sharon opened the door to the bank's agency office. A wad of tobacco bulged from his cheek.

"Sorry to keep you waiting."

"Another minute and I'd have become a snowman."

"A very distinguished one, though."

There was just enough light to see an outline of the teller counter and signs hanging from the ceiling: Receiving Teller and Paying Teller. The manager led the way back, and pulled up two chairs next to his desk so they could sit side-by-side. Sharon went to his desk and removed two heavy canvas bags from the drawer. These he handed to Will.

"From the Crown Point," Sharon said.

Though Sharon's face betrayed no emotion, Will divined that these humble bags, stained and tattered, were bursting with the hope of new life. He had been accumulating shares of the Yellow Jacket and Crown Point mines for several months, and now owned the majority of each. He set the bags down on the floor between his feet. He opened one, and bending down to take a look, was met by a gravid, loamy essence from the loins of Mother Nature herself, musky with the odors of vinegar, metal, and yeast all thrown together, as though She, or the Devil—who knew?—were cooking up something deep down. Moist and brindled, the sample gave way between his trembling fingers. He held up a fistful to the lamp and noted light bouncing back at him from mirror-like flecks.

"Here are the assays," Sharon said, handing him a sheet of paper before leaning over to spit into a cuspidor.

The assays ranged from $200 per ton to $1,500 per ton. This was rich ore. Very rich. How thick was the ledge? He knew from earlier discussions it had been no thicker than a strip of leather when Sharon first spotted it.

"It remained thin for a hundred feet." Sharon paused and the hint of a smile crept across his face, something rarely seen. "But it just opened up into a pod. And it keeps getting wider."

Will fell back into his chair, stunned.

"It's a bonanza," Sharon said.

"But, I thought we couldn't get to the deeper ore?" Will said.

"I have pumps running all day and night. The water has gone down a sufficient amount to reveal clues to those who know where to look."

"My God," exclaimed Will.

"Congratulations," Sharon said, "your bank is saved."

Vindication. Faith not disgraced, but justified. Downturns are followed by upturns, Will had told them. One must be patient, like waiting for springtime after a long, cold winter. He would be a gracious victor, and doubters would be welcomed back with open arms. His faith in himself, in Sharon, had gotten him through, and now he would reap the rewards and so would his beloved city.

"Now you know why I needed the additional fifty thousand dollars," Sharon said. He added more tobacco juice to the cuspidor. "We are in need of more pumps, and we must be aggressive with our loans to the other mines. Loans in bad times like these will conclude in foreclosure, and the bank will have no choice but to assume the collateral. The mills and mines will end up on our books. Or, I should say, the bank's."

"What about the water?" Will asked.

"Cornish pumps," Sharon answered. They were new, and costly, but had tremendous power and capacity. They would put in an order immediately, for as many as it took. "Don't concern yourself," Sharon said, "I will master the water. Assuming I get the fifty thousand."

"I'll get you your fifty thousand," Will said.

"And I," said Sharon, "will get you control of the Comstock Lode."

He listened with restrained glee as Sharon reviewed details and plans. They discussed which mills would handle the ore, what processes would be used, and how it would be transported. Sharon offered suggestions on how to profit from the rush to Virginia City, which would hit once word got out of the new bonanza. And then there was quiet. Sharon looked at him.

"I have one other request," Sharon said. "One I'd ask that you give your full and earnest consideration before giving a response." He paused. "I believe it would suit our mutual interests if we were partners."

"Partners? I am not in need of a partner."

Sharon stroked his moustaches as though contemplating his next move in a poker game. "It was my promise to you to work hard and orchestrate favorable investments in Virginia City. These objectives have been accomplished thus far, to the extent possible. The sacrifices required of me, however, have taken considerable toll, on me and on my wife, who refuses to relocate her household to a mining camp. I cannot blame her for this refusal. Life in Nevada, Mr. Ralston, is akin to being marooned on a desert island: the eye is met with an ocean of sand and sage brush from all vantage points."

"Take some time off," Will counseled. "Visit with your wife. Take her on a trip somewhere. Get out of Virginia City for a while." He could understand how this place would get a man down.

"I fear I haven't have been sufficiently clear as to my objectives," Sharon said. "Neither Virginia City, nor my wife, are the principal motives for making this proposal, and I have no urgent need of a holiday. What I lack is a presence in San Francisco. At the stock exchange, and in the real estate market. I am an investor, Mr. Ralston, but my exile, as it were, in Virginia, leaves me at a substantial disadvantage in my chosen profession."

Will could see where this was going and felt a twinge of anxiety. He needed Sharon here in Virginia City. "So, I would invest for both of us. Is that your proposal?"

"In San Francisco, yes. With a free hand. Here on the Comstock, I would direct our assets. We would own everything jointly, in equal shares."

If Sharon was a good investor, he was an even better gambler, having played this hand perfectly. He needed Sharon, and Sharon knew it.

"And you would remain here in Virginia City?"

"I would."

He told him he'd think about it and let Sharon know in a week.

Sharon gathered the bags of ore and carried them back to his desk. There remained the issue of Sutro and his tunnel. To Will, this was just more good news. Sharon listened, took in the scheme, worked his tobacco, considered the details. The ore would be removed more cheaply, but the ability of the tunnel to drain the water was enough to convince Will. Not so Sharon. An intriguing idea, he agreed, but had he, Will, heard of Sutro's prediction of Virginia City becoming a ghost town? Replaced by the Town of Sutro?

"What? He cannot be serious."

Sharon gave a shrug. "All mining activity and milling will take place at the mouth of the tunnel. In Sutro. Why would we need Virginia City?"

"The crazy, arrogant fool." Will stopped himself from attacking Sutro, but he felt betrayed. His mind raced ahead, thinking through every eventuality, imagining the Comstock and the tunnel operating in concert. Sutro would eventually control the entire Lode, once all the mines were dependent on his tunnel, and his town. Where would the Bank of California fit in? He had been keenly interested in the idea, but now saw only a threat. And a threat to the Comstock was a threat to San Francisco.

"Sutro," he observed, thinking out loud, "would become a very powerful man, if the tunnel were completed."

Sharon nodded in agreement. "Very powerful indeed."

"He could wrest control from us."

Again, Sharon nodded.

They sat in silence save for the wind howling outside. The battle was joined: Will knew it and he could see that Sharon knew it.

He didn't have the stomach for war. But Sutro could not be allowed to humiliate Virginia City and take over the Comstock. And San Francisco: his plans for the city depended on money pouring in from the silver mines. This wouldn't happen if someone else controlled the Comstock. It was, he knew, either the Sutro Tunnel or San Francisco. The choice was obvious.

Will needed to see Jess. Exuberant over Sharon's news, he was immune to the cold night air and unconcerned about being recognized. His pace was quick along C Street. At the Silver Queen Hotel he knocked on the door to Room 5b. When she opened, it almost seemed as if she were waiting for him.

There was little sleep to be had. Between desperate embraces, he learned that she was happy in Virginia City. The miners were gentlemen, treated her well, with respect, followed her at night to keep her safe. She was, he knew, a prize to be won, a vibrant flower in this town of industrious and lonely bees.

"There are, I suppose, many men in Storey County who would want to marry a beautiful schoolmistress."

"I don't intend to take a husband."

"Why not?"

"Someone of my character shouldn't have a husband, or a family."

"Yours is the finest of characters," he shot back. "The character borne of survival and prosperity despite the worst of circumstances. I have encountered no finer character in California or Nevada." He took her chin in his hand. "Jess, you've started anew. Your past is forgotten."

"But I cannot forget it."

His heart felt a tug. Her fear of judgment was palpable, the distrust of human nature probably justified. Few men would accept a bride tainted with her sins, if it were a sin, that is, to survive. She had neither the courage to confide in another man, nor the capacity to lie. He pulled her close and held her until she fell asleep.

Chapter 17

Sutro thought that perhaps he was dreaming. Can the dreamer know that he is dreaming? The answer must be yes, he decided, seeing the bizarre behavior around him, while the scientist in him, the engineer, said no, this cannot be possible. There had to be another explanation. His temperamental filly threw back her head and whinnied: Do we go or stay? He shifted in the saddle, and looked about again, and finally concluded that he was awake. Therefore, it was undeniable: the citizens of Virginia City were most assuredly ignoring him. Shunning would be more accurate.

The filly pawed the dust with her hoof. He flicked the reins. She swung her head around just to be sure, then headed down C Street. As they went, friends, acquaintances, shopkeepers all seemed to look away. Little children hid behind their mothers' skirts, the mothers herding them away like ducklings. He shook his head, baffled at what he was seeing.

"How are you, Mrs. Sanders?" he shouted to his seamstress. She, however, turned red in the face and rushed into the nearest shop.

This seemed proof enough. Sutro's face grew flush as the humiliation set in. He nudged the filly with his boot heels and headed to James Fair's office. Many Comstock superintendents were in favor his tunnel, or the concept of the tunnel, which surely would commence in the very near future. But Fair was a holdout. He would try the prickly super' once more, and find out at the same time what foolishness had gotten into the heads of the common man. He was too easily led astray, the common man. Fair, however, was a man of vision, and he didn't mince words.

The superintendent stared at him with steely gray eyes. He laid his quill into the crease of an open ledger book.

"If you're here to talk about your tunnel, you're wasting your time," warned Fair. "And mine too."

"Well, as a matter of fact..."

"Sharon and the Bank of California don't want a tunnel. Don't want it and don't need it."

There must be a misunderstanding. He produced Ralston's letter, held it up as proof: Ralston was in favor of the tunnel. It would remove the ore more efficiently, and drain the water.

"Sharon says he intends to use pumps to get rid of the water. Says the tunnel would be too expensive and isn't needed. And your plan for a town at the foot of the tunnel has everyone all riled up. Seems folks aren't too happy to hear that Virginia City will become a ghost town. The word is out, Mr. Sutro. Your tunnel is a threat to this community, and threat to business."

His thoughts fell into a state of turmoil. His own words, perhaps uttered indiscriminately, and in a rush of enthusiasm, were being used against him. But, he pointed out, his tunnel would benefit all. And the Town of Sutro would be well-planned and very modern, a great improvement over Virginia City.

Fair was growing impatient. "Sharon says there will be no tunnel."

Sharon? William Sharon? Did Sharon run the camp? Was it *Kaiser* Sharon now? His breathing was coming harder. Panic was setting in.

"But," Sutro exclaimed, grasping for a hold, any hold, "Sharon works for Ralston."

Fair lifted his brow. "That's true. Can't imagine Ralston would be any too pleased by your plans for Virginia, either." He looked at Sutro, then, without another word, picked up the quill and went back to his ledger.

He left in a daze. Somehow the filly found her way back down the mountain to his house in Dayton. He must speak with Ralston right away. It was true, he had hoped to build his new town near the river, but he never intended any harm to Ralston or the bank. He wanted to be their ally. This must be Sharon's doing, turning Ralston against him.

Leah couldn't hear of this. The years spent away from his family, not to mention the money spent, could not be in vain. It was absurd, besides. Pumps might clear the water temporarily, but what about the foul air? And the cost to move the ore down the mountain? Sharon was wrong and he was going to prove it.

"The Bank of California will find out that Adolph Sutro does not give up so easily," he said out loud. And he knew that this was not the end, but just the beginning.

***

If Finn had tried to imagine what sort of house Jessie lived in, it would have been this house on the north end of C Street.

With its coat of fresh blue paint and white-fenced porch complete with chairs and a swing, the house bore the hallmarks of feminine attention. A patch of garden along the side sprouted small white flowers. Lacy curtains hung in the windows.

He stood on the porch, in his hand the little book, the Poetry of Thomas Moore, which she had given him but of whose contents he remained ignorant. A mystery he hoped would soon be at an end.

When she answered the door, he half-expected the phantom girl to flee or disappear. But no, she stood still as can be and gave him a brilliant smile. She wore a simple white cotton dress, her hair pulled back and braided in the French style, leaving her face to shine out. He stared. Ah, splendid—

Soon he was seated in the drawing room across from Jessie and her stout landlady, widow Frieda. Mrs. Frieda, the protector of feminine virtue and her establishment's impeccable reputation, never said a word that Finn could recall, but sat and knitted and shot suspicious glances his way.

Tea was poured. Finn talked of old Éire, his daddy, the potato famine and the farm they had lost. Mrs. Frieda's needles clicked furiously while Jessie listened to his tale, sipping tea. He, too, had thought to sip some tea, wondering what the pale beverage might taste like, but he couldn't get his finger into the wee cup-handle, and, seeing the potential for disaster, he decided to forego the refreshment. He expected that next Jessie might share her family story, but was disappointed, and she asked if they should begin the reading lesson.

He gulped, nodded yes. She reached behind the couch and brought back a slate. She looked at him, expectantly. "You must sit next to me, so you can see the slate."

He thought that a splendid idea. He rose from his chair, glancing up at Mrs. Frieda, who glared at him with the eyes of a magistrate, as if deciding whether to send him to the gallows now or later. He settled in beside Jessie, and breathed deeply. Her perfume set his head to spinning. With a piece of chalk, she formed the letters of the alphabet, then sounded them out, one at a time, waiting to hear him repeat one letter before proceeding to the next. He tried to pay close attention, but found himself distracted by the nearness of her, by her intoxicating scent. When she finished, she handed him the slate to take home and practice. They would have another lesson next week.

"Now," she said, "for Thomas Moore." She picked Finn's book up off the table and held it in her hands for a few moments, studying the cover, almost caressing it, as though becoming reacquainted with an old friend. With reverence she opened it and began to read.

> *When he who adores thee has left but the name*
> *Of his faults and his sorrows behind,*
> *O! say wilt thou weep, when they darken the fame*
> *Of a life that for thee was resigned?*
>
> ...

Later, as he walked home with the afternoon shadow of Mt. Davidson now blanketing Virginia City, he was in the thrall of her, having sat beside her, trying to recall every detail of her face, her hands as they turned the pages—

"Hey, Irish!"

It was a voice he knew. One he despised. Coal-eyes. He continued on at the same pace, not allowing so much as one muscle to twitch or even the rhythm of his breathing to alter.

"Aye?" he said, stopping in front of him.

"So, this is where you ran off to."

He studied him for a moment, wondering why God would have created such a worthless creature. Hate-filled eyes stared back at him. Finn turned and spat. "One of us would have ended up dead if I'd stayed in San Francisco. So you can thank me for sparing your life."

Coal-eyes threw his head back and laughed. "I'm glad to see you, Irish. There's a score to be settled, and I aim to settle it."

"You never settle a score, don't you know? You only create new ones."

"Mine is dead friend."

Finn pushed past him and continued his walk with a practiced calm. He would have to settle the score eventually, as Coal-eyes said. And he was happy to think of it. He didn't want to live his life with revenge dangling over his head like a hangman's noose.

"See you around, Irish," shouted Coal-eyes.

***

A maid slipped into the dinning room with a platter of roast duck, set it on the table before Will and Elizabeth, then stepped back, curtsied, and scampered back into the kitchen. The long table sat beneath a great chandelier, and was set with their two place settings, opposite each other, at one end. The room was hung with a somber velvet wallpaper, and brightened with paintings of San Francisco Bay, tule elk in the Sacramento Valley, and snow-capped peaks in the Sierras. The children had eaten earlier and were up in the nursery.

"I haven't seen her before," Will said. "Is she new to the staff?"

"Yesterday was her first day," said Elizabeth.

"What's her name?"

"Rosemary."

Like the other girls employed in the household, the new maid was plain in the face. Homely, even. He wondered if this was intentional on the part of his wife—to eliminate temptation, perhaps. He gazed at Elizabeth, who did in fact seem all the more lovely by comparison in her blue silk gown, hair neatly pulled up behind her head. He adored beauty. Sought after it. Wished to be near it. Whenever possible, he surrounded himself with color, symmetry, and grace, be it fine art, manicured gardens, or comely maids. Wealth bestowed the privilege of beauty, that finest of luxuries, the costliest jewel in the crown of success. He was fortunate, he knew, to live in the light that other men only glimpsed on a rare sunny day. His looked again at Elizabeth, and it dawned on him that a lovely woman with a kind heart must be the most desirable kind of beauty.

"Toppie," Elizabeth exclaimed, adjusting her hair. "You're making me nervous."

"Sorry, but I was just thinking how lucky am I to have you."

Rosemary whisked into the dining room and set a plate of cooked vegetables on the table, then flew back into the kitchen. Steam rose from the cooked carrots and Brussels sprouts and Will frowned, not being particularly fond of the sprouts, and preferring raw to cooked carrots.

Elizabeth was watching him. Was something the matter? No, he said, the dinner looked delicious.

"Your face says otherwise," she said. "I thought you liked duck."

He did enjoy duck, and if he seemed distracted, it was only because he was thinking of the bank.

"Oh, that again," she said. "I wish you'd never started that ridiculous bank. It's been nothing but trouble and worry for you since the first day."

"It was worry, my dear, but now it's celebration. We have turned the corner to prosperity."

"Yes, I know, and I'm happy for you. Happy for all of us, I should say. This past two years has been most unsettling."

He wouldn't disagree with her. But, the turmoil of the past two years, which had seemed such a hurricane, proved only to be a gust of ill wind. He savored a sip of red wine, which lingered on his palate. A remarkable sensation, he thought, as if he hadn't ever tasted wine before.

"Did I tell you," he said, "that I'm off to Virginia City in the morning? To meet with Mr. Sharon. I'll be but a day or two."

She was incredulous. Virginia City? Again?

"Yes," he said. "Sorry. Something urgent has come up."

Rosemary came in carrying a bowl of potatoes. She set them down in the center of the table beside the other courses, then took up two serving spoons and began preparing dinner plates, one for the master of the house and another for the mistress. Will observed her work, noting the confident, practiced movements, the proper portions in the proper places with no drips or spills, the fine art of the plain girl, a thing to be appreciated. Once finished, and without any anxious glances at the mistress, Rosemary scurried off to the kitchen.

Elizabeth watched her go, then remarked how he, Will, seemed to be spending an extraordinary amount of time in that "dreadful mining camp." It was the focus of his attention, he admitted, and until certain matters were resolved, it would remain so. Wanting to change subjects, he asked how she felt about the property he had purchased on the peninsula, south of the city. Belmont. If he meant by that, she responded, was she interested in living there, the answer was decidedly no. She liked the city and didn't wish to leave it.

He took a bite of duck. She pushed the food around her plate. Perhaps, he thought, reaching for his glass of wine, if he remodeled the house, made it bigger, added a ballroom, built gardens, perhaps then she might reconsider.

"Where do you stay when you're in Virginia City?" she asked.

"At the International Hotel."

"Is it a suitable hostelry?"

"It's very nice."

With fork in one hand and knife in the other, she sliced at the duck breast, back and forth, slowly, precisely, absently, until the task was complete and, to her chagrin, she suddenly had a piece of duck to contend with. Did he ever see people he knew there, she inquired, pushing the fork into the tender meat. People from San Francisco, perhaps?

"Of course." he said, "Occasionally. Why do you ask?"

"No reason." With the bite of duck now attached to the end of her fork, she swept gravy around her plate. "Such as?" she asked. "Whom do you see, I mean?"

"For God's sake, Lizzie, why all the questions?"

She froze, set down her utensils and dropped her gaze, a chastened wife. Seeing her so, he was consumed with remorse. He apologized profusely. Would she forgive him?

She nodded, pensively. "I shouldn't be so nosy."

He didn't mind her asking. He saw some people they knew in Virginia City, but not often. Mostly it was just miners and shopkeepers and saloon owners.

"I see," she said.

"Now," he said, "I think I'll go up to the nursery. Would you like to come with me?"

"You go. I'll be up in a minute."

He rose to leave.

"You'll come right home, won't you?" Elizabeth asked, looking at him with grave, moist eyes. "After your business is finished?"

"Of course I will."

She nodded her acceptance of his answer and he leaned down and kissed her. He started out the door, resisting the temptation to glance back at her, afraid to meet her gaze.

Chapter 18

The Crown Point bonanza and a new routine at the bank. Will's mornings were spent in the business of charity, interviewing those seeking donations or employment, and listening to those with grand ideas for his city. He heard them all and gave generously, always with the proviso: his donations were to be in confidence. Hospitals, orphanages, museums, public works of all kind would receive the benefits of the Comstock Lode. In the afternoon he would meet with his tellers and accountants, write letters, send telegrams.

On this day he left the bank a little early to go by the corner of California and Sansome, where the new Bank of California headquarters building was under construction. He watched massive slabs of Angel Island blue marble being dragged into position, the siding of the new building. A stirring sight. Not yet completed and the building was already the talk of the city.

At home he found Elizabeth in the drawing room. She was in a quiet melancholy. He wondered if she abused the laudanum, and decided he would check with the physician. He sat down, suggested they go to see the new home under renovation in Belmont. Get some air. No, she thought not. Her moods were vexing: he prided himself on understanding and soothing the female temperament, but was at a loss as to his own wife.

She surprised him by sitting up straight. "I have in mind to go to Europe," she announced.

"Europe?" he said, laughing. "But Elizabeth—"

"And I intend to go."

"A vacation in Europe, I suppose, would be nice."

"I'm glad I have your permission," she said, "but I'm not speaking of a vacation. I have friends in Paris and have made plans to stay. Indefinitely."

His chest tightened. "Indefinitely? But, what about the children?"

"I'm taking the children with me, along with two of my maids."

He couldn't think what to say to this. He stared at her.

"I'll bring a tutor," she went on, anticipating his questions.

"You've thought of everything, it seems," he said.

"I tried to."

Seeing that she was serious, he turned to reliable measures of persuasion: honor, duty, responsibility, and so forth. How could she do this? She had obligations. He, too, would like nothing more that to move to Paris, but people were counting on him. And besides, he loved her and needed her. He was lying, she said, his one and only love was San Francisco. "San Francisco, and perhaps Virginia City," she added, glaring at him.

He winced. What implications came with Virginia City, he dared not ask. If she was determined to leave, he wouldn't try to stop her. But the children, he implored, they need their father.

"They hardly have their father now." She continued to meet his gaze, defiantly.

"That is not fair, Lizzie. I considered myself to be a good father."

Anger began to boil up. More talk would accomplish nothing. He swept out the door, slamming it behind him. A swim, he decided, would cool him down.

In the stables, James readied a horse for the ride to North Beach. Lizzie's announcement had utterly surprised him. She was prepared, he grudgingly admitted, and determined. How long had she planned this? For quite some time, obviously. Would she take a lover in France? Elizabeth was, after all, a beautiful and passionate woman. His insides burned at the thought. He hadn't anticipated this serpentine behavior, wouldn't have imagined Lizzie having the courage to do something so drastic. It was impressive, he grudgingly admitted. Bold.

He missed her already.

***

Sutro, having met stubborn resistance on the West Coast, found himself on the East Coast, where prejudice and misinformation against his tunnel would not yet have taken root. Hope rose anew as he trod the streets of New York, and made his way to 10 Washington Place, the home of Cornelius Vanderbilt, who had agreed to see him.

Minutes later, he stood at attention and gazed across the desk at the great man. The Commodore, as they called him, certainly must have known he was there, but showed no sign of it, so absorbed he was in his work. This was the man, Sutro mused, growing a little impatient, who had put his wife in an asylum when she had angered him, or refused to move, or had entered that time in life when all women became difficult. Which story was true, he didn't know, but the woman had borne him thirteen children! There were rumors, of course, that he had many more offspring of the illegitimate sort. Prostitutes, it was said, were his companions of choice.

Vanderbilt sat in a high-backed leather chair. His hearty build, wiry grey hair, and bushy sideburns, Sutro noticed, were much like his own. Finally, his host glanced up and motioned for him to sit. He obediently settled into a chair and looked across the gleaming mahogany desk at Vanderbilt.

"I hear you're a-wanting to build a tunnel," Vanderbilt barked without looking up.

"A tunnel. Yes," he stumbled, "under the Comstock Lode, yes, that is correct. You have heard of the Comstock and Virginia City?"

"We've all heard of the Comstock," Vanderbilt said, fingering through papers on his desk.

Sutro took out a map, some drawings, gave a brief explanation of the geography and geology of the Comstock. His tunnel would solve all problems, he told him, preparing at just the right moment to deliver the letter from Ralston.

"Transport the ore," he was saying, "drainage of water, and the tunnel will give air ventilation. The air in the mines, you see, is very bad."

Vanderbilt's attention had waned. Sutro fingered the letter. It was time.

Abruptly, Vanderbilt reached for a desk drawer, yanked it open and rifled through its contents. Papers flew. He recovered his own letter, then snapped the drawer shut and began to read. A frown spread across his face. He turned the paper around and laid it on the desk before Sutro.

It was on Bank of California letterhead. The signature of William C. Ralston flowed across the bottom—what letter was this? Sutro glanced over the words. Beads of perspiration sprouted on his forehead...a tunnel is unnecessary...will cost too much...isn't feasible...

"It seems the Bank of California is dead-set against yer tunnel, Mr. Sutro."

"Mein Gott," he cursed, forgetting himself. His plan was unraveling. Yes, Ralston had turned against the tunnel, but he was hoping word hadn't reached the East Coast.

Vanderbilt leaned back in his chair. He formed a steeple with his fingers and pressed them into the flesh of his ruddy, square chin. "Billy Ralston aught a bean married to my granddaughter. Did ya know that, Mr. Sutro?"

He looked at Vanderbilt, astonished. Had he heard correctly?

"Louisa was William Thorn's—my son-in-law—Thorn's daughter. Beautiful girl too. Damn good lawyer, Thorn. Anyways, Billy and her made a handsome couple, as I recollect." He paused. "Louisa died a-fore the wedding, though."

A silence fell over them. Sutro pondered this shocking information.

"I didn't much approve of him at first, that Billy Ralston. Just a ragged kid from the Mississippi Valley without a lick of polish. Not what you'd call a Knickerbocker, that much was certain. But I've picked many a son-in-law—got a slew'a daughters—and he showed promising signs. I like ambition and drive and hard work, Mr. Sutro. Anyways, Ralston worked for Garrison..."

Vanderbilt talked but he barely heard him. Panama and shipping and then San Francisco, the *North Star*, a voyage, his granddaughter became ill, Ralston had stayed with her until she died. Why had he never heard this? He glanced up to find his host staring at him.

"How much will this tunnel cost?"

"Three million dollars."

"Good God, man. Have you got West Coast investors for this project?"

"No. That is why I am here. With the Bank of California being against me, I cannot find investors in California."

Vanderbilt nodded while contemplating Sutro, then said he was sorry, but he wouldn't put in any of his own money until Sutro had some California investors. He would, however, offer free advice. Find their weaknesses, he bellowed. Don't trust anyone. And most important: don't be afraid to sell.

"Sell?"

"If ever I could make a profit on one of my steamers, I was a-selling a-fore you could say shipwreck."

Sutro stared at him, bewildered. The implication, the suggestion, if he understood correctly, was appalling. He thanked Vanderbilt for the advice, shocked as he was at the idea that he would ever sell his tunnel, should it be built, of course.

Outside the great mansion, he watched horses and carriages whisk by to their appointed destinations. He could not go back west without having found a single investor. Washington D.C. was not far away. Perhaps Congress would help. Yes, of course, Congress! And why not? The government knew the importance of the Comstock, and those very intelligent representatives would see that his tunnel was urgently needed and, therefore, deserved the benefit of public funding.

Chapter 19

It was morning at the magnificent new headquarters of the Bank of California. The lobby was full and Will was pleased that so many came to just to look, to gaze up at the painted Italianate ceiling, to admire the carved mahogany counters, the marble floors. John Fry was there and introduced his friend, Asbury Harpending, a tall, athletic-framed youth in an expensive black suit and tall stovepipe hat. He was friendly, this Harpending, direct, confident. Will took an immediate liking to him. When he learned that the young man had purchased his old Rincon Hill home, he was sure of lasting friendship.

The Rincon Hill home made Will think of Elizabeth and the years they had spent there. It had been their first home. Little Louisa had been born there. He missed Elizabeth and wondered how she and the children were getting on in France. He received short letters from her, but detected in those nothing in the way of remorse or longing to be home. In fact, she seemed to be happy.

He turned his attention to Harpending. He had ideas, this youth. And energy. Will listened while leading him on a tour. They ended up in his glass-walled office, looking out at the bustling lobby, discussing one idea that had captured Will's fancy: the

extension of Montgomery Street across Market. This would allevi-
ate the ever-present traffic congestion on Montgomery and, im-
portantly, open up the south side of Market to real estate development. Would the bank be interested in making a loan on the
project? Perhaps. He needed to see plans, budgets, details. They
would meet again, he promised the young man.

That afternoon Will fought through the traffic in his char-à-banc to
get to Mission Street, anxious to engage in his favorite sport. Train
racing. This he did as often as possible, sometimes with passengers and sometimes not, though he relished the former, what with
the gasps and yelps and white knuckles of astonished riders. Today's guest was an important one, and Will had other motives
beyond sport and entertainment. Their destination: Will's new
estate at Belmont. The Old County Road down the peninsula ran
roughly parallel to the train tracks, thus Will had, inevitably, in-
vented the new sport, a sport that was his foremost, and in which
he was the acknowledged expert.

Suddenly, the howl of a new era pierced the air like a
thousand horns, all blaring in concert. A cacophonic blast. His
passenger, Leland Stanford, flinched at the noise. Tension rippled
through the flesh of Will's four best horses.

"Dammit, we're late." He snapped the reins and the horses
jumped to a quickening cadence. Stanford grabbed for his hat.
Will surveyed the carriages and foot traffic that clogged Mission
Street: what daring maneuvers would be needed today? At the far
end of the busy avenue, just beyond the lush green of Woodward
Gardens, black smoke from a locomotive rose into the air.

"The train is right on schedule," Stanford said, checking
his watch and then slipping it back into his pocket. "Five thirty-

two." He seemed to take pride in a railroad that kept to schedule, even if it wasn't one of his own. Stanford, the former Governor of California, was also president of the Central Pacific Railroad, and part of "the Association" that was building the Transcontinental Railroad. Will had in mind that one day, the San Francisco-San Jose line would become part of Stanford's railroad portfolio.

"No matter," Will scoffed. God dammed efficient trains. "I like to give the beast a head start. Makes for a better challenge."

His trusted char-à-banc rumbled over the wooden surface in syncopation with the drumbeat of horse hooves.

"Look out," he shouted, snapping the reins. "Coming through."

Pedestrians leapt to the sidewalks. Mothers yanked their children to safety. Just then, another whistle floated high up over the roof-tops and trees. It began as a low moan, then soared to a high-pitched, plangent wail. The race was on.

The horses knew that bellicose whistle. They bolted ahead, now clear of the traffic. The rig jerked and creaked. Metal snapped against metal. Stanford fell to the seat-back, reaching for his hat again, and just in time to save it from the hungry wind.

Engine No. 5 soon appeared on their right, its black cow-catcher angled down onto the track like a giant broom to sweep away obstacles in the path of progress. Behind followed a half-dozen cars. The race followed the usual pattern: Will's carriage moved ahead when the train pulled into a station, then fell behind in between, over and over, as they flew by the Mission, Bernal, San Miguel, and School House stops. The route took them past Father Sera's old Mission de Asis, on to the hills south of the city, where the horses groaned and labored up, and then sweated foamy lather on the way down. Up and down, again and again.

The plank surface soon transitioned into a Macadamized road, a modern improvement funded by Will's own account, his horses much preferring, and making better time on, the even texture. Gravel now peppered the front of the carriage. He, too, peppered his captive guest with questions about his railroad. When would the Trans-continental Railroad be completed? Had he decided where to place the western terminus? Stanford was reticent, saying he deferred in these matters to his partner, Huntington. Will's fear was a terminus on Goat Island, in the middle of the Bay, instead of the more expensive, but vastly more beneficial, terminus in San Francisco.

Stanford, ever the politician, smiled and tipped his hat to the passengers on board the train, who watched the char-à-banc with fascination. The Central Pacific, Stanford said, could not make decisions based on what was best for San Francisco. He, it was becoming clear, had no concern for the effect on Will's city should the terminus be located elsewhere.

"Dammit, Leland," he shouted over the noise, "how can you be so cavalier? What would France be like without Paris? Or England without London?"

"Don't be ridiculous. San Francisco is not Paris."

"It will be," he said, tapping the brake sharply, the buggy having picked up too much speed down the hill, "If I have anything to do with it. We have a duty, Governor. We are stewards of the most magnificent piece of land any man ever dreamed of building a city on. How will we face future generations if we know we failed to bring San Francisco into her full potential? No, Leland, your plan would destroy San Francisco, and I can't allow it, not without a fight, at any rate."

"Don't be a fool. We're not out to destroy your city."

"If you locate the terminus on Goat Island, you'll do just that. And it will be on your shoulders."

"Hogwash." Stanford's face glowed crimson.

"Surely the railroad," Will said, "could afford to build a bridge to the city after coming all that way."

"Perhaps the city should pay for that bridge," Stanford replied.

Will said no more. He'd planted the seed and would now have to wait. He pulled up his frothing team at the Fourteen Mile House to change out his horses. His hostler was there with a crew, at the ready. He would lose some time, but even these fine animals couldn't survive the final dash after racing up and over the steep hills. Stanford complained: fresh horses hardly seemed fair. But Stanford, he pointed out, fueled his train without ceasing, did he not?

The new team shot out of the station at break-neck speed, knowing, it seemed, it was their duty to catch the big steel horse in the distance. The tracks and road were now side by side, the marshy Bay just to their left. They closed in on the train as it stopped at San Mateo, leaving only a straight, flat home stretch to decide the race. The train and horses now bore down on Belmont Station.

"Hang on! Almost there."

"Dammit all, Billy," Stanford yelled. "I am not a daredevil."

"Ha ha," he shouted, leaning forward. The train's engineer looked out at the char-à-banc from the little box-like compartment at the back of the locomotive, smiling at the quaint relic of the past. He tugged at the cord and sounded a loud, triumphant whistle. Stanford tipped his hat to him. Passengers leaned out the windows, cheering and whistling.

"Okay boys. Now!" Will shouted at the team, whipping the reins. The horses knew their master and broke into a full gallop. Stanford swore like a pirate when his hat suddenly blew off and disappeared in the trail of dust behind. The train began to slow into the Belmont station. Four hundred feet. The horses inched ahead, but not quite enough. Two hundred. They might make it. One hundred.

He barked at his team one last time, jerked the reins, and shot over the tracks in front of the train, shouting and cursing and bouncing off the seat as the rig jolted and cracked. Just behind him, the cowcatcher narrowly missed his rear wheels. Stanford gripped the railing and let fly a string of obscenities.

The race was over and Will had been the victor. Again. He rarely lost but never tired of winning. He eased the weary horses into a slow trot and checked his watch. A decent time. Stanford complained of the loss of his favorite hat as they meandered into the canyon and toward the glow of lights coming through the trees. The big man stared up at the enormous Italian-style mansion. Will's Belmont estate. The char-à-banc clattered up the gravel path and pulled under the porte-cochère. A waiting James Riker grabbed the bridles of the lathered team. A small pigtailed Chinaman scampered out to offer them a hand down. Will pointed to the buildings where his guest would find the bowling alley, gymnasium, and Turkish baths. And the stables, of course.

They entered the vestibule and climbed the stairs.

"Is Elizabeth still handling your affairs in Europe?" Stanford asked, the question posed delicately, as one would expect from a statesman. Prying, but with impeccable manners.

"Yes. Still in Paris." Elizabeth's official reason for being in Paris was to represent Will's interests at a world agricultural exhibition. The length of her stay in France, almost one year now, made such an explanation less and less plausible. In fact, it was becoming an embarrassment. Life without her and the children, he found, was empty and lonely, despite the constant stream of friends and guests.

An hour later, they sat in the opera-style boxes on the second floor, like Zeus and Apollo intent on mischief, watching other guests arrive for the weekend. A parade of black-suited dignitaries streamed through the front door, each accompanied by one or more glittering females bedecked with jewels, plumed hats and flowing silk gowns.

"Leland," he said, "I need your assurance on this matter of the terminus."

"Assurance of what?"

"That you'll do everything in your power to prevent the Central Pacific from locating the terminus on Goat Island."

Stanford protested that he couldn't do that.

He turned and looked him straight in the eye. "Do you recall, Governor, when you needed funds to start your railroad, and all the banks said no?" Stanford looked like a cornered fox, glancing about but seeing no way out. "And," Will continued, "do you remember who convinced the bank to make your first loan?" The railroad man gazed down at the entryway, but said nothing.

"It was I, of course. I arranged for your funding." And, he reminded him, he had had to put up a personal guarantee.

"I remember," Stanford said, "but that has nothing whatsoever to do with where we place the terminus."

"I came to your aid when you needed it, and by my way of thinking, San Francisco came to your aid. You owe us this much. The terminus must be in San Francisco."

Stanford sighed. "I make no guarantees, but I'll see what I can do."

"That's all I ask." Will stood up. "Shall we go down, then?"

Will's guest rose wearily from his chair. Had he been brought here so his arm could be twisted?

"Of course not," he lied. "I'll take you riding tomorrow just to prove it." The fear of a Goat Island terminus had lurched Will out of more than one sound sleep, his city naught but a ghost town, deserted and dusty and wind-swept. He would kill this plan, whether that meant bringing the other three, Huntington, Hopkins, and Crocker here to twist their arms as well, or even asking President Johnson to intervene. The railroad would not be allowed to condemn his city to irrelevance.

Chapter 20

Finn and Mackie hiked the steep curves that led up and out of Gold Hill until reaching the crest of the rise, then began the descent into Virginia City. In the four years Finn had been in Virginia City, he and Mackie had become like brothers. Mackie, having made a fortune on the Kentuck, was planning to marry a widow, though he lamented the unfathomable nature of the female species. Finn confessed to a vexation by that sex, and the schoolmistress in particular. There were sighs and chuckles.

"What do you think of Sutro's tunnel?" Finn asked.

"Just because a thing can be done, doesn't mean it should be."

But, wondered Finn, could it really be done?

As they parted, Finn to his saloon, Mackie to his widow, the elder renewed his longstanding offer of employment. He would teach Finn engineering skills, how to take assay samples and the like. It might require more time in the mines, but the pay would be better. Ten dollars a day. Finn said he liked his carpentry work, but he would give the offer serious consideration while he slaked his thirst at the Hibernia. Mackay laughed.

The Hibernia wasn't the biggest of saloons, but it was Irish, brewed a stout lager, and had a fine barkeep. He had a terrible thirst, he told O'Kelly, who placed a bottle of lager before him. In the main room, Irish miners played cards, drank whiskey, played billiards, drank whiskey, played cribbage and drank whiskey. Finn had finished his first lager when Joseph and the boys came in. They looked and smelled ripe from their shift in the mines. They dragged Finn and a bottle of whiskey to a table.

Joseph raised his glass. "God save all here."

They raised their glasses and proclaimed in unison, "God save you kindly." Each man then emptied his glass, it being bad luck not to after a toast.

Saloon talk rarely strayed from a few favorite topics: mining, prospecting, and women (or the lack of). Young Connor Murphy had his eye on the lovely schoolmistress, with intentions that were purely honorable, but his declaration brought a hushed quiet. That colleen, declared Joseph, belongs to Finn. Finn swore she was only teaching him to read, giving Murphy renewed hope, but the look in Finn's eye might have put doubts into his mind.

"Why do you want to read?" asked Murphy.

"I like poetry," answered Finn.

Murphy scratched at his chin. "So," he said, confused, "I can call on the schoolmistress, or no?"

Joseph cracked a fist on the table. "Jaysus. Are you daft, man?"

Murphy then wisely declared that she wasn't for him, he not needing to read or gain greater education accomplishments than what he already had.

The saloon door squeaked open; Finn glanced to see baggy breeches and woolen caps. Cornish. In the Hibernia? He looked again and saw Coal-eyes saunter in. Their eyes met. The Prod flashed a grin. The room fell into a quiet.

"I told you this saloon had a stench to it, Crowell," one of the Cornishmen said.

"It's that foul lager they drink," responded Coal-Eyes.

Finn now knew his name: Crowell.

"You boys can stay," said O'Kelly from behind the bar, "but I don't want any trouble here." He laid a pistol atop the hardwood counter.

Tomas Gallagher, his voice loud, as if speaking to a deaf man, explained for the benefit of young Murphy, that the Cornish were called Cousin-jacks in these parts, seeing they were always promoting their fellow Cornishmen at every opportunity: My cousin, Jack, he's your man.

Words shot back and forth between the groups like arrows, but soft-tipped arrows, the level of belligerence more in keeping with a hard game of football than a street fight. But then the word *schoolmistress* could be heard, and a Cousin-jack bragging that he'd *have his way with her—*

Finn shot up. His chair fell back and cracked on the floorboards.

Another, deeper hush fell over the room. Joseph stood up, shoulder to shoulder, with Finn. Then Sweeney and Gallagher, followed by Murphy and Ian. The billiard players laid their cue sticks on the table. Cribbage players set down their cards.

He said to Crowell, "But one chance I'll be givin' you to walk out under yer own power."

Crowell pushed his chair back and stood up. "The lads aren't ready to leave, are ya, lads?" His companions rose to their feet, chairs tumbling and slapping the floor like gauntlets.

Finn charged. He lunged at Crowell, and together they flew into the next table, crushing it into the floor. Behind him the room erupted, chairs and tables crashing, glasses breaking. The Protestants were out-numbered and the fight lasted but a few minutes before a Cousin-jack pulled a gun. Shots rang out. Smoke rose from the barrel of O'Kelly's pistol and the armed boy fell to the floor. Crowell went to him, kneeled, put his hand to the boy's neck, then declared him dead.

Everyone stood still in an ominous quiet. Crowell stared at his fallen companion.

"That's two of my boys you've killed," he said to Finn. He motioned to his friends, gave a hateful stare at Finn, then headed for the door.

***

Sutro looked at his watch. Ten after two. He was perched upon a thinly padded chair in the hallway outside the chambers of the House of Representatives in Washington, D.C. The august body was currently in session. He tapped his foot, scratched the scar beneath his sideburns, and grew generally restless. Pages darted in and out the wide doors. He strained to catch a glimpse inside, but the doors closed too quickly. The pages passed him as if he were a sleeping dog, casting wary glances at him before scampering off; a constituent seeking an audience with their employers, their glances said.

The smartly-dressed boys disappeared down the long hallway and past the paintings of famous men: George Washington, Thomas Jefferson, John Adams. And, of course, Abe Lincoln, the victim of a mad assassin. Thaddeus Stevens was not among the faces staring out from the gilded frames, but was in fact behind the closed doors and no doubt participating in some important debate. The Chairman of the House Ways and Means Committee was, after all, a very important man.

The minutes ticked by and turned into hours, and he filled the time immersed in his notebooks and maps, which were soon spread out atop his legs and the empty chair beside him, fine art to the eyes of the engineer. Mesmerized by the practical beauty of it all, he hardly noticed the giant doors swinging open. Congressmen and pages streamed out into the hallway, chatting and debating and hurrying off in different directions. He fumbled desperately with his papers, attempting to reorganize them while at the same time searching the faces for Thaddeus Stevens, whom he had been told bore a striking resemblance to Abe Lincoln.

And then he saw him. Abe Lincoln! No, Stevens—*Mein Gott*, he does look like him. He jammed the remaining papers into his rumpled leather satchel, trying to keep an eye on his man. He jumped up just as his prey whisked past, charging down the hall surrounded by pages and lesser peers. Sutro, maps under one arm and satchel under the other, followed in panicked pursuit.

All arteries led to the Capitol Rotunda, which appeared to swallow up the marching Chairman and his entourage. Crowded with desks and chairs and men in dark suits, the heart of the democratic world reverberated with the sound of what seemed a thousand voices simultaneously talking and yelling, discussing and debating, with Stevens at the center benevolently directing the flow of civilization.

Sutro stood back and watched, though he couldn't help but turn his gaze up to the magnificent cupola towering high above, light streaming in from what seemed like windows to heaven. He looked down, then around. Stevens? Where was Stevens? He scanned the room, the hallways. There, speeding from the rotunda, was his savior. He shot after him.

"Mr. Chairman," he cried, perhaps a little too loudly. Heads turned.

The congressman wheeled about and looked at him. His eyes darted to the arsenal of paper under Sutro's arms.

"I have been waiting to speak to you," he said, coming up alongside the chairman, out of breath.

"Is that a German accent?" Stevens asked, resuming his stride down a long hallway.

"I emigrated from Prussia."

"Immigrants are what makes this country strong, Mr. –?"

"Sutro. Adolph Sutro."

"The Negroes were immigrants. Did you know that Mr. Sutro? Forced immigrants, but immigrants nonetheless."

He kept pace with the Chairman's stride.

"You're not from the South, are you Mr. Sutro?"

No, he assured him. The West. Nevada and California.

"Good."

Stevens went on a tirade, outraged at the mendacious South and the spineless North that was tiptoeing around the idea of Reconstruction. Sutro listened patiently. Finally, as they approached his office door, the Chairman's fury began to cool.

"In the West," ventured Sutro, "we hear about Reconstruction, but the great story on everyone's lips is the Comstock Lode."

"Is that so?" mumbled Stevens, unimpressed. He pulled up in front of his office door. "Are you a Comstock miner, Mr. Sutro?"

"Well, no."

"Then what in damnation are we talking about?"

He hastily explained about his tunnel and lack of resources. He needed a loan from Congress.

Stevens reached for the door latch. "Ways and Means has its hands full with Reconstruction. If you need money, you should find investors." He pushed open the door.

His mind raced. The Chairman, he remembered, was a man of the people. "The Bank of California controls the Comstock," he blurted. "And they are against the tunnel. And because of their great influence and power, I cannot find investors."

Stevens stopped and looked at Sutro. "The Bank of California controls the Comstock?"

"They control the Comstock mines, all the mills, and Virginia City too."

"Is that a fact?"

"They have foreclosed on many mines and mills after the owners could not pay their assessments and the high interest rates. Two percent a month."

"Two percent a month?"

The fire was back in Steven's eyes. Why, if that wasn't usury, he'd swear an oath.

Sutro agreed wholeheartedly. He didn't mention that other banks were charging much more and that these interest rates were considered fair given the risks involved. But he didn't intend to quibble about such matters.

Stevens mumbled something about damn greedy bankers. Sutro was to come to his office at ten the next morning: the Chairman would hear more about this tunnel. He turned and disappeared into his office and the door slammed in Sutro's smiling face.

Chapter 21

From his desk in the new bank building, Will could see every employee and customer, and they could see him. And while most businessmen would deplore a glass-walled office and object to working in a 'fish bowl', he had designed his office for precisely this effect and relished being the center of attention, the object of everyone's fascinated stares. The common man was enthralled with how things worked and would look on with curiosity at an engine being dismantled, the inner workings of a clock, or the strings and hammers of a piano. Men wanted to know what was behind the veil and so Will had removed it entirely.

To one side of his office, below paintings of Yosemite Valley and the Giant Sequoias, sat a large oak table where he and William Sharon now huddled over partnership books and ledgers. Sharon grumbled about profits (too few) and expenses (too many). The woolen mills, he pointed out, were still losing money, to which Will responded that they were losing less than the previous year. But Sharon had the same objections to the sugar factory, the iron works, the furniture plant, and so on, and in the face of those complaints, Will's reasoning was consistent: All were necessary for San Francisco to be independent of Eastern influences.

Sharon quoted Shakespeare, as he was wont to do, something about weeds in the garden. Will didn't consider his enterprises akin to gardening, but held his tongue. Good business, all, he said.

"It would be preferable," said Sharon dryly, "if some of them actually made a profit before I am grown old."

The Comstock would carry them to their goal, Will reassured him. He counseled patience. Almost two years since the Crown Point, and surely the next bonanza would hit soon. Sharon, perhaps feeling the weight of expectation, shook his head.

They had their differences but reasoned through them. Now they put together a strategy to wrest shares of the Kentuck mine from John MacKay, an upstart Irishman that was becoming a thorn in Sharon's side. MacKay wouldn't sell, but his partner, Jay Walker, might. It still rankled Will, and he said so, that Sharon had let this MacKay gain control of a mine out from under their noses. Sharon ignored the criticism, saying they should put Colonel Fry on the board to keep an eye on things. Will had lost track of how many boards Fry was sitting on.

Foreclosures remained Sharon's notorious specialty. Due to the on-going defaults on their high-interest loans, he reported, they now controlled most of the mills in Virginia and Dayton, through Union Mill and Mining, and he was working to obtain the few remaining holdouts. Once they were all subdued, they could control milling prices, which meant they would eventually make greater profits from milling than from the bullion itself.

The agenda was nearly complete, except for Adolph Sutro and his tunnel.

"Sutro has been in Washington," he said to Sharon, "in case you hadn't heard."

"Has he met with any success?"

"All I know is that he gained an audience with Thaddeus Stevens, Chairman of Ways and Means, and the congressman was receptive."

"Goddammit," cursed Sharon. "Sutro cannot gain an ally in Washington."

Will assured him he had the matter under control: the best lawyers had been retained.

Sharon said, almost to himself, "He's naught but a bug, and I'll squash him before I'm done."

Will preferred that Sutro fly off somewhere to getting himself squashed. Sharon, however, had acquired a profound antipathy for the Prussian.

Colonel Fry arrived. His timing was impeccable: he had a knack for coming just in time for lunch, which would be paid for by his son-in-law. He listened to the discussion about Sutro. Had they thought, Fry asked, about a railroad? With a railroad from Virginia City to Carson, and then Truckee, the ore could be transported efficiently from the Comstock, and this would eliminate any royalties for Sutro and his tunnel.

"No royalties would assuredly put an end to the tunnel," mused Will.

"Good idea, but a railroad would be too expensive," said Sharon. "The terrain is formidable."

Will picked up some paper and began to tear: if his brain was working, his fingers needed employment also. "What if we could get the other mine-owners to help with the cost of a railroad?" he asked. "They too would benefit from a railroad, would they not?"

Sharon liked this idea. Yes, he thought he could get the other owners to help, and maybe even the counties between Virginia City and Carson. The cost would be staggering, but there was no question, a railroad would benefit all.

If they had a railroad, Will said, thinking out loud, Sutro's tunnel would be obsolete before it was ever built.

***

Finn stepped from the hoisting cage into the six hundred foot level of the Kentuck Mine. Mackay's offer of employment had been too good to refuse. He now took in a fine wage and was learning skills of a useful nature as a Kentuck lumberman and apprentice engineer. Mackie had shown him how to take samples, to assay them, and to convert the numbers into ore concentration maps. Fear of the deep still plagued his imagination, but he resolved to conquer that fear.

Today he was to head up the northerly drift toward the Yellow Jacket to catch a sample he was missing. Mackie had told him over and over to be thorough, don't leave any gaps. He held up his candle and felt his way through the dim passages. The wafer-thin Kentuck had only ninety-four feet on the Lode, or about thirty paces. Finn counted his strides through the adjacent mines, keeping track of progress until he reached, according to his reckoning, the edge of the Kentuck. He continued his pacing and counting.

A blast reverberated through the walls and he momentarily lost his balance. The candle flickered, threatening to go out. *Don't do it, you little demon.* He cupped the flame and steadied himself, then continued on, but as he took his next step, he couldn't remember if his last pace had been thirty-three or forty-three. Or was it twenty-three? Curse me.

He reached a cross-cut, turned, and followed it to the end. Twelve paces. There was no candle holder, so he pushed the waxy stub into some loose debris, took out two sample bags, and marked them with charcoal. On the wall he noticed a dark streak. A seam perhaps. He examined the thin line with the candlelight, following it down, across the wall. 'Tis a diagonal line, he thought, invoking a word he had just added to his vocabulary. A splendid word, *diagonal*. He scraped the seam with his fingernail.

A noise to his right startled him. He held his candle in the direction of the sound, straining to see into the dark. There was an adit he hadn't noticed before. Tapping. Then more tapping. Or was it knocking? Jaysus! He heard voices, saw a flicker of light.

"Who is it there?" he said with some conviction.

There was no response. The voices went silent. Light danced off the walls about ten feet ahead. A candle glowed in the adit, seeming to float in mid-air. Then an arm. A face appeared.

"Who are you there?"

"Finn Gillespie."

"What are you doing here?"

"Takin' samples for the Kentuck."

"Well, that's a hell of thing, seeing as this is the Yellow Jacket."

Finn peered hard at the man. He had seen those menacing eyes before. William Sharon.

"I didn't know 'twas the Yellow Jacket, Mr. Sharon. Suppose I lost count of my paces."

Just then, another candle appeared in the tunnel behind Sharon.

"Potato farmers can't count, as a rule." That voice he knew. Crowell.

Finn spat. "I can count the number of times I've dropped your arse into the mud."

Crowell started but Sharon put out his arm. "You best be on your way, then."

Finn turned and headed back to the drift.

Crowell works for Sharon!

He counted his paces from the cross-cut but kept seeing those two curs in his mind's eye. What were they doing in that cut? Had they found something? The wisp of a seam, perhaps? With his thumb he felt the dirt still collected under his fingernails, wondering if he had enough to test.

Chapter 22

Three of the Sutro children sat on one side of the long, narrow, pinewood table, and two more sat on the other. The parents occupied the ends and kept close watch on the territory in between. The boys, Charles, age six, and four-year-old Edgar, were seated as far from each other as possible to keep them from mischief. Emma, the eldest at 13, insisted she have the chair next to her father. Rose and Kate, ages 11 and 7, filled the remaining seats, while baby Clara sat with her mother. For this evening, the family had the dining room to themselves, Leah having arranged for the boarders to eat early and retire to their rooms.

"Father, will you take me with you to Europe?" Emma asked.

He looked up at Leah, who glared back at him with a frown from the opposite end of the table, as if to say, See what you've done?

"No, Emma."

Emma's hopeful gaze fell. Leah placated, Emma bruised. I cannot win, he thought. "I would like to take you with me, but you must stay in school. You want to be a doctor, no?"

"Yes, Father."

"Then you cannot come with me." His daughter had recently set her mind to becoming a physician. She and her mother had witnessed a carriage accident and the ensuing medical attention, much to the girl's fascination. He thought the idea a little farfetched, but then again, she was a Sutro.

"But I could study while we travel," Emma was saying. "And I could take care of you, and help with planning your tunnel."

Sutro chuckled, but Leah frowned. "Emma," she said, "I'll hear no more of this. It is bad enough that your father is never home. I won't have my children leaving me as well. And for the purpose of digging some hole in the ground, no less."

Rose asked, "Is it true that the President is going to help with the tunnel, Father?"

"Not the President, a congressman. Thaddeus Stevens."

"Why doesn't the President help, papa?"

"The President—" Sutro began.

"The President is too busy determining what to do with all the freed slaves," Emma blurted.

Leah tapped a fork on her plate. "Emma!"

"She is right, Mother, the President is too busy." Sutro looked to his younger daughter. "But do not worry, Rose, Mr. Stevens is a very powerful man and he will help with the tunnel. And do you know what else?"

Rose shook her head.

"I will build a town near the tunnel and we will all live there together, as a family. A fine town, too. Finer than Virginia City. And I will call it the Town of Sutro."

"Adolph," cried Leah. "You mustn't say such things." Baby Clara, sitting in her mother's lap, began to whimper. "Now you've upset the child."

"I would like to live with you in Sutro, Papa," Rose said.

"Enough, Rose. Please," Leah scolded. Rose dropped her eyes. The baby was now crying in earnest. Sutro rubbed his temples: though building a four-mile tunnel was a momentous undertaking, it seemed a trivial matter compared to the intricacies of domestic life.

Little Clara sat on her mother's lap taking mouthfuls of food. Sutro ate quietly, thinking that in a few years he would need to begin paying for Emma's education. Cultured families sent their children to college. But he had been working to raise money for over four years and hadn't generated much for all his efforts. He watched his wife, grateful at least for her self-reliance.

Leah seemed to feel the weight of his eyes and looked up. A faint smile lifted the unpleasant, down-turned features into an indulgent, if exasperated, gaze for the father of her children.

***

Mine he'll be, Galway's boy
To my ragged arms is fallen.
Mine he is, this wayward toy
If you lost him, don't be callin'.

No, you crooked windy byway
Claim him I do for a time.
Down your cage did he race and sway
'Till his feet did he plant on mine.

Silence, you fools, your claim is naught
To my domain he's all but takin'.
Tommy takes what Tommy aught
And to hell you can come knockin'.

Finn looked up from the slate.

"Very nice, Mr. Gillespie." Jessie smiled. "You're making excellent progress. And you've a knack for verse."

Her smile was his reward and the one thing he strove to earn more than praise from Mackie, cheers from his friends, or high wages. The students had scurried home and only two or three teachers remained in their classrooms at St. Vincent de Paul School. The sign outside the door read Miss Jessalyn Ohhlson, whose room had two large blackboards on adjacent walls and a window facing out onto E Street. Scrubby wooden desks formed neat rows front to back, with an opening in the center for the heating stove.

Jessie set down the slate. "Would you like to try to read Thomas Moore?"

"Faith I could try. If you'll help me, that is."

"Certainly." She picked up the little blue book and leafed through the pages. "Here," she said, handing it to him. "Try this."

Finn studied the black print. Some words he recognized, others he didn't.

> *'Tis the last rose of summer*
> *Left blooming alone;*
> *All her lovely ...*

She leaned towards him, looking at the page. "Companions," she said. He caught her sweet fragrance, and held it for a moment. She sat back, hers eyes still on the book. "Ah, companions indeed," he said.

> *All her lovely companions*
> *Are faded and gone;*
> *No flower of her...*

"Kindred—"

> *No flower of her kindred,*
> *No rose-bud is nigh,*
> *To reflect on her ...*

"You must attempt to sound the words out," she scolded, "even if you don't recognize them at first."

"Aye, but 'tis more fun when ye help me."

She tried to look stern. "Blushes. The word is blushes."

"Ah, splendid. A fine word, blushes."

> *To reflect on her blushes,*
> *Or give sigh for sigh.*

He closed the book, stood, and went to the window. Autumn leaves whirled about; winter would soon arrive in Storey County. Dust mixed with the reddish leaves: the Zephyrs were bearing their teeth. He wanted to know of Jessie's family, but when asked, she had always changed the subject, or simply refused to tell.

On an impulse, he reached for her hands.

"I've a great grá for you, Jessie. I want you for my wife. Ye needn't tell me about your past, or anything else, and I wouldn't be asking you. I would care for you, make a family with you." He squeezed her hands. "Will you marry me, then?"

Her eyes turned red and glassy. "I can't Finn. I...I can't marry you."

"I've put it before me to marry you, Jessie. I'll bend my knee, if you like."

"No. Please don't."

"But why then? You've feelings for me, I can see it."

She shook her head, wiping her eyes. "No, it's not true."

"I wouldn't call you a liar, but I don't believe you." He went to a knee.

"Stop Finn!" she cried. And a sob escaped.

He was taken aback. The violence of her protest, the flood of tears so strong, his conviction withered. Perhaps she didn't love him after all.

"I'm so very sorry," she said, looking at him with deep red eyes. "I don't want to lose you, Finn. You're the only real friend I have, the only person I really trust. Please tell me you'll remain my friend."

He couldn't say no to anything she asked. He supposed he could be a friend as easily as a husband, though it was a bitter potion. A sad smile fell across her face and she squeezed his hands.

Finn strolled home through darkening skies and blustery harvest breezes, taking out his frustrations on the dry leaves that crackled beneath his boots. He would make her his wife. One fine day. He just needed to know what stood between them.

***

Will contemplated the hush of his Belmont garden. Sharon stood fuming, a few paces away. Crickets, previously chirping with gusto, were now ominously quiet. The full moon above shined down through the huge oak trees, casting eerie shadows along the gravel pathway. The partnership was, he feared, tearing at the seams.

Light poured from the ballroom's tall bay window and spilt out into the garden. Elizabeth, just inside, finally back after nine months in Europe, looked blissfully unaware and happy in her white shepherdess costume as she chatted with guests. On the dance floor behind her, couples stepped and twirled to the orchestra, smiling, festive, carefree. His wife, he decided, looked most alluring tonight. Her diamond necklace, a gift to celebrate her return from Paris, sparkled in the lights, drawing his eye to the pearl-white skin of her long and lovely neck.

She had assembled the most illustrious guests from San Francisco for her masquerade ball, each arrayed in fine costume and playing their parts: Alvinza Hayward (Scaramuccia mask), Simon Eliot (Volto ghost), the Harpendings (Harlequin valet and Columbina maidservant), Judge and Mrs. McAllister (the braggart Capitano and poor Shepherdess). And from Virginia City, William Sharon: Doctor-of-the-Plague.

Enormous mirrors around the perimeter of the ballroom gathered light from the chandeliers. A pale moon shone through the skylight. The room, full of swirling dancers and humming with conversation, had grown stuffy. Will had given the signal: a Chinese servant pushed up a wall-sized pocket-door and fresh air flowed into the ballroom. The adjacent room housed a magician performing tricks, and a table of refreshments. The guests murmured in awe.

Sharon, however, was put off by the opulence. His humble abode, he pointed out from behind his Dottere Peste mask, would fit nicely within the confines of this very room. From whence the money for such extravagant living, what with many Comstock mines nearing depletion?

Will wanted only to enjoy an evening with his wife and guests. He gathered his patience. To avoid a scene, he suggested they move the discussion into the garden.

"Is it your belief that I spend recklessly?" he said a few moments later. His words caused a steamy vapor to form in the cool air.

"That man is the richest whose pleasures are the cheapest."

"More Shakespeare?" Will said.

"Thoreau."

"Do you think those people in there," he said, pointing to the masqueraders inside, "come here for *cheap* diversion? No, Mr. Sharon, they come here expecting to be entertained in grand fashion, and I oblige them on behalf of the Bank of California. If you believe Belmont is for my enjoyment, to satisfy a frivolous craving for luxury, you are mistaken. It is for those fine people inside the ballroom. Belmont announces to them, and the world, that San Francisco and California are worthy of their attention, of their investments. And I will spend what needs to be spent in order to insure their confidence."

"How you dispose of your income is of no concern to me. But the ventures in which you invest our profits trouble me to the brink of anxiety. They are hemorrhaging money and we can ill afford to continue in this fashion, especially now that the Central Pacific has achieved its connection to the East Coast."

"No one," he said hotly, "not even you, predicted the ruinous effect the Transcontinental Railroad would have on California's economy."

On this they agreed, that inexpensive eastern products, arriving aboard the newly completed railroad, were undercutting West Coast businesses. Will's determination to prop up the many factories and businesses of San Francisco was, to Sharon's thinking, futile and absurd. They should cut their losses and sell. No. His city would not be at the mercy of East Coast influences.

Sharon fumed. It wasn't just the railroad. John Mackay had formed a partnership with James Fair and two San Francisco saloon owners, Flood and O'Brien. The four Irishmen were maneuvering to take control of the Hale and Norcross, and Sharon feared they would soon have a majority interest. How did this happen? Will wanted to know. The mine had gone borrasca, Sharon answered, the stock was cheap, so they bought it up. Will asked what they were after.

"That is unclear," said Sharon. Their eyes met. Will had an uneasy feeling.

"There is some good news," Sharon said. "Potentially."

"I could use some."

"We've found a promising streak, deep in the Yellow Jacket."

Will's heart jumped. He knew the Comstock would come through. Sharon thought the streak would also be found in the Kentuck and Crown Point mines. How fortunate, then, that they had purchased Walker's interest in the Kentuck. The Comstock seemed to be toying with him, Will thought. Hot and cold she went, like a fickle mistress, burning with desire one day, cool and distant the next. But he was a faithful and constant lover. He would put up with her temperamental affections, knowing she would always come back to him with open arms in the end.

Sharon would know soon enough of assay values and would send a wire. "What is the current state of affairs with that crazy Sutro?" Sharon asked. On this subject they always found agreement.

"Despite our lobbying, Congress granted him a federal easement and mineral rights. Thaddeus Stevens, it seems, is a man of the people." Will shook his head. "When will our railroad commence?"

Sharon almost smiled. The other mine owners, as predicted, had been willing to advance funds for the railroad. Storey County and State of Nevada had also contributed. They would begin laying track in a few months, and the new line would be owned by the two of them, and Darius Mills. And now, Will smiled. Once the railroad was operating, it would put an end to Sutro and his ridiculous tunnel.

They ended the discussion on this high note, the crickets resumed their chirping, and together, puffing Cuban cigars, he and Sharon returned to the ballroom. There, seeing Elizabeth so happy, glowing like a debutant at her first ball, he felt a rare glow of satisfaction.

When she had returned from Paris, at his urging, Elizabeth seemed glad to see him. In his last letter to her in Paris, he had made promises to be a better husband, a better father, spend less time at the bank. How he could spend less time at the bank, he didn't know, but that was his intent, should his wife return. Once home, she revealed few details when he inquired about Paris. The children, however, gushed with information: where they visited, *who* they visited, what they had learned.

An effort on his part would be required, he knew that, and he was determined to see his wife happy. He approached her now, she with her feathered Harlequin mask. He put up his disguise.

"You are very beautiful, my lady, and I have been unable to take my eyes from you all evening. May I have this dance?"

She lowered her mask and smiled, and held up her hand to him.

Chapter 23

Sutro charged out the Virginia City telegraph office, a message from Washington D.C. pressed between his trembling fingers. Thaddeus Stevens, he hoped, with word of funding. The Chairman had been most optimistic in his latest correspondence.

He went to the edge of the sidewalk, trying to ignore the Virginia-Truckee Railroad terminus under construction down on E Street. The station house had been framed and crews were preparing a bed for the rails themselves. A grim sight. Devastating, almost. Sutro had been clear with Stevens, and the Chairman well understood, the threat that the railroad posed and the urgent need to begin digging the tunnel right away. The wire, he was certain, contained the good news he had been waiting to hear. A smile passed over his face, wondering what William Sharon would say when he heard: the United States Congress would provide funding for the Sutro Tunnel.

He ripped open the telegram.

...most tragic news...very sorry to relate...heart failure...Thaddeus Stevens deceased...

Sutro reached for the back of a wooden bench and steadied himself. With great effort he lowered himself onto the seat, his sweaty fingers still clutching the telegram. Those same fingers seemed to involuntarily wrap around the paper and crush it into a little, hard nugget.

God must be punishing him for his disbelief. That must be it. Over and over his hopes were raised, only to be dashed, like the miserable Sisyphus, his rock tumbling to the bottom of the hill after reaching the top for the thousandth time. His efforts in Europe, though of educational value, had also proved a failure: he had secured no investors despite several trips and dozens of presentations to the wealthiest and most influential men on the Continent.

"Are you all right then, Mr. Sutro? Faith, you don't look so well."

He looked up to see Finnian Gillespie standing before him, one of the few people in town that still had a kind word for him.

"I have just received some terrible news. My friend in Washington has died."

"I am in my sorrow for you, then."

"Thank you."

"Not Mr. Stevens, I hope."

"Yes, Mr. Stevens, I am afraid." He had hoped to convince Finn to come to work on his tunnel and had mentioned Thaddeus Stevens to him. How could anyone fail to believe in his tunnel if the Chairman of the Ways and Means Committee was supporting it?

"Oh but that's a woeful turn for you, Mr. Sutro. Will ye be giving up on the tunnel then?"

The sound of Finn's voice melted into the noise of stamp mills, horse hooves, and wagon wheels, and his thoughts drifted away. Where would he turn now? It seemed as though God did not want this tunnel built, and who was he to continue to fight with God? Leah, it seemed, had been right all along.

"Mr. Sutro?"

He heard a voice and turned to see Finn staring at him.

"Will ye abandon the tunnel, then?"

He might have to. How could he continue? There was no place left to go, no one else to turn to. He clenched his jaw. "I cannot bring myself to say I quit. But..." His voice trailed off.

He felt a hand on his shoulder. "Come on then, I'll be buying you a whiskey."

Though grateful for the kindness, Sutro declined. He wished only to be alone so he could think what he would say to Leah.

***

A clear blue-sky day along the Pacific Coast—he has been here before. The wind whips. Another swell and the boat lists, first to port, then starboard as the wave passes beneath like a silent and gentle leviathan. He holds the rail for balance. The wind hits the back of his neck; his ears ache, numb from the cold.

And then he sees it. An opening in the coast. Up ahead. Slowly, it comes into view. A yawning chasm. And there, in the middle, the narrow cleft. The nexus. The coast has laid herself bare, beckoning him in. He flushes with embarrassment, but cannot look away. The siren is calling and he must go to her. A man cannot resist. He must do as Nature intended. He approaches her, the hidden passage revealed, the froth of

treacherous currents, they take control and pull him in. He cannot es-
cape. Doesn't wish to. He yields to her.

And then, ecstasy. Deeper and deeper he pushes, and deeper
still. He is beyond the gate now. Heaven. Calm waters. Soft, rolling, tree-
speckled hills to his left. Deer nibble at the grass, calm and serene. Green
islands dot the blue waters. And on the right, the jewel. Ah, such beau-
ty…

Tell me, William, about San Francisco.

Another time, Louisa. You look so frail. You need your rest.

Oh, William, I long for the West. Tell me, please, before it's too
late.

Those words, too late. Do not say them.

Tell me, then.

All right, all right. But where do I begin?

How does it look as you come into the Bay?

Breathtaking. The city perches on the tip of a long peninsula
and kisses the blue waters of the bay. You see her carefree hilltops jutting
up here and there like children's toys: Russian, Telegraph, and Rincon
Hill. When you first behold her shores, you think you've discovered a
hidden paradise. What lucky men live here? Fairies, perhaps, live here,
and not men at all, you say to yourself. You look back and see white,
powdery fog rolling over the hills from the cool Pacific, like icing over a
cake. Soon the city is floating in a white mist. These San Franciscans,
you cry, they live on a cloud.

Oh, William, I can see it all so clearly.

But the muddy, filthy streets, the stench, the gambling houses
and parlor girls and gunfights. No, I won't tell her. She needn't know.
Someday the mud will be replaced by cobblestones, the gambling houses
by theatres, parlor girls by mothers toting their little ones to Sunday
School—

"Will, what would you say if I were to find myself...in a family way?"

He was jolted out of a deep sleep, his eyes popped open. In the bed next to him, Jess looked on patiently, waiting for an answer. They were in a room above the new Poodle Dog. School was out and she had come to San Francisco for a few days.

"What? Are you—?"

She wasn't, but what if she was? What would he say? He would say he thought girls like her had ways but, he stopped, ashamed of what almost came out of his mouth.

She finished the sentence for him: "That girls like me had ways of preventing those little inconveniences?"

He tried to think—

"Well," she said softly, "you needn't worry, we do have ways."

He tried not to look into her sad eyes, but they were impossible to avoid. She wanted something. Something all women wanted. Something he couldn't give her. A family.

"Is there someone else? In Virginia City?"

She hesitated. "Yes, perhaps."

Jealously dug its claws into him. He got up from the bed, his toes sinking into the plush carpet. He went to the desk to write, to answer letters, requests for assistance. One from a fellow horse-lover seeking advice, advice he now wrote out, giving details on breeding and stable practice. He wrote to the cemetery back east, funds to be sent for Louisa's gravesite. Every month there must be fresh flowers. He didn't want to think of losing Jess. He glanced at her now and saw Louisa: their resemblance still startled him, even after all this time. She stood, wrapped herself in a blanket, and went to the window, staring out.

"I imagine what it would be like to have a family," she said. "To have loved ones who care deeply about you and will sacrifice anything for your happiness. I imagine what it's like to eat supper with someone at night, to talk to them about the day, to plan for the future with them. I try to remember when I was a child and how it might have been to experience these joys, and what I recall only makes me yearn even more for the domestic life of a wife and mother. And I do yearn for it, William. I yearn for what you can never give me."

"I understand." He gulped hard. "I just don't know how to give you up."

She turned from the window and faced him. He went to her and they fell into an embrace.

"I'll try," he said. "If you can just give me a little time."

He dressed, kissed her goodbye, and walked down to the lobby, already thinking when he might see her again. Outside he turned to take a detour past the bank before heading home. He entered through the bullion door on Sansome Street and, once in his office, sifted through the papers: a note from Franklin, another from Mills, two letters, and a telegram from Sharon. He snatched up the telegram.

Yellow   Jacket   streak...expanded   into   pocket...assays high...extends to Kentuck and Crown Point...

This had been the news he had so anxiously awaited and fervently hoped for: a new bonanza. Hopefully. Sharon must be confident, else he wouldn't have wired. And just in time, if it was true. Business in San Francisco (all of California for that matter) had fallen into a depression. That damned Trans-continental Railroad. His many businesses, already suffering losses, were hemorrhaging money now at an alarming rate. The Comstock was the only thing that could save him. And it would, once again.

Chapter 24

Will kept a light touch on the reins. Elizabeth sat beside him in the phaeton, bundled up with a fur coat, looking out at the elegant South Park district. The rig, behind a two-horse team, jangled over the cobblestone street. The street, a parkway really, encircled a large oval lawn in the midst of fine, stately homes. The sun shown brightly in the November afternoon sky. A bright sun, however, didn't guarantee warmth.

"San Francisco," he said to his wife. "I think it's warm perhaps two, three days a year."

"I think two," she said, smiling at him.

He thought to mention that it was warmer on the peninsula, Belmont in other words, but reconsidered before the words escaped. He was careful with his words these days.

"I don't know what I'm to do with Samuel," she said. "He wants only to be at the stables in Belmont."

"He does love horses," Will said of his nine-year-old son. And he loves Belmont too, he thought, but didn't say. Sam had complained to him in private about the fact that there had been no horses in Paris, and his mother had grown tired of hearing him complain.

"Like his father, I suppose," Lizzie said.

He glanced over to look for a smile but didn't see one. He clicked the reins to keep the horse at an even pace, and tried not to think about the Comstock. He was still waiting on confirmation of Sharon's Yellow Jacket find. The days were passing in agonizing slowness.

"Will, Jr. has been asking me about a horse, lately," he said. "He sees his big brother riding and wants to imitate him."

"I'm grateful for Emelita," she said. "Someday she and I will shop together while you ride with the boys."

They drove by a particularly beautiful home, and Elizabeth's gaze lingered there. It was in the French Provençal style, and Will thought he could hear a little sigh. Or perhaps it was just a breeze in the air. After they passed it, she said, "I would like to see Samuel take more interest in his studies. Perhaps you can have a talk with him."

He said he would be happy to do that.

"Emelita has a cold again," she reported. "She does not take to this San Francisco weather."

"Well," he said, unable to resist, "there is Belmont. It is much warmer on the peninsula."

Elizabeth bristled at this. "You know I spend as much time at Belmont as possible. But we make our home in San Francisco, and I prefer the city life. It's just that the weather can be damp and cold. Today, for example."

"It is almost November," he pointed out.

"These fall months are often the warmest."

He had to agree. He asked if Emelita was eating well.

"The nurse tells me she eats well enough. She looks to be a healthy three-year-old, but she seems rather lethargic. I worry about her."

"Mothers worry about their children. It's what mothers are supposed to do."

She didn't respond to this. He had meant it good-naturedly, but knew good intent mattered little in married life. Words mattered a great deal. A change of subject was in order.

"Shall we drive up Market Street?" he asked.

"All right. Can we stop in at the milliner? I need to order a hat."

"Excellent," he said. "And I need to order a pair of boots."

He paused, then said, "Not at the milliner, of course."

She didn't laugh, as he hoped she would, but she did smile.

Chapter 25

It seemed like any other day. Finn went through his normal morning routine: get out of bed, stoke the fire in the wood stove, heat water, make breakfast, try to ignore the incessant clank clank—schurump, clank clank—schurump of the stamp mills, and, when the bells at St. Mary's rang the eight o'clock shift change, head down to the street, ready for another day's work. He and the other miners, who also imagined it a normal day, ambled up the hill to the saddle between Virginia City and Gold Hill, then looked down toward the Yellow Jacket and Crown Point mines.

A boy, running like a jackrabbit, raced out of the Kentuck hoisting barn and over to the Yellow Jacket. That's when Finn noticed a wisp of smoke. He bolted down the hill. Inside the Kentuck barn, he found MacKay.

"Where's the fire, Mackie?"

"We don't know yet. Deep, we think."

"'Tisn't much smoke. Perhaps the boys have it out."

MacKay sent him to the Yellow Jacket to see what they knew. He sprinted into the barn just as they dragged a miner out of the hoisting cage. It was young Murphy. They laid him out on a stretcher while he told his tale of the "devil himself" that he'd seen down below. He gasped and wheezed out his story: at the 900-foot station he was when a warm breeze started to blow and then a terrible rumble, and then the lights went out. "Just like that!" He had heard Gallagher and McGinley down below, yelling up to him that they were suffocating and to drop the cage.

"But I couldn't send him a cage. I couldn't see. I couldn't breathe." Murphy began to weep.

Finn ran back toward the Kentuck to report to Mackie, plagued by a frightful thought: McGinley and Gallagher may be trapped in a hell fire.

***

Sutro wandered out of his house and stood with the morning sun on his face, but felt little comfort from the warmth. The high plains of the Washoe Desert spread out before him like a wasteland of discarded vegetation, cast out of heaven, it seemed, and scattered over the barren soil. The prickly flora, starved for nutrients, water, and attention seemed as desolate as he, and equally accustomed to hardship and neglect.

The Sutro Tunnel, he morosely conceded, was a dying patient about to take its last breath. He would confess to Leah like a penitent sinner: you had been right all along, he would say. Perhaps she would receive the news with joy, thinking her husband would finally settle down once again to the life of a quiet merchant. Oh, that damned bank, that damned William Sharon.

He headed to the stable to feed his horses and noticed a trail of dust rising in the distance. Six Mile Canyon. A rider appeared. As he watched, his curiosity grew. The horseman flew like a Pony Express rider. What could be the hurry? He hustled to the stables and saddled one of his horses, then rode out to the highway. The galloping horse slowed, barely, as it approached him. "Fire!" the horseman shouted. "In the Yellow Jacket."

Sutro stared as if Mercury himself had flown past. A fire? He looked up in the direction of Mt. Davidson, but saw only blue sky. He kicked his horse into a gallop and headed up the canyon.

***

Gold Hill firemen pulled at thick ropes ahead of a clanking fire wagon laden with a heavy water canister. Finn charged down the grade, his legs barely able to keep up, and fell in behind the wagon, adding his muscle, his groans, his slipping boots. Other men joined and together they pushed while the firemen pulled, until the wagon finally reached the Yellow Jacket mine.

All around men darted this way and that. Some hauled water, others carried provisions: ropes, ladders and the like. Everyone seemed to have an urgent purpose, running just on the edge of panic, like a village under siege. Up above, on the divide, Virginia City fire wagons passed over the hill, heading down to join the fight. Women and children came down with them, faces anxious and white. Finn could make out the black silhouette of William Sharon hurrying to assess the damage to his most profitable mines. Beside him, Crowell kept pace like a vicious dog.

Inside the Yellow Jacket barn, smoke poured out of the main shaft and collected in the upper reaches of the ceiling. The superintendents were huddled together in one corner, in the other Father Manogue tended to the injured and maimed. Miners gathered around the shaft, all talking at once:

—the cages were full o' men going down for their shift...it hit 'em like a cannon ball...was operating the hoist but didn't know, you couldn't 'a known... Sammy sent 'em all the way down to 900 feet...drew up the cages, I did, for the next load and we sees Horace and Willy passed out on the floor...dragged 'em off and dropped the cages down lickety-split...we was lookin' at each other wonderin' what the hell had happened...like the devil was comin', scared senseless we were...waited a few minutes we did, longest fuckin' two minutes of me life... raised the cages again and it was the Bickle brothers...God help me, 'twas a fearsome sight...never forget it as long as I live...Richard's head chopped off it was and George's fuckin' arm...dead and mutilated, hadn't made it into the cage...ripped 'em to pieces on the way up—

Firemen began to stream through the door, one, then another, and another, pulling hoses and lugging big axes. They rigged a pulley for the water hoses and gathered into the cages, gave the operator a nod, and dropped into the smoky void.

Finn muttered a blessing and crossed himself. God help them. God help dear Joseph.

***

Sutro's old mare labored with each step, exhausted from the long climb. He urged her past the lower-most streets of Virginia City, anxious to learn of the fire. Black smoke was now rising into the sky forming a dark cloud over the mining camp. Sirens wailed. Women and children rushed out of their homes with fear-stricken faces, then began their grim, determined scramble up the hill.

His lethargic mount responded to a kick with a surging gait, an effort quickly abandoned until the next kick, an interesting cause-and-effect experiment, which, had he the time, might have occupied his attention for a considerable distance. Now, anxious as he was to see the fire, he just muttered a curse at the beast. A young woman, walking beside, looked up at him. Her penetrating green eyes captured him, held his gaze.

"Are you Mr. Sutro?"

"Yes I am."

"The fire, do you think it's a bad one?" she asked.

He didn't know, he said, but they would learn soon enough.

"I have heard of you," she said.

He reined in his horse, swung his leg over the saddle, and lowered himself down, relishing that sinful pride of fame. Or was it infamy? Was her husband a miner? Miss—? The girl's face was pale, but her stride, like the rest of her, was beautiful, confident, purposeful.

"Miss Ohhlson."

"Oh, pardon me."

"I am a schoolmistress, Mr. Sutro," she said. Ah, he said, it is very good to teach the children. She smiled, as if to say yes, it is very good.

"I understand you will build a tunnel, Mr. Sutro," she said.

"There will be no tunnel. I have given up."

She grew reticent, and they walked in silence. Then, glancing at him, she said, "Your tunnel, Mr. Sutro, were it in existence, it would rest well below the mines, would it not?"

"Yes, of course," he said, smiling. A simple creature. Charming, but simple.

"And should there be a fire up above, in the mines, the smoke and flames would rise to the surface, would they not?"

"Yes, yes, they would," he said, chuckling at these childish questions, but becoming a little curious.

"Down below, in your tunnel, were it in existence of course, there would be no smoke there, no flames, I suppose."

"No, I suppose not."

Now, suddenly, his thought raced ahead of hers. He bent his mind to a startling idea, envisioning miners descending on ladders below smoke and flames, scampering down into his waiting, benevolent tunnel where they would be led to safety, unmolested. There would be no need of deadly ascent up through fire and smoke to reach the surface. It had never occurred to him that the tunnel could be used as a fire escape!

"No, Miss Ohhlson, there would be no smoke," he cried. "No flames." He stood still for a moment, thinking, pondering the enormous black cloud gathering above Virginia City. *Mein Gott.*

He ran to catch up to the schoolmistress, tugging at the reins of his unruly mare, who tugged back disrespectfully, having scant patience for the world of genius. Questions swirled. What would the superintendents say? And who was this girl, so beautiful, yet unmarried? She was an enigma and yet he knew not to question fate—luck had brought their paths together and he would leave it at that. Oh, the wonders of his agile engineering brain. An incidental remark from a simple schoolmistress and it bursts forth in brilliant revelation.

***

With one hand Finn held the cable inside the hoisting cage of the Yellow Jacket mine, with the other he grasped a wet towel. A soot-covered fireman stood beside him, his temporary partner, and together they waited for the cage to drop. In the past hour, air currents had unexpectedly begun to flow down the Yellow Jacket and out the Crown Point and Kentuck, taking the smoke with them and giving crews a chance to enter the mine. They'd pushed back the flames, but many beams had collapsed and needed replacing, a job for which Finn had volunteered. In preparation, several loads of timber had been sent down to the 900 foot station.

The floor suddenly fell out beneath his feet. His nostrils burned. He thrust the wet towel up to cover his face. The cage floor rattled violently beneath him, sending vibrations up his legs and into his torso, his ears popping with the pressure change as each station whistled by.

The cage lurched to a sudden halt. His partner fired his lantern. They crept into the chamber, their feet sloshing in hot water. Soon their light fell onto a dead miner who lay against a beam, his face plastered to the wood. Nearby, another, with his head in a winze where he had gasped for one last breath. To one side of the station lay a stack of fresh timbers, which they hoisted onto their shoulders.

They sloshed into the smoky drift until reaching another corpse. He held his lantern up. Gallagher, face swollen and black, skin fried to a glaze. Mary, mother of God. He pushed grimly ahead to the next body, raised the lantern. It was Joseph, mouth gasping for one last breath of air, agony etched into still-opened eyes, ready to pop from their sockets, arms reaching out for the help that would never come. Finn crossed himself and laid a hand on Joseph's shoulder. "Oh, a dear broth of a boy you were, Joseph."

His partner continued past him. Another crew would be coming down for the dead, the fireman said. He then waded into the drift, his light growing dimmer and dimmer. He looked at the tortured face of his dead friend. "Ah, Joseph McGinley, you didn't deserve such a hellish death."

He forced himself to go on. Smoke gathered along the ceiling. He bent low to stay beneath it. The beams of light from their lanterns continued to illuminate the horrors: two scorched legs dangling from a dark shaft in the ceiling; a corpse mid-way up a ladder, both now turned to charcoal. The lantern light was remorseless, delving into crevasses and tunnels that he didn't want to see into. Silently, witnesses to the graveyard, they pushed on, deeper and deeper. He took little notice of the wheezing that gathered in his chest with each breath.

"We'll cut out the burned wood and replace it with fresh timber." The fireman's voice was calm, business-like. They dropped the beams and went back to the station for tools and more wood. They worked quickly, silently, save for their harsh, gravelly breathing. After replacing a ten-foot span of framing, it was agreed that they must return to the surface for fresh air. They stepped into the cage and pulled the bell chord, Finn trying not to think about Joseph, that he was leaving him behind.

Like a bubble breaking the surface of a pond, they burst out of the mine-shaft and into the hoisting barn. Another team took their place in the cage and soon disappeared down the main shaft. Finn and his partner sat to one side in silence, just breathing the lovely, cool air.

Men rushed about the barn in a blur. Finn was half-awake, half-asleep, or perhaps just dreaming. He couldn't decide which. A crowd of town-folk had gathered in the doorway. Jessie! What was she doing there? And Adolph Sutro next to her, talking and gesturing, and talking some more though no one seemed to be listening. Dreaming, I am, or 'tisn't day yet.

The air is poisonous down there, he heard someone say. He looked over at a group of men huddled in conversation. Mackie, with the other superintendents, and Jones, that bear of a man, super of the Crown Point, and the fire captain: *The men can't work for more than a few minutes at a time. Aye, they're comin' back up like drunken sailors. We can't afford to lose any more fire fighters. We should pump fresh air down, I tell you. Aye, we should. No, don't do that, it will only reignite the fire*—Mackie's voice, it was. *No, the fire's been pushed way back into the drifts. And fresh air will pull it right back out*—Mackie again: he was against the idea. *We don't have any choice, Mackie. The men won't last down there without fresh air. I say we try it.*

All the men agreed except Mackay. The foreman quickly put his crew to work on getting air hoses in place.

"Finn, are you all right?"

"He died, Mackie. Joseph McGinley, down in hell he is, and I've got to bring him up."

"Don't worry, we'll get Joseph." They were going to pump fresh air down there, Mackie explained. Finn was to be watchful. If he saw flames gathering, he was to run for the cage.

The hoisting cage re-emerged. He took another drink from the water barrel, and then soaked his cloth for the ride down. He followed his partner into the cage and looked back toward the doorway. Sutro, still talking and nobody listening. Jessie stared at him, her face pale and earnest. Their eyes met. She shook her head in slow, deliberate movements, as if warning him, and her lips moved, but he couldn't make out the words.

The fireman signaled to the operator. He grasped the cable and glanced again at the doorway. Jessie gave him a brave smile as the cage dropped into the darkness.

***

Ledgers and books littered the surface of Will's desk. He added figures in his head, reached for a ledger to check the numbers, subtracted, added more numbers, pulled a book out of the pile and checked the totals, then threw it down in frustration. The numbers did not balance. Too little income; too many expenses. It's nothing but a puzzle, he thought. And he only needed to make the pieces fit in some semblance of order for a short while longer, until Sharon's new Yellow Jacket ledge began producing. Down the hall, paper rustled in Tibbey's office, the head teller and treasurer probably frustrated by a growing stack of bills. He would go down and ease Tibbey's mind with a draft from his personal account. His money, after all, was the bank's money, and vise versa.

A knock came at the door. Will stood to greet his head teller. "Ah, Mr. Tibbey, I was just coming to see you."

Tibbey seemed wary of this revelation.

"I know the books are running in the negative, but do not worry yourself." Will handed him the draft. "This should get you through until the Comstock silver begins flowing again."

The teller took the draft with trembling fingers.

"What is it, Mr. Tibbey?"

Tibbey took a slow, deep breath, and handed a slip of paper to Will. A wire from Sharon.

Fire in the Comstock...rescues attempted...many men dead...Yellow Jacket, Kentuck, Crown Point...indefinite closures...

He crumpled the paper, dropped it on the floor, then walked slowly past Tibbey and out into the lobby, his footsteps echoing in the vast, empty space. He came to a stop and cast his gaze upwards at the angels on the ceiling. God, if you're there, tell me what to do.

"Perhaps you should go home, sir. In the morning things may not seem so bleak." It was Tibbey's voice, but they seemed like words from above. Yes, he needed to go home, see his wife and children. Sit by a warm fire. The answer would come to him, although at this moment no answer seemed possible.

***

The cage slammed to a halt. Finn waded out into the hot brine, gathered more timbers, then headed into the drift. He whispered a blessing as he pushed passed Joseph.

"After we've rebuilt the support," his partner said, "we can go into the drift to look for survivors."

Fresh air suddenly caressed his brow. Sweet, clean, and cool. The fireman stood up and took and deep breath. The air pumps. Blessed, blessed air. Invigorated, the two men worked quickly. One brace went up, then another, and another. Finn hoisted a beam and began to head into the tunnel, ready to work the next section. He noticed, as he went, a glow up ahead, far into the drift. He puzzled over this, at first thinking his eyes deceived him. The light deepened and grew brighter, changing hues from orange to red, glowing like a Pacific sunset. He stopped.

"Do you see that?"

His partner stood silently behind him. Finn waited for an answer. Just then, a dull roar seemed to come from the bowels of the mine. A tug came at his arm. Run, the voice said in a hoarse whisper. Fingers squeezed his arm and jerked him around.

"Run, for God's sake!"

Finn turned to see his partner splashing violently through the hot water. He ran too, lifting his feet high. Great sprays of water flew with each stride. He was hardly moving: time seemed to slow. He lost his balance and fell face first into the hot pool. Pushing with all his strength, he rose up and kept running, the skin of his face burning from the water. His feet, so heavy. Thick. The water groped him, claimed him.

You were right, Mackie, the fresh air will be the holy and redeeming death of me. Blessed damned air. Take me life if you will. But Jessie. Does she love me, or no? Oh, that he knew. He would not leave Joseph, he yelled ahead. If he didn't, the fireman yelled back, he'd be joining them in heaven. So be it, then. He tugged on the lifeless arm of his friend; rigid joints popped gruesomely. The fireman wheeled about, screaming that there wasn't time. There wasn't time.

"I've got you, Joseph. I won't leave you, boyo."

"You goddamn fool, you'll do them no good dead."

He hoisted Joseph, crackling and splitting and popping, onto his shoulders. Just then a wave of heat swooshed past, engulfing him, searing first his nostrils, then his lungs. Gasping, he glanced back to see an inferno thundering up the devil's tunnel. He back-peddled, wheeled around. The water tugged at his ankles. He slogged to a crawl; Joseph's weight pressed down upon him.

A lantern grew dim in the distance. What about Gallagher, he wanted to scream, but hadn't the strength. You can't leave Gallagher. The rock walls suddenly were aglow in bright orange light. His pant legs felt as if on fire, his skin burned. A wall of flames hit him from behind, just as he collapsed under the weight of his dead friend.

His last sensations were blistering hot air and scalding water. And then, nothing.

***

Will rode along the damp, quiet streets of the business district with his hostler. Will glanced at him and tried to imagine what sort of troubles plagued his life. Everyone had troubles and setbacks. An ill-tempered wife, perhaps? Sore joints in the morning?

"How is your family, Mr. Riker?"

The Negro turned to him, and a great smile shone out from his dark face. "Why, they're just fine Mr. Chap. And thank you for asking. We have everything we need, and then some."

They eased the horses to a stop in front of the Commercial Street residence. He dismounted, handed the reins to James and thanked him for the company.

"I'm the one that's thankful, Mr. Chap."

He pushed open the front door. Inside, the porter stacked crates and luggage just off the foyer. Startled, the young man met his eye, then turned and hurried down the hallway. Will stared at the mound of luggage. Someone, it seemed, had just arrived or was about to leave. He rushed up the stairs, taking two steps at a time. He called for Lizzie, but heard no answer. Voices drifted from down the hall. Just then she emerged from the bedroom, stopping when she saw him.

"Lizzie, what is all that luggage downstairs?"

"I'm going back to Paris."

"What? Why?"

"Why? Because I'm appreciated there."

"What in God's name do you mean? I appreciate you."

"Kindly do not swear at me, the children will hear you." She pushed past him and began to descend the stairs. He followed.

"But I thought you were happy. Lizzie—"

She continued with deliberate steps to the bottom of the staircase.

"What will I do without you? Without the children?"

"I suppose you can always move into a room at the Poodle Dog. I understand they are very accommodating."

This was as close as his wife would ever come to slapping him in the face. And he felt the sting.

"Lizzie, you mustn't go," he pleaded. "I need you now more than I ever have."

She turned and looked at him, considered his plea. A woman cannot resist a man that needs her, he knew, and he did need. Desperately.

"You need something that I cannot give you. Something no human being can give you." She reached up and brushed his face with her fingers. "Goodbye, Toppie."

Part Three

(1869-1872)

Chapter 26

"How is our patient?"

"Feverish."

It was a female voice—that one.

"Keep using the cool compresses."

"I replace them at regular intervals. But what of his breathing? It seems so harsh, so labored."

There it was again. Definitely a girl.

"He has the pneumonia in his lungs. There's nothing we can do except hope the fever breaks."

"I see." The female voice was quiet. Resigned. "Did he get this pneumonia from the mines?"

"Best I can tell, it must have come from the air down in the mine. During the fire. Disease is carried in the miasma, you see, and the heat of the fire and all that smoke made for a poisonous miasma. He surely breathed it deep into his lungs."

"Perhaps fresh air would help."

"No. Just the opposite. Keep the room closed up and dark."

"If you think that's best."

Footsteps. Then, "You're doing a fine job, miss."

"Thank you."

A soft hand caressed his brow. Finn attempted to open his eyes, but they seemed frozen shut. Was it Jessie who touched him?

The struggle had fatigued him. He dozed off.

***

In the Savage hoisting barn, the miners engaged in bawdy speculation on the possible uses of the long stick wielded by Herr Sutro. The Savage not being presently under the control of the bank crowd, Sutro knew his presence there wouldn't cause any great consternation with the superintendent.

"One thousand six hundred and fifty feet below us," he was saying, "the Sutro Tunnel will end." With the stick he sketched out the basic geometry in the dirt. "From there, one branch will go off to the north, and one to the south. The tunnel will lie beneath every mine of the Comstock Lode. Now, imagine a fire in the Savage, like the terrible Yellow Jacket fire that just killed forty-five men, God rest their souls. Forty-five miners, just like you. And now, we must expect that there will be a fire in the Savage someday." He carved a cross-section of the mine at their feet: squiggles represented the ladder he envisioned. "But imagine that all you need to do is climb down this ladder to the Sutro Tunnel. In a few minutes you would be safely out of the mine and the fire would not harm you."

The men suddenly began to take notice of his dirty scratches, jockeying for position to get the best view. Their clothes were still clean, their shift not yet started, so Sutro knew they would be rested and attentive. They stood amongst, and leaned against, the timbers of the hoisting works, murmuring and pointing at Sutro's crude drawings. They approved of this, he could tell.

"William Sharon and the Bank of California do not want my tunnel. They care nothing about the miners. Only one thing matters to William Sharon. Money. And his control of the Comstock. I care about the miners, though. I am the only one that plans for your safety. Who would take care of your families if you died in the mines? Have you thought of that? What has the Bank of California done to help the miners? Nothing."

"Are you sayin' you'll take care of us, Mr. Sutro?"

"My wife might have something to say about that."

"Is you a good cook?"

"No," said Sutro over the laughter. "Not me. But the Sutro Tunnel will protect you from fire and poisonous air."

A miner spoke up. "I'm agreeable with what you say, Mr. Sutro. Sharon doesn't give a lick about us. But what can we do? We can't build your tunnel for you."

"No, you cannot. But you can tell your union and the other miners to support the tunnel. The plans are complete and I only need a small endorsement to begin digging."

"We miners ain't rich folk, Mr. Sutro."

"How do you expect us to invest if you can't even get the big banks to?"

A murmur arose in accord with these sentiments.

If each miner gave but a few dollars, Sutro explained, he would have enough to begin. He sensed, however, that he was wasting his time. It was true, how much could these hardworking miners afford? And yet, something from them, even a little, would lend credibility to his project. Look, he could say, the miners themselves support the Sutro Tunnel.

He left them to consider his plea. A few minutes later he knocked on the door to Finnian Gillespie's room. Superintendent Jones was being called a hero for hauling young Gillespie out of the mine, but the lad's survival had been just as heroic, miraculous even. Very strong and brave, that young man, and possessed of great skills.

Miss Ohhlson appeared at the door bearing witness to the hardships of nursing in her dry, cracked lips, reddish nose, and hollow eyes. Through this innocent creature, he thought with some affection, Providence had shown Her wise and unpredictable hand, reviving his hopes for the tunnel.

He inquired after her patient. The doctor's diagnosis, she reported, was a pneumonia of sorts in the lungs. But God wishes that he recover, Sutro assured her. Why else would he be alive, no? She nodded tentatively. This was a very good deed she was doing, Sutro said, nursing him back to health.

"I will only be able to stay until the schools reopen," she said.

He followed her to the bedside. The Irishman's once-handsome face was now gaunt and pale save where darkened by stubble. His eye sockets were deep and bluish-black. His chest rose and fell with an awful noise, like a leaky pump. The schoolmistress lifted the damp towel from his forehead, dipped it into a bowl of water, squeezed out the excess, and then blotted the perspiration from his face. Gently, solicitously, she cared for him, and with noticeable affection.

"It is a miracle he has no burns."

"He has some on his legs," she said, "but they are healing."

"Do you know what happened to him down there?"

Superintendent Jones had gone down for him, she said. The knee-deep water, in his opinion, had saved Finn—Mr. Gillespie, that is. That and Joseph McGinley, God rest his soul, who had already perished. Mr. Gillespie had resolved to bring up his friend and must have had him on his back when the flames engulfed him. Jones believed he fell into the water as the fireball passed through, and that, and Joseph's body acted to protect him.

"Providence seems to have had Her hand in many things that day," Sutro observed.

She seemed not to hear him, staring at her patient. But then she looked at Sutro, puzzled. What did he mean by Providence?

"I do not wish to gain from the tragedy of these poor miners," he said by way of apology. "But the fire has revived the prospects for my tunnel, and I cannot help but think that higher authority is at work. Everyone agrees my tunnel would have saved many lives during the fire.

"But, I must have the support of the miners," he went on, engrossed with his burgeoning prospects. "I believe the miners will support the tunnel. I have spoken with many of them and they agree: mining would be safer with a tunnel beneath them. If the miners participate, others will follow. The miners first, investors next, then perhaps the government."

"I have been told that a congressional committee is coming to California," she said offhandedly. "Perhaps they would find the Yellow Jacket mine worthy of their consideration."

"What congressional committee?"

"I believe it's called the Ways and Means," she said as she blotted Finn's brow.

The Ways and Means? Could it be that Thaddeus Stevens' interest in the Comstock would survive his death? How did she know this? Mr. Mackay, she said, had told her.

Providence, oh Providence.

"Have you considered a speech to the miners, Mr. Sutro?" she asked, interrupting his reverie.

He had already begun speaking to the miners, he told her. No, what she was suggesting was that he speak to all the miners, at Piper's perhaps. But he was not a good speaker, he told her, and his English faltered when he was nervous.

"But you like to talk, don't you? Especially about your tunnel? Just talk to them all at once."

Herr Sutro had to admit that he did indeed like to talk, much more, in fact, than he liked to listen.

***

Finn heard voices.

"As soon as he awakens, I will feed him."

It was the female voice again. It must be Jessie.

"Food is not necessary. Just the opposite, in fact. His blood needs to be cleansed of impurities."

"But how will his body recover if it is weak? He wastes away, doctor."

There was an edge to her voice. Concern.

"Tea. You may give him tea when he wakens."

A damp towel was lifted from his forehead. Finn waited expectantly, knowing any moment the soft touch would come. His body burned, as if it were still down inside the Yellow Jacket, engulfed in flames. I'm sorry, he heard her say. I only have concern for our patient. Water splashed musically, then the cool towel touched his face, blotting his one cheek, then the other. He wished she would put the cool cloth to the rest of his burning skin. Once the fever breaks he can eat something, the male voice said, not before.

"You make an excellent nurse, Miss Ohhlson."

It was Jessie, then.

Footsteps echoed and then the door closed. She came close and stroked his brow. Finn was determined to open his eyes. He fought against the heavy weight of fatigue and finally, his lids parted ever so slightly.

"Oh, bless you, Finn." He watched helplessly as she swiped at the tears. Her face glowed, and he tried to lift his hand to touch her, but it wouldn't move.

"I'm going to feed you something," she whispered.

***

"Billy Ralston!"

Will, thoughts ensnared in a tangle of relentless speculation, stopped in mid-stride. All of his businesses, investments, and plans wove together in his head like a vast web, on the edge of which sat a hungry spider waiting to swoop down to collect her fat prize. Both spider and web, he knew, had become more formidable since the Yellow Jacket fire. Having Elizabeth and the children in France again didn't help his state of mind.

But friends beckoned. Fellowship called. An afternoon sidewalk confabulation was in progress and his presence was required. Come on over, Billy, one of the men cried. He was waiting for Sharon on a late-arriving stagecoach, and what better way to escape the entanglement of his own misery than an ad hoc, street-corner committee to discuss the problems of others? The new Poodle Dog restaurant, the evils of East-Coast influences, and the new President, Ulysses S. Grant, all were topics for debate by concerned citizens of the business district. When the stage finally arrived and Mr. Sharon climbed out, dressed in his trademark black broadcloth suit and white linen shirt, Will, now up to date on affairs of some import, took his leave.

He and Sharon exchanged greetings. His partner had not yet dined at the new Le Poulet d'Or, or the Poodle Dog, as locals called it, so they walked up to Bush and Dupont. Sharon settled into his chair, looked about the exquisite dining room, and allowed a sigh to escape. Fresh Olympian oysters had arrived that morning, said the waiter, so they ordered a platter, a couple of salads, and a bottle of wine. Polite conversation about theatre and social events eventually gave way to the Comstock and Virginia City. They needed another bonanza, Will said. Sharon assured him it was the focus of his daily attention. That, and the Virginia & Truckee Railroad, which would be completed by the end of the year. He hoped.

"Excellent," Will said. With the railroad, all aspects of the mining would be under their control: mining, milling, and now transportation. Revenue and profits would soar.

Sharon finished chewing an Oly, then took a sip of wine. He had hoped, he said, the Virginia & Truckee would put an end, once and for all, to the Sutro Tunnel. However, Sutro had been rallying the miners to his cause with the hypothetical argument that the tunnel would have prevented death in the Yellow Jacket fire. A ridiculous argument.

Will, about to take a bite of his salad, set down his fork and looked at Sharon. He didn't need one additional aggravation. Especially one so fraught with danger.

"What's more," Sharon continued, "he managed to corral the Ways and Means Committee and engage them in a tour of the Savage Mine."

"Dammit, Mr. Sharon, we cannot allow this."

Sharon assured him that no harm had been done. He, Sharon, had spent the following day with the committee, demonstrated their progress with the railroad, the large pumps installed for water removal, eventually convincing the politicians that the tunnel was superfluous. Besides, Sharon said, stroking his moustaches, Sutro was his own worst enemy, undoubtedly lecturing the congressmen as if they were schoolchildren.

Hearing this, Will resolved nonetheless to have his lawyers in Washington keep a close eye on Sutro. They finished their meals and dessert arrived.

Sharon, between bites, said he had heard talk of coin shortages. A problem, Will confirmed. He was writing weekly letters to President Grant asking for coin to be released from the Treasury. Jay Gould, however, seemed to have captured Grant's ear and was advising the President to hoard coins. All West Coast banks were facing bank runs. Sharon shook his head and together they lamented the end of the Johnson administration.

Will had been waiting for his partner to ask about the Montgomery South real estate auction. He decided to get it over with. "Our lots did not sell at the auction," he announced. There was no way to gloss over the disaster. "The market is in a terrible slump. And our enemies in the press poisoned the waters so thoroughly that all investors were frightened off."

Would it be a complete loss, then? Sharon wanted to know, pushing his plate away. No, Will said, trying to sound confident. He and Harpending planned to build an opulent hotel, The Grand, on the lots they had retained. It would have four hundred rooms and all the modern conveniences, and would undoubtedly attract other businesses to the area. Sharon grew tight-lipped: where would they find the funds for such expenditure?

From their principal lender, of course, Will said. The Oriental Bank in London.

Sharon stared at him, poker-faced. "How much?"

Meaning, Will knew, how much had they borrowed? "We've surpassed our credit limit. By a factor of two."

"What amount, exactly, have we borrowed?"

"One and a quarter million."

"My God," Sharon exclaimed, slamming his fist on the table. Near-by patrons glanced in their direction.

"I had counted on the Yellow Jacket," Will admitted. "And it would have come through if not for the fire. Damn, that fire." But, no matter, he told himself, refusing to give in to pessimism. Difficult times turn into prosperous ones. He looked at Sharon. "The Comstock will come through for us, Mr. Sharon. We just need to continue down to those deeper ores. And, once your railroad to Carson and Truckee is running, it will provide us with dependable income. That, combined with Union Milling, will give us the time we need to find the next bonanza."

Sharon had lost his appetite. He took out his tobacco pouch and pressed a wad into the side of his cheek. Will sipped his coffee. He would take care of the coin shortages by whatever means were necessary. Sharon, though, had to hit the next Comstock bonanza. And soon.

Chapter 27

The moon carved a lucent streak into the night sky. Montgomery Street, whose plank sidewalks were unaccustomed to the clatter of boots at this late hour, may have wondered at its ghostly insomniac: a strangely familiar shape moving with strides both gentlemanly and deliberate, wary yet confident.

He, Will, navigating the dimly-lit streets, made a left at California, and thereafter let the down-slope propel him toward the Bay. His eyes were focused, shifting, taking in every detail, the streets, the alleys, the buildings. A chilly gust of wind cut with seeming ease through his heavy black coat. Shivering, he nodded to a boy leaning innocently against a lamppost, collar turned up and cap pulled down. The lamplighter nodded back, a little grin creasing his lips. Will continued at a measured pace, imagining his progress to be slowed by a substantial weight. He passed the entrance to the Bank of California, then made another left at Sansome before stopping abruptly at the bank's side door. He pulled out his watch.

Twelve minutes, the wiry hands told him. Good.

He slipped the watch back into his pocket and there, nestled deeply, found a gold coin. Letting go the former and grasping the latter, he turned and walked back up California and stopped at the streetlamp. The boy, awash in light and sitting patiently, looked up the street, then down before turning his gaze on the great banker. Will quickly pressed the half eagle into his palm. The lamplighter looked both ways again before dropping the coin into his vest-pocket, then gave a conspiratorial nod.

Will hurried back down California Street, and as he turned the corner onto Sansome, the street began to go dark behind him, one lamp at a time. He glanced back to see a shadow fleeing up the darkened sidewalk. Events were going according to plan.

The silver slip of a moon was now the only light intruding on the black night. At the side entrance to the bank he inserted his key and pushed open the door. Asbury Harpending stood waiting inside, wearing dark dungarees and overcoat, as instructed. Behind him, James Riker formed the trusted rear-guard.

"Where's Dore?" Will asked.

"Not here yet," Harpending answered. He glanced at Riker, then looked at Will. "Are you sure Dore has sufficient stamina for this?"

"He'll have to." Maurice Dore had conducted the auction of their New Montgomery real estate; he figured the man owed him a substantial favor, given the abysmal outcome. "Besides, he's the only one I could find on short notice. That I trust, anyway."

Will pulled the watch out again and checked the time. Ten forty-five. He glanced at Harpending, glad the younger man still had his athletic frame: he would have to pull the lead-oar on this team. A tap came at the door. Harpending yanked it open and Maurice Dore stepped inside, rubbed his hands enthusiastically, and smiled.

"Do we proceed with this skullduggery?" Dore, a portly, middle-aged man, grinned like he was back in grammar school, about to commit a boyish prank.

"We do," said Will, "but don't look so happy. You're going to break the law first, and your back second."

Dore's smile turned to a frown, and James Riker chuckled.

Will led them into the bank, unlocked the main vault, and swung open the massive door. Harpending and Dore followed him inside. Stacks of silver and gold bullion lay in neat rows on the shelves; the two men gasped at the sight. Will, however, like the man who finds little excitement in an oft-seen petticoat, unceremoniously lifted a bar of gold off the shelf and handed it to Harpending.

"Take as many as you can carry," he told them. He opened a canvas bag, placed three bars inside, and waited for his friends to do likewise. "Now stay close and stay quiet," he said, wheeling around and heading out of the vault with the bag slung over his shoulder. When he reached the Sansome door, he told Riker to wait there, and gave him a wink. Riker grinned.

Will and his co-conspirators strode out the door and around the corner, past the front of the bank, and up California Street. When they reached Montgomery, he turned right and was relieved to see the lamplighter had darkened that block also, in accordance with their bargain. They moved along the sidewalk as quiet as alley cats. The heavy bag cut into his shoulder blade, the bars thumping his back with each stride. He stopped at the door of the United States Treasury and Mint. His men pulled up beside him, their breathing the only sound in the cool night air. The huge bronze door boomed like a kettledrum in response to Will's pounding fist.

They waited. Will studied his black boots. From the side of his eye, he could see Harpending and Dore glancing up the street, then down. The door, finally, creaked and began to open. Light poured out and swept an arc across the sidewalk until it illuminated Will, then Harpending, then Dore, exposing them one by one, raccoon-like creatures of the night whose thieving exploits would be discovered only upon the light of day.

A stern-faced guard appeared in the doorway. He looked, nodded, then stepped aside for Will.

"Give me your bags," Will said to his two friends. He took Harpending's bag and handed it to the guard, then took Dore's in his free hand. "Wait here," he said.

Will followed him into the bowels of the Treasury building through a series of hallways and doors, eerily quiet and yet strangely exhilarating. Soon, an enormous vault, already open, loomed before them.

"I'll be down that hall, in my office," said the guard, pointing. "Knock twice when you're finished." He set down the bag of gold, turned, and disappeared.

Will inched into the vault, half-expecting a trap to spring. "God help me," he whispered.

Slowly, crouching low, he passed the inner workings of the great door, creeping like a tiger, one careful step at a time. He passed a second door and entered a small chamber. The last opportunity for sanity stared him in the face. The last chance to call off the brazen heist. On one side of the room, bullion. On the other, coins. He stared with an equal measure of amazement and disgust: stacks of gold coin rose off the shelves, half eagles, eagles, double eagles, and all in that beguiling yellow color that no painter could mix save God Himself. And silver dollars, big and heavy, the riches of the Comstock. Row upon row of coin, the life-blood of the economy, sitting there like guarded jewels too precious for the hands of common men. Those fools in Washington. Coins horded by a puppet President taking advice from imbeciles who had no knowledge of the West, no understanding of the economy. They knew not the error of their ways.

He slung the bullion bags onto the floor. Working quickly, he moved the bars onto the shelves, noting the amounts delivered, and then re-filled the bags with the equivalent in gold coin. He ignored the silver: gold would give them more value for their effort.

Out the vault and through the corridors he hurried. He shoved open the heavy door and handed the bags to his waiting assistants. They were to give the coins to Riker, get more bullion, come back, he would give them the equivalent in coins, and so forth. They nodded and left.

Will stood guard at the door and waited, checking his watch from time to time to see how long a round-trip would take. When the two carriers returned, it had been 18 minutes. He took their bullion, went to the vault, exchanged it for coin, and sent them on their way. This process they repeated, over and over.

The night raced on. The moon traversed the sky in a great arc. After many loads—it seemed hours had passed—Will waited by the door once again, but the knock didn't come. He checked his watch, then pried open the door and peered out. Quiet. No one in sight. But in the direction of California Street he could see a light. Damn!

He eased out the door, closing it but making sure it didn't latch. Walking purposefully, but without hurry, he approached the light and soon recognized Harpending and Dore. The intruder was a policeman, a lantern in one hand and a gun, aimed at his friends, in the other. Will was incredulous: had he not paid the beat cop to leave this area alone?

"Good evening, officer," he said with thinly disguised irritation.

The policeman held up his lantern and peered at him.

"These men are with me," Will said, as if that would conclude the matter.

"Billy Ralston?!" The policeman gazed at him through the lantern light. "What the devil is going on here?"

"What do you mean, officer?"

"I mean, why are these men skulking about at three o'clock in the morning like a couple of alley cats?" The officer swung his lantern toward the bags; the pistol he kept trained on Harpending and Dore (alley cats would be more of a threat, thought Will). "And carrying bags of gold bullion?" said the policeman.

Will eyed the bags lying in a heap on the ground. No rational tale would explain why his two friends were carrying gold bullion at three o'clock in the morning on a dark street, just a couple hundred feet from the Treasury. He took note of the policeman, a man about forty, or less, big and barrel-chested, a footballer once, no doubt. Probably couldn't be outrun. Honest face. His badge said Sergeant.

"Those bars of gold belong to my bank," Will said. The truth in small doses seemed the right approach. He thanked the lucky moon that his thieves had been stopped coming from the bank, rather than the Treasury. "The Bank of California. It's right around the corner."

"I know where the Bank of California is. But how do I know that gold is yours?"

Whose would it be, if not his? He would take him to the bank, right then if he liked. Show him the books and match up the stamps, bar by bar.

The sergeant glared at him, his gun barrel still pointed at Dore and Harpending. "Let's say I believed you. Then why the devil is the gold out here, on the street? And what are these men doing with it?"

"I can't tell you that, Sergeant. But we have broken no law here"—that he knew of, he was thinking. "That's my gold and these men are with me. I can say no more."

"Is that so? Well, maybe we should just go down to the police house. A jail cell might free up your tongue."

"Now hold on, Sergeant!" Will assured him he meant no offense. What he could tell him was that he and his men were trying to avert a crisis, a crisis that would bring down every business in the city. Men would be out of work. Crime would rise. "All of our lives will be much worse off in the morning, if you interfere with our mission," he said.

The policeman scoffed. "You're saving the world, is that what you're telling me?"

"No. Just California. And San Francisco."

"Do I look like a fool?"

"Not at all, sir. And you know I'm not foolish enough to be out here in the middle of the night transporting gold without a good reason."

A gust of wind: the lantern creaked. The sergeant looked in the direction of the Treasury. "A crisis, you say?"

"Yes, sir. And if you'll be so kind as to come by the bank in a few hours, I'll show you the fruits of our labor. If you want to take me in at that time, I'll gladly surrender."

The policeman thought about this. His lantern swayed in the wind, its light glancing off the buildings and sidewalks. "All right. Fair enough," he said, as he holstered the pistol. But he was going to be at the bank later for an explanation. It was only because of Mr. Ralston's fine reputation that he would go on down the street as if he'd never seen any of this.

"You wouldn't have any idea where my beat cop is, would you? Or why all the street lamps are out?"

"No, Sergeant," Will answered. "I was asking myself those very questions just before you arrived."

The policeman chuckled, swung his lantern toward Sacramento Street, and went off in a half-canter into the night.

They were off schedule and so picked up the pace, laboring hard until five-thirty. The crescent-moon was gone and pale light began to glow in the eastern sky. They had transported less than he had hoped, having lost valuable time with the policeman. But, according to his tally, the Bank of California now had over a million dollars in gold coin.

At the bank, Will thanked Riker and told him to go home, but the faithful assistant wanted to stay until the opening. Harpending and Dore, utterly exhausted, left, with Will wondering out loud how he would ever repay them.

The secretary and head teller arrived at the bank on schedule. The bank would open in a few hours and they were to have the coin on display at the teller stations and ready to disburse. Will hadn't slept, but the excitement of the night still coursed through his veins as he washed up and changed. Back in the lobby, anticipation was building as the tellers stacked their coins. By eight-thirty, Will could see customers gathering outside the bank, milling around, talking amongst themselves. This was where rumors were hatched, he thought. He could almost see them coming to life on the lips of his customers, taking shape and spreading like little demons out into the street and beyond. Rumors, he knew, were what led to bank runs. In this case, rumors of coins shortages.

By quarter to ten, throngs pressed at the front door. Agitated. Ready almost to riot, it seemed.

At ten o'clock sharp, Will himself unlocked the doors. He stood aside as a tidal wave of bodies flooded the bank, rushing toward the teller counters, boisterous and determined. But then they stopped. A hush fell over the lobby.

"Look at the coin!"

"You told me the bank had no gold coin."

"That's what I heard."

"Would you look at that?"

"Gosh damn, ol' Ralston has done it again."

Will stood up on a stool he had placed by the entrance. He gazed out at the crowd and saw familiar faces. Across the huge lobby, against the wall on the far side, he saw his assistant. Will nodded to him and Riker gave him a salute. He continued searching until he saw the policeman. The sergeant touched the bill of his cap and Will nodded back in acknowledgement.

"Good morning, folks," Will announced. "As you can see, the rumors of a coin shortage are obviously exaggerated. There are among us, unfortunately, those who would drive wedges of distrust between commerce and the public, who would spark fear in hope of reaping illicit gain from the chaos they create. But please, ladies and gentlemen, always remember that your money is safe here at the Bank of California, and will be as long as I am its cashier. Today you are free to withdraw any and all funds you wish, but please do not do so out of fear, or based on false information. Thank you for your patronage and I will be here to answer your queries, should you have any." He gazed out at the stunned crowd, then, shoving his hands deep into his pockets, said, "And if anyone can lend me a few coins for lunch, I'd appreciate it. I seem to be a little short at the moment."

Laughter rose up and filled the room. Then carefree chatter, followed by more laughter. Like a war had just ended, a truce had been called. Relief. *Thank you Billy* and, *That Billy has done it again* echoed throughout the room. Many stared up at him, wide-eyed, mouths open. Where had he gotten the coin? How had they been so misinformed? It was a miracle! Some began to turn around and push their way back out the front door. Others followed.

The tide reversed course. Ebb and flow, ebb and flow. It had always been thus.

He stepped down from the stool and greeted his customers and friends as they passed out onto the street. They eagerly shook his hand, thanked him, apologized for doubting him. He was magnanimous in accepting their gratitude.

Chapter 28

Sutro gazed out at the faces of hundreds of miners. His canvas-clad audience sat fidgeting and mumbling among themselves, casting impatient glances up at the stage. Just imagine you're talking to a few miners, he said to himself, remembering the school teacher's advice. Piper's Opera House, normally the site of entertainment ranging from Shakespeare to dogfights and everything in between, had never seen a crowd gather for a speech. By simply attending, he knew, these citizens of Virginia City were braving the wrath of the Bank of California, to which they owed their very livelihoods. But every seat was taken. Miners filled the orchestra seats, boxes, and balcony, and some even sat in the isles. In the front row, local newspaper editors Dan De Quille and Alfred Doten sat with pens in hand.

"My fellow citizens," he began, "I am..." The noise in the crowd trailed off. He looked down at his notes, glad for the help Miss Ohhlson had given him in preparation, but nervous nonetheless.

He traced the tortured history of the tunnel, and his efforts over the last five years to bring the great work to fruition: the Nevada Act, which granted him a tunnel franchise, royalties he had negotiated with mine owners, and the Sutro Tunnel Act, which granted federal rights to build the tunnel. With the Tunnel Act in hand, he had gained pledges from many of the mine super-intendents for the use of his tunnel. But the Act, he exclaimed, had spurred the Bank of California into nefarious action and they set about to undermine him. The pledges he had secured from other mine owners were unscrupulously diverted by the bank to the construction of their railroad.

"Virginians," he cried, "have you ever been in a position where your friends shunned you? If you have you know how mortifying it is on meeting an old acquaintance to have him pass by you pretending not to see you, instead of shaking you by the hand and welcoming you. Have you noticed them cross over on the other side of the street when they saw you at a distance?

"The Bank of California thought I would be left helpless. Defeated by their great powers arrayed against me. But they got hold of the wrong man. I was not to be ousted so easily." A rumble began to spread throughout the hall. They had never heard the story told in this way.

He had been to New York and Washington and Europe countless times, but the great financiers would pledge funds only after Pacific Coast investors endorsed the project. He admitted that the Virginia-Truckee Railroad, paid for by the cancelled sub-scriptions to the Sutro Tunnel, would eliminate a major source of revenue for the tunnel: the tunnel would not be needed to remove the ore to the Carson Valley. Yes, upon completion of the railroad, the ore would be transported by train. But men, drowning in the great floods of hot water, or burned by scalding steam, or suffocat-ing in foul, poisonous air, would not benefit. In a fire, such as the great Yellow Jacket calamity, what good would the bank's railroad do for miners stuck down below with burning flesh and singed lungs?

"Miners and laboring men, what is the price of your health, your liberty, your independence? Who is there among you so impractical as to refuse to donate outright a few paltry dollars per month to a cause, so worthy and just as mine, which will insure to you liberal wages, safe passage into and out of the mines, a cause which will make you the power of this land, make powerless our oppressors, and break up your arch enemy, the Bank of California?"

He gazed out at his audience. Waiting. Silence greeted his stare. For a moment, he thought his effort had failed, his words fallen like quiet, weightless snowflakes. Then, suddenly, a man stood up and yelled out—*The bank crowd has swindled us all;* and another—*Because 'o them, our friends were killed in the fire;* and yet another—*Murdered, they were!*

Pandemonium broke out. Cries for lynchings echoed from the walls and flew about the room.

Sutro held up his hands to quiet them. He wanted their support, but lynchings perhaps might be too extreme. After several raucous minutes, he succeeded in quelling the uprising and told them that what he needed was their financial support. Someone began to clap. Others joined, and soon the room filled with applause and whistles.

They were behind him. After years of solitude, he, the outcast, reveled in the sweet vindication of their approbation and affection. They yelled his name and he waved, thanking them, and he wished Leah were there to witness his triumph.

Chapter 29

Will examined the interior of his California Theater with a critical eye. Beside him, Asbury and Mrs. Harpending tried their best to ignore the one awkward, empty seat in his box. Will found society's preoccupation with his marital problems amusing, but unworthy of his time: he preferred to focus on his new theater. Exquisite carpets, sumptuous upholstery, and fine tapestries all mingled together to create an air of refined excess and privilege. Rows of white, green, and red footlights lit the wide stage, which was complete with the latest in scene-changing mechanisms. He looked out over the heads of his fellow San Franciscans, prideful that they were finally becoming cultured citizens of the world, leaving behind that coarseness of Gold Rush-era Buena Vista, this theater but another milestone on his city's path to greatness.

The actress on stage sang a lovely aria. Mrs. Harpending glanced sideways, again, at the empty seat. He turned and caught her eye. Perfect fodder for conjecture and gossip that seat, ripe with scandalous rumor, which ladies such as Mrs. Harpending found irresistible. Caught in the act, she gave him a heartbreaking smile of sympathy, as if to say she understood his loneliness and would like nothing more than to hold him to her bosom and make him forget the bitterness that surely filled his days. He smiled inwardly. Nothing elicits more tenderness in a woman than a lonely man.

Elizabeth, of course, was the source of abundant speculation among San Francisco society. He received letters from her, and his children, from time to time, though there was no mention of when they would return. The official reason for her visit, to buy furniture for Belmont, surely would not have taken more than a month or two, and Will's embarrassment was turning, day by day, into resentment.

While his irritation simmered, he found his gaze lingering on the pretty actress playing the lead part in *Little Nell and the Marchioness*. Lotta Crabtree was a lively spirit and he wondered if she would enjoy a trip to Belmont. A private tour, perhaps. Of course, she wasn't Jess, but Jess was in Virginia City, and a man gets lonely for female companionship. Besides, Elizabeth, according to Will's sources, was not living the life of a nun in France. Rumor had it that she had been seen in the company of a French actor.

At the intermission, Will and his guests made their way down the wide, sweeping stairway and into the lobby. There, amid chandeliers and potted white camellias, a crowd gathered around to hear whatever story Will might have to tell. He related one of his many popular anecdotes to eager ears. It's the absolute truth, he was saying, the only entertainments in Panama were billiards and poker. That and watching the Pacific Ocean for approaching steamers. As for the natives, they passed the time smoking cigars and stealing from Americans.

A Mrs. Carrington exclaimed that she could not imagine him living in such a place. Her daughter, a young widow whose much older husband had died, leaving her rich and childless, said she thought it sounded quite exotic. "I wish I had been there," she declared. "In fact, I may just take the passage across the isthmus the next time I go to New York."

"Charlotte, whatever has gotten into you?" Mrs. Carrington colored and looked at Will. "I apologize for her manners."

"No need to apologize, I assure you. I find your daughter delightful and refreshing."

"No one travels through Panama now that the railroad has been completed," another woman added.

"I don't care if I ever take the Panama passage again," agreed her husband. "The mosquitoes are as thick as locusts in a Mormon desert."

"The railroad is certainly much easier," Will conceded. Then, turning to the young widow, he added, "I like your spirit of adventure, Mrs. Randolph. If you do decide to cross the isthmus, I would be happy to provide you with some travel advice."

She looked at him with a wry smile. "What does one eat in such a place?"

"Charlotte," the girl's mother protested. "Mr. Ralston has no time for this."

"I have nothing but time, Mrs. Carrington. Actually, the food in Panama is quite tasty. Many fine tropical fruits, of course. And, if you're particularly brave, you might sample the roasted monkey."

"Oh, my word," gasped Mrs. Carrington. Her daughter stifled a shriek; another woman looked near to fainting.

He smiled mischievously at the widow. "They look rather frightful, like a black baby almost, but they're quite flavorful."

"Dreadful." Mrs. Carrington looked sternly at him, but, he thought, with a touch of indulgence. "I simply refuse to believe that you lived among such barbarians, Mr. Ralston."

"I am only grateful that I lived to tell about it, madam. I apologize if I shocked you and to make amends, I want to extend an invitation to you, your husband, and lovely daughter to visit me at Belmont. I promise to serve you something far more elegant than roasted primate." He noticed Harpending across the room, signaling to him. He turned to the youthful Mrs. Randolph.

"I will count on you to bring your mother and father to Belmont," he said. "You'll find it most charming, I assure you."

She gave him the conspiratorial smile of a worldly woman.

"Now if you'll excuse me," he said. He made his way towards Harpending, thinking that young widows were like yesterday's flowers, though in the case of Mrs. Randolph, recently plucked and still displaying quite handsomely in the vase.

Will and Harpending moved to one corner of the lobby. Plans were in place for the Grand Hotel on New Montgomery and construction was due to commence. Harpending seemed nervous. There was, he said, still the matter of funding. He looked at Will with a curious grin, as though surely this minor nuisance had slipped his partner's mind.

What? Had not his last installment arrived? Not since he last checked, said Harpending. Will apologized, assured him the draft would be forthcoming. His mind turned over the problem: he didn't know where he would find a quarter-million dollars. More juggling would be necessary, and he already had too many twirling knives in the air.

Just then he spotted John Fry; it was like seeing the sun peek through the clouds. When together, they avoided the topic of Lizzie's absence and stuck to their common business interests, a discretion that Will appreciated. Colonel Fry had been reaping the rewards of Will's investments for many years now and sat on the board of every bank-controlled mine on the Comstock, as well as Union Mill and Mining. Why not the New Montgomery Real Estate Company? He waived his father-in-law over.

"Your young friend was just telling me about the Grand Hotel on New Montgomery Street. He promises it to be a spectacular addition to our budding hospitality industry."

"I have a faith in Asbury." Fry looked admiringly at the young financier. "He seems to have a knack for finding the best investments and turning hay into gold."

Will put his hand on Fry's shoulder and smiled. "Like an alchemist, you mean."

A chime sounded the end of intermission.

Will suggested that the three of them have lunch later in the week. He had a proposition for the Colonel. Fry seemed pleased at this: he was always eager for a new venture. As they climbed up the broad staircase, he knew Fry could be counted on in a pinch. But, he had to be careful: one mustn't dip into such a well too frequently else it run dry at an inopportune time.

***

Finn had gained sufficient strength to attend Sutro's speech at Piper's Opera House, and afterward he had cheered as loud as anyone. He remembered with a smile when he had thought Sutro a madman, and often told the story, to great laughter, of the day he had met the Prussian. Now, two days after the speech, he and Jessie worked their way slowly up D Street toward Piper's for another meeting. The sun had set and long shadows stretched across the camp.

"It was kind of you to walk with me," he said, breathing hard from the climb.

"The doctor doesn't want you to exert yourself too much."

"Oh, I see how it is then, you accompany me as a nurse-maid."

"Nursemaid and friend."

"A stroll with the nurse is something like a kiss from your grandmother. 'Tis nice, but who will remember it?"

A tickle settled in his chest and he fell into a gravelly cough, and she handed him a handkerchief. "I will remember," she said.

They passed Union Street and then stood before Piper's, a splendid monument to the frivolity of miners and their life in camp. Opera was never on the calendar of events at Piper's, unless cocks crowing before a fight could be considered singing. Finn took a deep breath, which sent him into a spasm of coughing.

Jesse took hold of his arm. "You should have listened to me and ridden the mule."

"You told me to ride, so you did. But I'll wear the poor beast out if I don't begin to walk again."

"The assembly is for miners only," a man announced as they reached the entrance. "But for you, Miss Ohhlson, we'll make an exception. Honored, we would be, to have you attend. And I'm sure Finn here wouldn't mind, either." He winked at her and grinned, his bulbous nose crumpling up like wadded paper.

"That's very kind of you, sir." Jessie showed her appreciation with a smile that would break any heart, and the old miner could only beam at his good fortune. His cheeks were ruddy as they passed by. "You just make yourself comfortable, miss," he said, tipping his hat.

In the auditorium of wooden seats and glass chandeliers, Finn approached John Mackay and James Fair, the former greeting him with an eager smile, the latter with steely gray eyes. If Finn was ready to come back to work, they had a position for him. Wary more than ever of the mines, Finn thanked them for the offer and said he'd consider it.

"Sutro gave a fine speech," Mackay said with a grin.

"So he did," agreed Finn.

"A speech is one thing," Fair grumbled, "digging a four mile tunnel is another."

A miner yelled out for everyone to take a seat. The assembly quickly grew raucous, with motions to pledge funds for the tunnel, denounce the mine owners and superintendents, and lynch the Bank Ring, with Sharon to dangle first and longest. The miners, incensed at the manipulations of the bank, now exposed to the light of day by Adolph Sutro, were in a surly mood. But calm was maintained, and finally, after arguments and debates galore, a vote was taken and fifty thousand dollars was pledged. All motions of a sanguinary nature were defeated.

Walking home afterwards, Finn sensed that the world had changed. A leavening was taking hold among the poor, he told Jessie, an awakening to power where previously there had been only obedient servitude. Mackay, Fair, Flood and O'Brien were mounting a challenge to William Sharon. Sutro, many years the outcast, was now a symbol of hope. The Bank Ring was in disgrace and their authority in the camp had waned.

"Sutro came to see me," he said.

She was surprised at this. Aye, 'twas true, he said, Sutro had asked him to work on the tunnel. And? Did Finn intend to? Well, God's truth, he wasn't sure. He was of a mind to see the tunnel built, and Sutro had even offered to give him tunnel stock, for what it was worth. But Mackie also wanted to employ him, so he was in the clutches of a dilemma.

"Whether you work for him or not," she said, "it's good that Sutro will finally begin his tunnel."

"'Tis good, I agree."

"And I'm glad you are going back to work, though I think you need a few more weeks of rest."

"You make a fine nurse, Miss Ohhlson," he said, happy that she would fret over him, "and I'll be thanking you for tending to me."

They strolled along, approaching an intersection. What, she asked, did he think would happen to the bank, now that the miners seemed to be turning against it? He hoped it would collapse but was doubtful of that result, as Sharon had his railroad now.

Suddenly, as they rounded the corner, they were face to face with two men. Finn pulled sharply on Jessie's arm.

"I'm glad to see you up and around, Mr. Gillespie."

"It's kind of you to say so, Mr. Sharon." Finn nodded to Sharon, but ignored Crowell, who stood beside his master like a dark shadow.

"You know Mr. Crowell, don't you?"

"I do."

"But I don't believe I've met your lady friend." Sharon turned his dark eyes to Jessie.

"Miss Ohhlson," Finn said, "Mr. Sharon. And Mr. Crowell." He fixed a hard gaze, first on Sharon, then Crowell.

"She's a schoolmistress," Crowell said.

"Ah, I see." Sharon stroked his moustaches. "The schoolmistresses I remember weren't nearly so...fetching."

Finn tugged Jessie's arm, as if to lead her away, but she resisted. "I am disappointed at your coarse behavior, Mr. Sharon. I had been told you were a learned man, fond of Shakespeare."

Sharon, ready to play the part, raised his hand in a sweeping gesture. "Lady, you know no rules of charity, which renders good for bad, blessings for curses."

She kept her eyes on him, unflinching. "Villain, thou know'st no law of God nor man; no beast so fierce but knows some touch of pity."

Sharon bowed ceremoniously. "Touché. Though she be but little, she is fierce."

"A pleasant evening to you, Mr. Sharon," Finn said.

"And to you, Mr. Gillespie." Sharon's poker face revealed no emotion. "Nice to make your acquaintance, Miss Ohhlson."

Crowell threw Finn an icepick smile. "See you around, Irish."

Jessie tried to keep up with Finn's long, angry strides. He had no fear for himself, but knew that Crowell wouldn't hesitate to use Jessie as a pawn in their war. A malice existed between them, he told her. Yes, she had perceived that.

"I don't care for him," she said, "but I care for Mr. Sharon even less."

"Aye, a demon-of-a-man, that one."

A coyote's ululation pierced the night air once, its voice quickly joined by a chorus of others, shrill and euphoric. A kill had been made. A chill ran up Finn's neck and he felt Jessie's hand slip into his.

"You needn't worry about me," she said.

The howling died off, beast and prey fulfilling their grim duties to Mother Nature. A bittersweet silence. Jessie, though, walked beside Finn with a gracious, feminine sway, Mother Nature redeeming herself.

Finn stopped, and, imitating Sharon's gallant hand, said, "I was prepared to lash out at Mr. Sharon with the verse of Thomas Moore, but you were too quick."

Her face erupted into a smile, and the smile grew bigger until she laughed. And Finn laughed, too. She squeezed his hand, saying she felt brave by his side.

They arrived at Mrs. Frieda's front door, said their goodbyes, and with a stern warning and wagging finger, the nurse prescribed no work for a fortnight.

He made his way home, weighing his offers of employment: MacKay, or Sutro? The tunnel must be built, he decided, and Sutro needed his help. I should work where I'm needed most, he thought.

Chapter 30

With one hand on the back of widow Randolph's silk dress and the other on the banister, Will descended the stairs leading to the first floor at Belmont. His leather shoes creaked but were otherwise quiet on the carpeted steps. The house was strangely silent: the staff had yet to begin their morning chores. James Riker, though, would be waiting outside, seated in the carriage, his big bright eyes staring straight ahead, neither questioning nor judging.

"I simply adore Belmont," Charlotte Randolph said. They had passed through the library and out the coachman's entrance. "A more delightful place could not possibly exist."

"And a more beautiful guest I've never had," he said.

"You flatter me, and I quite enjoy it."

She was worthy of flattery, he assured her with a broad smile. "I hope you will come again."

"Well, you did promise Mummy and Daddy they could come, and I know they're dying to see Belmont, what with everyone talking about the grandness of it all."

"Yes, I did promise them, didn't I? And how are you at playing the fool?"

She leaned forward and kissed him on the cheek. "Quite good, I believe."

She smelled marvelous. "Shall I have James take you to the station?" he asked. "The train will arrive in half an hour."

"Yes. I must get back to the city. Mother drops by at the most unexpected times. I don't think she trusts me, though I can't imagine why." She threw him a wry smile.

Riker hopped down from the carriage and helped the guest into her seat. Will, grateful for his faithful assistant, decided he and Riker would ride out towards San Jose later in the afternoon, knowing that his groomsman loved nothing more than to ride and hear stories of the Mississippi River, New Orleans, and Panama. He waved goodbye and slipped back inside as the carriage whisked across the gravel and out the gate.

He wandered into the cheerful sunroom and raised the walls up and into their overhead pockets. Warm, natural light flooded into the adjacent library, where he intended to keep his mind occupied with correspondence. He sifted through the day's stack of mail, and his heart jumped at the sight of Jess's handwriting.

My Dearest William,

It has been too long since we have seen each other and I miss you a great deal. Being the famous man that you are, I hear of you constantly and the sound of your name always brings with it a touch of sorrow, for in many ways you are the only family I've known.

The Yellow Jacket tragedy has altered the course of many lives in Virginia, including my own. It pains me to relate that much of what is being said here is critical of the bank, and I wonder sometimes if you know the full extent of Mr. Sharon's activities. He is not well liked by the general population and I worry that much of the business he conducts in your name will reflect on you in an unflattering manner. Many startling allegations were recently made by Mr. Adolph Sutro in a speech given to miners at the opera house. It would be most soothing to my troubled conscience if you could assure me that Mr. Sutro's allegations are in fact without merit or validity, or at the very least, that they are the machinations of Mr. Sharon and not of your making.

Mr. Sutro claims that the bank has undertaken to cheat the other mine owners by mixing worthless tailings with silver ore for the sole purpose of inflating its profits. As you might imagine, this allegation is very troubling to all decent citizens of the mining camp. It is also claimed that the bank has diverted funds intended for his tunnel and redirected them to the construction of the Virginia-Truckee Railroad, and that the bank wishes to assume control of the Sutro Tunnel for its own purposes, namely, to maintain primary control over the Comstock Lode and Virginia City. Other claims have been made by Mr. Sutro, and others, but I am confident that your hands are clean, you, like the rest of us, having been the victim of a fiendish man of low moral character. I hope to hear your own words on this the next time we meet.

I remain torn between the desire to establish a domestic life here in Virginia and the wish to maintain our close affections. These, I suppose, are mutually exclusive, but it would give great solace to my heart if you could provide your blessing and assure me that our friendship will continue in some fashion, if only that we will each maintain a solicitous feeling for the other. If this obstacle is surmounted, I can then proceed to grapple with the greatest of all fears, that of telling my husband, should I have one some day, of my sordid past, a past I dread he will not be able to understand or forgive. This torments me night and day and stands as an obstacle in the path of happiness, though I become convinced in my darkest hours that happiness is but a fleeting gift to which the damned are not entitled. I wish you were here to tell me it wasn't so. With all my affection, I am –

Sincerely yours,

Jessalyn

Will stared at the paper through blurry, tear-filled eyes. How could he answer such a letter? If he could take her into his arms he would, and never let go. But she needed another man now. Reluctantly, he took out a piece of stationery.

My Dear Jess,

You are a dear, sweet creature, too blessed for this world. I wish you were here so I could wrap you in my arms and shield you from all life's sordid inventions. I worry about you night and day and your letter gave me at least a momentary respite from those anxieties, knowing now that you are at least safe and in good health.

I will come to Virginia to answer your queries, face to face, but in the mean time, suffice to say that I am beset by challenges on all sides, not the least of which is Adolph Sutro. There exists a crucial link between the Comstock Lode and San Francisco, a link jeopardized by Sutro and his tunnel. Given the choice between San Francisco and Sutro, I must choose the city. For this I cannot apologize.

If I may change the subject, Lizzie and the children are returning home. This is welcome news, however, to my dismay she intends to stop while in New York and visit Mr. and Mrs. Thorn! The very parents of my deceased fiancée. I know not her motives for such an extraordinary visit, but my thoughts run wild with speculation. I have remained in contact with Emily Thorne over the years. This link to the Thorn family has always been a source of anxiety for Lizzie, and I fear her visit is intended to put an end to the relationship. I sit and imagine the meeting between these dignified people—whose only sin was to lose their beloved daughter—and my jealous wife, thinking all manner of things she might say to them and how they will respond.

Well, enough of my self-pity, though I'm grateful for your sympathetic ear. I hope to be in Virginia City soon and look forward with great anticipation to seeing you again. Until then, I remain,

Affectionately yours,

Will

The news of Sutro's speech had been related in a wire from Sharon, and Will had resigned himself to the inevitability of certain criticisms arising from it. But the miner's pledging money to the tunnel was an unexpected blow. He felt like a captain in the throws of a mutiny. A benevolent captain, whose only concern was for ship and crew, with never a thought for himself.

***

Finn tugged at the lapels of his coat and cinched the collar about his neck, determined to keep the freezing rain from slipping its icy fingers down his back. He peered out from beneath the bill of his rain-soaked hat at the muddy trail of Six Mile Canyon, and then looked over at Sutro hunkered down against the barrage of angry pellets coming, it seemed, from a diabolical enemy up above.

"The rain is not so bad." Sutro had to shout over the noise. Gale-like winds added their fury to the early winter blast.

"Ah well, I'll hold it's better than a snow storm," Finn yelled back.

"We will go into Dayton to greet the crowds before the ceremony. Perhaps the rain will stop by the time we get there." Sutro prodded his horse and pushed onward like an old and grizzled sea captain sailing confidently into a tempest. Finn watched him, grinning. A crowd in Dayton was as likely as the devil in a confession booth.

They continued down Six Mile Canyon and arrived in Dayton, soaked to the core. Cross's Hotel, where the grand assembly was to occur, resembled a garrison bombarded by wind and rain. The sloppy, wet street was empty except for some men wearing red and blue striped uniforms, huddled closely together like a herd of zebras.

"That'd be a colorful gathering," observed Finn.

"The Gold Hill Miners Band."

A sorry sight to be sure. As Finn had suspected, no one had come for the tunnel ceremony save those paid to be there.

Sutro, however, had expected a crowd in the hundreds. Undaunted, he asked the band leader what they could play.

"Marches, m-m-mostly."

Sutro peered out from beneath the bill of his hat. "How about Dixie?"

Yes, the band knew Dixie.

"Good," he cried. "Play loudly. As loudly as you can."

The eleven members responded, to Finn's surprise, with a rousing rendition of the popular song, which, as they tooted and honked the melody over and over, seemed to mysteriously ward off the rain. And as the music played and the rain slowed to a mist, a crowd did indeed begin to gather. A crowd that, after half an hour, reached about 200 people. Dayton, Finn knew, was a town so sleepy and unaccustomed to excitement that any stimulation whatsoever could give rise to a spontaneous holiday.

"There will be a barbeque after the ceremony," Sutro announced to the gathering. A loud and persistent cheer went up.

The music stopped and, as if on cue, the rain began to fall again. Wagons were hitched and the assembly moved in a long train some distance away to the foot of the Flowery Range.

The Town of Sutro was still being surveyed, but the namesake himself led the parade up the only street so far graded, and to the façade standing at its far end. The wooden structure, which looked like the front of a small store, had the words "Sutro Tunnel" painted across the top. Finn had built this to the boss's exact specifications, and even in the rain it seemed grand and important. Like the monument to a great struggle. Sutro, staring up at the portal, swelled with pride.

The rain fell harder, blown sideways by the wind. Finn, like everyone else, receded into his woolen coat. Sutro, though, seemed not to notice the elements.

A limp, wet flag was raised up the flagpole until, at the apex, it flapped in the wind like a broken bird wing. The Miners Brass Band played a tortured version of the Star Spangled Banner, though Finn could scarcely discern between the whistling wind and the musical notes. The former, he decided, was probably more on key. He watched Sutro stride to the speaker's stand. Freezing rain driven by terrible gusts of wind, lashed at the Prussian's face.

The speech, he promised, would be brief. He thanked his audience and was sorry they didn't have better weather. This was a proud day, he told them, a day he had thought might never happen. But when you know you are right, that Providence is behind you, you must have the conviction to keep going no matter what the obstacles. Great men never give up.

"How are we going to have a barbecue in this weather?" someone in the crowd shouted.

"We can take everything back to Dayton," yelled another, to a general murmur of approval.

Sutro smiled reassuringly. Yes, they could move the barbecue to Dayton. The tunnel, he went on, would save many lives and make the miner's work easier. And this little Town of Sutro would become the next Virginia City, where everyone would live and work together, and enjoy all the conveniences of modern America.

"Will there be enough food for all these people?" a man asked. "At the barbecue, that is?"

Sutro assured them there would be, and if they could wait another minute, he would be done with his speech. The wind peppered his face with raindrops; he wiped the water away from his eyes with his sleeve. His bushy sideburns looked like two sponges, saturated and dripping from the sides of his face. In conclusion, he told them, a great dream was about to become a reality and they would all be able to tell their grandchildren that they were present for the historic birth of the Sutro Tunnel, which—

"Where should we have the barbecue, Mr. Sutro? Where in Dayton, I mean?"

"How about the old Courthouse?" came the answer from somewhere in the crowd.

That seemed a popular choice.

Sutro grimaced. He finished the last of his speech, and stepped down from the stand to a soggy applause. Finn stood to one side with a shiny new pick in hand. Sutro grasped the implement and strode resolutely up to the opening in the façade. Cheers and whistles went up through the torrents of rain. He hoisted the pick far overhead, holding it for a moment as if realizing his life was about to change, then with a great heave and groan, buried the prong to the hilt in the rock-filled mud.

The Sutro Tunnel had commenced.

After the handshakes and smiles and congratulations, the band broke into a spirited march. Finn took that as a signal and led the gathering back into Dayton, like Moses leading the faithful to the Promised Land, or barbecue, as it were. Sutro said he would be right along.

A bit later, in the warmth of the Dayton Courthouse, while the good people of Dayton ate their manna and danced to the tunes of the Miners Band, Finn stood to one side with Dr. J.C. Hazlett and John Bethel. The heat from a nearby fireplace caused steam to rise off their wet clothes. Hazlett, a diminutive man with a soft voice and spectacles on the end of his nose, looked more like a librarian than a doctor. Besides caring for the tunnel workers, the middle-aged physician would oversee assaying as well as stock sales. Bethel, a miner by trade, was wiry and fit, with an abundance of energy, seemingly unable to sit still for any length of time. He was to be the tunnel superintendent. Finn would work with both men as the assistant foreman and, since he knew assays, take samples for Hazlett. He wondered if the five thousand shares of tunnel stock Sutro had given each of them would ever be worth anything. It all depended on the man with the enormous salt and pepper sideburns, wiry gray hair, and intense gray eyes, the man everyone in the courthouse now waited to see: General Superintendent Sutro.

In the mean time, they huddled by the fire, and partook of the barbeque.

"He cut the crew back to nine men," Bethel groused. He put a drumstick to his teeth and tore off some chicken, then added, "And we haven't even started digging yet."

"That's a wise strategy, in my opinion," said the doctor, eyeing Bethel and his drumstick with some disdain. "He can make his money last longer that way. Fifty thousand dollars is a paltry sum when you consider the work we have to do. With a full crew we'd consume that in less than a month."

"I won't be blamed for the slow progress, then." Bethel rotated the drumstick back and forth, planning his next bite.

"I'd be thinking," Finn added, "that slow progress is what he wants."

"Precisely," agreed the doctor. "He must be able to tell investors that the tunnel is being dug. It won't do to run out of money and have to stop digging."

The foreman finished off the drumstick and tossed it onto a platter, then wiped his hands on his pant-legs. "Well, with three crews of three men each, we might as well be digging a hundred mile tunnel. Either way, it'll never get done."

"Mr. Sutro," explained the doctor, "expects France to lend him millions of dollars. He told me it is a certainty. Once this money arrives, you will be able to dig in earnest, Mr. Bethel."

Just then the door swung open and Sutro burst into the room as if blown in by the storm. The crowd paused momentarily and the room grew quiet. Congratulations, Mr. Sutro, someone yelled. It'll be a fine tunnel, Mr. Sutro, shouted another. And it's a fine barbecue you have here! This brought great applause. Sutro waved, then charged across the room to where the three were standing. His eyes were red. Fierce.

"What is it, Mr. Sutro?" Finn asked.

The Superintendent cursed under his breath before answering, as though spitting out vile phlegm. "I must go to Washington right away. I have just learned the bank is about to pass a bill." He muttered something guttural to himself, then said, "They are trying to eliminate royalties for the tunnel."

"That goddamned bank," muttered Bethel.

Sutro looked like he might burst into flames. Intense heat could generate spontaneous combustion, Finn had heard. But then, unexpectedly, an idea seemed to grab his fancy. Slowly his eyes softened. He cooled. A moment passed and his bearing melted into calm serenity.

"But you see," he said with a little smile of satisfaction. "The tunnel has begun and they are desperate to stop it. Now they fear Adolph Sutro more than ever." Without warning, and oblivious to the room full of well-wishers, Sutro turned and charged toward the door as if there weren't a moment to spare. He grasped the doorknob, then wheeled back around to look at them.

"Do not worry. You begin digging. I will stop the bank."

Chapter 31

Snow fell like dollops of icing outside the window of Will's room at the International Hotel in Virginia City. It didn't fall so much as float down with quiet authority: what man or beast dare interfere with something so mysteriously delicate? Will stared until the picture blurred in the wavy panes of leaden glass, the flakes becoming ghostly little masks, quivering and whispering to frighten the lonely. Jess stood before the window, enshrouded, it seemed, in snow. He wondered if she, too, was mesmerized by the vision, or if her attention had been captured by someone down below on C Street. Perhaps, like he, she sensed the mood in camp and contemplated its significance. He had noticed it the minute he arrived: icy stares and silence where there had once been jovial greetings of, "Hey, Billy!"

Things had changed in Virginia City and he knew why. It was Sutro and that infernal speech.

"I can see the schoolhouse from here," she murmured. "The snow is halfway up the front door."

The same snow that had cancelled school for the last few days. This has been a cold winter, was all he could think to say. She remembered, she said, playing in the snow as a girl. A little sled, riding down the hill, the excitement, being happy—had it really happened? Yes, he told her, just as he remembered swimming in the Ohio River.

"Were you ever fearful?"

"Never," he said with too much bravado. "Well, perhaps a little. When the currents were strong and we feared being swept down into the Mississippi. Terrible tales were told of boys caught in the confluence and never seen again."

"I was never afraid of the steep hill until I crashed the sled into a tree. After that, I was always fearful."

Yes, children were fearless until they discovered their vulnerability. That terrible moment, the beginning of the loss of innocence. Tell me more about your childhood, he said, but she seemed not to hear. Why, she wanted to know, had he treated Mr. Sutro so badly? He let go a great sigh.

"I'll tell you everything," he said, "though it may shock you to know the truth." The Yellow Jacket fire had nearly ruined him, burned up any hope when they shut down the Crown Point and Kentuck mines.

She interrupted: "I almost lost a dear friend in that fire, not to mention the forty-five dead miners and firemen. That is the real tragedy of the fire."

It was a terrible tragedy, he agreed. But she must know that miners die at their work, and firemen likewise. So did policemen. These were hazardous professions. The miners willingly chose their work for which they were paid commensurate with the risks they took.

Other blows had landed, he said. Mills selling most of his shares, a harsh vote of no-confidence; President Grant's policies toward the West—Lincoln and Johnson had listened to him, why wouldn't Grant? Then there was Sutro and his damned tunnel. Did she have any idea what disaster would ensue should the tunnel be completed? And traitors like superintendent Jones and Alvinza Hayward, who had just stolen the Crown Point out from under their noses. Jones, he said bitterly, had discovered a deep ore body and failed to report it to them. This left them no choice but to buy up the adjoining Belcher mine, though little consolation that was. No, no, the wolves were circling. And they smelled blood.

How, she wondered, could he buy the Belcher if he had no money? And he couldn't help but laugh.

How indeed?

"I will find the money, in that place where I find all the money, everywhere and nowhere, shuffling accounts, shifting resources, notes, promises, my father-in-law, it doesn't matter. The money is always there for something so important. We mustn't lose control of the Comstock. It's the one reliable asset keeping us afloat. Do these traitors here in Virginia not understand that Sharon and I built this town? That we supported it through bonanza and borasca, through the frantic rushes and the great depressions? God-blessed, none of these fools would have jobs if it weren't for the Bank of California. Traitors, all of them. Adolph Sutro then comes along and weaves a tall tale for them and suddenly, Billy Ralston is the devil, and we cheated them."

"It troubles me," she said, "that you would associate with a man like Sharon. Make him your partner, even."

"I'm sorry if it troubles you," he said testily, "but he is an astute businessman."

"An unethical, astute businessman."

"There are allegations only." His voice was growing louder.

"You know in your heart the allegations are true."

"I know no such thing," he shouted. This wasn't a lie, but it was close, and he looked away, unable to meet her gaze.

He was a trapped man, he told her. Trapped by his duties, his responsibilities. San Francisco was his burden, but also his posterity. Louisa's posterity.

"Oh, William," she whispered, taking him into her arms. "You poor, tortured soul." She did not agree with his sensibilities, but he knew at least that she understood them. And she asked him about Elizabeth, was she back from France, and what had she said of her visit with the Thorns? How were the children, and had he been happy to see them? Samuel, he reported, had grown up so much he had hardly recognized him. The same for William, Jr. And Emilita, such a beautiful little girl.

She grasped his hands. "William, you must go home and try to save your family. They are so very much more important than the Bank of California and the Comstock. Even San Francisco. All of it means nothing if you lose your family."

In the world he knew of no one wiser than Jess. She who had no family knew best the value of loved ones. He helped her with her coat. They pulled on gloves and scarves, and then he escorted her down to the second floor, where they slipped out onto B Street and a waiting coach. The falling snow would, he hoped, give them cover from prying eyes. The driver, seemingly impervious to the cold, held open the coach door, and Jess, holding Will's hand for balance, stepped up and quickly settled herself into the corner. He leaned in and kissed her, then stepped down and closed the door. A rap on the side of the carriage to alert the driver, and then Will stood back.

The coach pulled away, but a gaze from across the street diverted Will's attention. A big, handsome youth stared directly at him. He looked familiar. Will tugged on the hotel door, but then glanced back. The young man remained there, staring at him intently, like someone who'd seen a terrible vision, or witnessed a crime. Will darted into the hotel, trying to remember where he had seen that face. Through the lobby and up the elevator and down the hall to his apartment, he struggled with his memory. He pushed open the door and caught a hint of Jess's perfume lingering in the air. Then he recalled that jaunty boy, years ago, strolling down the street in San Francisco, stopping to gaze at Jess and to give her a flower, a flower now dried but still redolent with wistful youth, that she carried to this day, close to her breast and near to her heart.

And then he knew. There was another man in Jess's life. And it was this Irishman.

***

Sutro, back in Washington D.C., watched with a mixture of fascination and annoyance as the printer, a short, powerful man named Schreiber, methodically plucked cast metal pieces out of tiny wooden compartments and placed them, one painstaking letter at a time, into the rectangular form. The work of building a typeset page for the printing press was, in the engineer's view, a laborious process in need of improvement, though the end result of a neatly printed page was quite impressive. Mr. Schreiber, looking down his nose through wire-framed spectacles, attempted to extract the next letter from the cramped box with his short, stubby fingers. Like an elephant trying to pick up a peanut with his foot, thought Sutro with considerable impatience. He turned his hat around on his finger, spinning it a little faster each time. Sutro's business was urgent, but the printer took no notice: he was happy to have someone to converse with. Typesetting could be a lonely business.

"You are from California?" Schreiber inquired, having finally grasped the elusive letter between thumb and forefinger. He spoke with a heavy German accent, a fact that annoyed Sutro, who was convinced he now spoke nearly perfect English and felt that those who couldn't were either inferior or lazy.

"Yes. California, but also Nevada." Sutro watched in agony, fearful the printer was about to drop his hard-won specimen at any moment, which would mean waiting for the elephant to pick up the peanut again. Why didn't he use an implement, he couldn't help but ask. This seemed obvious, though what was obvious to the engineer was not so to the ordinary man or dim-witted pachyderm.

"I have been meaning to try that, but always forget. Old habits, as they say," Schreiber chuckled. He turned his attention to placement of the piece in his expanding puzzle. And did Herr Sutro come by the train or the boat?

By train, he told him.

"Excellent. What did you think of our transcontinental railroad, then?"

Our transcontinental railroad? As if it belonged to the East Coast, or Washington D.C. Crocker and Stanford would find that interesting. It was a great feat of engineering, Sutro answered, thinking this man asked too many questions.

"I agree," enthused the printer. "And before California, where are you coming from? I am guessing from your accent, somewhere in Prussia."

He is a fool, thought Sutro. I have no accent. Aachen, he said with a frown.

"Ah, you see? We Austrians know our accents. Yes, yes. And Aachen is sometimes called Aix-la-Chapelle, is it not?"

Austrian! No wonder he was so obnoxious. By the French, only, Sutro explained curtly. He began twirling the hat on his finger again. It would only be polite to ask the printer where in Austria he was from, but he couldn't bring himself to.

"I am from Prague," the printer offered good-naturedly. "Although many consider Prague part of Bohemia."

"Ah, I was about to ask you where you come from," he lied. "Very fine city, Prague."

The printer began poking for his next letter, then said: "Did you know that Prussia and France are close to war?"

Sutro grimaced. The hat slipped off his finger and tumbled to the floor. "Yes, I have heard. I have agreement—an agreement, with France for a loan, so I hope there is no war."

"A loan from France? You must be an important man, Herr Sutro. Important men do not borrow from other men, they borrow from a country. Am I right?"

Sutro did indeed consider himself an important man, even a visionary, and his feelings toward the printer immediately began to soften at hearing this astute observation. He protested that he was not so important, but that he was building a very important tunnel in Nevada. The French, he said, understood this idea and had agreed to lend him three million dollars.

"Ho, ho! Three million dollars. That is a lot of money." Herr Sutro must have very fine tastes; did he wish to look at his collection of printing plates from Austria? There was one in French and several in German. The printer started to get up from his seat.

The stroking of his ego was like a dose of laudanum, lulling him into complacency. But then he remembered his schedule. "Perhaps another time, Herr Schreiber."

The printer's happy expression drooped. Sutro hoped to cheer him up with a proposal. If they could come to an agreement, he would like him to print something for Congress.

"For Congress?" Schreiber said, resuming his seat. "They have their own print shop, no?"

Yes, this was true, but this particular bill had never made it to their printer. And, in addition to the bill, he also needed a speech printed. A speech? What sort of speech? Was Herr Sutro a politician?

"No. I am an engineer," Sutro declared, always proud to announce this remarkable fact. "The bill is hand-written. My enemies slipped it onto the Speaker's desk and hoped to pass it into law without notice. I plan to expose their little plan. It seeks to eliminate royalties for use of my tunnel."

"You have devious enemies, I would say. I, thank goodness, do not have enemies." The printer paused and looked up. "Except, sometimes people are not happy with what they read and then I get complaints. But these are not the same as enemies. You agree?"

Sutro supposed he did, yes. And would the people be happy with Sutro's speech, the printer asked.

"Some happy, some not." His speech to the miners had been so well received that he was certain Congress need only read it, and would likewise be persuaded to support his tunnel. The Bank of California, of course, was another matter.

"Yes, it is always that way," the printer sighed. He poked at his almost-complete frame, making minor adjustments.

Sutro produced the hand-written legislation, House Bill 1179, and a copy of his Piper's speech, and handed them to Schreiber. They discussed the number of pages and copies needed, haggled over price, then reached an agreement. Fifty dollars. A huge sum, but an expense that could not be avoided. He would give a copy to every member of Congress, he told the printer, so they could see for themselves the treachery of his enemies and the benefits of the Sutro Tunnel. A brilliant plan, was it not?

Mr. Schreiber peered over his spectacles at him. "You are a very clever man, Herr Sutro."

Yes, this was true, Sutro conceded.

"I was a friend of your predecessor, Thaddeus Stevens," said Sutro, as he hurried along beside Henry Holt, the new Chairman of the Ways and Means Committee. Snow covered the Capitol Mall and Sutro's feet were numb. But he had been tracking Mr. Holt for days and was not going to miss this chance, even at the risk of frostbite.

"Mr. Stevens' death was most unfortunate," said the Chairman, without much conviction. He walked at a brisk pace.

"Most unfortunate," agreed Sutro, struggling to catch his breath. "He was a big supporter of the Sutro Tunnel."

"So I've heard."

And had the Chairman also heard of the Sutro Tunnel Act? He had. Mr. Holt's pace seemed to quicken. Moisture vaporized near his nostrils with each breath.

"Then you might be aware of House Bill 1179, which would gut the Tunnel Act."

The Chairman had never heard of such a bill.

"Well," said Sutro, playing his interlocutor as if an opponent in chess, "that is because it was never printed, but only slipped in among other bills on your desk."

Holt glanced over at Sutro. And why was that?

"Opponents of the tunnel hoped to avoid a debate. Very underhanded."

"Humph," grunted Holt, accompanied by a burst of steamy vapor from his nose. "When does it come up for a vote?"

"Next week." He reached into his satchel and handed him the bill and a copy of the Piper's speech. The miners, he explained, had pledged fifty thousand dollars and with that sum, his crew had bored 1,390 feet, so far. But the money was nearly gone.

Holt took the papers without breaking stride. Sutro then made his next move in their little chess match. He proposed that Congress create a commission to investigate the Sutro Tunnel and then make recommendations to Congress.

"Recommendations for what?"

"On whether the tunnel would, as I claim, increase efficiency and output of the Comstock mines." Then he added, "Mr. Stevens agreed with the proposal."

Holt shot him a skeptical look. "Mr. Sutro, I've a meeting to attend. Come to my office in a few days, after I've had a chance to read your materials."

Sutro slowed his pace and watched the busy Chairman speed away. His toes were nearly frozen, but the match had gone well.

The next morning, Sutro flipped through the Critic-Record as he sipped his morning coffee, still feeling the cold in his feet. The headlines looked familiar: Benson-Smith, the Woman Insulter; Education Contributes to Low Morals; Rising Emigration from Europe; Gold Supplies Running Scarce. This last one caught his attention, and he carefully tore the article out to save it for future lobbying efforts. Then he found what he'd been looking for under Congressional Business: House vote on Bill 1179: 124 nays, 42 yeas. With a smile he tore the article out and placed in his vest pocket.

Then he caught sight of an innocuous headline at the bottom of the facing page, like a little weed sprung up in his just-planted garden: France at War with Prussia. His fists clenched. He shoved aside his coffee cup and read the short story, then rose, fumbled through his coin pouch, and slapped a nickel on the table.

"Damnation!"

In the telegraph office, he prepared a telegram to Dr. Hazlett.

Western Union Telegraph Co.
Washington, D.C.

Dr. J.C. Hazlett
Dayton Office of the Sutro Tunnel Co.
Dayton, Nevada

France at war with Prussia; loan unlikely. Cease digging —A.
Sutro

Chapter 32

Finn and Jessie, enveloped in a throng of Catholics anxious to depart the church for their Sunday afternoon recreation, moved slowly toward the exit of St. Mary in the Mountains. A great crucifix adorned the wall above the exit and Finn dutifully crossed himself as he passed beneath it. Jessie glanced up, then quickly dropped her gaze as though she couldn't make herself look at the poor, tortured man nailed to the cross with blood dripping from his wounds.

Outside, the crowd dispersed into the unseasonably warm March sunshine. The air, though, still had a cool bite. Patches of snow dotted the ground here and there, the last remnants of a harsh winter.

"How are you, Mr. Gillespie?" Mrs. O'Brien spoke to Finn but her eyes fell on Jessie. A child was clutching either leg. Her husband tipped his hat to them.

"Ah, how but well, Mrs. O'Brien." He fingered the bill of his hat. "May I introduce the schoolmistress, Miss Ohhlson?"

"It's a pleasure to meet you, Miss Ohhlson," said Mrs. O'Brien with a frosty gaze.

They exchanged curtsies. The matron quickly took her measure of Finn's guest with an efficient and practiced eye, an examination he knew would be the subject of much discussion later that afternoon.

"And are you a Roman, Miss Ohhlson?"

Jessie glanced at Finn.

"Roman Catholic, she means."

"No, ma'am. But Mr. Gillespie was kind enough to invite me to attend mass with him."

"Oh but I suppose I should have known it. I noted the look of a Protestant about you, though one can't be sure in these times."

"What times would those be, Mrs. O'Brien?" inquired Mr. O'Brien.

Mrs. O'Brien shot a fearsome glare at her husband. "We live in a land where the blood o' the Irish is frightfully tainted," she said. "As polluted as a stream in a raging storm, it is. Make no mistake, the Exodus of the Great Potato Famine was a cruel enemy to the Irish, Mr. Gillespie."

Perhaps, suggested her husband, the Irish race would benefit from a wee bit of new blood.

"Ah 'tis that I wouldn't see that day, Mr. O'Brien."

He smiled at Jessie. "Don't mind me wife. She'd be the one to leave her religion at the alter, she would."

Mrs. O'Brien flushed a deep red. "It's time we get the childer home, Mr. O'Brien."

"Aye, 'tis, Mrs. O'Brien." The husband shook Finn's hand, then tipped his hat to Jessie. "You'll be a welcome visitor to our parish any time, miss. A friend of Finn's is a friend of ours. Isn't that right, Mrs. O'Brien?"

"It is, Mr. O'Brien. A good day to ye, Miss Ohhlson. Mr. Gillespie." She grasped the hands of her two children and dashed off. Mr. O'Brien gave a knowing look at Finn, then followed after her.

He and Jessie began the walk up Taylor Street.

"She's altogether full of the blather, that woman is. But don't mind her, she'll take to you after a time."

"I have me doubts, if you go to that of it, Mr. Gillespie."

He laughed. "As do I, Miss Ohhlson."

They strolled slowly up the grade toward C Street.

"Oh, but the sun feels blessed," he said.

"I enjoy the spring but don't look forward to the heat of summer."

"Aye, but today I'm in my gratitude for the spring."

"As am I," she said, smiling. Had he been reading any good books?

Jonathan Swift and Gulliver's Travels, he reported. A strange tale entirely. He lately dreamed of being swarmed over by silly little men, rapping his shins with their tiny cudgels.

They reached C Street, then strolled down the main thoroughfare. Something had been nagging at him and he decided he must rid himself of the burden.

"Jessie, there's a question I am after needing to ask you. Do you know William Ralston? Of the Bank Ring?"

She stumbled slightly, caught herself, then continued walking beside him, though she didn't answer. He was wondering if he should ask again, when she finally responded.

"I do. I knew him before I moved to Virginia. I met him in San Francisco."

He thought about this. He tried to remember if he'd ever seen Ralston in San Francisco. Certainly he'd heard of him. Everyone had. If San Francisco had a king, Ralston would be it. An image flashed in his mind—the first time he'd laid eyes on Jessie, outside a restaurant in the city, she with a proper gentleman. Finn had given her a flower. Their eyes had met. Had that been Ralston with her?

"And have you seen him here in Virginia?" he asked.

"I have."

"And why would you see Mr. Ralston, then?"

"Because we're friends. We exchange correspondence."

He didn't detect any insincerity in her answer, or her voice. But it was odd, inexplicable even, that a man like Ralston would have a friendship with a young, unmarried woman. That miserable Sharon was a known adulterer, but he had never heard such talk about Ralston. Tawdry images began to invade his thoughts. He tried to cast them out, vile images of Jessie...

"It has been a long time that I've waited for you, Jessie. Is Mr. Ralston the reason you put me off?"

"No, Finn."

"Well then," he pressed, "which is it? Do ye love me or no?"

She looked straight ahead and continued walking, her eyes becoming red.

"You're dear to me, Jessie. You know that. And I'll wait longer if ye ask it of me. But not if Ralston is in the midst. It's either him or me, but you can't have both."

With one hand she reached for a handkerchief and then dabbed her nose. Still she said nothing.

He grew frustrated. "Have you no more to say?"

She shook her head.

They walked. Then he said, "I saw Mr. Ralston at the International Hotel a while back. He was with a fine young lady."

She stopped and looked at directly at him. "Finn, you mustn't ask me these questions. Don't you see? I can't be called to explain myself. I have never promised you anything. I have never told you I was something I was not. There are some things in a person's past that are private. And if you insist on pressing these inquiries, I fear our friendship will suffer irreparable damage."

She turned and ran. He wanted to chase after her, but he feared the spectacle that might ensue. Her skirts and petticoats fluttered and danced as she ran down C Street. People stood aside to let her pass and whispered to one another.

Dejected, he could only think to drown his sorrows at the Hibernia. But no, that would solve nothing. Had he been wrong to question her? The words they had spoken and her expressions crowded his thoughts. Then, as he turned to go home, he noticed a dark figure leaning against a post on the other side of the street, hat pulled low, a thin cigar dangling from his lips. Sinister eyes trained on him. Crowell. Like a bird of prey, staring, silent. Watching.

***

A knock came at the door to Will's office and Franklin appeared. Will's fingers, busy at tearing shards of paper, ceased at the interruption, making him suddenly aware of the fatigue in the muscles of his hands.

Franklin handed him an envelope. "A wire for you. From Sharon."

"Thank you." He tossed the telegram aside and looked out the glass wall of his office into the bank lobby. Franklin slipped out the door.

Will's troubles seemed implacable, his enemies relentless. Sutro was making trouble in Washington and it was only a matter of time before the Prussian would commence digging again. Congress had, it seemed, given in to his ludicrous demands for a commission to study the tunnel and report on its feasibility. The commissioners were due in Nevada any day, but Sharon would be ready for them, or so he had assured.

Will glanced at the newspaper lying on the corner of his desk and clenched his fist. Of all his nettlesome problems, nothing galled him more than being painted by local newspapers as, depending on the day: an industrialist, monopolist, or greedy capitalist whose only interest was self-aggrandizement and the accumulation of obscene wealth. They attacked him at every opportunity. He had thought they would heap him with praise for saving the Pacific Coast economy: after his raid on the treasury President Grant had seen the wisdom of releasing the hoarded coins into circulation. Businesses were now operating without fear of bank runs. Ironically, those same San Francisco businesses continued to devour his, and the bank's, resources while investors still expected their one percent a month dividend. The city was draining him like a thirsty babe its starving mother.

Angrily, he snatched up the envelope. He read, but thought perhaps his eyes deceived him. He read the wire again in disbelief. The Belcher, it said, had hit a bonanza. And not just any bonanza, but the biggest Sharon had ever seen. The Belcher, the mine they had grudgingly traded for after Jones and Hayward had stolen the Crown Point.

He rushed to the door, looked down the hall and shouted for Riker.

Riker appeared, his eyes big and round and white. "Yes, Mr. Chap?"

"Get my horse ready, please."

Ten minutes later, Riker held Sir Walter by the bit as Will swung his leg over the saddle. Riker then climbed atop his own mount.

"James," he declared, "all is well with the world."

"Yes, sir, I can see that it is." James' smile was joyous and sincere: nothing seemed to please him more than to see his boss happy.

Astride his favorite horse, Will gazed at the city and she greeted him with her raw splendor. Pacific breezes were cool on his face; the sun warmed his back. All around him in the business district, commerce proceeded in orderly fashion: trains moved along their tracks, horses pulled wagons and carriages; men conducted business, women darted in and out of shops. Where else on Earth, he asked, could one find a place more appealing to the sensibilities of man? More in harmony with his pursuit of happiness. Why, nowhere, Mr. Chap.

Nowhere indeed, he thought.

Sir Walter trotted handsomely toward the apartments on Commercial Street, their city residence and where Lizzie preferred to spend most of her time. She was growing more accustomed to Belmont, of this he was certain, accompanying him there more and more often. That she had a fondness for city life, he couldn't hold against her. They would always maintain a home in the San Francisco, he had reassured her. And now, as he rode along, he could not help thinking that, with the Belcher strike, they would be able to afford a bigger house in the city. Perhaps the lot he had seen at Pine and Leavenworth would make a nice location.

Oh, the many plans he had for the flood of silver that would soon come pouring into his vaults.

He found Elizabeth sitting in the library, reading beside the window, bathed in sunlight. The maid, Rosemary, danced a feather duster over the bookshelves. Lizzie had returned from France

"My dear," he said, "you look like a vision."

She raised her eyes to him and smiled. Why was he home at this hour?

"I have some news. We have discovered a great new bonanza in the Comstock, according to Sharon." He could barely contain his elation.

She put her hand on his, saying that was very good news. She knew he had many worries lately. They talked, the way they had talked when life was simpler, after they had first been married. He apologized for his irritable behavior of late, and she suggested that it was more irascible than irritable. He laughed. They should throw another ball. Would she enjoy a ball?

"Yes. I would enjoy it very much."

"Excellent," he said. He leaned over to kiss her on the cheek, and as he drew near, was captured by an enticing fragrance. Her perfume was subtle: light and fresh, not overly sweet. He kissed her, but then, rather than pull away, hovered by her cheek, feeling her warmth, taking her scent deep into his lungs.

Elizabeth sat up, straightening her dress. "Rosemary, I believe Mrs. McMurty needs some assistance in the kitchen."

Rosemary curtsied and scampered from the room. As she dashed by, her foot caught a table leg. The table jumped; a tall vase rocked, threatening to tumble. Will watched it, holding his breath. The bottom of the vase tapped, metronome-like on the tabletop, then settled. He leaned over and whispered in his wife's ear.

"I need to go upstairs to change. Would you care to escort me?"

From his intimate vantage point, he could see her skin turn a deep red. Heat suddenly radiated from her neck and shoulders.

"Now?" she whispered back.

He pulled away and looked at her. She was in the thrall of a profound blush. Their eyes met for a long moment. Then, without another word, she rose and went to the stairs, put her hand on the banister, and began to ascend. Regally. Seductively. He couldn't remember when she had looked so desirable. So beautiful. Each elegant step she took with care, as if she knew the wait she imposed would be sweet torture. He watched, astonished at the spell she so easily cast, and he was surprised at his own desire, compounded with each step until he was certain he could not wait another moment. And yet he did, and it was marvelous. Such a perverse pleasure, anticipation.

After, he closed the bedroom door behind him and walked down the dim hallway. Jess had been right, he decided, stepping leisurely down the stairs. Domestic bliss was something not to be taken for granted.

It had been months since he had last swum in the Bay and he was eager for some vigorous exercise. Sir Walter, too, seemed enthusiastic, high stepping over Russian Hill and down to North Beach. When the first surge of water swept over Will's feet, the cold nearly snatched his breath away. Fall in San Francisco was the warmest time of year, yet the water remained perpetually cold. Undaunted, he plunged in with the usual abandon and began his stroke. Take this slow, he counseled himself.

Elizabeth, as Jess had suspected, was indeed a more passionate lover now. Had France made her so, he wondered. He couldn't deny that she had grown from the chaste prairie girl he'd met thirteen years ago, into a warm-blooded and sophisticated woman. She had clung to him in their bed, as if grasping at their closeness with a sort of desperation, refusing to let it go. And in the end, she had cried. Wept, even. He had held her tenderly, though he knew not what to say, or perhaps knew what to say, but couldn't. And sometimes words were unnecessary, he knew. He marveled at the complexity of these female creatures, who wept for joy and sadness alike, unions and separations, births and deaths.

His arms ached. Alcatraz still lay far in the distance. He resolved to get back to a regular schedule of swimming, but for today he had gone far enough. He turned back and began a slow retreat to the shores of North Beach. His thoughts drifted with the currents to Louisa. He had long thought of building a great monument to her but could ill afford such an extravagance. Now, however, with the Belcher, everything had changed. An idea began to take form in his imagination as he took slow strokes though the cold water. Something so extraordinary, so magnificent, the entire world would stand in awe.

Chapter 33

In the tiny office of the Sutro Tunnel Company, the General Superintendent and Engineer-in-Chief Adolph Sutro sat with his lieutenants at a round, rough-hewn table, with a view out onto C Street in Virginia City. The plank walls were bare save a large map of the Sutro Tunnel, and beside it a drawing of the Town of Sutro with its many yet-to-be-built streets stretching out from the tunnel entrance like branches from a tree trunk.

Herr Engineer was fuming that the Congressional Commission was spending all their time with William Sharon, touring carefully selected mines. See for yourselves, a tunnel is not necessary, Sharon would be telling them.

He looked at his assistants. Dr. Hazlett looked back but said nothing. John Bethel chewed a giant wad of tobacco, his eyes shifting back and forth from Sutro to passers-by on the sidewalk outside. The bank's discovery of a new bonanza was a blow that Sutro had not yet absorbed. That damned Sharon seemed to have a nose for the silver, he'd give him that. He asked Finn what the miners were saying.

"It'd be mostly bad news, Mr. Sutro. Sharon is proud as a peacock of his new Belcher ledge and has taken the commissioners down to see it. But he only takes them into the coolest shafts and drifts and is careful to keep the air pumps going at all times. And every miner on the Comstock has fearsome orders to breathe nae a word in favor of the tunnel, under penalty of dismissal."

"They'd cut their balls off is what he's sayin'," groused Bethel.

"I heard they're serving fine champagne in the hoisting works when they come out of the mines," added Dr. Hazlett.

"It's a fucking, jolly party they're throwin' for the Commissioners." Bethel leaned over and spat colorful juice on the plank floor. "Why would we need a goddamned tunnel when they've got mine shafts as pure as a maiden's privates, and air as clean as a fucking sea breeze?"

Ideas were bandied about, but there was general agreement that Sutro must steal them from the grip of William Sharon, and get them to see the tunnel. Use the bank's tactics, Finn suggested, give them a party, a steak dinner, fine wine, the works.

Sutro thought this an excellent idea. He would invite the Commissioners to the International Hotel where he would ply them with food and drink, then take them to the Town of Sutro.

"Now I must go meet my visitors from San Francisco," he told them.

Later, Sutro strode across the hotel lobby to shake hands with George Coulter and Lewis Price. Coulter was a San Francisco broker whom he knew and didn't care for; Mr. Price he didn't know but took an immediate liking to. Price was a man of many talents (reminding Sutro of himself) and had been sent to investigate West Coast mines as potential investments for McCalmont Brothers Bank, in London.

He led them on a tour of the camp, talking, explaining, pointing out important mines and mills, then down into the tunnels and adits to sample the foulest air and hottest temperatures and worst flooding. James Fair, superintendent of the Savage, had given him permission to take Coulter and Price into the mine. At the 1100-foot level, sweat dripped down Sutro's forehead; water seeped from the clay walls. It was beneath this very spot, he explained, stomping his boot, that his tunnel would intersect the Comstock, the Savage being the mid-point along the lode. This mine alone, he went on, spent $65,000 a year on fuel to pump its water. Price scribbled notes in his little book. Sutro raised his lantern and peered over Price's shoulder, the note read: "$65,000: This will be saved by the Sutro Tunnel."

Sutro smiled.

"I understand you have been looking at gold mines in California, Mr. Price."

Yes, Price's employer wished to invest in mining activity, and he was to report to him the best prospects.

"Ah, I see. But of course you must also consider the Sutro Tunnel. You will not find a better investment. As you have seen, the Comstock needs the tunnel very badly." He explained its many advantages: efficient ore removal, water drainage, air circulation, and, of course, escape from fire.

"If the Sutro Tunnel were operating right now," he said, "the miners would be able to work longer shifts and work with more vigor. So, you see then? My tunnel would be a much better investment than a gold mine. There is no risk. We know it is needed and I have federal right of way to build it. And I have agreements with the mining companies to receive two dollars for every ton of ore removed."

Price penciled more comments in his notebook.

The following day he took the two men through all 1300 feet of his tunnel. He unfurled his map and pointed to the Yellow Jacket Mine. It was a terrible tragedy, he told them, but had his tunnel been built before then, all the lives would have been saved. They murmured and nodded, and he thought, seeing them receptive, that this was good practice for the commissioners. Later, back in Virginia City, Price mentioned he would be departing for London in two days.

"Mr. Price," Sutro exclaimed—an idea had popped into his head. "What a great coincidence. I too am leaving for Europe. I will trail behind you by only a few days. And it would be no trouble for me to come to London and meet with the McCalmonts. I will make myself available to answer any questions they have about the Sutro Tunnel. This is a fine coincidence, do you agree?"

Price glanced at Coulter, who had cocked one eyebrow but was otherwise speechless. Price cleared his throat.

"Well, I see, jolly good, Mr. Sutro. The McCalmonts will be most surprised. Surprised indeed...and delighted, I'm sure."

Good. It was settled, then. But before he could leave for London, there was the matter of the tunnel commissioners. Two were engineers in the Army Corps of Engineers: John Foster and H.G. Wright; the third, Wesley Newcomb, was a Ph.D. Sutro had already decided: they were well-educated men, therefore they would conclude that the tunnel was essential to the Comstock Lode.

The four men rode on horseback down Six Mile Canyon, and he attempted to make pleasant conversation. Hadn't the dinner last night at the International been very nice? Yes. Had they enjoyed the fine wine? Indeed, they had.

"I am told you are a paleontologist," he said to Dr. New-comb.

Of a sort, said the scientist. He studied seashells.

Sutro frowned. Seashells?

"Yes. That is my specialty. Conchology is the technical term."

Ho, ho, his children liked to collect seashells. Did that mean they, too, could have a Ph.D.? Dr. Newcomb, however, didn't seem to have heard the joke.

"Have you seen the Hoosac Tunnel, in Massachusetts, Mr. Foster?" he asked his fellow-engineer.

"General Foster." And yes, they had conducted a thor-ough study before commencing their trip out West.

"Ah. Excuse me, General Foster. I forgot that you are in the Army. But the Hoosac Tunnel proves what I have said all along: an engineer can build anything, including a four-mile tun-nel. Do you agree?"

"Are you an engineer, Mr. Sutro?"

"Herr Engineer was my title in Prussia."

And where did Herr Engineer earn his degree? In Prussia, Sutro answered, a degree was not necessary for such a title. Expe-rience was necessary. He had learned by experience.

"Hmm. I see. An honorary title, of sorts."

Sutro fumed, but held his tongue. He doubted that these American engineers had suitable experience and training, other than learning from a book. Still, the general was an engineer, a like-minded soul, and now he must make his case to him against the bank.

"Mr. Foster—General Foster, you must be careful not to believe all you hear from William Sharon. The Bank of California

and Sharon believe they own the Comstock. They have misman-
aged the mines for many years and refuse to accept that my tunnel
would make production more efficient. And that it would make
mining much safer. No men would have died in the Yellow Jacket
fire if the tunnel had been in place."

He saw no visible response to these remarkable facts.

"Sharon and the bank have manipulated the Lode for their
own selfish purposes. They care nothing for the miners or citizens
of Virginia. The miners were my first investors. This tells you,
Mr.—General Foster, that the miners support me and not the
bank. And no one knows better than the miners."

Was that so?

He continued to attack the bank, but his guests seemed
apathetic. An hour later he led them up the main street of his in-
choate and eponymous town and to the mouth of the tunnel. From
there, he, Bethel, and Finn led them into the tunnel and deep into
the mountain. The commissioners took notes and asked a lot of
questions, then, at the end of the tour, promptly shook hands with
Sutro and Bethel, got back on their horses, and headed up Six Mile
Canyon.

"Those three pricks don't know a tunnel from a whore's
ass," grumbled Bethel as they watched the three ride off. As always, a wad of tobacco bulged at the side of his cheek.

"Sure but they're anxious to get back to Virginia," Finn
said.

"And the fuckin' arms of William Sharon."

"They are engineers," said Sutro, trying to remain optimistic. "They understand how valuable the tunnel is."

"Ah, shit. Dandies is what they are. Dumbest fuckin' questions I ever heard." He mimicked them, pretending to hold a note-

book and pencil. 'Have you encountered any ore bodies thus far?' Shit, if we had, do you think we be standing here like goddamned jackasses?" He leaned over and dribbled tobacco juice onto the sand. "Goddamned dumbest assholes I ever seen," he said, wiping the residue from his chin.

Hazlett had joined the group. Had the Commissioners been impressed? Yes, of course, Sutro was quick to respond. Was he still planning to leave for Europe? Yes, he would leave day after tomorrow. But did he not think it a bit risky, leaving them in Sharon's hands?

"It cannot be helped," Sutro stated flatly. "The McCalmont Brothers are ready to invest and I must bake the bread while the oven is hot, if you understand me. Besides, I am not worried. The benefits of the tunnel are obvious to intelligent men such as these commissioners."

***

"My daughter tells me I am to be a grandfather again." Colonel Fry sat lazily in his saddle. He looked over at Will with raised eyebrows, as if to declare that his son-in-laws' bad behavior had been found out.

Will smiled like a Cheshire cat. "Remarkable, isn't it? I, a father at age forty-five, and you a grandfather at…at what age will it be, Colonel?"

"A very ripe, old one," Fry mumbled, and Riker, who rode a few paces behind, chuckled quietly. Rocking from side to side in his saddle, Fry said, "Emelita showed me her new horse. A fine gift, but is that wise? I mean, do you think she can handle such an animal?"

He knew what the Colonel was thinking: that he couldn't lose another granddaughter. He reassured him that it was only a pony, and that she always rode with either Riker or her father.

They rode along First Street toward Market, and pulled up the horses at Mission. Fry remarked, off-handedly, that he hoped Elizabeth had no plans to take his grandchildren back to France. This, Will knew, was his father-in-law's way of prying into the state of the marriage. He couldn't blame him, and assured him all was well in the Ralston household and that Lizzie would not be returning to Paris. They approached Market Street, which was coming to life at this early hour with wagons, carriages, and horses.

"You've said nothing about the furniture factory, Colonel. Were you not impressed?"

"All I can say is, there is an overabundance of sawdust which I can still feel it in my breeches, and other unmentionable locations, and I suspect it will remain there until—until I have my next bath, at a minimum."

Will laughed. "I thought you were going to say until you were in the grave."

He could feel the dust too, but he didn't mind, much like a farmer doesn't mind the soil beneath his fingernails. Fry and Riker had accompanied him on his morning inspection of the West Coast Furniture Manufacturing Company, as fine a factory as the West Coast had to offer, he assured them. The Colonel was skeptical of the venture into another furniture business, given that the last one had failed. But Will was about to show him why this one was different.

They veered left at Market Street. Gigs and broughams jangled up the wide boulevard. An empty lot lay in the distance. It had come to him during a swim in the Bay: a new hotel, so glorious that even the Grand would want to hide its head in shame, so astonishing that it would be talked about in every circle from New York to Paris. A hostelry to attract visitors from all over the globe. And, the monument to Louisa Thorn that he had long wanted to build.

New Montgomery, that troubled real estate project no longer. Now, the Grand Hotel rose on the east, to their left. Directly opposite, on the corner, lay an empty, two and a half acre lot. Weeds grew out of the sand, bent over in the wind like thirsty vagrants begging for water. Empty boxes and splintered boards lay scattered about.

Fry eased up to one side of Will, Riker the other. "I fail to see how your fine furniture will enhance the appearance of this property."

"That, Colonel Fry, is because you lack vision."

In Will's mind he saw a seven, maybe eight-story hotel, and he held up a hand, waved it in an arc. The name over the entrance: The Palace Hotel. He could see a lobby so enormous that a barouche-and-four could drive right in and hardly be noticed. Wide corridors, high ceilings, fabric wallpapers, Axminster carpets, wainscoting, each room with running water and fireplace. "The furniture, of course, will be the finest, and made right here in San Francisco." Will gave one of his patented winks at Riker.

Fry was incredulous. What would such an undertaking cost? No matter, Will said, the cost would be more than covered by the Belcher. Fry bristled at this: no ledge goes on forever. Not to worry, was the argument, after the Belcher there would be other bonanzas. The deeper they went, the more silver they would find. All the geologists agreed on this point.

Fry shook his head. "That is all true, but I caution against reckless spending. Overly generous contributions to charity, struggling businesses, public buildings; all worthy causes that consume much but contribute little."

"You're becoming a reliable pessimist in your old age."

Harpending, he told him, was just back from London and wanting to discuss what he called a "very lucrative investment." He must get back to the bank.

"Be wary of young Harpending," cautioned Fry, as they crossed Market Street. "I like the young man. He is quite charismatic. But Pyramid Range investors were enticed with his pronouncements and promises of great wealth, only to discover they had been bilked."

Will had heard no solid evidence that Harpending knowingly bilked investors. He diverted the conversation to Sharon: had the Colonel heard he was running for the Nevada Senate? That traitor Jones, of all people, would run against him. The Colonel worried that Sharon would leave the Comstock, and who would run the camp in his absence? Will hadn't decided that yet, but suspected that Sharon had too much at stake there to abandon his post entirely.

They turned onto California Street.

"Has the Sutro Tunnel Commission issued its report?" Fry, on the board of, and stockholder in, almost every bank mine in the Comstock, had almost as much at stake as Will in seeing the tunnel stopped.

"I have on good authority the report will be highly unfavorable to the concept of a tunnel." Any intelligent man, he thought, could see the tunnel was not needed.

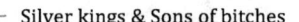

Chapter 34

To Sutro, the most charming feature of the McCalmont Brothers' banking house on Philpot Lane in London, was its antiquity. Everything on the Pacific Coast was new and awkward, everything in London ancient and hoary. Unlike the blue-marbled Bank of California, so big and elegant and ridiculous in its vain attempt to appear European, this bank seemed to possess the dignity of Father Time.

Philpot Lane. Why didn't we have streets named Philpot Lane? He loved the excitement of the West, but missed Europe. These visits refreshed his soul. And the fatherland, Prussia, was just across the Channel. There, people understood the value of his experience and upbringing. The title Herr Engineer meant something in Prussia!

"I say, Mr. Sutro, my cousin tells me your tunnel will be a bully success."

"Yes," he said, "And your friend, Mr. Coulter, has purchased some Sutro Tunnel stock himself."

"Can't get a more ringing endorsement than that, what?" exclaimed Hugh McCalmont, beaming at this brother.

Sutro always found himself a little uncomfortable around the British and their unfailingly good humor. Chipper, he thought they called it. And they employed a version of English he could barely understand, much less speak. Robert McCalmont was a pleasant-enough looking fellow: tall and thin, with sweeping moustaches into which the tip of his long, curved pipe disappeared. From the bowl of that pipe wafted flavorful smoke, reminding Sutro of his tobacco merchant days. Hugh, several years younger, with the hair to prove it, had by contrast a bald, clean-shaven face.

Had the McCalmont brothers heard that the Comstock miners had also endorsed his tunnel?

"There's a jolly-good guarantee," Hugh exclaimed, looking at his brother. "The miners themselves, old chap. Who better than the miners to know if the tunnel is a top-drawer investment?"

He struggled to understand through the sing-song accent, but was fairly certain this question had positive implications. He glanced at the older brother.

Robert plucked the pipe from his moustaches and jabbed it in Hugh's direction. "That's the ticket. But tell me, old chap," he said, turning to Sutro, "is your tunnel off and running? Has the pick met the rock, as they say?"

"We have begun boring the tunnel, but had to stop, I am sorry to report. I was to receive a loan from France, but it cancelled when the war with Prussia began."

"Nasty business." Hugh shook his head earnestly.

Robert took a puff from his pipe. "Bismarck is a man to be reckoned with, no doubt of that. Napoleon-the-Third didn't know what he was getting himself in for, attacking Prussia."

"You don't put your hand into a bloody hornet's nest," added Hugh, "unless it's a sting you're after."

"A ghastly mess, what." Robert puffed sagely on his pipe. "But, back to your tunnel, Mr. Sutro. Coulter and Price have given us the low-down, as you Yanks like to say. What we want to know is, what sort of investment will it take to get this wagon train moving?" He winked conspiratorially at him.

Sutro stared, confused.

"How many Greenbacks do you need, is what Robert wants to say," offered Hugh.

He wondered if he heard correctly. Had they already decided to invest? He hadn't anticipated this and now had to shift his focus—did anything ever go according to plan? How many Greenbacks? He still needed a considerable sum, though would prefer gold to Greenbacks.

"France was to lend me three million dollars. In gold."

"That might be a bit rich for our blood." Robert drew from his pipe, then blew the smoke out in a long, hazy trail. "Hugh and I discussed an investment of six hundred and fifty thousand. Gold for shares of stock. We would consider further investments in the future. What say you, Mr. Sutro? Will that put the pick to the rock?" He smiled. Smoke seeped out between his teeth.

It was less than he had hoped for but still a considerable sum of money. With it he could commence digging with a full crew. But the real benefit would be the ringing endorsement that he could take to other investors. Now, he thought, the money will pour in. The floodgates were opening.

At his hotel, he strode down the hallway, scarcely believing his good fortune. He had sent a telegram to Dr. Hazlett on the way to the hotel: "Prepare to commence work again!" had been his enthusiastic message.

He opened the door to this room—a telegram lay on the floor. Reading it, he cursed himself for thinking his troubles were over. It was from Hazlett: friends in Washington reported that the Tunnel Commission would issue a denouncement of the tunnel as unnecessary. Sutro must get to Washington as soon as possible.

It was clear what had happened. That fool, General Foster, had been bribed by William Sharon. Of course, General Wright had seemed a very competent engineer, but he must have been led astray by Foster. Sutro knew what needed to be done: rally his supporters in Washington and demand hearings be held before the Committee on Mining.

And while he waited for passage, he could secure a contract with the McCalmont brothers, then wire Bethel to begin work again.

If Sharon thought he had won, he was in for a surprise.

***

Finn, John Mackay, and James Flood had the bar mostly to themselves. MacKay and Flood sipped Irish whiskey, Finn a strong lager. The Hibernia Saloon was in its afternoon quiet.

They chided Finn about Jessie. Mackie, now a married man, had a keen interest in seeing Finn safely domesticated. He hadn't seen Jessie in weeks, Finn reported. That he missed her dearly, he kept to himself.

"The four of us," said Mackie in a low voice, "Fair, O'Brien, James, and I are moving into a new prospect. I can't tell you which one yet, as James here is still acquiring the shares, but Fair thinks highly of it."

"And you know," added Flood, "Fair has a bit of the leprechaun in him."

Finn said it sounded like malarkey.

Mackay laughed. "It does indeed. But Fair is a wily one down below."

Finn wondered to himself what mine they were pursuing. He glanced at Mackie. "You'll make an enemy of Sharon, once he finds out you've taken over one of his mines."

"We agree, but Sharon has had control of the Comstock long enough. We've decided it's time for someone else to run the place." Besides, Sharon would be off running for the Senate.

"We know the tunnel is shut down, Finn, and that you're in need of work. We'd like you to come into our employ. We'll make it worth your while." They would give him shares in addition to a good wage, and he'd make a handsome profit if they hit the lode they expected.

Finn thought for a minute. "I've got shares in the tunnel, you know."

"Aye, we figured you did."

And Sutro was paying him with more shares while the tunnel was shut down. "Will you let me consider it? He's away raising money, and I'd need to talk with him before I make my decision."

"Sure. But we need you sooner rather than later."

During the walk home, Finn decided he fancied the idea of working for his friends. But, if Sutro still needed him, he would stay. He'd made a commitment.

***

"I am told they want to name a San Joaquin Valley town after you." Harpending, with his great, resplendent beard and ruddy complexion, grinned at Will.

"I have declined the generous offer." Will drew hard on a cigar he had just lit, trying to establish the ember.

"I think Ralston, California has a very nice ring to it." Harpending sat across from Will's desk in a forest-green leather chair, peering at his host through a growing cloud of smoke.

Satisfied his cigar was lit, Will took several puffs. "They have already named a town Ralston. In New Mexico."

"Well," persisted Harpending, "I believe they will honor you at any rate, but with the name Modesto, instead. They believe you to be a modest man, it seems."

"I think they chose wisely." Modesty, after all, was his Midwestern creed: anonymous charity, avoiding the press, hard work, exercise. "Are you sure you won't have a cigar? They're Havanas."

Harpending declined.

Will looked at his guest. "Surely your urgent business wasn't to tell me about Modesto."

"No." Harpending paused and looked around, as if he suspected eavesdroppers. "I have a most extraordinary discovery to relate. The principals have authorized me to speak to you, but you must keep this under your hat."

Harpending leaned forward. "Diamonds," he intoned. He withdrew a pouch from his coat and emptied it onto Will's desk. The stones clicked across the hardwood surface like little marbles. Harpending gathered them into a neat mound.

"Where...where did you get these?" Will gazed at the stones, skeptical, yet wide-eyed. There appeared to be at least fifty diamonds of various sizes, still stained with the earth from which they came and yet dazzling nonetheless.

"I'm not authorized to give the exact location. But I can tell you they came from a western state."

"I've never heard of diamonds being mined anywhere on the continent." He frowned at the absurdity of it, but couldn't look away from the precious stones. So primitive. Raw. Spectacular.

Harpending leaned back in his chair with an arched brow. "Did you know they discovered diamonds in southern Africa a few years ago?"

He had heard that, yes.

"No one had ever heard of diamonds in Africa, either. And now they're mining millions of dollars worth each year."

Will rolled the cheroot in his fingers. What his friend was saying struck a chord. If in Africa, why not California? Or Arizona? If he had learned anything about the West, it was that everything was possible. Great harbors, bountiful harvests, timber, gold, silver. And quartz mines were known to yield precious gems—why not diamonds?

"And there is something else to consider." Harpending withdrew an envelope from his jacket, took out the contents and handed it to Will. "Shreve and Company did an appraisal on the big stone." He pointed. "108 carats."

Will quickly read through Shreve's appraisal until he reached the conclusion: $96,000 for the large stone; $600,000 for the whole lot. Could this be possible? He examined the letterhead: yes, it was definitely Shreve.

"Who are the principals?" he asked as nonchalantly as possible.

"Philip Arnold and George Roberts."

Will remembered Roberts from the Mineral Hill Mine. He had made a tidy profit on that mine when Harpending sold their interests to a British investor. The name Mineral Hill, cloaked with the reassuring aura of a past success, elicited an inner smile.

"Billy Lent, too," Harpending added. "From Mineral Hill, and the Comstock, of course."

Was Lent a director? Everyone knew Lent to be, in addition to a pompous, self-centered prig, an astute investor. Harpending shook his head, no, but Lent had endorsed the venture by purchasing an eighth interest.

Now his chest tightened, but he hid his excitement. "Is that so?"

"It is. He and his friend, George Dodge. General George Dodge. Both are investing."

Will put the cigar to his lips and drew the whiskey-like smoke into his mouth. He held it there, thinking and tasting, then blew it out straight in the direction of his friend. His luck had changed for the better, there was no question of that. It was odd, he thought, how luck ran in streaks. Now, with the Belcher, it was certainly the time to move boldly, while luck was on his side.

His guest watched him, briskly rubbing his thumb and forefinger together as if trying to smooth a callous.

"What sort of deal did Arnolds and Roberts offer?"

Harpending relaxed his busy fingers and leaned forward. "Due to the prestige of your name, which the principals desire to have associated with the mine, they will grant you a one-sixth interest. Roberts and I will also have a sixth. Lent and Dodge purchased one-eighth, and Arnold, the discoverer, holds one-fourth."

The offer of shares at only the cost of his name was generous, not to mention gratifying, to see that his reputation had such value. How could he refuse such an offer? He still had his doubts, but it would cost him nothing and if the diamonds did exist, it could be a bonanza perhaps even greater than the Comstock. He admired the Comstock like a fine racehorse that continued to win, but the idea of diamonds was new. Thrilling, even. And diamonds, he reasoned, would add a luster and allure to San Francisco.

He puffed his cigar thoughtfully and looked at Harpending. He trusted this man, he decided. Their New Montgomery venture hadn't gone well, but the young man had vision, daring, and yes, charisma. He trusted Lent and Roberts too, from his days with Mineral Hill, and his instinct told him to accept the offer. And he liked to follow his instincts.

"Tell Lent and Roberts they have a new partner."

Harpending smiled broadly and scooped the diamonds back into the pouch. "I'll arrange a meeting so we can discuss the particulars."

Chapter 35

The train steamed eastward. Will, looking out the window from time to time at the vast American landscape, was taken with a sense of awe at this transcontinental railroad. He had failed, to his chagrin, to secure a western terminus for San Francisco. It had not been for lack of effort: he had maneuvered, negotiated, and called in favors, but it seemed an unsolvable puzzle. Everything had conspired against this crucial piece, this intended marriage of geography and industry, from short-sighted voters (who failed to approve bonds), to ignorant politicians (who vetoed funding), and so on. Ferries would have to do for now, while he gathered the pieces for yet another go at the puzzle.

Now he was headed for Washington, D.C. His newest friend, Mrs. Fielding, sat directly across from him, the powder on her face failing to hide the deep wrinkles and pockets under her eyes. Eyes that nonetheless retained a keen perspicacity and languid condescendence. She was returning east from a visit to California, and their conversation, unhindered by any constraints of time or noisy children, touched on many topics: politics, theatre, art, and the railroad itself. And what did Mrs. Fielding think of California?

"I can't see what all the fuss is about," she said.

"Did you visit San Francisco?"

"Of course. Nothing but a poor cousin to New York, if you want my opinion."

He flinched. But, was she not impressed with the California Theater? And what of the Grand Hotel? Perfectly adequate, she sniffed. He consoled himself that she was a partial jurist. Soon, his Palace Hotel would win over all skeptics, including the Mrs. Fieldings of the world.

The train whistle blew as it approached a crossing. Watching the heartland of America pass by his window along with the days on his calendar, Will grumbled at having to make an appearance before the Sutro Tunnel Commission. He had thought the issue decided. Sutro, however, had convinced Congress to postpone their findings until hearings could be held. His attorney had urged Will to attend. The bank, he said, would appear "cock-sure" of victory were he absent from the proceedings.

After learning all he could from Mrs. Fielding about the ways in which New York was superior to San Francisco, he turned his attention to the Pullman car and the details of its design. He intended that his own Kimball Car Manufacturing Company would soon make luxurious cars to compete with Pullman. Thankfully, the Central Pacific Railroad, and his old friend Leland Stanford, were customers at the bank.

***

Will, in the capital, settled into his chair near the back of the walnut-paneled hearing room, its high ceilings and historical tapestries declaring an eminent purpose. John Mackay, James Fair,

Isaac Requa, T.B. Shamp, Charles Batterman, Henry Day: all Comstock mine superintendents who had submitted statements, now took their seats, appearing even less enthusiastic at being there than Will.

The bank's attorney, Thomas Sunderland, strode into the hall with a dramatic flourish, followed by a ponderous Sutro, with his attorney and the ever-present arsenal of maps and papers, all three taking seats at the long table at the front of the room. The committee members then filed in and assumed their seats at the rostrum, facing the hall, and Chairman Negley rapped his gavel. The Committee on Mines and Mining was in session.

"Gentlemen," said Negley, "we are here to take argument and testimony in regards to the Sutro Tunnel and the Commission report on the same, after which this committee will make recommendations on whether or not to adopt the Commission's findings, and for such other relief as this committee deems fit. Now, if there are no questions, Mr. Rice, you may proceed on behalf of Mr. Sutro."

Rice stood up. "Mr. Chairman, my client will proceed with questions on his own behalf." He resumed his seat.

Sunderland shot up out of his chair. "Am I to understand that Mr. Sutro wishes to proceed without counsel? If so, I object. He is not an attorney."

Chairman Negley waved his hand. "This is not a court of law, gentleman. If Mr. Sutro wishes to ask questions, he may do so."

"But—" Sunderland glanced back at Will, shrugged, then sat down. Will watched Sutro with fascination. Would this Prussian emigrant with his thick German accent actually attempt to conduct these hearings on his own? Preposterous.

The first witness, General Foster, was called and duly sworn before taking the stand.

"Mr. Foster," Sutro began, "do you remember when we met in Virginia City?"

"It's General Foster, and yes, I remember."

"Yes, yes. General Foster. Excuse me. And you are an engineer, are you not, General Foster? With a degree from an engineering school?"

"I am."

"Now, sir, I was reading from page 8 of your report, as follows: 'The cost per ton of hoisting ore is $.5117; cost of pumping for the fiscal year ending June 30, 1871, was $124,674.' Now, I want to ask you General Foster, how you arrived at these figures, if you had an opportunity of examining the books as to the correctness of those statements?"

Foster replied, "It was decided by the Commission to address each of the superintendents. We did not seek access to the books."

Sutro glanced at the chairman, then asked if the general had seen them hoist water at the Comstock, and did it make any difference if whether the water was hoisted or pumped? The general could not say in that regard. Did the general know how much a gallon of water weighed? Not without consulting his tables. Did he know how much a miner's inch would discharge by minute? No, he did not.

"Is the rule 17 4/10 gallons?"

Foster didn't answer.

Sutro rifled through the superintendent's statement, then read for a moment. "It is stated that 17 4/10 gallons are discharged per minute. Mr. Day says the water has decreased from 18 to 5 inches in the Ophir mine—that's after they've been pumping for several years. Now, if we have 87 gallons per minute, or 5220 gallons per hour, or in 24 hours 125,280 gallons, which is 8 34/100 pounds each, this gives us 944,835 pounds of water raised in 24 hours, or 472 41/100 tons. We know they are hoisting 12 tons of rock out of the Ophir every 24 hours, and in order to get out that 12 tons of rock, they have to hoist 471 tons of water. Do you think that is a considerable proportion, as compared to the quantity of rock they take out, General Foster?"

Foster could only stutter that he wasn't sure, but could make some figures if given the time.

And, to Will's astonishment, Sutro proceeded in this vein, to inflict upon General Foster a thorough humiliation that went on for most of the day, destroying the witness's, and the bank's, credibility with one inquiry after the other which the hapless Foster seemed incapable of answering with any authority.

"Do you think," Sutro said to Foster, "that if 1700 tons of water had been let out of the Ophir by a tunnel, it would have saved any money?"

Foster's voice was weak. "You want me to answer these questions here and now, and I am not prepared to do so. If the Committee wants it, I can make the figures." He wrung his hands. "If you ask the question, I will answer it, though I suppose you want to undermine my testimony by it."

Sutro responded that he did not want anything of the kind.

"Please answer the question," said the Chairman, "would it have saved money?"

"Certainly," Foster hissed.

Sunderland flopped down into his chair, casting his papers onto the table.

"I believe," said the Chairman, "this would be an appropriate time for a recess."

***

Sutro rose to greet the Committee members on the following morning. His examination of Foster the day before had gone better than expected—Rice had joked that he should have been an attorney. Engineering was much more challenging, Sutro informed him.

Dr. Newcomb (the conchologist) took the witness stand. Sutro, not wanting to debate science with the scholar, asked about opposition to the tunnel, and how the mines were controlled. The mine owners manipulated stock prices, Newcomb said. Stock-jobbing, it was called. They would discover a new ledge and wire buy orders to the stock exchange in San Francisco before word got out.

Again, Sunderland objected, but to no avail, and Sutro made his point: the bank crowd, as they were called, were only out for themselves.

***

That afternoon, Sunderland rose, chest out and hands on his lapels, and cross-examined Professor Newcomb. How deep, he inquired, were they working the Chollar and Potosi mines at present, to which the witness responded, 300 feet. And was there any show of water?

"None to produce any disturbance," answered Newcomb.

"Was there any that required pumping?"

"Of course not!" Sutro blurted. "Not at that 300 feet." Any fool knew the water was much deeper now, after all the pumping.

Sunderland protested and Sutro was admonished to give the other side their equal time. The professor further testified, to Sunderland's delight, that ore was taken out and up through the shaft, and that the tunnel, had it been in place, would have cost the owner $166,000 in royalties for the year.

"Now," Sunderland said, "I will call Mr. William Ralston to the stand."

Attorney Rice shot out of his chair. "I object, Mr. Chairman. William Ralston did not submit a report or statement of any kind to the members of this committee."

The chairman raised his hand. "As I said earlier, the committee is not obliged to be too particular."

Will assumed the stand and was sworn in. Sunderland began his questioning.

"Mr. Ralston," he said, "you are the cashier of the Bank of California, are you not?"

"I am."

"Now, can you explain to the committee why the Bank of California is opposed to the tunnel?"

"The tunnel, very simply, is not needed." The water was drained by pumps, the air ventilated by blowers, and the ore removed by the railroad.

"And do you believe, Mr. Ralston," Sunderland inquired, "that the Comstock would have survived if the Bank of California had not continued to pour money into it during all these years?"

"I doubt it."

Sunderland nodded to the committee that he had no further questions.

Sutro stood. "I would like to ask the witness just one question."

Sunderland and Rice exchanged a flurry of objections and protests, but the Chairman, however, urged flexibility.

"Do you recognize this?" Sutro asked, showing him a letter.

Will did indeed recognize it.

"And can you tell me what it says? Just read the first paragraph, please."

Will tried to focus on the writing, worried about what he might find there. It had been so long. Seven years, in fact. "This letter will be presented to you by Mr. A. Sutro, with the view of laying before capitalists, a tunnel, in the State of Nevada. This tunnel is designed to cut the great Comstock Lode, which contains our richest silver mines, to drain it of water and render it easily accessible. Too much cannot be said of the great importance of this work."

Sutro took back the letter and pointed to the signature at the bottom. "That is your signature, is it not?"

"Yes. It is."

Sutro stared at the paper for a moment. "And my question is, why did you change your mind?"

Many thoughts ran through his mind, answers he could give: Circumstances had changed...Sutro would destroy Virginia City...the tunnel was too costly. But he knew the answer, the only one that mattered. He met Sutro's gaze with an assured calm.

"I changed my mind because of San Francisco. The tunnel would have destroyed San Francisco, and I could not allow that to happen."

***

Will tugged at his collar, pulled it up under his chin. He felt a chill and it was hard to swallow. His head ached. The comfort of the Pullman enveloped him, and the train rocked gently. He needed sleep.

He relived Sutro's triumph in his mind, saw the flustered lawyers, the embarrassed experts. It was as if Sutro had planned the whole thing, the Committee, the investigation, the report, and the hearings, anticipating, waiting for his chance to humiliate all his critics. His passion for this thing was beyond Will's comprehension.

He had wired Sharon already: they must gain control of the tunnel stock, at any cost. This was the only solution.

He closed his eyes, pulled a blanket over himself. He saw Sutro, shovel in hand, digging his tunnel, laughing like a mad man, destroying the world. He wished Elizabeth were there.

***

An icy drizzle fell on Virginia City, and Finn crossed his arms and pushed through the cold. C Street was in its state of winter muck. About to cross Union Street, he noticed Jessie, her head covered by the hood of her woolen coat. Their eyes met. To his surprise, she gathered her skirts and stepped down from the sidewalk into the street. A wagon careened toward her. The driver whistled. Finn yelled and she jumped back up to the sidewalk. Undeterred, she looked both ways, then charged across the street, wading through the sludge until she stood below him, the hem of her coat and dress stained brown with mud. He helped her up to the sidewalk.

"You gave me a start, stepping in front of that wagon."

She brushed vigorously at her coat and dress. "I always seem to forget that streets are made for horse traffic." He watched her efforts with amusement; the mud refused to yield. She finally gave up, laughing, and he led her to a nearby bench where they sat, side-by-side. From beneath the shelter of an awning, they watched the rain descend on the camp in a grey drizzle.

What was he reading now? she asked after a few moments. Mostly Thomas Moore, he admitted. "And you?"

She had, it seemed, become entangled in the cause of Don Quixote.

"Not a book I've heard of."

Don Quixote, she explained, was a gallant man who sacrificed all to pursue his dreams, ridiculous though they may have been. He loved books and chivalry and wanted a life of great adventure. Jessie looked out at misty rain. "He was," she said, "the most romantic of all men."

And what happened to him? Did he have his adventures, achieve his dreams?

"It's rather tragic, I'm afraid. His friends betrayed him and he died a lonely man in the end."

"Ah, 'tis a sad tale, then."

She nodded. He glanced up to see her eyes glistening at the thought of poor Don Quixote. He decided he wouldn't read that book.

"Finn..." Jessie bit her lip. "I owe you an apology. I should not have run off and left you that day, when we last spoke. I have suffered the sting of self-recrimination ever since. You confronted me with a sincere grievance, and I owed you an honest answer. I have had time to consider that answer, which I wish to give you now."

She paused, then looked at him.

"I will not see William Ralston again. I am ready, Finn, to give my entire attention to you, and you alone."

Her gaze was level and sincere. But during their time apart, questions had crept into his thoughts. He had seen her on occasion, arm in arm with the public ladies, talking, counseling, and he had wondered. Was she offering advice? Urging them to a higher purpose? Consoling? And now, as he gazed into her lovely, sad eyes, he wondered, as he had so many times before, why that sadness seemed to reach into her very soul. Where did she come from? Where was her family? Why had she been with Ralston to begin with?

The cold, gray rain continued to fall.

Now he began to recognize something in her face, some-thing that alarmed him. Her eyes recalled those forlorn, with-drawn eyes of the women of North D Street, that God-forsaken district where pitiful creatures sold their bodies to lonely men. Could this be a coincidence? Had Jessie...? He stared at his boots, his mind racing, blood pulsing in his temples.

"Finn, is something the matter?" She reached out and put her hand on his arm.

Unable to meet her eyes, he stared at her hand. Smooth and delicate, the fingers tapered, translucent, achingly beautiful. But who else had those fingers touched? What shame had they known? This terrible notion of her past—he could keep it buried no longer.

"I'm sorry, Jessie—I..." He rose, unable to think, not knowing what to say. "I...I must be getting back to Sutro. The men—they'll be needing their wages."

She sat still as a tomb save the trembling hands in her lap pressed into the folds of her dress. Her pale complexion had lost any vestige of color, as if death had come to claim her.

He tried to speak but couldn't, a great lump having gathered in his throat, choking off his voice. Her tiny chin began to quiver and he had to tear his eyes away, else all reason be lost. He turned away, forced his feet into a march, to where he didn't know. A great battle raged, to turn back, or no? But he knew what he'd see if he did, and knew he couldn't bear it.

***

Will tossed in his sleep, in a cold sweat, had vivid dreams. Jess was troubled, but the dream was vague. Her fortunes, too, had turned. But she was a strong girl, stronger than he. The Pullman car rocked him gently, soothingly, but then Sutro was there, pick in hand, hacking gleefully at the walls of the Bank of California. He thought of Elizabeth, how he wanted to be home with her, and with his children.

Part Four

(1872-1875)

Chapter 36

Will's head ached from deep within. Actually, he realized, his entire body ached. He tried to lift his head but could not. Elizabeth gazed down at him with that benevolent look mothers give their little ones: a comforting look, even to a grown man.

"How long have I been in bed?"

"Two weeks." With a warm hand she caressed his face. "You sound terrible."

"I think my head is going to burst." He ran his fingers along the bridge of his nose, pinching and squeezing. The pressure was at the same time painful and soothing.

A nurse appeared, dipped a sponge in a bowl of water, and wrung it out. Elizabeth laid her hand across Will's forehead. "His fever is gone," she reported.

"Yes, mum."

Elizabeth took the sponge and gently wiped his forehead, then the rest of his face.

"That feels wonderful," he murmured. His mind wandered, and he began drifting back into sleep, seeing images of horses, locomotives, gold coins, silver, and then, a terrible thought. His eyes popped open.

"Who is managing the bank?" he asked, trying to sit up.

"Franklin. And Mills, I suppose."

Mills? Mills?! His pulse began to race. The blood surging to his head throbbed in his temples. He rubbed them, trying not to imagine the worst, Mills delving into matters of which he knew only enough to create havoc. Had word gotten to him of the fiasco in Washington?

"What is it, Toppie?"

"I should get down to the bank." He sat up and attempted to swing his legs over the side of the bed, but they refused to cooperate.

"You mustn't worry so much. You need rest. The bank will not collapse without you."

He slumped back onto the bed.

The nurse handed Elizabeth a fresh sponge and she used it to wipe his face again. "You just rest," she said firmly.

He closed his eyes and drifted off…Mills, in his office, giving a stern lecture on the importance of conservative banking practices, and then Colonel Fry, to counsel on family solidarity and familial duty…

Hearing voices, he opened his eyes, sat up, then leaned back against a mound of pillows. Elizabeth was holding a cup of broth, which she served him, one spoonful at a time. He could feel the nourishment flowing into his body, feel the strength returning. Tomorrow, or the day after, he hoped to be in his office.

Elizabeth was telling her father about little Bertha, but then, seeing Will awake, she said, "I'll leave you two and go check on the nursery." Her complexion ruddy and eyes twinkling, she kissed her father before dashing off, filled with a renewed sense of purpose. To be needed was a potent elixir.

On his fingers, Fry nervously twirled his brown derby. Will observed the exercise, wondering. "What's the latest at the stock exchange?" he said.

"Rather dismal, I'm afraid. Prices are down and trading thin."

"Do you ever see Sutro Tunnel stock?"
"Of course."

"I want to begin acquiring all available shares. This is to be kept close, you understand."

The Colonel, still toying with his hat, said he would do what he could.

"While you have been ill," Fry began, now setting aside the hat, "an audit was conducted at the bank. I heard of it from Sharon."

Will recoiled slightly, caught off guard. He stared, waiting. "And?"

"The results of the audit were...not favorable."

Not favorable? In what way? And who called for this audit?

Fry glanced at the hat, then tried to settle his gaze on Will. "Mills. Mills evidently had requested the audit."

"What is he doing requesting an audit?" Will said.

"He is the president of the bank."

The president in name only, Will thought, seeing Fry sheepishly drop his gaze. The moment Lizzie had mentioned Mills, he knew there'd be trouble.

"In what way was the audit not favorable?"

"They discovered loans, I am told. Numerous loans. Loans you made to your factories. The Kimble Car Company—"

Stanford had promised him an order for that factory. He need only maintain the workers until the Central Pacific order came through, then the loan would be paid back. That the order seemed to be always coming but never arriving, worried him, but Stanford had promised, and he trusted him.

The Colonel continued. "There are also loans to Adams Lock Company, West Coast Furniture, Consolidated Tobacco. And more, it seems."

What had prompted Mills to conduct an audit, he didn't want to think about. It didn't matter, he thought, rubbing his temples. These fools didn't understand. All they wanted was their damned dividend. Had he ever failed to deliver one? On time?

"What does the board propose to do?" Will asked.

"I'm not privy to all their communications, but I hear rumors, of course. I believe the question has been posed as to whether you should sell certain assets to repay the loans."

"Sell assets?" he cried. "I will do no such thing." How dare they? Such a drastic measure would be an unjust punishment, disproportionate to the problem. If indeed there were a problem to begin with. "It had been my intent to pay those loans from my Belcher income," he said, fuming. "I just hadn't thought it to be a matter of any urgency. I will not be treated in this way, like some common thief. There will be hell to pay when I return to the bank, which I intend to do first thing in the morning."

Fry took up the hat and commenced to spinning. "Look here, Chap, why don't you allow me to lend you some money to pay off the loans, and that way there needn't be a great uproar. I hate to think of you having a nasty falling-out with Mills and the board."

"Thank you, but there will be no need. By God, I'll pay the loans off when I'm good and ready."

The Colonel's face twisted with anxiety. "I'm sure this is all quite unnecessary, Chap, and that it isn't nearly so bad as the board has painted it. But if we pay the loans off, then we can just get back to business. No ruffled feathers, if you know what I mean."

Will couldn't fathom that he was being challenged in this way. He had fallen ill and the board had turned on him like vultures. But what offended Will, worried Fry. The future of the bank, and Fry's stock, were in jeopardy, and he was determined to put the matter to rest with a bridge loan. It was, for Will, a bitter potion. To pay the loans off was tantamount to admitting they were improper.

"This is very kind of you, Colonel," he said after a moment of consideration. He was greatly offended by this betrayal of the board, and though tempted to fight, he could see the wisdom in the Colonel's approach. They would meet there in his office tomorrow to work out the details.

***

"Oh, Father, I wish I could have been there."

Sutro couldn't help but smile at Emma, her expression so ardent and sincere. She was his most loyal supporter. In her new dress, from the East Coast, with its billowing sleeves and tight bodice, she appeared older than her fifteen years. The small study at the Sutro house doubled as his office, and his oldest daughter made a habit of spending much time there when he was home.

"I wished that as well," he said, "but you had school."

"What better education than to watch my father defeat the lawyers of the great Bank of California? And before Congress, no less."

Yes, Sutro thought, she had a point. It would have been a fine lesson for her to see how he had brushed aside the bank's attorney, and their witnesses. Embarrassed them, even.

"Well," she said, "you must promise to tell me every detail. Leave nothing out."

What could he do but oblige the dear girl? The testimony had taken many days and he could not tell her all of it. What he could say was: she must always be prepared. He defeated the bank because he was better prepared. They thought they could come in and wave their hands and put up ridiculous witnesses with impressive credentials, and the Committee would believe everything they told them. That did not happen because he had studied their reports and statements and found their weaknesses. It was then an easy matter to show the Committee that these statements were false and without a true foundation in engineering.

"Yes, Father, I understand. But please tell me more. What sort of room was it? What did the congressmen look like? Were they old and decrepit? And who was there? President Grant—was he there?"

No, the president had not been there. But every word spoken would be printed by the Committee on Mines, and he would get her a copy.

Emma smiled, then leaned forward and kissed him on the forehead. "I will read it cover to cover."

Sutro, trying to resist the spell she cast, stood and began to pace the floor.

"We must address your education, Emma. I have decided to send you to a boarding school." This he could afford due to the rise in value of his tunnel stock.

If the school was in San Francisco, she said, or Oakland perhaps, she would gladly go.

It was in Pennsylvania, he told her.

"Then I shall not go." She folded her arms, emphatically. Her jaw was set in firm resolve.

"Emma. You must not tell me where you will and will not go." He loved her dearly but did not know where she got this stubborn streak. Leah, of course, could be quite stubborn.

Her eyes glistened. He couldn't look at her. With his recent successes, his stature had surely risen, and so now his children's must do likewise. It was time to take her education more seriously. She had great potential, and he did not want his children to suffer the same humiliation he had. She must earn a proper degree.

"I don't want to go to Pennsylvania," she cried. "I don't even know where it is."

"Pennsylvania is a fine place," he implored, vexed by her emotion. "Where the Constitution was written. You will like it there."

She wiped a tear from her eye. "No, I won't, Father. I wish to stay here, with Mama, and Rose, and..."

In Prussia, all children of means went away to school, he explained, certain she would see the clear logic of this.

"We are not in Prussia, Father."

He did not appreciate this tone, but chose to ignore it. "But it is the same. Children must have the finest education, especially children so smart, like you."

Leah came in and took a seat, as if having sensed that one of her children needed her.

"Mama, Father intends to send me away to school."

"Yes, dearest. I know."

"But you cannot allow it. I don't wish to go."

"It is your father's decision, not mine."

Emma rose, holding her chin high. "May I be excused, Father?"

Sutro bristled at her insolence, but admired her strength. Yes, she could go.

She strode defiantly out the door. Sutro turned to his wife, who looked at him as though he were sending their daughter to the gallows. There were fine schools in California, she reminded him.

He barely heard her. The issue of Emma's schooling was already decided. He had come home with an astonishing report of congressional triumph, certain Leah would finally be happy. Thrilled, perhaps, and proud of him. But he was disappointed, for she seemed unmoved, as if his great achievement in Washington had been a trivial matter of little consequence. "Yes, dear, that is very good news," had been her response.

Now he grasped Leah's hands. His plan, which he had long anticipated, would surely bring her to tears of joy. He would build her a house in the Town of Sutro, Nevada. A big house. A mansion, in fact. Finally they would all be together under one roof.

She, hearing this, stared out the door and said nothing.

"Leah, do you not wish to celebrate?"

"I have grown accustomed to my life, Adolph," she said. "I do want our family to be together, but this would be a great change for me and for our children. We have lived in this house, in this city, and now you would have us move to the desert? There will be no people, no church, no shops. It will be a very big change. You must understand this."

Try as he might, he could not understand. Where would the children go to school, she asked. Was there even a market in Sutro, Nevada? He tried to console her. She needn't worry. He would build schools and shops, and anything else she wanted. But the children! What about the children?

"If their mother is happy," he declared, "they will be happy." Besides, he thought, how could they not like a town named after their own father?

She nodded, her face blank, seeming to understand the expectations he had for her. She wiped away the tears in her eyes.

Sutro watched sympathetically but knew that people eventually came to realize that he knew what was best for them.

Chapter 37

The contents of Finn's lunch box looked entirely familiar: boiled eggs; boiled potato; stale bread; tin of salt; strip of jerky. Lunch in the tunnel: sustenance, not fine dining.

But Oh!—a piece of cake from his neighbor, Mrs. Murphy.

This he eyed, thinking it a splendid idea to begin at the end. A fine cook, Mrs. Murphy, make no mistake. To eat the cake now would be shameless gratification, but if he ate the potatoes first, he would only devour them so as to get to the cake that much quicker. Gratification, he reasoned, was a sin easily disposed of in confession. But then he would actually have to go to confession, and what other tales would he have to tell once inside that dismal booth?

He gave in and reached for the cake, put it to his mouth and paused. Closing his eyes, he savored the rich vanilla fragrance, allowing his imagination to anticipate the buttery texture that would soon delight his waiting palette.

A gust of sharp, foul breath accosted his face. A gentle nudge to his shoulder. He opened his eyes to see Old Peg staring at him. He scowled fiercely at the beast, a worthless strategy due to overuse, he knew, that would lead only to further, more insistent, nudges. He ignored Peg, and turned to Tomas.

"Peggy is after me cake again, Tomas."

The mule's keeper was unapologetic. "She likes cake. Has a sweet tooth, she does."

Finn, resigned to an act of charitableness toward one less fortunate, held aloft a moiety of his cake, which Peggy devoured with her leathery lips.

Old Peg gratefully moved on to the worker seated beside Finn, looking at the boy with big, hopeful eyes. Jeremiah, of a less generous nature, simply glared at Tomas McTerry.

"Call yer mule, McTerry. I'll not be sharing me pie with her, no matter how much she begs."

"Go on, Peg." McTerry waved at the mule. "Jeremiah is a gluttonous soul with no concern for God's gentle creatures."

With the feast in progress, Pete and Jenny, Old Peggy's companions, had wandered into the impromptu dining room in the Sutro Tunnel and, following her lead, began to beg for food with gentle nudges and forlorn eyes. The mules, each adopted as a pet by one or more of the men, were the principal source of transportation in the tunnel. Sutro, of course, had purchased steam engines and even a locomotive, preferring, Finn knew, the mechanical to natural power. But the machines were always broken down, and the crew inevitably turned to the mules, who reliably hauled the ore carts and trains in and out of the tunnel, now about two miles in length.

One of the lads chewed on a heel of bread. "Will there be any ore left in the Comstock by the time we get there, Finn?"

Finn considered for a moment, reluctant to say anything against his employer. The Virginia-Truckee Railroad had been completed to Carson, and ore was being shipped out daily by rail.

"Not likely, at the rate we've been going," someone answered for him.

"They say Sutro trembles with rage at the sight of the Virginia-Truckee," Tomas added.

"Aye," said Jeremiah. "Every ore car hauled out is like silver coin slipping through his fingers."

"And into William Sharon's greedy hands."

"Ah," said Finn, "don't worry yourselves. They say the Comstock goes clear down to hell and beyond. The ore'll never run out, so they say." He'd heard this, but didn't really believe it.

"I hope so," said Tomas. "Don't fancy the thought of diggin' this tunnel only to find no silver when we get to the end."

"If you'd feed yer damn mule better," said Jeremiah, "we might finish the tunnel sooner."

Finn chuckled and made for the heading to take a sample. Perhaps this one might show some signs of ore, ore which the government had granted to the tunnel, should any be found along the way to the Comstock. When he finally emerged from the tunnel a few hours later, he came upon a bleak, dusty village of shanties and a boarding house. Sutro had plans for a grand house, which Finn was to build, but looking at the thirsty land, Finn wondered why anyone would want to live in such a place. Of course, there was no reasoning when it came to Adolph Sutro.

Later, in Virginia City, he dropped off his sample at the assay office. A funnel-shaped column of black smoke rose above the camp, coming from a train leaving the station with five cars of

Comstock ore and thousands of dollars of wished-for tunnel royalties. His throat was dry: the Hibernia was calling.

"Hey, Finn." O'Kelly reached for the lager he knew would soon be ordered, opened the bottle, and set it on the bar. Had Finn seen Mackie lately?

"I haven't," said Finn. "He and Fair have been mighty quiet for a couple of Irishmen."

O'Kelly leaned forward—there were rumors of a stupendous ledge.

Finn, remembering what Mackie and Flood had told him, raised his bottle. "Faith, 'tis my wish they found one."

"As it is mine," the barkeep said. Jobs were scarce in Virginia and they could use another big strike. "They say the Belcher is nearing her limits."

"Do they now?"

"Aye, they do. Sharon wouldn't say so, but the miners talk, you know."

It was well known that a miner could pass a secret faster than Western Union. He sipped his lager. Sharon, he murmured, would turn rabid dog when he heard what Mackie was up to.

"If he weren't so busy running for the Senate, maybe he'd have taken notice by now."

'Twas true, Finn thought. Virginia City had been a more neighborly place since Sharon had left to run for office. The guard seemed to be changing, and the new one had a more kindly soul.

"Have you seen your schoolmistress?" the barkeep asked. "A fine slip if ever there was one."

Finn sighed and finished off the bottle. Yes, she was indeed a fine slip.

***

To an innocent eye, all might appear just as before, although Will knew differently. From his office, the clerks and tellers were about the bank, occupied in their customary chores, but with unnerving quiet. His staff had greeted him sheepishly that morning, as if guilty of treason in his absence. He knew, however, the audit wasn't their doing.

His first order of business upon retaking the helm had been to check with Fry on the acquisition of Sutro Tunnel stock. He had no word on Sharon's simultaneous efforts in Virginia City, and so composed a quick telegram. This he gave to Riker: the former hostler now occupied a desk outside his office as his full-time assistant. If anyone was loyal, it was Riker, and he suddenly valued loyalty above all else. The broad-chested Negro had always been a proud man, but with the promotion his pride had grown into a quiet dignity, and Will's affection likewise had grown into a kind of brotherly love.

Shortly before the lunch hour, Asbury Harpending arrived, anxious to see him. He sat across from Will's desk, his eyes bright and cheerful, as always.

"You look awful," were Harpending's first words.

"Thank you," he said, "it's good to see you as well."

He laughed. "Well, I have news that should assist in your recovery. I went to New York with your power-of-attorney in hand. Lent and Dodge were there. Naturally, we took the bag of diamonds and met with attorney Barlow, as planned."

Will listened intently; much was at stake. Harpending had met with Congressman Benjamin Butler, General George McClellan, and Horace Greely of the Tribune, all sworn to secrecy. The man they had come to see was the renowned jeweler, Charles Tiffany. Tiffany had inspected the stones, and had a gemologist look at them, and it was their informed opinion that the sample was worth one and a half million dollars.

Astonishing.

Harpending's eyes sparkled, gem-like.

"What has been proposed," the young man was saying with barely-contained enthusiasm, "is the formation of a new company to be named San Francisco and New York Diamond Company. I knew you'd insist on San Francisco coming first," he said, grinning. "The company will have 100,000 shares with a par value of $100."

Will did the arithmetic in his head—ten million dollars!

"That's right," Harpending said. "Ten million. You, me, Arnold, Roberts, Lent, and Dodge will be granted share rights. Our attorney will be paid $250,000 in stock for his services."

These numbers were almost overwhelming, the news too good. This would rival the greatest of mineral discoveries and cement the West as the new frontier of unparalleled wealth. And why not? Mother Earth had indeed blessed the Pacific Coast.

"This is very exciting, Mr. Harpending. Incredible, even. But I think we need to see the diamond fields with our own eyes. Don't you agree? After all, these diamonds could have been flown in from South Africa, couldn't they?"

Harpending seemed to hesitate, but then agreed. Of course, they must do their due diligence. He would select a geologist and have him prepare a report.

"Good," Will said, trying hard to keep his imagination in check.

Later in the afternoon, architect John Gaynor leaned over blue prints spread across a work-table in Will's office. Will had great respect for the man who had transformed Belmont into a Tuscan masterpiece, and he had complete confidence the Palace Hotel would be Gaynor's magnum opus. The architect had traveled for months to examine the world's finest hotels. From these he had drawn inspiration for the plans they now examined. The hotel would cover the entire two and a half acres on New Montgomery.

But Gaynor had some bad news. The foundation, he now estimated, would cost about $1,750,000. This, Will recalled with a grimace, had been the original estimate for the entire hotel. Since they would need revised estimates for Sharon's approval, they may as well include other changes. Bay windows were essential on every floor. And each of the eight hundred rooms must have fifteen-foot ceilings. They reviewed the framing, electrical, the flooring, and hydraulic elevators. Guests would receive their mail through ingenious pneumatic tubes. On the roof, lush gardens would look out on the Bay.

The plumbing intrigued him, for he knew matters of creature comfort were of utmost importance. Theirs would be the first hotel in the world with fully-plumbed private baths in each room, and flushing toilets designed to carry off water without the usual "horrid noise," that Lizzie so despised. It would require six miles of wrought iron pipe, Gaynor warned. Worth every cent, Will responded.

He and Gaynor were kindred spirits, Will decided, as the architect rolled up his plans now scribbled over with notes, and together they would give the world a remarkable treasure.

Chapter 38

John Mackay held the cage door open for Finn, who hadn't been down in the mines, or even stood in a hoisting cage, since the Yellow Jacket fire. Even three years later, the cage gave him shivers of apprehension.

"You're bound to snap that cable, squeezing it so hard." Mackay climbed into the cage and gave Finn a kindly elbow in the ribs. "Don't you worry, Fair runs a safe mine."

"So they say."

Down they went, flying past station lights, ears popping, air growing hotter and hotter, and then the familiar abrupt stop. Mackay opened the cage door at the 1200-foot station and grabbed a lantern. Into the crosscut they went, stooped over beneath the low ceiling, Mackay a ghostly shadow tripping along ahead of Finn. After a minute they emerged into an open gallery, dark except a few candles flickering from their high perches. Throughout the chamber, a lattice-work of immense beams strained against the clay walls and ceiling that squeezed inward. Mackay greeted his men, who dropped their picks and hammers and smiled, as if someone had declared a holiday.

"Is that Finn Gillespie?" one miner cried. "Are ya gonna work for the Con-V, Finn?" "Oh, but Finn, Mackie here's a fine man to work for. But don't box with him!" "Aye, fierce in the ring, he is." These jabs were followed by considerable hysterics. Finn followed Mackie to the back of the chamber, hearing the unceasing badinage, the miners' bond and sole entertainment.

Mackay stopped and held up his lantern. The ceiling lit up like a splendid galaxy in the night sky.

"Jaysus, Mackie."

Mackay smiled sheepishly. "You should buy some Con-V stock, Finn. You'll be able to retire."

He stared agog at the spectacle. He had never seen such rich ore. It shimmered and glittered in the light: reds, yellows, greens, like a rainbow of jewels. Except there were no jewels, just humble quartz crystals with a crown of silver ore gilded with flecks of native gold.

Mackay ducked into an adjacent chamber. Again, Finn stared up in disbelief.

"Jesus, Mary, and Joseph." He reached up to touch to it. The surface was rough and jagged. "'Tis a vision, Mackie. Like a holy revelation. The saints would fear and tremble at the sight."

Mackay laughed. "Don't be blasphemous, Finn. 'Tis bloody ore is all, and one we're going to mine till it's gone."

A shame, thought Finn. The most beautiful sight he'd ever laid eyes on.

"Have you heard that Sharon wants your tunnel stock?" Mackay asked as they made their way back.

"My tunnel stock? Sharon?"

"The men tell me he's after Sutro Tunnel stock. Has he not made you an offer?"

"He hasn't," said Finn. "Why would he want it?"

"Don't know for certain, but the bank is a wee anxious about Sutro and his tunnel. Rumor has it that Congress is set to lend him millions of dollars."

"Aye. We've been hoping for it."

"Well, be aware. Sharon gets what he wants. I'm not sure your stock is worth crossing him over." Mackay glanced over his shoulder. "Sell it and buy Con-V. You won't be sorry."

Ah, but how could he do that to poor Mr. Sutro?

They reached the cage and climbed in. Mackay looked at Finn, his eyes smiling. "You're a fine, honest boy, Finn."

In the hoisting barn, he shook Mackay's hand. "Congratulations to you Mackie. I'm proud to see you on the shank of advantage and wealth."

"I hope the same for you someday, Finn."

Perhaps Sutro's tunnel will strike a ledge along the way, he mused as he left the Con-V, though nothing in the tunnel, or any of the mines for that matter, would ever look like what he'd just seen.

He ambled along Sutton Street, perplexed at Mackie's warning. He crossed D Street. Suddenly, appearing like a black cloud, Crowell slipped out of an alley. He stood in Finn's path, belligerent and sullen. Finn stopped in mid-stride, his reverie broken. They stood, face to face. Neither spoke, but only stared at one another. A long piece of straw dangled from Crowell's lips.

"Mr. Sharon sends you his regards." He took the straw out of his mouth, pointing it in Finn's direction. "You and Miss Ohhlson."

He started—just to hear Crowell utter her name was enough to justify a terrible beating. But he would attempt civility. "Tell Mr. Sharon his regards found my ear."

Finn took a step to go around, but Crowell moved in front of him.

"I believe you own some tunnel stock." Crowell thrust the straw between his lips. "Sutro Tunnel stock."

"What if I do?"

"Mr. Sharon wants to buy it. He'll pay a fair price."

"Tell Mr. Sharon I'll be thanking him for his offer, but I'm of no mind to sell."

"Don't you want to know the offer?"

"Nae. I don't."

Crowell studied him, chewing on the straw, his eyes as black and impenetrable as a mineshaft. Much like Sharon's, if you go to that of it. "Not that I give a damn, Irish," he said, "but yer makin' a mistake. A big mistake."

"The name's Gillespie." Finn took a step, then stopped. "I'll be going now. And I wouldn't be getting in my way if I were you."

He brushed past Crowell and moved with a deliberate ease down Sutton Street, thinking he had better check under the floorboard in his room to make sure the certificates were still there. He had moved them long ago, at Jessie's suggestion: they had been under the mattress. They'll be safer in the floor, she had said, but you should put them in the bank, Finn. Nae, he had answered. He didn't care much for bankers.

Morning cool had given way to afternoon heat. He turned off of Sutton onto E Street, pulled a cap from his back pocket, and with a flick of his wrist, settled it atop his head. His eyes shielded from the sun, he could see St. Mary's in the Mountains, her spire as slim as a sewing needle, tall enough to reach clear to heaven's gate. St. Mary's, where he had gone to Mass with Jessie. Oh but it had been grand to sit next to her.

'Twas different now entirely. Now the sermons fell on his tormented ears. He avoided confession, though he would confess for her if he could. His only sins were guilt and remorse at having left her, frozen in her shame like a pillar of salt, condemned to an eternity of solitude. The vision of her utter dejection haunted him in his sleep.

Her sins must be forgiven, the priest would say, 'twas Jesus that forgave Mary Magdalene. Aye, and he turned water into wine, Father. Next thing I know, you'll be tellin' me to turn the other cheek to the slithering Crowell.

He detoured to the cemetery and stood before Joseph's grave. "You should see it, Joseph. The Con-V. It's like the stars of heaven down there. Except I don't believe it, not for a minute. I believe it's really hell disguised as heaven, luring the unwary." His friend listened. He was a good listener, Joseph. "You're all wise now, aren't you?" he said. "Up in heaven, and all. Tell me what to do, then. About Jessie." Joseph didn't answer. Finn put his hand on the gravestone; it was unexpectedly warm. He pulled back, suddenly, seeing a vivid image of Father Manogue in his mind's eye. "Ah, damnation, Joseph."

He took his leave of the graveyard, and approached Taylor Street. St. Mary's rose serenely on his left. A wind-blown cloud passed overhead in the rarefied air, casting a shadow that rose up the spire, ascending to the tip of the heavenly pinnacle like an angel's prayer. And then it slipped off the top, leaving the symbol to shine like a beacon. Father Manogue, that saint of a man, stood below in the cathedral doorway, smiling at Finn, his kindly face like a welcome sign.

Finn slowed his pace, then slowed some more. Finally, he stopped. He glanced at the father all clad in his long, black robes, the white of his collar gleaming like a halo. The spire seemed to point the way. Finn sighed deeply, then turned and marched toward the church.

"G'day to ya, Finn," said Father Manogue.

"Good day to you, Father."

"Splendid afternoon."

"Aye, 'tis." Finn stood before the doorway, staring down at his boots, which he scuffled against the gravel path. He looked up. "Might I be having a word with you, Father?"

***

Louisa smiled across the desk at Will, brown curls framing her pale skin, laughing eyes declaring the world a joyful place. She looked so young in that portrait, he noticed, as if seeing her for the first time. How long ago had it been? Twenty years. Twenty years since she had died. Would she be pleased, he wondered, with the Palace Hotel? Did she know that he had built it for her? This would be his farewell gift to her. It was time, he now knew, to go back to Lizzie, heart and soul.

A stack of telegrams lay on the desk, awaiting his attention. He picked up the latest wire from Sharon, bending one corner back and forth while gazing out through the glass into the huge lobby, customers making their deposits and withdrawals, posting their payments. Sharon's bid for the Senate had fallen prey to bad press: the bank's Virginia City agent, it seemed, was not well liked. He was not one to accept defeat, however, and was already laying plans for another run. And, as Will had suspected, Sharon couldn't divest himself of the Comstock, and remained in control of its affairs through a network of agents and informants, even though he spent little time in camp.

He opened the telegram.

Have defined the Belcher seam.

The ore boundaries had been reached, in other words. This news was unwelcome but not entirely unexpected. It had to happen eventually. He wasn't concerned: the Comstock fissures extended deep into the earth and more Belchers were waiting to be found. He read on.

Mackay, Fair, Flood, and O'Brien control Con Vir.

What were those Irishmen up to? There must be something. MacKay and Fair were Irish, but they were clever Irish. God dammit, this wouldn't have happened had Sharon been on the Comstock instead of out running for political office. He swore under his breath. Rifling through his desk, he found a Comstock map and unfolded it across his desk, pressing out the creases with impatient thrusts of his hand. He ran his fingers over the words Con Virginia. It was, he recalled, originally comprised of several small mines: the old California, Central, Kinney, White and Murphy, and Sides, all 1310 feet of which had been joined together and renamed the Consolidated Virginia. And now these four upstarts had taken control of it. Why? Had they found something? That didn't seem possible—Sharon's men would have reported any important discoveries.

He read on. *Ophir just north, urge buy.*

Will studied the map. The Ophir lay north of the Con-Virginia, as Sharon had said. The name Ophir held a certain magic on the Comstock, having been the site of the original shallow discovery, and Will very much liked the idea of purchasing this mine. Neither the Ophir nor Con-Virginia had been explored at depth, mainly due to water problems. He knew what Sharon was thinking: if the Irishmen were to make a great discovery, it would likely extend into the Ophir, just as their Belcher find had extended into the Crown Point.

He perused the telegram for mention of Sutro Tunnel stock. Nothing. It could be that Sharon had the matter in hand, or, conversely, was having no success. He would have to send him another telegram. On a piece of paper, he scratched out instructions to purchase Ophir stock.

"Give these instructions to Franklin," he told Riker. "Tell him to send a clerk to the stock exchange immediately."

Riker whisked the note upstairs to the secretary's office. Will returned to his desk and opened Harpending's telegram.

Arnold was to accompany geologist...has disappeared. Trying to locate.

Trying to locate? At Arnold's demand, Will and Lent had paid him fifty thousand dollars each, for Christ's sake. This supposedly was a good-faith payment, without which the promoter refused to reveal the location of the diamond fields. As it was, Arnold had agreed only to lead the geologist to the site for an inspection. And now he could not be located?

"That filthy scoundrel," Will spat. Arnold had their money but refused to disclose the mine location. Was he a thief? What was Harpending doing about this?

He grabbed for paper, dipped a pen in the ink well, and wrote to Harpending in furious and belligerent cursive.

Received your wire...Arnold pledged his honor as a man to carry out faithfully the program as agreed. We did not then nor do we now believe he intended doing so and consider ourselves swindled out of the fifty we paid.

About to make revisions after quelling his anger, he noticed Darius Mills standing in his doorway. Mills had always presented to stockholders and the public, as he did to Will now, a Quaker-like appearance and demeanor. Stable. Frugal. Long-time friends, they greeted each other and traded particulars of family milestones, marriages, births and so forth.

"What is the latest with your diamond prospect?" Mills asked with a steady gaze.

The telegram to Harpending lay on his desk, a reminder that he may have been swindled, a fact he had no intention of admitting to Mills. Across from him he saw a man who would never discover gold, silver, or diamonds, never build a Palace Hotel or California Theater. But, in his methodical, phlegmatic way, Mills had accumulated a great fortune. A banker's fortune.

"We're still investigating at this time. But it certainly appears to have tremendous potential."

"It seems hard to imagine diamonds in California," said Mills.

Will had to be careful here, not wanting to admit he didn't even know where the fields were. Best to go on the offensive: was Mills aware that diamonds were recently discovered in South Africa?

The president nodded. He had heard that, yes.

"Chap, I've come to speak with you about a matter of great importance. A matter I have given careful consideration of late."

Will sensed that his partner intended a fatherly lecture on one of his investments. Or perhaps he was still unhappy about the unauthorized loans. Surely he didn't wish to complain about the Comstock, what with the Belcher windfall still pouring in, at least for the time being.

"Please, Darius," he said, smiling. "As friends, we must speak freely."

"Very well." Mills appeared to choose his words carefully. At its inception, the bank was a bold innovation, one he proudly associated with. The bank had been very successful and Will was to be congratulated. Their agreement had allowed Will to direct the bank with a free hand, an agreement mutually beneficial to them both.

Mills paused. So, he wishes more control, Will thought.

"At this time," said Mills, sounding philosophical, "the bank directs its resources into an ever-widening array of non-productive and risky avenues, the faults of which are too lengthy for me to enumerate here. This is the stage of the bank's life when, in my opinion, we should be directing its resources into more conventional, and conservative, banking investments."

Again, he paused, and Will knew what would follow. They had discussed it before: Mills did not approve of investing in the Comstock Lode.

"I am no longer able to continue in my position with the Bank of California. And rather than insist on a change in direction or policy, I think it best that I resign my office as president."

"But you still own shares," Will said in disbelief.

He, Mills, would retain a small number of shares, and remain on the board of directors.

This did not placate the cashier. The hypocrite, he thought. "You have become rich from these investments you so ardently oppose," he said evenly.

"I will not deny that my association with the bank has been most lucrative. But now it is time for me to focus my attention on other pursuits."

Will didn't hear most of the remaining conversation. Empty words, mostly. His concern now was how other stockholders would react. And customers. Would this show of no-confidence frighten off other investors? Mills was highly respected. Revered, even. And who, now, would assume the mantle of bank president?

After Mills left his office, he found Riker and waited for his assistant to ready two horses. They climbed into the saddles and began the ride to the new Pine Street residence. The sun was low in the western sky, casting long shadows. The summer air was turning cool as evening approached. Mills, he thought, another friend who was no friend at all.

"Do you have any old friends, James?"

"Mostly you, sir. And my wife, I suppose. If it's proper to call your wife a friend."

"I think it is proper. And thank you, James, I consider you my friend as well."

They turned onto Pine Street and the horses began a gradual climb, their heads high and proud in standardbred fashion. Carriages rattled by and people waved: San Franciscans loved him, if nothing else, thought Will.

"A true friend is a rare invention, don't you think?" Will observed.

"Rare indeed, Mr. Chap."

"Why is that, do you suppose?" If they were willing, he would have been friends with everyone.

Riker sat atop his horse in quiet contemplation. "I suppose God knows we won't treasure somethin' if we have too much of it. Like a warm day in San Francisco, Mr. Chap, there ain't many of 'em, but them's we get are mighty fine. Mighty fine indeed."

Will threw his head back and laughed—the man had the wisdom of Solomon.

They had reached Montgomery, where, across Market, workmen moved like industrious ants about the frame of the Palace Hotel, carrying bricks, timber and pipe. The sight stirred his imagination: a dream coming true right before his eyes.

"I had many friends, once," Will said. "But now they're disappearing, one by one."

"Oh, Mr. Chap. Ain't no one has more friends than you. Look at 'em all waving, like you was their king."

Ah, but will they be there for me when I need them? Will asked himself. Not likely. "Investors. Customers. Admirers. But not friends, James."

Riker shook his head. "Even if you was to lose every friend, Mr. Chap, you still has your family, and they loves you more than anybody else."

Will glanced at Riker with a rueful smile. Yes, this was true, he did have his family.

Chapter 39

Sutro handed his horse off to the stable boy and looked in the direction of his new Nevada home. To the left, down 27th Street, the main thoroughfare of the Town of Sutro, he imagined one day would be occupied with houses and stores, rather than scrub brush and rabbit holes. Up ahead, a stately mansion rose out of the desert sands like a monument dropped mysteriously from the sky. Three stories, a lookout above, sides of whitewashed wood shingles, a covered porch along the front, shading four, tall, east-facing windows. Atop the lookout, an American flag waved in the stiff breeze. That breeze, he knew, would gain strength as the day wore on until it became the irksome Zephyr wind.

He approached the front door, pleased with the house despite the absence of landscaping—the native vegetation was perfectly adequate anyway. Pushing open the front door, he marveled at the well-lit front rooms, the furniture selected by Hazlett that was utilitarian but attractive, and the large parlor where the Town of Sutro would entertain its guests and dignitaries. He strode down the hallway to the sitting room to find his wife and all his children, except Emma and Rose, who were away at school.

"Papa," cried Kate. She jumped up and ran to her father, throwing her arms around his substantial waist.

Charles, Edgar and little Clara followed. Sutro hugged each of them, then kissed his wife. The children gathered around him on the couch. The room was large enough for several chairs, a couch and a desk. A bookshelf, mostly empty, covered one wall. The other walls were still blank and uncovered above the wainscoting save for the green-patterned, paisley wallpaper. The floors were wood-plank but covered by a large, plain wool rug.

"We don't like it here," Edgar announced.

"Hush, Edgar," scolded Kate. She, the resident elder at eleven years old, assumed a motherly role with Edgar and Clara, eight and six.

"But—" The boy seemed to quickly realize his co-conspirators had abandoned him. He glared at his sister. "It is much nicer in San Francisco," he insisted.

"It is not," said Kate.

Sutro patted Edgar on the back and glanced at his wife, who had dour expression. He preferred to focus on his son. "You will like it here, Edgar. This is beautiful country, Nevada. It is just different from San Francisco, but you will get used to it."

Charles said he liked riding horses, and his father promised to take him riding. They could even ride to the tunnel. Sutro picked up little Clara and asked her if she liked it there.

"I don't know. It's hot." She frowned, then added: "And windy."

"But," he said, feigning surprise, "San Francisco is windy, too."

"But it's not windy and hot," she explained.

He chuckled. Daughters were a delight. "Did you know this town is called Sutro?"

"Yes. Why are there no people here?"

"There will be many people here very soon."

"Will there be a school?"

He began to wonder if Leah had put the little one up to these questions. That his wife sat looking at him with eyes asking the same thing, convinced him it was so. Yes, of course, there would be schools and churches and stores, a big city one day. No, not as big as San Francisco, but very big. He scooted the children out to play, wanting to talk to their mother.

"The children miss their schoolmates," Leah said.

"They will make new friends."

"But there are no children here."

"There are a few."

"And I have assumed the role of teacher. Something I fear I am not adequately prepared for."

"You will make a fine teacher for our children."

"I feel I have been dropped on a desert isle in the middle of nowhere. How can you possibly expect us to live in a place like this?"

He glanced about the room and, satisfied that it was new and well constructed, said, "But this is a fine house. Better even than our houses in San Francisco. And you do not have boarders any longer. I thought you would be happy. We are together as a family, as you always wished."

She sat staring straight ahead. Her eyes grew red—an unhealthy sign. How long did he intend that they remain in Nevada? Until the tunnel was complete, of course.

"How long will that be?"

He had been thinking about this himself. "A few years," he said, reluctant to be more specific.

"A few years?" She put her head down. "I am confident that this tunnel will be worth it, considering what you are putting our family through."

"It will be worth it," he said boldly. Doubts, however, were beginning to gnaw at him. The Virginia-Truckee Railroad transported huge quantities of ore out of the Comstock on a daily basis, ore that would have paid him two dollars for each ton had the tunnel been finished. Would there be any ore left when the tunnel connected to the Comstock? Would the superintendents even agree to use the tunnel? Mackay and Fair and a host of others were all pleased with the railroad.

"Yes," he said, "when the tunnel is completed, Sutro will grow like the weed in springtime."

***

Finn knocked on the door of Mrs. Frieda's Boarding House. Breezes, carrying a hint of winter's coming chill, played a melancholy song on a nearby wind chime. The formidable landlady opened the door but said nothing, glaring as if he were a wolf there to prey on the innocent lambs.

"A fine afternoon to you, Mrs. Frieda. Would Miss Ohhlson be here?"

She considered him for a moment, then, without warning, closed the door in his face. It would take more than cheerfulness to win the frau, he realized. Inside, footsteps clapped down the hall. The minutes ticked by. He listened for their return. Or voices.

Nothing, though, only silence. Thinking perhaps he should leave, he heard the latch.

The door creaked open. Jessie looked out at him with a blank expression. Whether hurt, angry, or just apathetic he couldn't ascertain.

He took off his cap, suddenly nervous. "Are you in the midst of your school papers? Or would you be in idle time at the moment?" He stuffed the hat into his back pocket. "That is, might I have a word with you?"

She stepped out onto the porch and closed the door, then turned and walked past him without meeting his eye. As she passed by, her blue dress, swaying gently back and forth, brushed against his grateful leg, and he leaned in so as to catch the scent of her perfume. She took a seat on a rocking chair, and he settled on a bench, across from her.

He tried to think what to say. How to begin. Perhaps he had he lost his only chance with her. From the side of his eye he could see Mrs. Frieda spying on them through the window.

"You look as pretty as an Easter Lilly," he said. And oh, but she did.

She nodded in acknowledgement, rocking, rocking, ever so slowly in her chair. The silence of a female is terrifying noise, he decided.

"Mackie and Fair will reap a great harvest, so they will," he said, vexed by his sudden loss for words. "In the Con Virginia, that is."

She rocked in the chair, glancing at him but still saying nothing.

'Twas cruel for God to give woman such awful power, he thought, suddenly irritated with his Maker. He stared out at the street, quiet at this far end of town. The chimes babbled their random notes. His chest grew tighter and tighter.

"I am here to apologize, Jessie." He looked at her to see a reaction. She just rocked. Back and forth.

"I was a fool, and I'll never forgive myself for leaving you in your sorrow on that terrible day. I'm ashamed. Greatly ashamed, so I am. Nightmares plague me and I can't stop worrying over you."

She put her feet to the floor and stopped rocking. "Are you here because you're worried about me? If so, you can rest assured there is no need."

"No. It'd be more than just worry." He tried to think. "I'm after thanking you. Thanking you for what you said, about, well, about Ralston. You came to me in a generous spirit and I behaved like a horse's arse."

She blushed and looked down.

"That is, I'm ever so sorry," he stammered. "I shouldn't have used such foul language and I'd be after begging your forgiveness. Jaysus. I don't know what's come over me. 'Tis a spell I'm under. A terrible spell." Using his sleeve, he wiped the perspiration from his forehead. "What I meant to say is, I behaved like a jealous cur, and I'd be beggin' your forgiveness."

"I don't mind that you're jealous," she said quietly.

This must be good, that she didn't mind, though he wasn't entirely certain. "But it's more than that, Jessie," he said. "I was after thinking vile thoughts and accusing you in my mind of all manner of transgressions. But now I see what a fool I was, and how your past doesn't matter to me, and that you are the loveliest creature I've ever known."

She sat as still as mouse. He thought she would be glad for his confession, but instead she seemed taken aback. Her face grew pale. Had he said something wrong? He waited, looking at her. A gust of wind whistled down from Mount Davidson: the afternoon Zephyrs were gathering. The chimes protested in a cacophony of music.

"I must tell you about my past, Finn."

"No. You needn't do that, Jessie. What a fool I'd be if I cared about things that can't be changed."

"But I must," she said ardently.

And so she told him, starting at the beginning, as far back as she could remember. She told him things she'd never told anyone. And he looked right into her eyes and listened, and he didn't judge her.

***

"I need a new horse, Father."

He knew why ten-year old William wanted a new horse, but asked him anyway. "Why is that, William?"

"Because," interjected the older Samuel, "my horse is bigger."

"And faster," complained the younger son.

Samuel was a fine horseman and could handle a spirited animal; Will, Jr. liked fine things, including horses, but didn't appreciate the sacrifice, or the expense involved. They returned from the morning ride, the horses sensing the barn and increasing their gait. It was a glorious fall morning, and dew still clung to the blades of grass, though it was drying quickly in the warming air.

"I like my horse." Emelita sat proudly on her small filly, Pepper.

"That's not a horse," Junior said. "It's a pony."

"It is not. Pepper is a fine horse, isn't she, Father?"

"Of course she is."

Will himself had taken one of his older mares out for a ride, and she seemed grateful. He reached down, stroked her neck, and she flicked her tail like a filly.

"If you want a faster horse, William, you'll have to look after it. A younger animal needs more attention. More riding, more walking, you have to keep their hooves trimmed, brush them. Are you sure you want to take on such a responsibility?"

"Yes." It wasn't an earnest yes, but a stubborn, defiant one. How does one teach a boy like William to appreciate what he has, when he has too much to begin with? The only horse Will's parents had owned had been strictly for work; a horse just for pleasure would have been inconceivable.

They rode up the trail out of Cañon Diablo and through the terraced gardens below the house. James Riker greeted them at the stables with a big smile, asking about their ride.

"It was very good," said Emelita, "because Papa was with us."

Will helped her down. "Can you make sure your brothers take care of these horses?"

"Of course, Papa."

"They need a good brushing."

"Oh, I know, Papa."

He turned for the house knowing she and Riker would keep the boys in line. This was the rare day when there were no guests at Belmont, though several were due to arrive within the week. Elizabeth sat in the sunroom with Bertha and a nursemaid, at the end of the long room, closest to the barn, so as to watch her children on their horses. The space was warm in the morning sun. He leaned over and kissed his wife, then sat beside her. They watched Bertha test her newfound legs: her steps from chair to chair are tentative, but quite entertaining. The three sat in rapt attention.

"How was your ride?"

"Excellent. A fine morning to be out."

"Where are the children?"

"Tending their animals."

She was silent. The silence of disapproval.

"They will appreciate the horses more," he added, "if they have to care for them."

"I just don't think Emelita should have to brush and feed her horse. James can do that."

He preferred not to have this discussion again. "William thinks he wants a new horse, but I'm not sure he's ready for it."

"He mentioned this to me as well. Why do you say that?"

"He doesn't appreciate the horse he has and I won't buy him a high-bred animal if he won't care for it properly."

"The boys are due to leave for school soon, so I hardly see what difference it makes. The hostlers will care for the them anyway."

This may be true, but he wouldn't give in on this. He said, "I have to meet Sharon at the train station in an hour."

She glanced at him, and didn't like that he'd changed the subject. "Is he coming here?"

Will knew of her distaste for Sharon. "No. I'm picking him up and we're going straight to the city, to inspect the Palace Hotel."

She contemplated this for a moment. "This hotel, Toppie, it just seems beyond extravagant. I imagine Mr. Sharon must think so as well."

"He defers to my judgment in these matters."

"But fireplaces and baths in every room? Bay windows? Silver-plated chandeliers? I concede that I know nothing of these matters, but why does San Francisco need such a grandiose hotel?"

It frustrated him that she didn't recognized the value of this great undertaking, recognized the benefits that San Francisco would reap. All the world would speak of this hotel, he knew, wish to see it so they could tell their friends, saying, I have seen the remarkable Palace Hotel. To visit it would be like a pilgrimage that must be accomplished before one died.

"San Francisco needs such a grandiose hotel, as you say, because it is, or will be, the most beautiful city in the world. Why should San Francisco's hotels and theaters be outshined by New York's? New York is nothing but an older, plainer sibling to San Francisco, and the East Coast is just a jealous rival to California. Have you seen the Atlantic? My goodness, the Pacific is infinitely bluer, wilder, and more beautiful. Why would anyone sail New York harbor when they can pass through the Golden Gate into the finest harbor in the world? What is Long Island compared to the Peninsula? My God, Lizzie, nothing is too good for San Francisco."

"You needn't swear." She took Bertha's hand and helped her walk between chairs.

"When will you return?" she asked.

"Tomorrow."

"I intend to go the city with the children tomorrow," she said.

"I promised the boys I would ride with them."

"There will be other times to ride."

"They will be leaving soon for school, as you say."

She handed Bertha off to the nursemaid and together they went to the window.

"I do not like it here, William. I can only stay so long before needing to return to the city. I have told you that."

Yes, he sighed, she had.

At the Belmont station, Sharon emerged from the luxury car made by his, and Will's, Kimble Car plant. Dressed in his usual black suit, his moustaches drooped at the corners, following his mouth into its customary frown. He put his luggage in the back of the char-à-banc and climbed up into the seat beside Will.

"Our Kimble car is superior to the Pullman, is it not?"

"Most assuredly, though Pullman seems the master salesman."

Will lamented that a superior product should not be so easily out-sold. He expected to receive the promised order from the Central Pacific any day. Stanford, thankfully, recognized quality.

They traversed the Peninsula Road, the train coming up alongside them before slowly pulling ahead. Sharon put a slug of tobacco into his cheek. They held an impromptu partnership meeting: purchases of Ophir stock, of which they now held a majority interest, and Sutro Tunnel stock: neither partner was finding many shares available. There were persistent rumors of a strike at the Consolidated Virginia, owned by the four Irishmen, but with their Ophir shares, they should be protected.

The road turned from the Bay and now rose up and down, wave-like. The hills were golden brown.

"Speaking of rumors," Sharon said, "talk of diamond fields has reached my ears."

"More than just rumors. Harpending is involved."

"Harpending, huh?" Sharon didn't seem impressed. Montgomery South was still a fresh wound.

"Where are these diamonds located?"

"Somewhere near Colorado," Will said. This revelation had surprised him, having been led to believe the fields were in Arizona or New Mexico. "Henry Janin, the geologist who has worked for us in the past, just returned from an inspection. His report is favorable and concludes that the investment is safe and attractive." He decided not to mention that Janin's report was limited to a confined area: Harpending had cut the expedition short to return home to his sick wife. This had seemed odd, but Harpending had always been attentive toward his lovely bride.

"We have set up an office for the company in the bank," he said. "The stock is being snapped up by prominent investors, in case you're interested."

Sharon leaned over the side of the carriage and spat. "I haven't the capital at the moment."

No matter, Will thought. Doubters would be sorry. He had been granted shares, had purchased more, and lent money to friends who wished to buy. It was a bargain relative to the great potential, he had told them. They passed San Bruno Peak, then crossed into San Francisco County, and finally the road became

Mission Street. He turned the char-à-banc onto New Montgomery, then stopped before Market Street in front of the Palace Hotel.

Workmen scrambled amid the enormous structure, carrying bricks and pipes to the upper floors. The immensity of the building was startling. He glanced back at the Grand Hotel, which seemed a trifle. Will pointed out the retail spaces that would deliver considerable rent.

Sharon worked his tobacco in silence.

"And note the bay windows for every room," he said. "Each guest will have natural light."

"What I note," Sharon said, articulating the words concisely, "is that we are far over budget given the progress of construction. I had expected to see the structure nearly completed, but find it still in the early stages. How in God's name are we to pay for this?"

He studied Sharon, then the hotel. It was true, the costs had run over. Dramatically. "I had hoped we would be closer to completion as well. But as the building progresses, questions arise over details. It is my position that we must employ only the finest quality throughout, though this approach has necessarily created some inflation."

"Some inflation?" Sharon said. "How many millions will it take to finish this grand debacle?"

"Debacle? Whatever the costs of this...debacle, I will cover them if you do not choose to participate."

"I have assumed a one-half share of this hotel," Sharon said, "but you have failed to consult with me and keep me informed, as is your duty."

"It has always been my *duty* to administer our affairs in San Francisco, while Virginia City is your domain. I do not meddle in your management and expect the same restraint from you."

"That has been the arrangement, I agree." Sharon's face was flush with anger. "But this has altered the landscape. The investment you are making here is unprecedented."

"I did not complain of the cost overruns on the Virginia Truckee Railroad."

"You may recall that I managed to defray substantial costs on that railroad to the other mine owners and the surrounding counties." Sharon spit what was left of his tobacco onto the ground. "These investments of yours, they must come to an expeditious conclusion. You are burning through money on one ill-conceived notion after another. That furniture manufacturing plant, what will happen to it after this hotel is finished? I warrant it will sit idle. I understand that you've invested in the Spring Valley Water Company now, an enterprise that has no hope of profitability any time soon."

Will grew angrier with each word. "San Francisco needs the water and I have political connections to ensure the success of that venture. I did not complain when Jones and Hayward outmaneuvered you on the Crown Point, nor did I say a word when you were bested by four illiterate Irishmen. You, who have made your share of mistakes, have no right to question my judgment."

Sharon turned a deep red. Will, regretting his outburst and the rapidly descending argument, thought to take a conciliatory tone.

"Perhaps we need to take a moment to cool off," he said. "We have had a rewarding partnership and I do not wish to have it degenerate into back-biting and second guessing."

Sharon furiously bit off a fresh chunk of tobacco, then said: "Nor do I."

"Shall we go to the bank?"

"I think I'll walk," Sharon answered.

A short time later, Will was sitting at his desk, pondering the argument with his partner. Unlike Sharon, he had great faith in his investments and knew that eventually, each of them would turn the corner to profitability. He picked up a letter from Leland Stanford and tore it open.

...I regret to inform...the Central Pacific cannot engage the Kimble Car Company in a contract at the present...

He crumbled up the letter and slammed it down onto his desk. Sharon, learning of this, would raise a knowing eyebrow. But Stanford, Huntington, Crocker, and Hopkins (the railroad Association), whom he had helped to get started, lent them money when no one else would, and now the greedy sons-of-bitches would not honor their promise. A letter. They sent him a letter. They wouldn't even look him in the face, and they wouldn't repay a debt of loyalty.

Friends, as the wise James Riker had said, were as rare as a warm day in San Francisco.

Chapter 40

John Bethel emerged from the boarding house, tugged at his rumpled felt hat (which he appeared to have used as a pillow), and shuffled toward Sutro, a cloud of dust rising behind him, his red flannel shirt and canvas trousers caked with that very dust, and a healthy measure of bacon grease. Bethel suddenly stopped and began rooting around in his pant pockets. Sutro watched him, stupefied. From the eyes, which began to twinkle, he concluded that Bethel's fingers must have found something: out came a dark chunk that recalled hardened cow-pie. Bethel inspected his treasure carefully, twisting and turning it before putting it to his teeth and gnawing off a sizable chunk. Now with a brown smile he turned to Sutro, stuffed the remainder of his breakfast into the pocket from whence it came, and said:

"Mornin'." Vapor streamed from his nostrils and, though it was a cold December morning, Bethel wore no jacket.

"Good morning," said Sutro, with no attempt to hide his exasperation. "Shall we go?"

"I'm ready when you are."

In silence, they proceeded to the hoisting works of Shaft Number One. This was to be the first of four shafts dropped from the surface down into the tunnel, although it was the only one completed so far. They climbed into the cage; the operator, at his signal, dropped them into the shaft, and a moment later they hopped out of the cage and into the tunnel. A cool draft of air passed down the shaft and toward the tunnel entrance, whistling as it blew. Sutro smiled: ventilation was an added benefit of the shafts.

They took seats in the waiting mule cart. The driver clicked the reins. "Get up, Fanny," he said, sounding apologetic. Fanny obeyed and the slow ride to the heading began. Sutro fumed at the pace: the shafts, if they could ever finish them, would cut this trip short by a factor of ten. The foreman, engrossed in his breakfast, didn't appear to be in a talkative mood, so Sutro studied the tunnel, much as one might study his own offspring. The walls were a rough texture but mostly covered by heavy timber, and the braces on the sides and ceiling, at right angles to each other, gave the circular tunnel a square appearance. The ceiling was high enough for man and beast to pass beneath without bending. The floor was dirt with a track to the right side, the track on which they now travelled. All according to the Chief Engineer, and General Superintendent's, plans.

Sutro, satisfied with what he saw, asked Bethel how far they had progressed with the second vertical shaft.

"Three hundred feet. Rock as hard as fucking steel. Then, soon as we hit a soft patch, we're swimming in water. God dammed holy fucking mess." He leaned over the side of the cart and spat tobacco juice, then worked the plug with his fingers until satisfied that all was in order. "The same on three and four, except worse. You best give up those shafts, they're a waste of manpower."

"They are worth the manpower," Sutro retorted. "Once they are completed, the tunnel will go much faster." And they needed to go much faster, he knew. Precious time was being wasted.

"You've got three times the men working on those goddamn shafts as you do the tunnel. It don't make no sense."

"It makes sense to me, and that's all that matters." Sutro had no intention of arguing with his foreman. There was but one General Superintendent of the Sutro Tunnel.

Just then a blast rumbled though the tunnel like an earthquake: first the loud thud, then the vibrating ground and walls. At the tunnel heading they had encountered hard porphyritic rock that only gave way to dynamite and expensive hydraulic diamond drills.

"If you don't mind me askin'," said Bethel, "why the hell haven't we gotten that government money yet?"

Sutro did mind, not wishing to think about the debacle. "The committee has recommended the loan," he said tersely, "but the bill hasn't passed." The mule plodded along. Bethel plied his tobacco. Sutro, watching the wood-framed walls of the tunnel pass by and now, thinking about Congress, grew more and more aggravated at political foot-dragging with each step Fanny took.

"These politicians cannot be trusted," he muttered, thinking out loud. "They make promises but never keep them. Like thieves and liars, taking from us but giving nothing back. They have given no assistance to Nevada or the mining interests. But we send them all our gold and silver, more than they get from any other state. You would think we would be important. Respected. But they treat us like we are their slaves."

What truly aggravated him: Congress seemed determined to nullify his great triumph before the Mining Committee. That vile Sharon was behind it, he knew it as sure as his name.

"If you are worried, you shouldn't be," he went on. "The McCalmont's are going to lend me more money." He gritted his teeth: the $800,000 loan would, unfortunately, require mortgages on the tunnel property. What could he do? He was running out of money.

"I ain't worried."

"Can you estimate how much longer before the tunnel is to the Comstock?"

Bethel scratched his chin. "We've hit this hard porphyry and even with dynamite and diamond drills, the boring is damn slow. If those shafts..." He chomped his tobacco for a moment. "We've got over two miles to go, and I'd say, based on this pace, we're lookin' at another three years of hard digging." He spat. "That's my best fucking guess, anyways."

Yes, thought Sutro. That had been his calculation as well. They were a very long ways from completion. In distance and time.

The mule continued her methodical journey. The explosions grew louder. As they moved inexorably, methodically, toward the tunnel heading, it began to dawn on him that the tunnel may never make any money. A sickening knot grew in his gut. A great bonanza had been discovered in the Con Virginia, or so the rumors went, but its ore was being mined already and hauled out by the Virginia-Truckee. Would there be any left in three years? Would there ever be another great bonanza like the Con Virginia?

***

A fine Belmont morning. From his bedroom window, Will could see his hostlers readying carriages and bridling up teams of horses. In the room behind, Elizabeth was speaking, though his attention was directed more at the former than the later. He regretted this, tried to listen to her, but his horses were such fine athletes, the muscles so sculpted, the coats so sleek, he couldn't take his eyes, or attention, from them.

"The carriages will be ready in half an hour."

"Don't wait for me," she said, looking in the mirror and making adjustments to her silk dress. "You should go back down and breakfast with your guests."

He had been down to breakfast already but wondered what delayed her appearance, and so had come back to the room.

"Your dress is very nice. But aren't you concerned—that is, do you think it will be comfortable? After all, the drive to the Cliff House is a long one."

"I had thought I would stay home today, if that's all right with you."

"Lizzie, these Japanese bankers consider you their hostess. They will be greatly offended if you do not accompany us."

"I'm not feeling well today."

"You look quite well to me."

"My head aches."

"Your head aches a lot lately."

"I have a lot of worries."

"What worries?"

"Our sons, off at boarding school. I worry about them day and night. Are they eating properly? Are they dressing warmly enough? Are they attending to their studies? William, you know, has developed bad habits. And then there's Bertha; she's become a very fussy eater. I have gone through three nurses already: they say she is a willful child. Emelita is the only one I don't have to worry about."

"The boys will be fine," he said. "They're strong and healthy. And Bertha has a capable nurse to look after her."

"It is my job to look after the children," she said tersely, "not the nurse's."

She turned to the mirror. The room was quiet; he could hear the horses whinny and neigh outside. He remaindered her gently of their Japanese guests waiting downstairs.

"You know very well that I am weary of playing the hostess of Belmont. Every week you invite dozens of visitors and it is left to me to make arrangements for them. To decide which rooms they will take, what they will eat, what sort of entertainment they will like, arrange balls and dances and music. You expect too much."

"I expect what any man does of his wife. To be a good hostess. You do not, it seems to me, have such a difficult time of it."

She became very still. He glanced in the mirror to see her face take on heightened color. "I resent the implications of such a statement."

Stubbornly, he resolved not to apologize. "These are very important guests of the bank, Lizzie. Today of all days I need you to be a proper hostess."

"Every guest at Belmont is important to the bank."

"But these visitors are from Japan. They have traveled a very long way to be here. They wish to reform their currency system, among other things, and they've come to me, and to the Bank of California for advice. They would learn from us and we should be honored to oblige them. I'll teach them and they, in turn, will bank with us. And if all goes well, the Bank of California will be first to associate with the Japanese. It will be a stunning triumph. Imagine it. By the time they depart, we will have entered into agreements to lend them substantial amounts of American gold and silver." As he spoke, he was envisioning San Francisco as a center of international banking.

She seemed unmoved. "I fail to see how my presence is necessary for reforming Japanese currency problems."

Will looked at her in the mirror. Their eyes met.

She blinked.

In her wardrobe he found a dress of fine, lightweight wool, green in color, long sleeves, buttons up the front.

"I think this will be appropriate and comfortable." He laid the dress across the bed.

She turned and stared at the garment. Outside, the sound of gravel crunching. Horses stomping their hooves: impatient, high-blooded horses.

"I'll call Betsy for you on my way out," he said.

He turned and walked out of the room, closing the door firmly, but not too firmly. Downstairs he could hear the strange chatter of foreigners. He found Betsy waiting nervously beside the skylight-railing and assured her all was well and would she mind helping Elizabeth, who had decided to change.

Lizzie would play her part, he knew, and play it well. Descending the stairs in deliberate, thoughtful steps, he pondered the great bonanza, now confirmed, at the Consolidated Virginia mine. The heart of the Comstock, some were calling it, discovered fourteen years after the initial find. It worried him that their own systematic surveys of the Ophir, just to the north, had turned up no hint of the Con-V ore. He entered the dining room. The long table, crowded with Oriental faces, became suddenly still and quiet. Simultaneously, they all stood up. A small, distinguished man stepped from the table and turned to meet Will.

"Ambassador Iwakara," Will said, bowing with his best Oriental manners, "my wife will be down very shortly and sends her deepest apologies. Women are delicate creatures, but one could sooner move a mountain as to make them come to breakfast before they are ready."

Mr. Iwakara, laughing and bowing, seemed greatly amused by this. Wives, it was agreed, are the same no matter the country.

Chapter 41

The St. Patrick's Day Parade in Virginia City always began with respectable floats and songs of the Emerald Isle, and ended in resolutions to die for Old Éire amid public drunkenness and utter foolishness entirely. If not for Jessie's ardent desire to witness the grand spectacle in person, having only seen it from afar at Mrs. Frieda's, Finn would have declared his intention to stay home, sat trying to read while hearing the pipes and whistles, then given up and joined the celebration, only to swear by the end to not go the next year. It was his own fault: he had bragged about the parade like a fool. 'Twas the grandest spectacle an Irishman could dream of, and the like. How could she have not seen it? I was waiting for you to take me, she said.

They found a bench near the Delta Saloon on C Street; the crowds poured in and spectators took their places along the side-walks. Spring was in the height of its glory, the sun beginning to dry out the bog-like streets. Jessie, in her paisley dress with green trim, which she had made especially for this day, looked as bright as a daffodil.

"Your childers will be agog," he said.

"At what?"

"To hear we kept company at a St. Paddy's Day parade."

She turned as red as an apple. "Hush now, Finnian."

The parade began. Virginians and their many guests joined the gambol all along the parade route. Miners in their red shirts mostly stayed close to the saloon doors while families lined the sidewalks, the children dangling their happy feet into the street. A pair of splendid horses with silver-trimmed saddles kicked off the celebration, the riders carrying flags, American and Irish, side by side. Red, white, blue, and green, stars and stripes and harps all waved proudly together to ecstatic applause. Next came the parade Marshal, newspaper man Dan De Quille, and Finn roared his approval. De Quille's paper, the Territorial Enterprise, had printed Sutro's speech in its entirety.

Behind the marshal, the Reno Engineers Marching Band played a fine version of the Star Spangled Banner. Horses pranced; wagons were festooned with hand-painted signs; firemen pulled their polished fire wagons, wives cheered and threw flowers at the heroes of the Yellow Jacket fire. Dancing broke out along the sidewalks. Finn pulled Jessie to her feet and taught her a jig, and she laughed so hard he had to catch her from falling.

When the Piper's Opera house float appeared, the men erupted in a clamorous celebration of the dancing girls and actresses, who waved like sirens at the riotous crowd. Wives turned children's faces away, but kept their own eyes glued.

Across the street, Finn noticed something. A face perhaps. But then it was gone.

The parade finally ended with a leprechaun tugging a wee wagon and his pot of gold, to the delight of the miners. And again Finn noticed something. Across the street. Eyes. A gaze. Crowell's face.

He tipped his hat to Finn and disappeared.

The leprechaun passed by. The crowds began to shift and surge like a herd of cattle, pouring out onto the street. The sidewalk quivered. Mothers tugged at their children's arms. Miners pushed through the masses toward the saloons: their celebration would continue long into the night. Finn grasped Jessie's hand, keeping an eye out for Crowell. They pushed along the sidewalk. Piano music tripped out the saloon doors as they passed by the various establishments: the Delta, Daley's Exchange, the El Dorado, the Palace, each filling up quickly with rowdy and thirsty miners.

They heard a ruckus behind them. Finn spun around and Jessie's hand slipped from his. Miners pushed and shoved their way into the Palace Saloon. Curses flew. Fists began to swing, jaws cracking. A man crashed through the saloon doors. On the sidewalk outside, mothers shrieked and children screamed. The fight spread like a fire in dry kindling. Bystanders fled in all directions.

Finn reached for Jessie, but suddenly felt a blow to his head. A terrible pain blinded him. He put a hand to his head. There was warm, slick blood on his fingers. The crowd spun, then became a blur. Jessie? He tried to look back for her, but saw only a fog. Then blackness. His knees buckled. His head, the pain, blood...

***

Will took up Jess's letter again from atop his desk.

"...*committed* to Mr. Finnian Gillespie..."

Committed, he thought, committed to, future wife of? Confident penmanship, exclamation points, words like beautiful and wondrous and forever spilled from her pen, her joy leaping from the page. He was happy for her, and yet, he read the words like the sailor whose beloved had found another, someone not forever at sea, someone not forever on a voyage. The sailor can't blame her, and yet the pain is deep. He will long for her, the sailor knows, until he drowns in some terrible shipwreck, or hangs in a mutiny.

According to his pocket watch, the St. Patrick's Day parade would be over now. He had in mind to visit John Fry at the stock exchange but would not subject himself to throngs of unruly Irishmen.

Outside, the street appeared calm. He set off for the Exchange, but stopped short at a newsstand. Headlines cried out:

Con-Virginia, the Heart of the Comstock

...

MacKay, Fair, Flood, & O'Brien: Silver Kings!

...

Four Irishmen Hit Huge Bonanza

The goddamned Irish, were they everywhere? He scanned over the stories: The Consolidated Virginia would be the greatest bonanza ever seen, not only on the Comstock, but possibly anywhere. Further down, another headline read: *Silver Kings to Open Bank*. Not only had the Bank of California missed the biggest bonanza in the Comstock, it wouldn't even handle the bullion. And the Irishmen were building their own processing mill—more profits lost. A complete and utter catastrophe.

"Did ya see the parade, Mr. Ralston?" asked the news vendor.

"I missed it this year, Mr. Brown."

"St. Patrick himself made an appearance. Tossed out free cigars, too." Brown took a smoldering cigar butt from between his lips and held it up as an offer of proof.

"It seems I should have gone."

"What do you think of the great discovery?" The vendor motioned towards his newspapers.

Will put on a smile for him. "It's great news, Mr. Brown. The more you search, the more silver you find on the Comstock. It's one of the wonders of the world, no doubt about it."

"Yes sir, Mr. Ralston. And those Irishmen are gonna be the richest men in San Francisco. Mark my words."

"Well, my friend, they just might be."

St. Patrick's free cigar, from the aroma, was probably made of cheap South American tobacco. Will took a *figurado* from his jacket and offered it to Mr. Brown. "Here, try this. It's from my own cigar company. The tobacco is excellent, better than Cuban."

Mr. Brown's cheroot was on the ground so quickly, and replaced by the *figurado*, that Will had to smile. He tucked a *Bulletin* under his arm and fumbled through his coin pouch for a half-dime.

"No," mumbled Mr. Brown around his *figurado*, "that one's on me, Mr. Ralston."

He forged ahead to the Exchange. *The richest men in San Francisco.* Not likely, he scoffed, tossing aside the newspaper (he didn't care to read it). He tipped his hat to friendly faces. People shouted: "Hey, Billy Ralston!" And he returned enthusiastic waves and smiles.

At the Exchange, Fry looked like a boy at the arcade. "Have you heard what Con-Virginia is selling for?"

Will had to chuckle. Investors rise and fall, but brokers are always happy: they made fees whether the market went up, or down. Con-V, the broker related, was selling for an astonishing seven hundred fifty dollars, the Ophir at a respectable three hundred. Will quickly estimated his paper-profits in the millions, although his Ophir gains were paltry in comparison to the windfall on Con-V stock. MacKay's boys had bought at six dollars per share, they, Will and Sharon, at about twenty. But the share prices, Will knew, were only anticipating rich ore bodies. And it was a rich ore body in the Ophir that he needed now. And badly.

He was having little success at finding Sutro Tunnel shares for sale, Fry reported. Those he did buy were selling at around five to ten dollars.

"Congratulations, by the way, on your promotion," he said.

"I'm still the Cashier in my mind," Will said. He received no joy from his new title, President of the Bank of California; he would rather have had Mills back.

"I went by the Palace the other day." Fry gave him a sideways glance. "I have never seen so many bricks."

"We've secured every brick the state can manufacture."

Fry could only shake his head. "You must have an army of masons."

"Armies of masons, armies of plumbers, carpenters—I think we've employed half the city."

"Employment the city desperately needs."

Yes, he thought. The great financial depression that had begun in the East had now reached California. Jobs were suddenly hard to find and coin shortages loomed once again.

"Sharon would like to see that hotel finished," Fry went on. "Says he's going broke with the escalating costs."

"It will return his investment one hundred-fold." He grew weary of Sharon's carping over the Palace. He excused himself, having to get back to the bank for a meeting with the diamond company geologist, Henry Janin.

***

Mottled grayish-blue Comstock ore tumbled out of huge hoppers, down long articulated chutes and into the waiting cars of the Virginia-Truckee Railroad. Sutro, sitting in his buggy, observed the orderly process, torn between disdain and admiration. It was, admittedly, an engineering achievement of the highest order. The railroad itself was an abomination, an insult to God, but the process of collecting and transporting the ore from the steep-flanked Mt. Davidson down to Carson City was something an engineer had to admire.

Damn that Sharon. Only through sheer determination and vengeful spite had he traversed endless canyons, steep grades, and treacherous passages, all with the sole purpose of defeating his tunnel. The station house was a cheerful red little *geschäft*, like a quaint hut of his Bavarian Alps—surely a fiendish stab at Herr Engineer's Prussian heritage.

The last of the St. Patrick's Day revelers were stumbling down Union Street. He watched them, thinking the celebration ridiculous, even if one had time for such things, which he did not.

As he observed the ore move in its remarkable, mechanical process toward the inevitable profits of mining and transportation, he did calculations in his head: each car could hold 250 tons of ore times 4 cars at $2 per ton came to $2,100. Two thousand dollars in royalties lost. In just one train-load. If they ran two trains per day, seven days a week, for a year...

He couldn't bear to think of it. About $760,000, his brain finishing the projections anyway. And the arrived-at figures didn't include the charges for draining water, moving equipment and timber, and other assessments he would be entitled to. Two years, maybe three, to finish the tunnel. Three times seven hundred...

Knowing how long the other great bonanzas had lasted, in two or three years the Consolidated Virginia would be in decline. And even if newer ores were found at depth, he continued to worry that the superintendents might not agree to use the tunnel. Might prefer the train. Fools, he had long since learned, came from all walks of life.

He watched the procession and considered his options. He could still hear, from years ago, Cornelius Vanderbilt's shocking words of advice. *If there's a profit to be made, I'll be a-selling a-fore you can say shipwreck.*

The cars were fully loaded, the ore heaped up in pied mounds. The locomotive blew its shrill whistle. Black smoke began to billow out of the smokestack. He watched, pondering his predicament as the train left the station and headed for Carson where the ore would be milled and turned into silver bullion. He shook his head. An impressive feat, that damn railroad.

***

Will found Henry Janin, and a companion, waiting for him in his office. The geologist introduced Clarence King, a broad-shouldered, rugged man with a well-trimmed, sandy blond beard. He looked Will straight in the eye while greeting him with a cool, dry hand. Janin, however, seemed nervous, his handshake clammy, eyes darting here and there.

Janin said: "Mr. King here is a surveyor." He stopped to swallow. "The government hired him to survey a railroad line in Colorado. Near the diamond fields."

"I see." He looked hard at him, but the scientist would not meet his gaze. King glanced at Janin, then at Will.

"I'll let Mr. King here tell you what he found."

He nodded. His pulse began to quicken.

"The government asked me to survey the area for natural resources, Mr. Ralston. I had heard rumors that Mr. Roberts and Mr. Janin here had found diamonds in the area, so I began a systematic search. The government, you understand, would want to know if the land were rich in precious stones before they sold the land to a railroad company."

"Of course."

"I completed my survey of the area, but didn't find any diamonds, sir. I figured I must have missed something and got to wondering where exactly the fields might be. As it happens, two of my men took a train the next day headed for San Francisco, and Mr. Janin here was on board along with your friends, George Roberts and Philip Arnold. My boys got to talking to your men and from casual conversation, were able to figure out where your boys had been working. So I went back out, you see, and my men and I spent three days in the area. We saw Arnold's tracks, so we knew we were in the right place. Anyway, Mr. Ralston, I'm here to tell you that we didn't find a darn thing. Mr. Janin and I are certain you've been taken, though I'm mighty sorry, sir, to be the one to have to tell you. I truly am."

"Harpending." Will looked from King to Janin. "Where is Harpending?"

Janin cleared his throat. "He's gone back to London, Mr. Ralston."

King leaned forward, placing forearms on his knees. He looked at Will. "I have contacts in London, say they saw Mr. Harpending with Arnold. They were there buying in the diamond markets. My friends know all the brokers and thought it was strange, these two Americans buying diamonds. So they noted it, you see."

No diamonds. Swindled after all. And not just by Arnold, but by Harpending! Will tried to maintain his composure, but felt a nausea coming on. So much hope he had invested this.

And Lent?

"Best I can tell," Janin said, "they were swindled just like you."

Will turned in his chair and stared at Louisa. What's next? Her gentle eyes and loving smile were there, as always, to see him through the darkest hours. But how much more upheaval could he endure? He had counted on the diamond fields and their substantial income, income that would now have to come from another source. Which source, he didn't know.

And Harpending. A traitor. Another friend who was no friend at all. Setting up an intricate ruse, playing him like a fiddle, luring him in with the guise of friendship, closer and closer, until he sprang the deadly trap. Was there a faithful man anywhere to be found? Did they all just lust after money, no matter the consequences?

He left for home early. Emelita ran to his arms when he came through the front door. His nine-year old daughter was still unabashed in her affection, a state that would change in a few years, he supposed. And so he treasured the innocence and lifted her up.

"What are you doing home, Papa?"

"I came to see you, of course."

She beamed, then kissed him on the cheek. "We're leaving," she informed him with a smile.

"Where are you going, my little dear?"

"Mama says we're going to see Samuel and Billy."

"Is that so?" Sam and Will, Jr. were away at boarding school in the East.

Elizabeth suddenly appeared, a little out of breath. She looked at Will, then at Emelita.

"What's this?" he said. He let his daughter down. She held his hand, but looked at her mother. "Emelita says you're planning a trip."

Flustered, Elizabeth sent their daughter to the nursery. Her trip, she said, was just to see their sons, whom she missed dearly, and besides, railroad travel was so convenient now it was just too much of a temptation. Simply put, she could not resist. Why she had not mentioned it earlier, she was not able to say.

"Lizzie," he said, trying to remain calm, "the state of affairs here, at the present time, is rather dire. The depression has hit us full on, there's talk of more bank runs, and, well, you have chosen an inopportune time to leave."

"Oh, but you'll be fine, Toppie. You always are. You come through every crisis better off than before. Certainly you don't wish me to plan my life around the Bank of California and all its ups and downs."

Of course, he suddenly thought. She was right. Just another crisis in a long series. They always looked the worst while in the midst.

"I asked father to come along, but he doesn't like to travel."

"What about Bertha?"

She looked down, perhaps sad, perhaps embarrassed. "She will remain home with the nursemaid."

In his disappointment, he studied her for a moment, she avoiding his gaze before leaving the room. She had appeared ready to speak, but evidently could not find the words. He loved her still, but, he decided, more like a sister than a wife. Her welfare was of great concern to him and he would always want the best for her. But the flame was almost extinguished. Her constant dissatisfaction and unhappiness were wedges driving them apart. And now, when he needed her, she was leaving. Again.

Chapter 42

Finn could hear voices. In the distance. Perhaps in another room, if it was a room he was in. Blindfolded, gagged, and tied, he couldn't know where he was. His head ached something awful. He struggled against the rope around his wrists, behind his back, and, when they didn't give way, he fell into a thrashing struggle, fighting the rope, the gag, the blindfold.

It was all for naught. He dropped his head to his knees, gasping for breath.

A door opened. Boots thudded on the floor. Then a blow to his side, in the ribs—he screamed into the rag. Pain radiated from his ribcage into his chest and stomach. He moaned, crumbling to one side.

"Hey, don't be passin' out on me."

He knew the voice. Coal-eyes. He was dragged into an upright position.

"We just want you to answer a question. Where is your tunnel stock? Tell us, and we'll let you go. Of course, if you weren't such a stupid son-of-a-bitch, you'd have sold it. But y'were too fucking dumb to do that."

Crowell hawked, then spit, the sound echoing in the small chamber. Phlegm sprayed Finn's arms and face. He didn't give a damn about the tunnel stock. He only cared about one thing.

"Now, you dumb Irish spud. I'm gonna ask you one more time, and yer gonna tell me where that goddamned stock is."

Fingers jerked the rag out of his mouth. Finn maneuvered his jaw, slowly; the muscles ached.

"Where are the certificates?"

"Where is Jessie?" Finn answered in a harsh whisper.

A blow to his face. Bare knuckles. Dull pain shot through his jaw and into his head. He wanted to yell out, but wouldn't give Crowell the satisfaction.

"That wasn't the answer I was lookin' for."

"I'll not tell ye a thing 'till I know where she is." He waited for the next blow. It didn't come. The stock, he reasoned through the throbbing pain, was his only leverage to make sure Jessie was safe. His trump card.

"How would I know where your little whore is? Do I look like her pimp?"

"If you'll bring her to me," he whispered, "so I can see her with my own eyes, I'll tell ye where to find the stock."

Now another blow to his face. He groaned in agony.

"I'm afraid it don't work that way. I'm the one's makin' the rules you dumb Irish potato farmer. Now, are you gonna tell me or not?"

Finn moved his head to one side, then the other.

"Have it your way, then."

A loud crack. His knee. A great, throbbing pain in his knee. Then another blow, and a cry of pain escaped his lips.

The rag was shoved back into his mouth. Then a smack to his head, adding to the already terrible pain. He fought for consciousness, but lost.

***

Sutro stood on the corner of Washington and Montgomery. To one side the stock exchange edifice arose, imposing and austere, to the other stood the Auction Lunch Saloon, gay and frivolous by nature. He clutched his satchel with a vise-like grip. And while on any other day he would enter the stock exchange without so much as a glance at the saloon, today he did the opposite.

Inside, his eyes adjusted to the dim light. Men, sitting at tables or at the bar, inspected him with quizzical glances as he walked in and took an empty table. He put the satchel on his lap and waited. A player-piano mechanically spilled out a rapid-fire version of Darling Nelly Gray. The barkeep chatted with his customers at the counter, each drinking whiskey. Sutro checked his watch: ten minutes early.

Now was the last opportunity to change his mind. Six years since he'd begun digging, eleven years since he'd conceived of the great work, and he could fight on, perhaps should fight on, but he was out of money and Congress (that club of fools and liars) had refused to fund the loan. The very loan recommended by its own committee. The body of fickle citizens known as the House of Representatives was more persuaded by avarice and power than by duty to their constituents. The bank crowd had their ear. Or their pocketbook. So, what was a sensible engineer to do?

A man dressed in a dark, broadcloth suit appeared in the doorway, scanning the room. His gaze rested on Sutro. He stood and motioned to him. The man weaved his way through the tables, then settled into a chair opposite Sutro.

"Do you have them?" the man asked.

He wastes no time, he thought. Good. A German, perhaps. He peered through the dim light but couldn't make out the features. In his satchel he found a large envelope, which he slid across the table.

"Yes. Here they are."

The man took the envelope, opened it for a quick inspection, and shoved it into his own bag. He looked at Sutro. "Any instructions?"

Sutro swallowed past a lump in his throat, then said, "Sell the shares in small lots so you do not attract notice. Otherwise, sell them quickly and at the best price you can get. Take your usual broker commission and deposit the rest in a Wells Fargo account in my wife's name. Leah."

The man nodded, stood up, shook his hand, then turned and retraced his steps through the saloon. Sutro, thinking he might reconsider, rose from his seat and opened his mouth. No words came out.

The broker disappeared out the door like a fleeting shadow. It was done.

Chapter 43

Finn opened his eyes to impenetrable darkness. Hot. So hot. Stifling, unbearable heat enveloped him like a steam bath. He tried to move but couldn't. Something was cutting into his flesh. Cold, sharp steel lanced his sides and back. The reek of filth overpowered him.

I'm alive, he thought. At least I think I am. Or, could this be hell?

Perhaps it was.

Silence. Ferocious silence. He tried to listen but there was nothing save the sound of his own breathing, and air passing through his nostrils, whistling in, then back out.

Jessie! Where was Jessie? There had been a fight after the St. Paddy's Day Parade. What had happened to her? Perhaps she was safe. Teaching school. Wondering where he was. Mary help me. Help Jessie.

He began thrashing about in a wild rage, but the restraints cut into his skin. Forced him into submission. He gasped for air, which came stale and heavy into his lungs. He knew that air. A mine shaft. Crowell had thrown him down a mine shaft, he realized with growing terror. He struggled desperately, but to no avail. The rag in his mouth had given way to his constant attempts to dislodge it with his tongue. Now, again, he moved his chin and jaw and tongue, fighting to push it out. Little by little, it moved, pressed against his teeth, which acted like a dam, stopping it. He bit down, trying to compress it, then pushed again with his tongue. Finally, it worked past his teeth and began to trickle out of his mouth. He spat out the last of it.

"Jessie," he screamed. "Jessie!"

"Mackie. Anyone." The blackness swallowed the sound.

He imagined what he could not see: ghoulish faces laughing at his terror, bony fingers poking, razor-like fingernails scratching. Rats, he was certain, gnawed at his toes. He flinched, violently, and pain stabbed at his ribs. He couldn't breathe and tried in vain to suck air into his lungs, gasping and wheezing. He heard a thud, thud, thud and thought it must be a Tommyknocker, Jesus, they'd come for him. But then realized it was his own heartbeat.

"Mary, help me," he said. And fervently, he prayed.

I'm here, Finn.

He heard the words, clearly, as if a church bell had sounded, the familiar calling. Was he dreaming?

"Joseph? Is that you?"

Aye, 'tis me.

"Ah, Joseph, you shouldn't be down here, down in this inferno."

You stayed with me, Finn, and I'll stay with you.

***

Will strolled into the dining room of the Pine Street house to find the nursemaid supervising Bertha's noon meal. At two years of age, his daughter had already developed strong opinions, at least with regard to food.

"I wasn't expecting you, Mr. Ralston." Henrietta glanced at him between attempts to coax food into Bertha's mouth.

"I've just come from the Palace and decided to lunch at home."

Bertha looked at him and smiled. "Poppy," she said. A cross between papa and Toppie, he always figured.

"I'll have the cook make you up some lunch, sir."

"No, Henrietta, you have your hands full. Don't concern yourself with me."

"You can have Bertha's lunch, I suppose," she said, trying to look sternly at her charge. "Little miss here doesn't seem to want it."

"No," declared Bertha, shaking her head. "Mine."

He chuckled. His daughter looked much like her mother: thick brown hair, porcelain complexion, eyes ablaze with passion. Her face, though, still round and cherubic, was part baby and part toddler. She sat in her special raised chair at the dining table, a piece of furniture that suddenly seemed ridiculously large. Empty. Forlorn, almost: a table in need of its family. He sat in the chair next to his daughter.

"Do you not like your lunch, Bertha?"

She vigorously shook her head.

He glanced at the nurse. "What is it?"

"A mush of corn and, well, I'm not sure what else. You'll have to inquire of the cook, sir."

He grimaced. Who could blame the child for not wanting to eat it? The bread on her plate appeared to have received some attention, he noticed.

Bertha, whose lips were sealed tighter than a locked vault, suddenly looked at him. "Mama," she said. Her eyes were big and brown and earnest.

He patted her head. "She is with Sam and Billy."

"Emmy," she said, inquiring of her sister.

"She's with Mama and Sam and Billy."

Her lower lip began to quiver.

"She asks me a dozen times a day," said the nurse, frowning. "I hardly know what to tell the child."

The little one seemed ready to cry at any moment. He stood, lifted her off her seat, and planted her feet on the ground. He grasped her hand. His daughter stared up at him, as did Henrietta.

"Come with me," he said. "We shall find ourselves something suitable to eat."

Will and his daughter strode past a smiling Henrietta into the kitchen. There they found the cook, Mrs. McMurty, polishing the bottom of a big brass pot, which she nearly dropped upon seeing the master.

"Good day, Mrs. McMurty. My daughter and I require some lunch. What can you recommend?"

The cook, dumbfounded, jumped off her stool, adjusting first her dress, then her hair. Bertha stared up her, then gazed in wonder at the kitchen: brass pots hanging from hooks, big wooden spoons in ceramic jars, vegetables spread out on the chopping board.

"Bertha is not especially fond of corn mush, it seems."

"I see." Mrs. McMurty looked terrified. "Well, sir, I'm beside myself trying to find something she'll eat."

"Very well then, why don't we ask her? What do you like, Bertha?"

His daughter just looked at him. The cook stared incredulously, first at little Bertha, then at Will. The world, it seemed, had just slipped off its moorings.

"How about bread?" Will knew Mrs. McMurty baked delicious bread.

Bertha nodded, smiling.

"All right then, Mrs. McMurty, bread it shall be. And put some jam on it, if you don't mind."

The cook grinned. "No sir, I don't mind at all. The missus wouldn't like it, I don't suppose, but if the master says so, who am I to question?"

"Precisely, Mrs. McMurty. You're a wise woman."

The door swung open behind them.

"Excuse me, Mr. Ralston," said Henrietta, "James Riker says, if you can spare the time, he has a message for you."

"Very well. Henrietta, see to it that my daughter has all the bread and jam she wants."

He smiled at his daughter and she smiled back. Her perfect little baby teeth and big dimples made him wonder if there was anything more delightful than a little girl.

He found his assistant waiting for him outside the front door. Riker bore his usual, unruffled demeanor. "The Colonel says he needs to see you right away."

"Where is he?"

"Says to meet him at the bank."

As Will threw his leg over the saddle, he wondered why Fry needed to see him. And why the rush? It could be that he had found a block of tunnel stock and needed instructions. Or maybe there was news on the Ophir: had they found the vein leading from the Con Virginia?

They rode at a brisk trot to the edge of Fern Hill, from where he could see Goat Island, and beyond that, the hills of Oakland. The pain of the diamond hoax still haunted him to distraction. In the middle of conversations, his friends would look at him, perplexed. He would be forgiven, naturally. Billy Ralston had a lot on his mind, they all knew.

"Now don't get me wrong, sons is just fine," James crooned (Will had told him about little Bertha), "carrying on the family name and all, but when yer daughter looks at you with those honey eyes, why you just melts. Least-wise I do, Mr. Chap."

Will smiled. "As do I, James."

At the bank, Will found Colonel Fry sitting stiffly in a chair outside his office. Fry stood when he saw his son-in-law. His shirt was unbuttoned at the top, tie loosened. Will noted his ashen face and knew something was amiss.

"Have you seen the Palace?" Will asked. They took seats at the opposite ends of a couch.

"I went by yesterday," said Fry.

"I was there for an inspection this morning. It seems our hotel has become a popular source of free entertainment. If you didn't know better, you'd think I was building a big stage."

A smile creased Fry's lips, then quickly vanished. "Hard times, I suppose. Lot's of men out of work."

Yes, he thought, and the Palace gives them hope. "You needed to see me, Colonel?"

"There is no easy way to tell you this, so I'm going to just say, straight out. Ophir stock has crashed. Your profits have vanished and you may even have a loss."

He stared at his father-in-law. Did he say the Ophir? But the Ophir was the next big bonanza. No, his information was wrong. A temporary swing in price perhaps, but nothing to get so worried about, surely.

"There must be some mistake."

Bloodshot eyes peered out at him through dark, cavernous sockets. The wretched expression sent a shiver of fear though him. No Ophir silver. No Arizona diamonds. No rail car contract. The hand of fate, once so generous, so benevolent...

"What happened?" He was determined to remain calm.

"There are rumors the Con-V ledge doesn't extend to the Ophir."

"But, that wouldn't explain a crash. Rumors of that nature would cause a drop in price, but not a complete collapse."

Fry, his facial muscles drawn taut, spoke with difficulty. "They are, perhaps, more than just rumors." He rubbed his hands on his pant-legs. "It appears that someone unloaded a large block of shares. Someone knowledgeable."

But no one else owned any large blocks.

"Who?" he demanded, his heart suddenly racing.

Fry seemed to have difficulty breathing. Will, concerned the elderly man's heart might fail, put a hand on his shoulder. "It's going to be all right, John. Just tell me."

His eyes red and close to tears, Fry focused his gaze on him. "It was Sharon. Sharon sold all his Ophir holdings. It caused a panic." Fry put a hand over his eyes and dropped his head.

He was certain he hadn't heard correctly. William Sharon? This could not be true. He and Sharon had had their disagreements, but after all these years, surely his partner would not betray him. He refused to believe it. There must be another explanation, or a mistake. Was the Colonel sure?

Fry remained hunched over, his whole body convulsing.

Will stared straight ahead, unable to blink or move. A full-grown man reduced to tears, gave him his answer. There was no other explanation. William Sharon, his partner, had betrayed him.

A clock chimed somewhere. He vaguely recalled Fry trying to console him before slipping out the door. Alone now, he stared at nothing, his mind a blank, unable to fathom what had happened. And then a noise out in the street roused him, and he pushed himself up and out of his chair. Outside his office, the bank had closed and was now empty. He must find his way home, to his wife, to his family. They were all he had left.

But Lizzie, he remembered, was gone.

Chapter 44

Finn heard voices.

Oh, voices. And kindly ones, at that.

The air was fresh. Cool even. He was flying. Or maybe floating. Oh but sweet angel wings must be carrying him. Either that or he was on a silver cloud. Ah, 'tis heaven, to be sure, he thought. I've made it to heaven and that's fine thing.

He opened his eyes, expecting to see Joseph. But it was John Mackay who looked down, studying him as if he were a strange creature from another world. The room was small with bare wood walls. Behind Mackie, he noticed a woman. She looked like Mrs. Robertson. Yes, Mrs. Robertson. That's why it looked familiar. He was in Mrs. Robertson's Bath House.

He suddenly became aware that he was, in fact, floating. In water. He jumped up, making a great splash but instantly put a hand to his side. Pain shot through his ribcage. His head ached something terrible.

"Hey, son, calm yourself. You need a bath."

Finn settled back into the warm water, taking shallow breaths to avoid the pain in his ribs. Purple welts covered his torso. He touched the lump on his head and winced.

He clutched Mackay's arm. "Mackie, I've got to find Jessie."

"Miss Ohhlson?"

"Aye. Have you seen her?"

"Not for a few days."

His mind raced. "I need some clothes. I've got to find her."

Mrs. Robertson picked up a kettle of water. "Don't you want some more hot water, Mr. Gillespie?"

"Nae, Mrs. Robertson, just my clothes, if you don't mind."

"I threw your foul clothes away," Mackay said. "But we got you some new britches."

He gingerly pulled on his clothes. He couldn't bend one leg—his knee was too swollen. He asked Mackie how they had found him.

"Sutro and Bethel were searching for you, said they hadn't seen you since St. Paddy's Day. Then we got word you were in an old winze in the Yellow Jacket. Not sure where the word came from, but that's where we found you, thanks be to God. Stuffed into a hoist bucket, you were."

"It was Crowell. He wanted the tunnel stock and I wouldn't part with it. Not unless he showed me Jessie. So he left me in the mine to die."

He sat to pull on his boots but couldn't bend that far. Mackay knelt down to help him.

"Have you seen that black snake?" Finn asked, trying his best to stuff his foot into a boot.

"Crowell? Nae, I haven't."

Boots on and dressed, he thanked Mrs. Robertson, and declared himself forever in debt to Mackay. He hardly remembered limping and running, limping and running, through the streets of camp, his mind intent on but one thing. In his room, he dislodged the floor board and peered inside. The stock certificates were gone.

He stood up ever so slowly, staring down at the floor. Jessie was the only one who knew of the hidden compartment. Had she given the certificates to Crowell? If so, where was that roach? And where was Jessie? He gazed about the room. Nothing seemed out of place. No one had ransacked it, to be sure. Then his eye caught something. On the desk. His Thomas Moore, that little blue octavo, a flower draped forlornly across its cover. An old, dried flower. He stared, disbelieving.

He rushed to the desk. It was his flower. Jessie's flower. The one he'd given her so long ago, that she'd kept it all these years, and yet, here it was, left behind, like a forgotten souvenir. Why? She had been with Ralston the day he had given it to her, in San Francisco.

Ralston.

***

Sutro found Leah sitting in the sunroom, her hands busy with knitting. He had always been fascinated by the speed with which her fingers accomplished their needlework, little digits repeating with precision and accuracy a rudimentary task. Impressive, but if given the time, which he would soon have in abundance, surely he could devise a machine that would do the work more efficiently, and faster too. The future, however, called for grander schemes than knitting. Their lives were about to change forever. The stockbroker had sold his tunnel stock, and just before the big crash. He now had over a million dollars sitting in Wells

Fargo Bank in San Francisco. That grand dame Providence continued to bless his life, impressed, no doubt, with his hard work, determination, and agile, forward-thinking mind.

Behind Leah, through the window, the desert stretched out as far into the distance as he could see. He had come to know this land better than any man. No one understood the hills, the soil, the water, the geography, and geology the way he did. He had lived with this land for fifteen years in a close partnership. The land would miss him, miss his ideas, miss his stewardship, but another land, another city, needed him now. Alas, the worthy are pulled in many directions.

This house he had built now belonged to the Sutro Tunnel Company. The town of Sutro, Nevada, also belonged to the company. And the Sutro Tunnel was now without its founder, its Chief Engineer and General Superintendent. Some might criticize him for selling out and leaving the McCalmonts with a mostly-worthless tunnel, of double-dealing, reaping unjust rewards, but those accusers didn't know the facts. Had he not been the victim of double-crossing, bribing, cheating, and sundry obstacles thrown maliciously in his path for the last fifteen years? Was it not just, that he finally reap some small reward for all his years of labor? Surely, no impartial jury would disagree.

He would now turn his attention to San Francisco, a growing city in need of his skills, his ideas, his foresight. Like Virginia City decades ago, San Francisco was a city in need of Adolph Sutro and his unique ability to investigate, analyze, and solve problems, and the city on the Peninsula had many problems, to be sure. He would humbly offer his services as Mayor, and should the fair citizens accept, he would take the helm and straighten out the mistakes of the past.

He sat beside his wife. She looked at him. Her hands stopped.

"Leah," he said, "I have some very good news."

***

He dreamed in the night of bank lines. They grew longer, in his dreams, longer and blacker until they reached like spidery appendages across the lobby floor, creeping all the way to the massive bronze doors before disappearing out into the street. Of the street, outside, he could see only a swirling fog. Chaos. In his dreams, panic reigned. But today, today he wasn't dreaming. Today there was calm. Lines, but calm lines. Orderly. Yes, he could almost convince himself. Almost, if not for their faces. Through the glass he could see the darting eyes, the tight lips, he could see his customers and friends, queued up like orderly, foolish lemmings about to go headlong over the cliff.

Will swept up a piece of paper, grasped the corner between his thumb and finger, and commenced the ritual tearing. A cone of white confetti grew atop his desk. He averted his eyes from the lobby. Withdrawals had been heavy all day, but nothing to worry about, as long as no one panicked, he thought, picking at the frayed edges.

A cruel thought kept coming to him: Sharon—his partner for Christ's sake—had betrayed him. The Ophir, his last and best hope to stave off disaster, to prevent the unthinkable. Ironic, the Ophir, where the Comstock Lode had been discovered, now a mere instrument of revenge. Oh yes, Sharon had finally gotten his revenge. He had always resented Will's San Francisco, the fine carriages, the high-blooded horses, the majestic Golden Gate. And

Belmont, of course. Sharon coveted the Peninsula estate, a bucolic gem to make any man weak with jealousy, but especially one so arrogant, so convinced of his—

A knock at the door startled him. Riker's black face appeared in the doorway. His aching fingers gratefully let loose the paper.

"A Miss Gustavson here to see you, Mr. Chap."

He grimaced, exhaled sharply, then nodded. He wasn't in the mood for solicitors, but could use a better distraction.

A blue satin dress swooshed into his office and floated toward his desk. He stood and exchanged a firm handshake with a surprisingly handsome spinster. The dress, he observed, directing her to a chair, was handmade but not without fashion. She gave him a pamphlet. He pretended to read it but studied her instead, surreptitiously. Little dimples winked at him from her rosy complexion. Tresses of blond curls betrayed only hints of gray.

"A fine Scandinavian name, Gustavson," he said, setting down the un-read pamphlet.

"Thank you."

"And where were you born?"

"Stockholm."

"Ah, I should have guessed it. Swedish women are the most beautiful in the world." She turned crimson from neck to high cheekbones. He observed the display with relish—he never tired of seeing a woman blush. "Pardon my loutish manners, Miss Gustavson. I couldn't help myself."

Composing herself, she looked at him with smiling welkin eyes that boldly held his gaze. He really needn't apologize, she assured him, her eyes mesmerizing with seeming ease. As the pamphlet explained, she was there on behalf of a group of Scandinavian women with a common purpose: to purchase a home in San Francisco. It would be a gathering place, and a shelter for those ladies who had fallen on hard times. By chance, there was a house on Clay Street, which they thought perfect, and they were now in search of donations. "We believe," she said, "that a small contribution from William Ralston will lend our cause great credibility."

He found her irresistible. Her eyes were playful, her smile beguiling yet innocent. He must help her. He rose from his chair and extended his hand. "Miss Gustavson—" he began...

She stood up, crestfallen. "Miss Gustavson," he laughed, "you needn't worry. I have been blessed with great fortune in my life. I would be honored if you would allow me to give you the entire sum to purchase your home."

Her eyes swam with tears. She grasped his hands. Her face was for a second time overcome by a deep and gratifying blush.

"Mr. Ralston," she exclaimed. "How can we ever thank you? Goodness, you are an angel from heaven."

He assured her it was only a trifle and begged that she keep the donation quiet. She was to see his secretary, Mr. Franklin, who would draw the funds from his, Will's, personal account. She left, dabbing her eyes with a handkerchief.

He took up his mail, read letters, penned a few responses. Men and women seeking advice, needing employment—and donations, of course. These he would give, if only he had more, to his friends, his fellow-citizens. To San Francisco. Noise from the lobby stole into his office, distracted him, one worry displacing another. He rose and went to the window. The crowd had grown even larger. Closing his eyes, he refused to let his imagination run away. Perhaps I'd better check with Tibbey, he thought. His trusted head teller was as steady as a mountain and almost as big, giving off an air of confidence through his sheer size and booming voice. But before he could reach the door, it opened and the teller himself stepped into the office.

"Coin supplies are starting to run low, Mr. Ralston."

"Send someone to the Treasury."

Tibbey's eyes darted here and there. "We've already been to the Treasury this morning. But, you see Mr. Ralston, it's not simply a matter of coin."

Will stared at him. "What is it?"

"Customers are withdrawing all their funds and closing accounts. If this continues, our loan portfolio will soon be out of balance with deposits."

From the corner of his eye, the lobby vibrated like a simmering caldron, and the dreaded word pushed against the barricades of his mind. Out of balance with deposits, he thought. Is that what tellers fear in those endless dark hours of the night? He almost smiled.

"I'll see if I can calm them down for you, Mr. Tibbey."

He strode out of his office like a headmaster off to quiet a bunch of rowdy schoolboys, his trusted enforcer two steps behind. Wading into the crowd, he saw familiar faces. With an easy smile and dry handshake, he greeted them, and the customers buzzed around him as if he were there to dispense money, goodwill, confidence.

"Billy Ralston! It's Billy Ralston."

"How are you, Mr. Johnson." He shook hands with his long-time customer.

"Just fine, Mr. Ralston, sir."

"If it's too crowded for you, Horatio, you can come back tomorrow. Your money is safe with the Bank of California. You know that."

"The misses, Mr. Ralston. She insists I get our money out. What little we have and all."

"You're welcome to do that. Your money is right there waiting for you."

He turned, undaunted, to another customer, smiling as if he hadn't a care. "And Mr. Marshall, is your wife worried as well?"

"Oh, no sir, not my wife. It's just that there's rumors, you see."

"Now Jasper, how long have you been banking with me?"

"Going on two decades, I suppose."

"And have any of the rumors ever been true?"

Mr. Marshall hesitated while he considered this. "Well, no, I suppose not."

"Of course they haven't. And any rumors you've heard lately are not true, either."

Mr. Marshall looked down at the papers in his hand, then glanced at the surrounding crowd. They seemed to be waiting for his response, as if he had been appointed as judge and jury on the spot. The man whose reasoned decision, after hearing all arguments, would decide the fate of the great bank.

"I, uh, I suppose you're right, Mr. Ralston. But meaning no disrespect to you, because you're the finest man in all of San Francisco, and I trust you like my own brother. But I need to withdraw today, then wait and see, and if all the trouble settles down, well then, I'll bring the money right back. You have my word on that, Mr. Ralston."

The hungry quake, Will knew, had arrived.

The crowd buzzed louder, the vibrations surging through the packed lobby and out the great bronze doors to the dark, unruly mob outside. He turned and calmly walked back to his office. Standing behind his desk, he stared at the little image of Louisa Thorn. What shall I do, he silently inquired, knowing her wisdom had never failed in an hour of need. What will become of our city?

He looked up to see Tibbey, solemn-faced, then glanced back at Louisa. He wished she didn't have to witness this. Beyond the glass, the crowd had fallen into the dreaded panic. Swallowing his fear, he examined his options. Who could help him? They would need access to substantial capital. Sharon, of course, wasn't an option. Fry had gone back east to join Lizzie. Leland Stanford, Harpending, Mills...

He had to face the truth: he was alone. No one would see him through this crisis. No one could help him.

"How did it come to this, Mr. Tibbey?"

The head teller's eyes glistened; he could find no words, it seemed. "You'll be fine, sir," he managed. "You always find a way."

"No, Mr. Tibbey. Not this time."

"Don't say that, sir. Billy Ralston can do anything, anything he sets his mind to." The poor man's voice almost cracked.

"I'm sorry, Ed." This is the end, he wanted to say. I can do no more.

Tibbey's gaze fell to the floor.

Will stared aimlessly into the chaotic lobby, hands in his pockets. There was liberation in finally giving up. Policemen could be seen outside the giant front door, waiting to do their duty should chaos turn to riot. He felt the gaze of the dark-haired girl who sat serenely on his desk, her confidence in him as unwavering as her smile.

"Lock the doors, Mr. Tibbey." His eyes went to Louisa. "The Bank of California is out of business."

Chapter 45

That night there were no dreams of bank lines. He rested well in the quiet, empty house in the city, like the soldier after a terrible battle, a battle that was lost and yet now, for the moment, left him at peace. He had fought the good fight. In the morning, he headed for the bank: he had been summoned. In the streets, life was oddly normal, with pedestrians, carriages, horse traffic, greetings from perfect strangers. At the bank, however, policeman guarded the entrance and crowds lingered outside, they, his customers, hoping for some miracle that their savings might still safe behind the great bronze doors.

He entered on Sansome and climbed the stairs to the second floor, legs weary, feet like anvils. His steps echoed behind him, the empty lobby as silent as a tomb. No customers or employees. Like a Sunday, except it was Friday. The day after the Bank of California had closed its doors. Last night, while he slept a dreamless sleep, auditors had pored over the books.

He knocked on the door. A meeting of the board of directors was in progress. His old friend, Dr. Pitman, opened the way for him. At the long, mahogany conference table he knew all the faces: Lewis McLane, John Earl, Rich Jessup…but his eyes were elsewhere. Mills sat at one end, at the other, William Sharon. Why was Sharon there? This was the penultimate insult, to have this villain participating in a board meeting. In this board meeting.

One seat in the middle of the table was empty.

Mills stood and motioned towards the empty chair. "Please sit down, Chap."

He took his seat. A hastily prepared report sat on the table, staring up at him.

Mills shuffled through papers. "The accountants have worked all night and prepared balance sheets and income statements. These are before you." He glanced at Will. "The results are alarming."

Will recognized his cue to open the report, which he had no intention of doing. "Give me a summary, if you would be so kind."

"You are indebted to the bank," Mills said, referring to his papers, "for various unauthorized loans, in the sum of $9,565,907." He enunciated the figure with careful precision.

Will gathered a deep breath, then exhaled slowly. "I am aware of the amounts. The papers are in order and the loans will be repaid."

"In order," said Mills, "except they were unauthorized."

"I authorized them."

"This is not your personal bank," Mills said. "You of all people should understand, this is a corporation, and you are a stockholder, just as I am. All the men in this room are owners of this bank and none of us is allowed to borrow money without proceeding through the proper channels. You have, it seems, abused your position as president."

"These loans will be repaid."

"With what?" It was Sharon. All eyes turned in that direction. Except Will's. He refused to so much as look at the man, the Benedict Arnold whose treacherous self-dealing had created this disaster. A traitor if ever there'd been one. He focused instead on Darius Mills, the man he knew carried the most influence.

"I have substantial assets," Will said, "that can be liquidated, if necessary, although I can assure you such an extreme measure is not warranted under the circumstances. We are facing a terrible depression, one that began, I hasten to add, on the East Coast. But regardless, this downturn will be followed by a powerful expansion. They always are. My holdings are well situated to profit from the inevitable rebound. The woolen mills, the cigar factory, the furniture plant, the water company—all will generate significant revenues once the depression ends. And I will gladly assign mortgages to the bank on each of these companies, so it will be protected."

"Mortgages will not suffice, I am sorry to say." It was Sharon again.

Will steadfastly refused to look at his former partner. "I was not aware that Mr. Sharon's view in these matters was dispositive."

Mills leaned forward and rested his forearms on the table. "We discussed this option before you arrived and reached the conclusion that the businesses are worthless. They are unprofitable. Mortgages on them will not, as Mr. Sharon says, suffice."

"They aren't profitable at present, but they are well-established businesses. To say they are valueless is absurd."

"Nevertheless..."

This word hung in the air for a moment. Will's slumping shoulders began to give way to stiffening anger. The instinct to stand and fight was taking hold. He straightened his back, then looked at each man. One at a time.

"As I look at you," he said, "men I have known and worked with for many years, it strikes me that each of you has reaped untold profits from our association. You have profited from the sweat of my brow, from my intimate knowledge of banking, from my hundreds of contacts and relationships with bankers and businessmen, from California to New York, from Europe to Japan. Each of you who cared nothing about the intricate operations of this enterprise as long as you received your one percent each month. A dividend I maintained and paid, month after month, without ever missing a single one until now, despite any difficulties I may have been experiencing, or depressions in the economy. These you received like clockwork with a greedy hand and knowing smile. And now, after having become rich beyond measure on the back of my innovations and hard work, you would watch me dangle from a tree, the vigilante lynch mob having found its scapegoat."

He tried to make eye contact with each of them, but most looked down. The room was silent. Will's anger continued to boil. That they would turn on him in his darkest hour was despicable. Bloodthirsty leaches, all.

Sharon sat up and cleared his throat. Now Will fixed his gaze on him. Black irises stared back, dark, remorseless: a panther, scarcely believing his good fortune, ready to pounce.

"That's a commendable speech. Except you've forgotten something. I warned you. Mr. Mills warned you. Even Colonel Fry warned you, or so he has told me. Your investments faltered and yet you continued to pour money into them. And rather than take the prudent course and sell, you invested in ever more speculative ventures."

He alluded to the diamond fields, Will knew, his face growing hot. This man who had himself been swindled once, long ago, but evidently forgot that it was William Ralston who offered a helping hand, a loan, and a job.

Sharon continued. "We all attempted to counsel that you were spending recklessly, investing poorly, and living too lavishly. But you refused to heed our warnings."

"I live only to benefit this bank and this city," he shot back. His damp collar chaffed at his skin. "What would you have me do, entertain the Japanese ambassador at the Poodle Dog?"

"Your infatuation with this city is notorious, and frankly ridiculous," Sharon responded. "No man can support an entire city. This obsession with San Francisco borders on lunacy."

"It is far less offensive than avarice and jealousy," said Will. "Your obsessions of choice."

"Any supposed obsessions I am accused of having do not threaten the wellbeing of our fellow stockholders." Sharon was now becoming red in the face.

"What is good for San Francisco is good for the Bank of California, and vise versa. I have lived by this tenet and it has never failed me."

"Until now."

"All that has failed me is you, sir," Will shouted. "A backstabbing, greedy traitor."

Sharon shot up out of his chair. "I will not abide any man to address me in such a fashion."

Mills stood, raised his arms. "Gentlemen. We must conduct ourselves with a modicum of decency. These are difficult discussions and we mustn't make them any worse with incendiary remarks."

Will fumed. These arrogant fools. Did they think they could do better? Let any one of them run the bank and return the dividends he had over all these years.

"What do you propose then?" he said, impetuously. He had grown weary of the sparring. Time to get to the point.

No one spoke. He waited.

Mills cleared his throat. "We have drawn up an agreement here, which requires your signature. This, I am afraid, we all see as the only solution."

The papers were passed down the table and placed before him. He read for several minutes, disbelieving.

"I agree to resign my position, effective immediately?" he read out loud.

"I am afraid so," said Mills.

He read further, then stopped and looked at Mills, mouth agape. "This requires that I assign all my assets..." His voice faltered. "It requires that I assign all my real and personal property over to William Sharon?"

Darius Mills looked at him as though at an errant child. His eyes were sympathetic. "If Mr. Sharon takes control of your property, he will have the utmost incentive to manage those assets to both his advantage and the bank's. We are unanimous in our agreement that this is best strategy."

Belmont. His horses. *The Palace*. It was to be Louisa's Palace. No, God. He couldn't comprehend this, like being asked to give up your children. Inconceivable. And Lizzie, and the children, where would they live? How would he support them?

William Sharon withdrew a pen from his shirt pocket and handed it to John Earl, who sat beside him. From man to man, director to director, the pen was relayed down the length of the table until it finally landed in Will's hand. He stared at the signature line, feeling the eyes of his once-friends upon him, vultures waiting to feast on his corpse.

He wrapped his fingers around the pen, staring at the agreement. If he signed, he would have nothing. But, of course, he had nothing anyway: all his friends had left him. Belmont and the horses and the bank, it all meant nothing if he was alone.

He grasped the pen and firmly scratched his signature: William C. Ralston—founder, and former president, of the Bank of California.

Chapter 46

Finn limped along behind an employee of the Bank of California, who marched soldier-like across the black and white marble floor. The lobby was eerily quiet except for the footsteps of two or three clerks who moved about behind the imposing wooden counter. An hour earlier, he had worked his way through the crowds mingling outside only to find the bank locked and guarded like a giant, blue fortress. An Irish policeman had gotten a message inside that Finnian Gillespie needed to speak to William Ralston.

And then he saw it, just ahead: a wide, glass wall, and inside, William Ralston, sitting at his desk. The great man with a kingly girth and bearing, clad in a white shirt and bowtie, impeccable beard trimmed short, seemed occupied in deep thought. Finn's guide paused before the office door.

***

Will was sitting at his desk. The envelope stared up at him, the envelope that he could ignore no longer. He picked it up. Grasping it in his fingers, he thought back to that day, some fifteen years ago, when he had visited Jess's apartment, the mementos collected on a little table, and underneath them, an envelope, embossed with a grandiose letter V. Jess, given it by her dying mother, had entrusted it to him. He unfolded the parchment paper, its yellowed edges frayed and worn.

Dear Miss Ohhlson,

I showed your letter to my attorney. The claim that I am responsible for your maternal condition is unfounded, even libelous, or so he tells me. Be forewarned, I am not one you wish to have as an enemy. I have aught but fond memories of you, and our friendship, and prefer to keep it that way. If you will cease in making such claims, I will honor the enclosed bank draft. These funds you can use to become established in some arrangement suitable to you and your little girl. I wish you the best, but please do not contact me again.

Sincerely,

Cornelius V

He stared at the letter, disbelieving, his heart pounding. Could this be true? That damned, selfish scoundrel Vanderbilt, the son-of-a-bitch who had taken Louisa to Europe on a death-voyage, father of children he probably didn't even know existed. Well, here was proof enough of one child. Jess, the family resemblance, she and Louisa of the same blood, which meant Jess was...

A knock came at the door. "Someone to see you, Mr. Ralston."

He stuffed the letter into his pocket.

***

"Mr. Ralston says you may go in," his escort announced.

Finn stepped into the office feeling like a Christian entering the Coliseum. So, he thought, this is the heart of the mighty empire, where insignificant lives are manipulated and sacrificed for nefarious purposes. Had it been under normal circumstances, he would have been nervous, but today he was afraid of only one thing: hearing the truth about Jessie. He strode up to Ralston's desk. As he drew near, the banker's face came into focus. Finn stopped, taken aback. This was not the face of Caesar, but that of a tortured soul stretched out on the rack for too many agonizing days. Deep lines etched the skin, lines that told a sorrowful tale. The eyes, too, cried out in pain. Here was a man who had known of bitter calamity. The tragedy in that face tugged unexpectedly at Finn's heart. What had made him so, this great man?

"Please, have a seat." Ralston motioned for him to sit.

They looked at each other for a moment. Jessie was the only connection between them, and both wondered what she saw in the other.

"You said you needed to see me." Ralston studied him, as if curious.

"Aye. I am here to find Jessie. 'Tis my belief she has come to San Francisco, and that perhaps she was after seeing you."

"If you're asking have I seen her, then yes, I have. A day or so ago."

Finn was relieved and distressed at the same time. So she had come to Ralston. "If you don't mind me asking, could you tell me why she was here?"

"She was here because of you."

"Because of me?"

Ralston studied him. "And perhaps you can tell me what brought you here to my office."

"She took my stock and I'm after thinking she gave it to you. All of Virginia knows you and Sharon covet Sutro Tunnel stock. And Jessie made off with mine. I don't care about the stock, truth be told, but she's dear to me and I need to know why she would do such a thing. If it's you she loves, and not me, I only need to know it."

The banker smiled ironically. "You have it all wrong, son." He opened a drawer in his desk and withdrew an envelope, which he slipped across the desk. Finn picked it up, turning it in his hands. Then, warily, he pried it open and removed the paper inside.

"What is it?"

"A bank draft. A Wells Fargo bank draft. I told her a Bank of California draft wouldn't do you much good."

Finn studied the paper. $62,000 was printed across the front.

"Jaysus. Where did she get sixty two thousand dollars?"

"She sold your tunnel stock."

He looked at Ralston. "And why would she do such a thing?"

"My boy, no one can comprehend the ways of that mysterious girl. But suffice to say that, right after she sold it, Sutro unloaded all his stock, the market crashed, and if you still had it, the stock would be worthless."

"Jesus, Mary, and Joseph." He stared at the note. He suddenly winced at a pang of guilt. *Oh what a great, cowardly fool I am.*

"But where is she, sir? Did she have the mark of fear on her? Had she been harmed?"

"No. Although she did seem anxious."

"Did she say why?"

"Just that she was worried about you."

"I was fearful that Sharon's men had done her harm, as they did me."

"Sharon's men did that to you?"

"They did."

Ralston sighed deeply and closed his eyes. "So that's it," he muttered. "The cursed Sutro Tunnel stock."

"What do you mean then, sir?"

"It seems she won your freedom with that stock. Counterfeited stock, that is. Not sure how she did it, but she's very resourceful. They won't be happy when they discover it."

He studied Ralston, trying to piece it all together. Then he remembered the Thomas Moore book. He took it from his pocket, turned it in his hands, then laid it on the table. He opened the cover to reveal the flower, still there, quiet and forlorn.

Ralston seemed transfixed at the sight. "Mr. Gillespie," he said, "I suggest you go and find her right away."

"Aye, I must. But is everything all right then?"

"She has told you where to find her," he said.

His knee buckled with pain as he stood. He steadied himself, took a step toward the door, then stopped and turned back. He extended his hand to Ralston, who took it, and they looked each other in the eye.

"Goodbye," Finn said.

"Goodbye."

***

Will's gaze followed the limping Finn Gillespie out of his office, across the empty lobby, and out the front door. Jess's letter burned in his pocket. Her secret, forever safe. He could never have imagined these things, Jess's parentage, that his decade-old war with Sutro would have had such consequences.

The empty desk before him, cleaned of all paper and books and other items, he no longer had use for. Empty save one thing. Louisa. There she sat on her delicate pedestal, looking at him. Smiling. Always smiling. This is what he had come for, and he lifted the picture off the desk and slipped it into his vest pocket. There was something he needed to show her. He strode out of his office, into the lobby, past the great glass wall through which he could see his now-clean desk, then continued over the marble floor and beneath the angels high above, until he reached the main entrance. The enormous bronze doors swung wide to let him pass, then closed with an emphatic boom.

***

"There's eight hundred rooms."

"Eight hundred?"

"And each has its own fireplace and bath."

"I don't believe it."

"It's God's truth."

Will, standing among the Friday crowd gathered to witness the finishing touches to the Palace Hotel, watched, and listened. And the men talked.

"Underneath, in the sub-basement, there's a 630,000 gallon reservoir. That's what supplies all the water for the baths and such."

"Where does all the water come from?"

"Artesian wells."

"That's a lot of water."

"Yes, it is. But, up there, on the roof, is another tank that holds 130,000 gallons. That's for the fire hoses. The Palace will be completely fireproof."

"Fireproof?"

"And impervious to earthquakes, too."

"I was here for the earthquake in '68. Those walls would have to be mighty strong to hold up to that kind of shaking."

"The walls are extra thick and the bricks laid with special mortar. And they're all connected with metal ribbon. I seen it with my own eyes. No earthquake will knock down the Palace Hotel. I guarantee it."

"How do you know so much about this place, anyway?"

"I've been standing here every day for months, watching it grow like it was a child. I know everything there is to know about her. Made some good friends here, too. See over there? That's Hank. And that there's Isaac. They're out of work, just like me. Seeing this hotel go up, somehow it just makes us feel good. Like there's hope, you might say. So we just keep comin', day after day."

"Yeah. I see what you mean, I suppose."

"You see those bricks? When the masons were workin', they laid 300,000 a day."

"Jimminy Cracket!"

"That Billy Ralston bought every brick around."

"He must have more money than the King of England, that Billy Ralston."

"England don't have a king. Haven't you heard of Queen Victoria?"

"Ah Christ. He's a rich son of a bitch, that's all I know."

"Yep. You're right about that. Good to know if you ask me. As long as Billy Ralston is watchin' out for San Francisco, we'll be all right."

Will patted the outline of ivory in his breast pocket. Yes, Louisa would be proud of this, his greatest triumph.

"I've been lookin' for ya, Mr. Chap."

Will turned to see James Riker. "It's always a safe bet to look for me here, James."

"That'd be true, which is why I came here first."

"It's a beautiful hotel, don't you think?"

"Yes, indeed. The grandest, most wondrous thing I ever laid eyes on."

"I'm glad you think so."

Together they watched. Men carried huge rolls of carpets through the front entrance—a giant doorway big enough for carriages to enter and drop off the guests inside, right at the registration desk. Painters could be seen through the windows, busy with their brushes. The final details. Soon it would be ready to open.

"I'll be needing my horse, James. I'd like to ride Sir Walter."

Riker had a look of profound concern. "Where are you goin', Mr. Chap?"

"For a swim, James. A swim in the Bay."

Chapter 47

Where could she be? San Francisco had been his home, but now it seemed a hostile place to Finn, a place where one could hide and not be found amid the sea of faces. Jessie had melted in among that sea of faces. He traversed the streets of the business district with an ache in his knee, limping, craning his neck this way then that at every blond head or fair complexion. Rushing carriages banged and clattered across the wood and cobblestone streets, charging through intersections, intent on pedestrian murder if one didn't know better. He found himself flinching at the giant horses, flying by so close he could hear their groans and creaking leather. The sidewalk, too, a cattle stampede of jostling and pushing, everyone off to save civilization or buy a new hat.

Gray and cool, the day seemed as disheartened as he, unable to shake the gloom. If not the business district, then where? Limping on, he knew only that he must keep searching. Time was precious. Ralston's anxious face kept appearing: find her right away, he'd said, as if fearing some impending doom.

Had he just sold the bloody stock to Sharon.

He began the climb up Pacific Street. Ahead, Russian Hill seemed like an insurmountable obstacle. He heaved a great sigh.

Like a blind man in the wilderness, I am. His knee and ribs hurt more with each step. But those pains seemed minor irritations compared to the guilt. She was as true as the North Star, Jessie was. How the wily Devil had tricked him into doubting this, he couldn't fathom. He would fall at her feet and beg forgiveness, yet again.

The book, tucked in the jacket pocket, bounced off his hip, as if demanding attention. What an odd rhythm it made with his limp, hitting his side with each step. Thump. Thump.

Jaysus!

He stood still and thrust his hand into the pocket. The book, suddenly stubborn, became entangled with the fabric and refused to come out. He wrestled with it, aggravated, pulling and twisting. Finally, the jacket released its grip. Out came the little blue book. With a fingernail he opened it to where the flower lay hidden.

'Tis the Last Rose of Summer.

And the answer came to him. He knew exactly where to find Jessie.

***

A man lives with the knowledge that his labors will be in vain, that the ravages of time, whether human or geologic, will ultimately raze the structures built with his blood and sweat. But a man will build nonetheless, and with a quixotic zeal, driven, as if by some demon. Such a man can only hope that his particular Great Monument will outlast all the rest, it being the work of his singular genius, worthy of a distant time and solemn tribute. The blood is spent, the sweat invested. The goal comes nigh, complications arise, pressures mount, human frailty, espe-cially human frailty, undermines the foundation.

To Will, there could be no greater ambition than to transform a crude, lawless outpost on the edge of civilization into a magnificent city. To recognize the God-given charm of a golden peninsula, and to build there something worthy of its grace. The land and the city, the one beau-tiful to begin with, the other painstakingly crafted to enhance that beau-ty. Like the perfectly fitting gown on a shapely woman.

Atop Sir Walter, Will rode up and across Russian Hill. He steered the big chestnut gelding onto Larkin Street, heading to-ward the Bay, and they climbed up the grade past fine houses, all freshly painted, their terraced gardens bursting with daisies and poppies. At Union Street, the Bay came into view. The wild beauty of it struck him nearly blind, as if seeing it for the first time. To the left, the Golden Gate, on the far side, Marin with its green grass and tree-spotted hills. And just below, Alcatraz, so vivid and close he could surely jump off of Russian Hill and land atop it.

At Greenbush, his faithful mount began the steep descent to the beach just as a billowy, white vapor of fog pushed through the Gate and into the Bay. Sir Walter was skittish on the steep downgrade and suddenly pulled up, tossing his head, as though not wishing to go any further. Will patted him on the neck. "On you go, now." He nudged the horse with his heels and began a slow, uneven descent.

At the foot of Larkin, he tied the reins to a post. Stroking his nose, Will fed his favorite horse an apple. Flecks of whitish hairs around the snout told of the animal's advancing age. He hoped his old companion would have a long and easy retirement.

Neptune's Beach House hadn't changed over the years. Brought to life, it seemed, as a dilapidated shack, it stood like an old, ravaged spinster, skin gray and gnarled by the salty air. He put on his swim attire, then made his way to the end of the pier. Today he would dive off the pier, something he had thought to do but never had. It was a day for firsts. Not far off shore, a small, sternwheeler lay anchored, its decks quiet, waiting patiently for her crew to return.

His toes curled over the edges of the wooden planks. Six feet below, gentle swells passed through the footings before lapping against the sandy beach, which today was free of children and dogs and grandmothers. He flexed his arms, swung them back and forth, then around and around, warming the muscles before delivering them up to the shock of icy water.

"Hey, mister!"

A boy waved from the other end of the pier.

"Have you ever been swimming in the Bay?"

He had, Will assured him.

"All right then. Watch out for the currents. They're flowing like the Mississip' out there today."

He waved a thank you. He turned his gaze back to the Bay, unconcerned about the currents that he knew better than anyone. Alcatraz loomed out of the water like a defiant challenge. Today he would swim to the stony fortress. Why not?

He dug his toes into the planks, bent his knees, and dove, head first into the water.

***

Finn stood across the street from the little bookstore, the memories flooding over him of a day long ago. Jessie leading him there, toying with him, then disappearing entirely, but not before leaving the little blue book for him at the counter. The prig-of-a-merchant, disgusted at Finn's illiteracy. Now, thanks to Jessie, he could read.

Through the wavy panes of glass he could make out blurred figures inside. The name on the window, Russian Hill Books, obscured his vision further—he hadn't been able to read those words years ago. On the street of this more genteel neighborhood, the horses stepped grandly and the carriages rolled quietly and with less urgency. A half a block up, a large wagon sat idle behind two, enormous black steeds, its driver asleep beneath a hat. Horses were tied to a post outside the bookstore, swishing their tails at flies. An afternoon fog was rolling in through the Gate; the temperature beginning to drop. Finn's knee grew stiff, aching. He lifted his foot up and down, trying to keep the joint free, buttoning his coat for warmth at the same time.

He heard a jingle and looked up. The door to the bookstore swung open. In the doorway, she appeared, her arms full of books. Jessie. Her green dress, pressed by a breeze to reveal long shapely legs, mimicked the white bodice, fit snuggly to her torso. And before the door had even closed behind her, she looked straight at Finn, as if she expected him to be there. She came to the edge of the sidewalk wearing a lovely, heartbreaking smile. The mists passed between them. He went to the edge of the walk but, about to step, his knee suddenly gave way. His step faltered. She reached out to him, her face drawn with concern.

From the side, he noticed the sleepy driver stirring in the cold fog. Finn tried to step off the sidewalk, but his knee buckled again. He grabbed hold of a post, steadying himself. Jessie took handfuls of green fabric into one hand, holding her books in the other.

The driver, now awake, gathered his reins.

She stepped down off the sidewalk, her eyes unwavering, looking straight into Finn's. The wagon driver clapped his reins. The horses bolted.

Jessie, like a ballerina, seemed to glide across the wooden street, her slipper-clad feet racing toward Finn. He could see her eyes, full of affection, earnest and tender.

The wagon sent up a great clamor. Horse hooves pounded like kettle drums. Finn glanced toward the noise, suddenly fearful. And then he saw him. Coal-eyes.

Crowell drove the wagon straight at Jessie, clapping the reins. Curses rained down—"double crossing whore," he spat—

"Jessie," Finn shouted.

She stopped to look at him. Questioning. Then she saw the wagon.

Finn leaped off the sidewalk, but his knee refused, and he collapsed.

The wagon and horses thundered down.

***

He dives off the pier and into the frigid water. It's so cold he can hardly breathe; he had forgotten how cold the water could be. He forces his arms into a crawl, moves his feet—they flutter meekly against the surface, a glaze of murky green. He glides slowly away from North Beach. Towards Alcatraz. There is a ship moored in the cove, a sternwheeler, its anchor rope burly and taut, holding fast against time and current. He sees the ship with each breath, each turn of the head. There is no one on board, that he can see.

Stroke. Kick. A methodical rhythm. Slow and steady. Already he can feel the currents, their inevitable tug toward the Golden Gate. He adjusts his course, estimating the geometry in his head, a moving triangle: he, the Gate, Alcatraz. The fog lies just above like a great downy blanket about to settle over the bridal bed.

***

Finn pushed himself up through stabbing pain. He jumped into the street and lunged for Jessie. His knee cracked. The two of them tumbled over the blocks. Crowell's wagon flew past and, carried by momentum, crashed a moment later.

***

He has made it beyond the ghostly ship, out into the restless Bay. He feels the turbulence just beneath him. The currents tug at his limbs, his swimming attire heavy, sail-like, pulling him off course. Alcatraz lies ahead, the Golden Gate to his left. Pacific fog is poking its long, gray finger into the harbor. He is numb to the cold now, stroking the water with heavy arms, kicking with reluctant feet. Waves slap rudely at this face when he turns to breathe. It has been several years since he swam and his body protests against the exercise, his lungs heave for air.

He swims. He can see Alcatraz up ahead, under a veil of mist. Waves beat against its rocky limbs, all elbows and knuckles and foam. It seems very distant, unattainable. The numbness is failing him; he can feel the cold, icy and penetrating. The fog approaches.

***

Finn and Jessie huddled close in the middle of the street. Books were strewn about, splayed open with pages torn and flapping. Some pages drifted across the street in the breezes.

"The doc tried to save that man," a woman said to someone. "He's dead as a wagon wheel though."

"Looked like he tried to run her over," another woman said.

Jessie was shaking. Finn held her close. So Crowell was dead, he thought. Try as he might to feel some Christianly sorrow, he couldn't muster it. "That wee blue book there," he said to one of the woman, pointing, "if you'd be so kind and bring it to me."

The woman jumped to her chore like an eager spaniel, sifting through the scattered books and papers. She picked up Thomas Moore and delivered it to Finn, then stood back as if waiting for her next task. Jessie smiled at the sight of the book, and he tucked it between them.

***

Visions loom in the murky waters...

Leland Stanford stares out the window of a Pullman car, deep in thought. A regal man, Stanford. Does he think about Billy Ralston? The promises made and broken? The face is serene and content. There is no sign of remorse.

Asbury Harpending gazes up out of the depths. A handsome face, a face to trust, but at your peril, beguiling, clever. He recognizes the room: his library, in the old home on Rincon Hill.

Harpending, too, seems at peace with his career, enjoying the spoils of his treachery.

Slow and steady, another stroke, another kick, onward—

Mills, standing tall amid the waves, an unmovable force holding firm against the excess of the age. Steady, reasoned, philosophical. A fatherly man, Mills, ready to give his fatherly advice, advice that the son will hear, but not follow. A timeless tradition…

The vision blurs into William Sharon, a great wad of tobacco bulging from his cheek. He spits, poisoning the water with an inkish cloud, squid-like, to blind his prey. *When Fortune means to men most good, She looks upon them with a threatening eye*, he says. Now he stands in a room amid familiar belongings—bed, table, lamps. Will chokes on mouthful of water, realizing it's Belmont and his own bedroom, and out the window, the beloved stables and horses.

A brawny Adolph Sutro stands astride Virginia City like a giant Colossus, pick in hand, striking and laughing at the feeble and the weak, his pockets overflowing with ill-gotten coin. Suddenly, the town collapses in an explosion of dust, every building and citizen swallowed up by the Sutro Tunnel, that mad creation of a fanatical would-be engineer.

But where is Elizabeth? He searches but can't see her. Where has she gone? With the Colonel, perhaps. She must be with the children. Caring for them like a good mother. And she is a good mother. Oh, Lizzie, I am so sorry. I have failed you.

***

The doctor came, looked them both over. Jessie had some broken bones, but would recover. She was shaking and the doctor told Finn to keep her warm. "Bring her to my office so I can set those bones," he said. And he would take a look at Finn's knee while he was at it.

The blanket enclosed Finn and Jessie like a cocoon.

"I've been looking for you," he said.

"I knew you would be."

"I've been meaning to ask you something, Jessie."

***

The Bay is formidable. Wind sweeps the water into angry whitecaps. He should turn back. But why? He pulls up, looks around, treads water. North Beach seems a long way. Very long. He touches his chest and feels the outline of the little porcelain tablet, tucked safely away. I am exhausted, he whispers to her. I don't think I can go on.

Waves slap at his face. He swallows water, coughs and spits. The tablet escapes, floats out, and Louisa sinks, slowly, drifting back and forth and down, like a fallen leaf, down, down, the serene face staring up at him, the image fading, fading, dissolving into the icy waters. He reaches out but she eludes his grasp, sinking lower and lower, into the depths. Down he swims after her, the precious remembrance, grasping desperately, but to no avail, a lost ideal just beyond reach. And then the likeness is gone but Louisa herself is there, suddenly before him, arrayed in silk that glows iridescent, her gown a corona of light, her face bright with hope.

"Go back," she says. Her voice is like a sad song.

But he will not go back, not now, it is too late.

She is determined. "You must return to your family, your city, there is work to be done."

Again, he refuses. He will stay with her.

The light of her gown shines brighter now. In her eyes he can see a tender compassion. He reaches out, but she remains untouchable, wavering in the numinous currents.

He glances back to see his city, his family, his friends. Out to the west, beyond the fog, the sun melts the horizon into a blur of color, the firmament tinged with joy and sorrow. The currents of memory sweep through him, fleeting images, children along the banks of the Ohio, steamboats paddling down the Mississippi, bawdy New Orleans, roulette wheels and arcades, the Isthmus of Panama, the Pacific, sleepy Yerba Buena clinging to the tip of a steep-banked peninsula, and now, San Francisco, churning with men and women, babies and children, friends and neighbors, gamblers winning and losing, cheaters, stock jobbers, miners and merchants, silver kings and sons of bitches, bankrupt widows, adulterous wives and cuckolded husbands with ragamuffin children playing in the streets until great, black horses roar down and pull fine carriages to a country villa, serene amid vast fields bright with flowers and green terraced gardens and chandeliered ballrooms, and oh the beautiful women with their glances and perfume, how he loved their smiles, was there anything more charming than a woman's smile? And, turning to her, so bright now that all he can see is Louisa and she, goddess-like, luminous complexion and silken hair, and those emerald green eyes that take him back to the garden, in bloom again, its wall enclosing all memory and longing, joy and sorrow, birth and death, until desire becomes reality, dream becomes warm embrace, and he wonders, can she be so warm?

She reaches for him, and her hand is warm.

THE END

Epilogue and Historical Notes

Shortly after Ralston's death, William Sharon made Belmont his permanent residence.

Colonel Fry took in Elizabeth and her children.

The Belmont mansion has been a part of Notre Dame de Namur University since 1922. The mansion itself (now called Ralston Hall) is maintained by the Friends of Ralston Hall. In 1966, it was declared a National Historic Landmark.

Sharon completed construction of the Palace Hotel; it opened on October 2, 1875, five weeks after Ralston's death. To this day, it is still one of the most magnificent hotels in San Francisco. Portraits of Ralston and Sharon hang in the lobby, fittingly, about twenty feet apart.

Shortly after Ralston's death and the bank closing, and by sheer coincidence, Virginia City burned to the ground. Most buildings were rebuilt, but not the International Hotel.

Sharon became president of the Bank of California. It reopened its doors six weeks after closing.

In December, 1875, Sharon finally won a seat in the U.S. Senate.

Sutro took the proceeds from the sale of his tunnel stock and moved to San Francisco, where he purchased a large tract of land overlooking the Pacific. The development was named, of course, Sutro Heights. He also purchased the nearby Cliff House.

Adjacent to the Cliff House, Sutro developed the Sutro Baths, which became a San Francisco recreational landmark and remained in use until the 1950s. My father-in-law swam in them as a boy. Roman-like ruins of the old baths can be seen to this day at low tide.

Sutro served a term as Mayor of San Francisco from 1895-96.

Emma Sutro realized her dream of becoming a physician.

The Consolidated Virginia bonanza was, in fact, the "heart of the Comstock."

John Mackay and his wife retired to France. They donated heavily to the church. His wife endowed the Mackay School of Mines at the University of Nevada, where his statue stands today.

James Flood built a mansion atop Fern Hill (now Nob Hill). It still stands and houses the Pacific Union Club.

James Fair began construction of a mansion across the street from Flood on Nob Hill; it eventually became the Fairmont Hotel.

Ralston's original bank building was damaged in the 1906 earthquake, but rebuilt. It remains to this day at the corner of Sansome and California, although now operating as Union Bank (originally, Union Bank of California), owned, fittingly, by the Japanese. The basement houses a Ralston museum.

When word spread of Ralston's death, black banners were draped over all the buildings of the business district.

During Ralston's funeral, all businesses and offices in the city were closed. Thousands of people lined the streets to observe the funeral procession. James Riker was seen following behind the hearse, weeping.

Comments on historical and chronological inaccuracies/liberties

Jessie and Finn are fictional characters. All interaction between them and the historical characters is intended to shed light on those characters, as well as historical events.

In order to weave history and fiction into a comprehensible story, certain liberties were taken. Most of the events are actual and occurred as presented. Some, however, were fabricated for fictional purposes. The following are departures from historical chronology and fact.

The Yellow Jacket fire occurred in April, 1869. The story has Elizabeth leaving for France at this time, however, she actually left in February.

Ralston did not attend the Congressional hearings on the committee report. John Fry did lend Ralston money, however, it was about a year after the committee meetings.

Sutro did sell his tunnel stock, however, not until three years after Ralston's death. This was also the year (1878) the tunnel was completed; the tunnel was never used. The McCalmont Brothers sued Sutro for, in essence, insider trading; the litigation continued into the 1880s.

Ralston and Sharon did not, as far as the author knows, attempt to buy up tunnel stock.

The Diamond Hoax occurred from 1871-72. For story and dramatic purposes, the hoax continued through 1875, ending before Ralston's death.

Elizabeth had returned from the east before Ralston drowned. St. Patrick's Day is in March, and although the story implies Ralston's death shortly thereafter, he actually died in August (1875).

Reader: My website, www.mdmcgranahan.com, has historic photographs of the main characters, maps which will help to orient you to the different places in the story, the geology of the Comstock Lode, and other things of interest.

Acknowledgements

This book would not have been possible without the remarkable support and assistance, over nine years, from many friends and fellow writers. My thanks and appreciation to:

Jude Berman, Mary Ellen Boyling, Chic DiFrancia, Susan Hall, John Hartnett, Kathyrn Kopple, Aviva Layton, Pamela Madison, and James R. Smith (www.historysmith.com). A special thanks to John Hartnett, whose unwavering enthusiasm and support for this book motivated me to keep going; and to my son, Andrew (www.ajmcg.com), who designed the book cover and website. Thank you to the Bancroft Library, Stanislaus State Library, and San Francisco Public Library, each of which generously allowed me access and provided valuable assistance.

To all who read the manuscript along the way and offered encouragement, or gave me a bed to sleep on during a research trip, or just pushed me to keep going, thank you very much, your support has meant a great deal to me.

I wish to thank my very fine editors, Mary Ellen Boyling (who worked for free and out of her love for Ralston and Ralston Hall), Jude Berman, and Karen Thompson Walker. Thank you also to Talbott Smith for his last-minute proof reading.

And finally, my heartfelt gratitude to my wife, Mary, for her patient support and refusal to give up on this book, long after I was ready to call it quits. I couldn't have done it without you.

About the Author:

Michael McGranahan was born and raised in San Diego, California, and holds degrees from San Diego State and Stanford Universities. He now divides his time between Modesto and Santa Cruz, enjoys rock climbing, surfing, and going to Giants games. This is his first novel.
Website: www.mdmcgranahan.com

www.ingramcontent.com/pod-product-compliance
Lightning Source LLC
Chambersburg PA
CBHW071245250626
47163CB00002B/339

* 9 7 8 0 9 9 0 5 9 8 0 3 9 *